Deadly Alliances

Candle Sutton

This is a work of fiction. Names, characters, dialogue, incidents, and locations are products of the author's imagination or are used fictitiously and should not be construed as real. Any resemblance to events, places, or people, living or dead, is purely coincidental.

Prologue

The late-May sun beat down with the mercy of a Columbian drug cartel as prosecuting attorney Reilly Tanner crossed the parking lot. Heat radiated off the blacktop and his car would be hotter than Death Valley in August, but nothing could bring him down. Not today.

The jury had reached a verdict.

After months of preparing, mounds of evidence, and two weeks in the courtroom, Al Rosetti was finally going where he belonged.

Prison.

Reilly glanced at the intern walking next to him. Will Underwood. Without his invaluable support and eager determination, they might not have brought this case home. "Thanks for the long hours you put in on this one."

"No sweat. I'm glad we got that dirtbag."

Dirtbag? The kid watched way too many old cop movies.

Although it was a fitting description.

A white sedan with black windows glided into the lot. The passenger window slid down. A small cylinder extended out the opening.

Gun!

The word caught in Reilly's throat.

A sharp crack shattered the silence. Reilly dropped his briefcase and tackled Will to the ground.

Two more shots echoed through the air.

Reilly slammed into the blacktop and rolled twice before stopping. He pushed himself up.

Scarlet stained his moist fingers.

A dark pool crept across the asphalt, pouring from Will, whose wide eyes stared at him without blinking. No sound came from Will's parted, twitching lips.

Reilly scrambled to Will's side.

A faint, erratic pulse flickered under Reilly's searching fingers.

Not a good sign.

The slight gurgling coming from Will's open mouth was even worse.

Tires squealed.

Across the parking lot, the car turned around. Reilly's gaze traced the barrel of the gun and the hand connected to a well-defined arm before resting on the shooter's face.

Tan. Deep set eyes. White-blond hair.

The shooter's gaze met his.

He had to find cover. But what about Will?

If he didn't run, they'd both die. Surviving was the only way to bring the help Will needed.

Focusing on Will's nearly colorless face, he leaned in. "I'm gonna get help. You hold on."

The gun swung his direction. He threw himself to the right and rolled to his feet. A shot echoed across the lot.

Had to find cover. A light gray minivan about fifty yards away was his closest option.

He ran.

Zigged to the left, zagged to the right. Anything to avoid running a straight line and being an easy target.

A bullet dinged off the asphalt, another ricocheted off a street light.

Each breath came harder and shorter than the previous one, but he couldn't worry about that now. Only three yards separated him from the van.

He dove.

Numbness tingled down his arm as his shoulder slammed into the pavement. Sliding several feet, he came to a stop by the front passenger tire.

Pain radiated down his body.

Keep moving.

He pushed himself up and scrambled around the front of the

van. Pressure built in his chest as he hauled in air.

A cough scraped from his lungs, followed by another, and another.

He plunged his hand into his pants' pocket and fumbled for his inhaler.

Just breathe.

His body refused to obey. Cough after cough shredded his throat. His clumsy fingers curled around the inhaler.

Where was the shooter?

He straightened slightly to peer through the windshield. The sedan eased past the van's rear doors.

The shooter's eyes locked on his and the barrel of the gun swiveled toward him.

He ducked as the back window exploded. Another bullet struck the windshield, raining glass on his head.

Every rasping breath stole precious energy. He ripped the inhaler from his pocket.

"You think that van's gonna save you? You're dead meat, Tanner."

He wrenched the cap off the inhaler and pumped the life-saving medication into his mouth. The coughing abated; the pain in his chest did not.

He needed help. And he needed it *now.*

Digging out his cell phone, he punched at the numbers, managing to hit 911 and send. The phone beeped twice and shut off.

Dead. Just like he'd be when those guys caught up to him.

He skirted the corner of the van and hurried down the driver's side. Keeping the van between them should buy him a little time.

A shot split the air. The window above his head shattered. Glass cascaded over him.

Weren't they out of bullets yet?

Wheezing rattled his lungs. His neck muscles felt as brittle as the broken shards beneath his feet.

The inhaler wasn't cutting it. And he was spent.

He rolled underneath the van. The sedan's tires rounded the front of the vehicle.

Shallow breaths lurched from his body. His hands shook so violently he had to use both of them to get the inhaler to his mouth and press down the vial.

Calm down. Breathe.

He watched the tires round the back of the vehicle.

The stall tactic wouldn't hold them off for long. Sooner or later, they'd get out of the vehicle and come after him on foot.

Sirens!

The welcome sound grew louder by the second.

Would the shooter leave? Or risk capture to get to him? His body shuddered as he fought for each breath.

The sedan's tires slowed, then stopped.

Leave. Please leave!

After a hesitation that lasted a lifetime, the tires turned away, smoking as the car flew across the lot.

The license plate!

He rolled out, pushed to his feet, and tried to focus on the plate, but it was too far away.

Tremors wobbled up his body. The deafening wail of the siren burped to silence.

Was Will…?

He managed four steps, barely rounding the back of the van, before his knees buckled. He pitched forward, then rolled to his back and stared at the sky.

The asphalt seared his skin. He tried to find the strength to get up, but his weighted limbs refused to obey.

Sit up. Sit up!

Years of asthma attacks screamed at him to get upright, but his body remained unresponsive.

Numbness clouded his mind.

Somewhere he thought he heard footsteps pounding, voices yelling.

A hand closed around his wrist. A muted voice, a man, said something about blue fingers and lips.

Paramedics. Speaking urgently. Their words swirled around him.

Blurry images swam through his vision. Then the images dimmed, the noises faded, and everything went still.

⊡ ⊡ ⊡ ⊡ ⊡

"Sir? Sir, can you hear me?"

Reilly forced his encumbered eyes open. A serious faced African-American kid stared back. Emblazoned on the kid's blue uniform were the words "First Response."

The siren and bumpy, rocking motion confirmed he was in an ambulance.

"Easy now." The kid's lips moved, but the words sounded distant. "Just relax and keep breathing. We're administering oxygen."

Thoughts blasted through his head.

Severe asthma attack.

Will had been shot. Someone had tried to kill him.

Des would freak.

His parents would worry.

Lana would smother him.

Lana. Suddenly there was no one he wanted to speak to more than his sister.

"Call...."

The word croaked into the oxygen mask, unheard by the EMT leaning over him. Reilly reached a hand to the mask, but the EMT forced it back to his side.

"You need to keep that on. Whatever it is can wait until we get to the hospital."

No. No, it couldn't.

He shook his head, brought his other hand around. The EMT caught it before it touched the mask.

"Hey, you almost died. Frankly, I'm surprised you're awake now."

The words barely penetrated Reilly's thoughts. Had to call Lana. Before some well-meaning person took the initiative to track down his parents.

He tried to pull his hands free.

"Calm. Down." The EMT sighed, released his hands, and reached for the mask. "What's so important it can't wait?"

"Milana Tanner." Pushing words through his scorched throat felt marginally better than swallowing gravel, but he forced himself to continue. "Deputy. U.S. Marshals."

"Milana Tanner, deputy, U.S. Marshals, got it." The EMT replaced the mask. "That who you want us to contact?"

Reilly barely had the energy for a slight nod.

Every part of his body screamed for relief. And in spite of the high flow of oxygen pouring through the mask, his lungs couldn't seem to get enough.

The vehicle slowed and the siren stopped.

The EMT leaned in. "I'll give the nurse the message. You relax and let the doctors do their job."

One

The cell phone vibrating against Deputy Milana Tanner's hip interrupted what had been a perfectly good run. As much as she wanted to ignore it, she slipped it from her pocket and checked the display.

An unfamiliar number.

She accepted the call anyway.

"Deputy Milana Tanner?" A woman's voice bit out the words.

She stopped mid-stride. "This is Deputy Tanner."

"Mildred Barton. I'm a nurse at Jacksonville General."

The hospital. The realization hit like a fist to the gut. Someone was hurt.

Her parents were out of town.

That left one person.

Reilly.

"Reilly Tanner requested that I call you."

He requested. Meaning he was alive and at least conscious enough to give a nurse her name and number. "Is he okay?"

A pause.

The hesitation spiked her pulse.

Barton cleared her throat. "He will be. I really can't release any information without his written consent."

Dang medical privacy laws. "I'll get there as fast as I can."

She ended the call and sprinted toward her house. Did this really need to happen when she was two miles away?

At least she could run a mile in less than eight minutes. Under normal circumstances. With the adrenaline coursing through her right now, she bet she could do it in five.

In spite of what Nurse Barton said, she wouldn't really believe Reilly was okay until she could see it for herself.

ꕤ ꕤ ꕤ ꕤ ꕤ

Lana strode down the nearly empty hallway, her sneakers squeaking on the polished tile. The room numbers indicated she was getting close. Should be just around the next corner.

She whipped around the corner and jerked to a halt.

A uniformed police officer sat in front of the closed door of room 413.

What were the police doing here?

For now, she didn't care. Reilly was her first priority.

Lana whipped out her badge. "Deputy Tanner, US Marshals office. I'm here to see Reilly Tanner."

The clean-cut officer who barely looked old enough to drive glanced at her badge before spearing her with a dark stare. "You're with the Marshals?"

"I didn't buy that online."

He stood, towering over her. Sarcasm might not have been her smartest response. Without a word, he reached for her badge.

Which she released. Grudgingly.

He examined it, looked at her, then returned his attention to the badge.

Sheesh. Okay, so maybe she should've changed out of her workout clothes. But she'd barely taken the time to grab her keys and badge, let alone worry about something as silly as her appearance.

He handed back her badge. "I was told no one gets in."

For crying out loud. Reilly was on the other side of the door and this rookie wouldn't let her past.

Maybe she should pull her gun.

Like that'd get her anything but shot. Or arrested. At the very least, banned from the hospital.

"Who's the lead on this?"

"Detective Sanders. He should be back soon."

At least Sanders knew her. "Soon isn't good enough. Call him. Now."

A twitch at the corner of the rookie's jaw told her she'd pushed too hard. "As I said, he'll be back soon."

Time for a new tactic. She softened her tone, adopting the ultra-persuasive manner she'd perfected over the years. "Look, I'm sorry. But that's my brother in there. The nurse wouldn't tell me anything. I need to make sure he's okay."

Hesitation flickered across the kid's face. "Your brother?"

"My only brother."

He stared at her for several long seconds. "I'd expect some family resemblance if he's really your brother."

Not good. The doubt in his tone told her she was losing him. "I'm adopted."

"Uh-huh."

She gestured at the closed door behind him. "Ask him yourself."

"No one gets in without Sanders' approval."

What were the odds she could skirt past him and get inside the room before he realized what was happening? Slim. And she'd probably get herself kicked out of the hospital for trying.

This was ridiculous.

So what if most people's image of a US Marshal didn't match her five-foot-two petite frame? The badge ought to speak for itself.

Although she'd learned long ago that most people placed her closer to twenty-two than her actual thirty-two years. Whether it was her slight frame, long dark hair, deep skin tone, or something else remained an unsolved mystery.

Someday she'd probably love it. Today was not that day.

"Look, you might as well have a seat in the waiting room. I'll let you know when Sanders gets here."

She crossed her arms, but didn't move. "I'll wait here."

"Suit yourself." The rookie dropped back to his chair, his gaze never leaving her.

Figured. All the cops in this city and she had to get the newbie trying to prove himself.

"Why are you guys here, anyway? What happened?"

"You'll have to wait for Sanders."

Seriously? Was that all he knew how to say?

She leaned against the wall across the hallway.

There were only a few reasons the police would be stationed outside Reilly's hospital room. There'd been a direct threat, he'd witnessed something, or he was a person of interest.

She discarded the last option. Reilly was about as clean as they came.

Seconds dragged.

Forget this. She didn't have the patience to wait all day.

If the rookie wouldn't try to get ahold of Sanders, she'd do it herself. She still had some friends at the precinct. Surely one of them could get in touch with Sanders and send him up.

She'd just palmed her phone when a tank of a man appeared. "Well, looky here. Deputy Tanner. What's up?"

Not bothering to hide her frustration, she gestured to the kid. "Would you please tell him to let me in to see my brother?"

Sanders' eyes momentarily widened. "Reilly Tanner's your brother?"

"Yes. And he asked the nurse to call me, but *someone* refuses to let me inside."

"Well, you gotta admit, you look more like a co-ed than a deputy. Especially in that getup." A glimmer of amusement lit Sanders' eyes.

"Funny." Her tone said it was anything but.

Leaning against the wall next to the door, Sanders eyed her. "I would've thought you'd appreciate our efforts to protect him."

"Protect him?" Her stomach lurched. A dull buzz rattled inside her ears.

"Yeah. You don't know what happened?"

"No one's told me anything! I don't know what happened, how Reilly's doing, or even why he's here."

Sanders stuffed his hands into his pockets, his eyes never leaving her face. "Your brother witnessed a shooting."

Reilly. A witness.

"Was he shot?"

Sanders shook his head. "At this point, we don't know a lot. Been waiting for your brother to come around so we can talk to him."

While the knowledge that he wasn't shot should've eased the coil in her stomach, it only squeezed it tighter. "So can I go in or what?"

"Yeah." He nodded at the door. "If he's up, lemme know."

The rookie slid aside and Lana pushed the door open.

The drawn blinds cast darkness around the room, but she didn't wait for her eyes to adjust to the dim lighting before approaching the bed.

Uncharacteristically messy dark blond hair topped a face that looked much too pale. Minor scratches marred his cheeks and something resembling a rug burn darkened his arms in splotchy patches.

The reddish stain on his hands told the rest of the story. Not only had he witnessed the shooting, he'd tried to help.

An ache settled in her chest. Hopefully he hadn't known the victim.

She gently touched his arm. "Ri?"

His eyelids flipped open and he jerked to a sitting position. The tempo doubled on the heart monitor next to his bed. Dilated eyes flicked from one end of the room to the other before locking on her.

A sigh slid out as he relaxed against the mattress. "Hey, you."

"No, hey, you." The response followed automatically, as it had ever since they'd created the exchange as teenagers. "How are you?"

"Alive." His raspy voice sounded painful. "Feel like crud."

"Sound like it, too."

"Thanks." He reached for the wire-rimmed glasses on the table next to the bed and slid them on.

"What happened?"

"Shooting–"

"No, to you. Was it your asthma?"

Moisture glimmered in his eyes as he nodded. "Yeah. Will was shot. Dead?"

"I don't know." Judging from the way Sanders had spoken of the shooting, she guessed the answer was yes. "Let me get the detective."

She went to the door and waved Sanders in. A chair scraped across the floor as Sanders dragged it closer to Reilly's bed.

Reilly shifted to look at the detective. "Will… okay?"

"The kid was gone when the EMTs got there."

A tear clumped Reilly's lashes as his eyes slid closed. Lana squeezed his hand. The news didn't seem to surprise him, but he'd likely clung to a sliver of hope that this Will guy had survived.

Will. Not a name she recognized. And she knew most of the attorneys working at the prosecutor's office. "Someone from work?"

A slight nod answered her. "Intern. Will Underwood."

Will Underwood. That was odd. There was a Will Underwood at church…

No. It couldn't be.

One look at the misery on Reilly's face confirmed the truth. Still, she couldn't stop herself from verifying what she already knew in her heart to be true. "Bob and Myra's son?"

"Yeah. Got him the job–"

"Ri, this isn't your fault. He could've died doing anything."

While Reilly was the one with asthma, Lana was finding it hard to breathe. Barely concealed tears scorched her eyes and the lump blocking her throat rivaled her fist in size.

Will. The dark-haired kid she'd spent several summers babysitting. Who'd gone from being short and scrawny to standing a good head taller than her in a single summer. Who, in spite of the eight years between them, had always had a not-so-secret crush on her.

Who would tell Bob and Myra that their only child had been gunned down?

Any question as to whether or not she'd have to call her parents had been put to rest. Bob and Myra had attended her Dad's church for as long as she could remember. They'd want him to perform the funeral.

And given that Reilly was involved, it'd be better if her parents heard the news from her rather than an outside source.

She hoped the news didn't put a damper on the wedding her Dad was set to perform this weekend in Daytona Beach.

The chair creaked as Sanders leaned forward, his elbows on his knees. "Walk me through what happened."

"Leaving work. Little after seven. Car pulled in the lot–"

"What kind of car?"

"White sedan. Four door. Volkswagen. Tinted windows."

Lana tried not to cringe as each word grated through his throat. Years ago, she'd witnessed one of Reilly's worst asthma attacks and even now, remembered the intense coughing. His throat had to be completely raw.

Not that he'd be likely to complain about it.

If Sanders noticed anything off about Reilly's voice, he didn't let on. "Did it look like a newer car? Or was it pretty old?"

"New."

Sanders jotted it all down. "Okay. Then what?"

"Gun at passenger window. Will shot–"

"Did you see the shooter?"

"Light blond hair, tan skin."

"Did you recognize him?"

Reilly shook his head.

Dang. Reilly knew just enough for the killer to consider him a threat, but not enough for them to make an arrest.

"I'll get a sketch artist down here." Sanders leaned back in the chair. "Go on."

"Shot Will. Tried to shoot me." What little voice he'd had was practically gone.

Reilly's hand shook as he reached for the glass of water sitting on the table next to his bed. She beat him to it and brought it close so he could drink.

Enough was enough. If Reilly kept talking, his throat was going to hurt even worse. "Look, Detective Sanders, his throat's had enough. Any chance we can finish this up tomorrow?"

"No can do, deputy. You of all people should know that."

She did, but figured it wouldn't hurt to try.

"I'm okay." Reilly coughed and couldn't quite hide a wince. "Ran to van. Hid underneath. Sirens scared them away."

The fragmented description was evidently enough to satisfy Sanders, who simply nodded. "Anything else?"

"They knew my name."

This was not good. In fact, it was bad. Really, really bad.

Reilly wasn't a celebrity. Or well-known. The only way those guys - who Reilly hadn't recognized - would know his name was if Reilly had been targeted.

"They spoke to you?" Surprise tinged Sanders' voice. "What'd they say? Exact words."

"Dead meat, Tanner. Van won't protect you."

Sanders jotted down the words. "Okay, you said the sirens scared them away. Did you get a plate number?"

"Tried. Too late."

"Okay, then what?"

"Woke up in ambulance."

Silence stretched. Lana watched Sanders make a few notations. "Has forensics uncovered anything useful?"

Sanders leaned back in his chair. "Well, the one slug that wasn't mangled appears to be from a .38. Got a few tread impressions from where they burned rubber taking off. So far, that's it."

Reilly's eyes slid from Sanders to Lana. "Think… try again?"

That was really the big question here, wasn't it? The killer hadn't come right out and said they were after Reilly, only that they'd missed him. The second threat could've been more about eliminating a witness than a targeted attempt on Reilly's life.

Except that they'd known his name. She couldn't dismiss the importance of that little detail.

Without a clear, definitive threat, securing the protection under which she wanted to bury him would be challenging.

She sighed. "I don't know. But until I feel better about this, you're staying with me."

"No. Bad enough Will's dead. Not you, too."

"I'm not giving you a choice in the matter."

Reilly's eyes narrowed. "Pulling rank. Older."

"You're taller, too. But I carry a gun and handcuffs. And you're not in any condition to argue."

A muffled sound from across the bed drew her attention to Sanders, who appeared to be barely containing his laughter.

Okay. So maybe it was kind of funny. All the more so since Reilly seemed to think he had a shot at winning this argument. "Do you have a stubborn older brother, detective?"

"Or pushy sister?" Reilly didn't remove his blood-shot blue eyes from Lana.

"I do have a kid sister. But she's pretty docile."

"Lucky you." Irritation bled from Reilly's tone.

"Any idea why someone would want to kill Underwood?"

"No. Nice kid." Reilly's words were growing harder to hear.

"Let's say you were the target. I imagine you've got lots of enemies. Anyone in particular stand out?"

"Rosetti."

No trace of emotion flickered across Sanders' face, but his voice carried a note of surprise. "You worked that case?"

"Yeah. Frank hates me. Saw it on his face."

"Anyone else?"

Several seconds passed before Reilly shook his head. "Don't know."

"We'll look into it." Sanders pushed to his feet. "I'll get a sketch artist down here tomorrow."

Pulling her card from her pocket, Lana passed it to Sanders. "I doubt we'll still be here. Call me and I'll make sure it happens."

Sanders nodded and left the room.

When Lana turned back to Reilly, she found narrowed eyes regarding her. "My job. Protect you."

"I know." Had to be a big brother thing. She gentled her tone. "And you've done a great job, but it's my turn to step up."

"Watched Will die. Not you, too."

"I appreciate the concern, but I'll be fine." With her job, she had training that Will had lacked. "Do you know if they're keeping you overnight?"

He nodded.

Okay then. The next thing on her agenda would be to find out if Sanders planned to keep the officer posted outside the door all night or if it'd been temporary until Reilly had given his statement.

If the officer stayed, she could head home and try to get a good night's sleep.

If not, the chair in which she sat would be her perch for the night. Under no circumstances was she leaving Reilly unguarded, especially in his current condition.

"After you're released, you can stay in my guest room. Or I can crash on your couch. It's your call."

"Neither."

"Fine. I'll park my car outside your apartment and stay up all night watching the place."

A breath hissed through his clenched jaw. "Stupidest thing... heard."

"Stupid or not, I'll do what I have to do. I've seen too many cases end badly where people thought they were safe or that they could handle a threat on their own. You will *not* join that list."

The pause lengthened. His silence spoke of displeasure more clearly than his words ever would.

"Your place. More room."

Safer, too. If someone was after Reilly, his place would likely be their first stop.

Straightening, she placed a hand on his arm. "Thanks, Ri. Just a few days, maybe a week, and if there's no sign of danger, I promise I'll back off. Now, you should probably rest that voice."

Not to mention the rest of him.

Creases marred the skin by his eyes and she couldn't remember the last time he'd looked so pale. A few hours of sleep - assuming he could sleep - would go a long way toward making him feel better.

She stepped into the hallway, only to find the corridor empty. No sign of the police anywhere. Even the chair the rookie had sat in was gone.

Well, that settled the matter of where she was staying tonight.

Maybe the nurse would bring her a blanket.

She turned back into the room and rang for the nurse. Next she'd have to call their parents.

While she waited, she prayed she was blowing this thing out of proportion. But the trepidation settling in her gut warned of unrivaled danger.

Two

When a phone rings in the middle of the night, it's never with good news.

It was the first thought to cross Lana's mind as her cell phone jerked her from sleep. The clock read four-thirteen.

Definitely not good news.

Thirty-two hours since the attempt on Reilly's life, less than twenty-four since he'd been released from the hospital. How much more disaster could be crammed into a two-day period?

She grabbed the phone and glanced at the caller ID. An unfamiliar number.

"Hello." Sleep made her voice scratchy.

"Deputy Tanner?" The booming voice seemed slightly familiar.

She sat up, all sleep slipping from her mind. "Yes?"

"Detective Sanders here. Is Reilly with you?"

"He's across the hall. What's going on?"

"There was a fire. Preliminary findings indicate arson."

"Reilly's place." So much for any question of whether or not Reilly was being targeted. "How bad is it?"

"It's a total loss. I tried calling him, but it went to voice mail."

"I'll let him know." How was she going to tell Reilly? Part of her was glad that Sanders hadn't been able to reach him. Maybe she could find a way to soften…

Wait. Sanders worked homicide. "What's homicide doing with an arson case?"

"There was a body inside the apartment."

Reilly lived alone. His apartment should've been empty.

The air solidified in her chest. Her fingers gripped the phone so tightly they throbbed.

Could Reilly have gone home for some reason?

No. Not possible.

It'd only been an hour since a nightmare had awoken them both. The timeframe wouldn't allow…

At this time of night, the drive would take less than twenty minutes.

But she'd made him park his car in the garage so it would be out of sight, and her car was parked in the driveway, blocking access to the garage. In order to get his car, he would've had to move her car, something he wouldn't do without asking.

Maybe.

But what if he'd felt guilty about disrupting her sleep? Or needed something important from his place and hadn't wanted to wake her? That sounded very much like something he'd do.

And she'd made it easy by leaving her keys on the kitchen table.

She threw off the covers and raced for the door.

"Tanner? Everything all right?"

Dang. She'd forgotten that Sanders was still on the line. "Give me a sec."

She crossed the hall and tapped on the door.

No answer.

A tremor shook up her legs.

She knocked again, but didn't wait for an answer before twisting the knob and pushing the door open. "Ri?"

The lump on the bed bolted upright. "Lana? What's wrong?"

Thank God.

She steadied her breathing. "I'll explain in a minute."

Stepping into the hall, she refocused on Sanders. "He's here and he's fine. No ID on the body?"

"No. Bone structure makes us think male, but it's gonna be impossible to run through facial rec. We'll be waiting on dental or DNA."

"Thanks for the heads-up. Keep us posted?" She held no illusions that he'd actually follow through, even if he agreed, but maybe he'd extend a little professional courtesy.

"Sure thing. I'd get your boy into WITSEC. Now."

"That was going to be my next call." Witness security - with all of its rules, routine disruption, and lack of privacy - would be torture for Reilly, but at least it would keep him alive.

She turned and almost smacked into Reilly's chest.

The eggplant rings under his eyes looked more pronounced and lines creased his forehead. He really could've used about eight hours more sleep.

"What body?" Some of the scratchiness had dissipated over the last twelve hours, but his voice still contained an unusually rough edge.

Ugh. The hall was not the place to have this conversation. "Let's head into the kitchen."

She brushed by him and led the way to the table, turning on lights as she went.

As soon as they were both seated, Reilly asked again, "What body?"

Sugarcoating had never been one of her strengths. "There was a fire at your place tonight. A body was recovered inside."

Seconds slid by.

He didn't blink, just stared at her as if trying to determine what her words meant. "Inside?"

"Yes. Any idea who it could be?"

"No." He rubbed the back of his neck. "Maybe I'd recognize–"

"I guess there was too much damage."

"Oh." A breath shuddered from deep inside his chest. "Someone else is dead because of me."

"Don't. This isn't your fault." There had to be something that would make him feel better. "There shouldn't have been anyone inside your place. Maybe whoever set the fire didn't make it out in time."

"Great. I've attracted the world's worst arsonist." He tried for a smile, but it looked more like a grimace.

The truth obviously hadn't quite hit him yet. "You know what this means, don't you?"

"I'm homeless?"

"You're going to need official protection."

Several seconds dragged as his unblinking gaze locked on her.

"Protection." The word came out dull.

"At least until we catch the guy."

And possibly through the trial, depending on who was behind it. If it really was Rosetti, as Reilly suspected, then they'd be looking at months, maybe a year or more, before the case went to trial.

Reilly straightened. Life sparked in his eyes and his jaw twitched. "I want you on the detail."

Why hadn't she seen that one coming? "Good luck with that.

It'll never happen."

"Why not?"

"Conflict of interest, for one thing. Plus, I'm in fugitive tracking, not witness protection."

"Would you do it if you could?"

"Absolutely." Family couldn't be entrusted to just anyone. "But they'll never go for it."

"Leave that up to me. I know a few tricks."

It'd have to be one heck of a magic trick to get her on his detail. "If you can talk them into it, I'm in."

His lips settled into a firm line. If the matter weren't so serious, she'd be tempted to laugh.

No matter how stubborn Reilly might be, he was no match for the US Marshal's office. The lawyer in him might be incredibly persuasive, might be able come up with some compelling arguments, maybe even lay out a solid case, but this was one battle he stood no chance of winning.

Lana glanced up from her computer as the door closed with enough force to vibrate her chair.

"Tanner. Pack your bags."

The clipped words brought her to her feet. She was going?

It took only a glance at Barker, her superior, to determine that she'd heard correctly. And that he was less than thrilled about the arrangement.

He stood outside the door to the conference room where he'd spent the last twenty minutes speaking with Reilly about the requirements for being federally protected. Raised voices had drifted through the door on more than one occasion, but never clearly enough for her to determine what was being said.

Maybe she'd misunderstood.

Rounding her desk, she crossed the still-empty office to join him. "I'm being assigned to his detail?"

Barker's lips pressed into a tight line. "Wasn't my decision. Your brother knows some people with pull and he called in a few favors."

Wow. After all these years, she knew she shouldn't be

surprised that Reilly had gotten what he wanted, but for some reason, she was. "Who's heading this op?"

"Hill."

Thank God. Reilly must've been doing some hardcore praying, something she sure hadn't thought to do. She couldn't ask for anyone better than Alex Hill.

Barker leaned his shoulder against the wall. "When she heard who it was and that you wanted in, she pushed to have you on the team. The deputy marshal finally caved."

"Um, okay. Let me finish this report and I'll head home to pack."

"Don't let Hill convince you to jump ship, got it? She's been trying to recruit you for the last six months."

Longer than that, actually, but what he didn't know wouldn't hurt him. "Jacksonville is home. I have no intention of leaving."

"Make sure it stays that way."

The cell phone on her desk rang.

A grunt accompanied Barker's nod. "She said she'd be calling you."

Without another word, Barker crossed toward his office. She snagged her phone. Caller ID confirmed Barker's suspicion and she accepted the call.

Alex didn't even bother with a hello. "I finally got you on my team."

"It's one case. And it's Reilly. I had to."

Alex's rich laugh filled her ear. "It's a start. Besides, this work is addictive. You'll see."

She could have guessed that would be Alex's response. Almost word for word. "So where are you guys at?"

"My team's getting ready to go. It'll be a few hours before we get there."

"How many are with you?"

"Four."

Four people she didn't know would be protecting her brother. *Her brother*. "And you trust them?"

Alex's voice dropped. "Relax. We're not gonna let anything happen to him."

Oh you of little faith. Why did you doubt? Jesus' words to Peter flashed through her mind.

Her eyes slid closed. Prayer should've been her first recourse, not her last resort. God wouldn't let anything happen to Reilly. "Thanks, Alex. You reminded me that God's in charge of this and I shouldn't be worrying."

Silence blanketed the air between them for several moments. Alex cleared her throat. "Uh, sure. Glad I could help."

One of these days Alex would listen. And Lana refused to stop pointing Alex in the right direction until that time came.

"I better get going. Just wanted to touch base with you before we left. See you soon."

"Safe travels."

She ended the call and set the phone back on her desk.

It'd only been a few months since she'd last seen Alex, but it had still been too long. She glanced over at the desk next to hers, the one Alex had vacated over two years ago, the one currently occupied by a quiet kid who'd come to them from New York.

I miss you, Alex.

Dwelling on the past would accomplish nothing. There was still work to do. Starting with checking on Reilly.

She opened the door to the conference room. Reilly jerked as she stepped inside.

If possible, he looked even worse than he had earlier. The lines pleating his face had deepened, the dark rings under his eyes were puffy, and the whites of his eyes had turned pink.

He'd aged ten years in the last thirty-six hours.

"How're you holding up?"

A light shrug lifted his shoulders.

She sank into the chair across from him. "Well, Barker is not happy."

A glimmer of a smile drifted across his face. "Told you I'd get you assigned to the case."

"Do you have any favors left to call in or did you use them all on this?"

"It was worth it. Thanks for doing this."

No matter how hard she tried to slip into work mode, the emotions roiled beneath the surface. If she didn't lighten the mood, she'd probably fall apart. "Someone has to keep you in line."

Normally he'd throw back some comment about him being the one to keep *her* in line, but not today. Today he sat like a zombie, staring at a spot on the wall behind her.

She nodded at the sofa in the corner of the room. "Why don't you stretch out for a little while. Try to get some rest."

"Maybe I will."

She stepped into the hall, paused long enough to see Reilly collapse on the couch, and softly shut the door.

Hopefully he was exhausted enough that he could get a few solid hours of sleep before the nightmares kicked up again.

ꟷ ꟷ ꟷ ꟷ ꟷ

"The powerhouse pair is back together again!"

Lana couldn't help laughing as Alex swept into the room, short blonde hair swishing around her pale face. "For a limited time only."

Ocean blue eyes studied her. "You look awful."

"Spoken like a true friend."

Alex stepped forward and gave her a hug. "Are you okay?"

"It was a long night."

"How's Reilly?"

"Okay, I guess." Lana glanced back at the conference room, where the door was still closed. "He's trying to act all tough, but it's hard."

"That's why you're here to help him through it."

"Really. And here I thought it was because you were trying to recruit me."

Mischief sparkled in Alex's eyes. "Two birds, one stone. The timing's perfect. I think there's going to be an opening on my team soon."

"Much as I'd love to work with you again, I'm happy here."

"We'll see." Alex jerked her head. "Come on, meet the team."

Lana followed her to where four men stood speaking with Barker.

"Guys, this is Milana Tanner."

An Asian man with a cap of black hair and broad shoulders offered a firm handshake. "Raymond Chow. It is a pleasure to make your acquaintance."

Next to him, a beanpole of a man nodded. Button-down shirt, round glasses, nervous smile. Looked like someone who would be more at home teaching history at a university. "Eugene Beckman."

She nodded back.

The next deputy stood barely under six feet tall. Thick, well-defined arms crossed over his chest and dark eyes bored into her. "AJ Peters."

The sharp tone made her blink.

A Hispanic man with a shaved head and a tattoo visible on his forearm socked Peters' arm. "Lighten up, dude." Turning back to her, he grinned. "Jaime Rodriguez. Don't mind Peters here. His bark is worse than his bite, you know what I mean."

She hoped so.

"So what's the plan?" Lana's eyes flicked over the group before resting on Alex.

"We hole up here in town until we can assess the threat level. Once we know who or what we're dealing with, we'll know how to proceed."

The safe house, located at the southeast end of town, overlooked a marshy swamp that undoubtedly housed snakes and alligators and all sorts of nasty critters.

As long as it didn't hide a snake in human flesh, Lana could deal with the rest.

She set her bag in the room at the top of the stairs that she and Alex would be sharing. Beckman and Chow had the room across the hall, Peters and Rodriguez were in the room next to them, and directly across from Peters and Rodriguez, right next to her and Alex, was Reilly's room.

If anyone breached security, and if he or she somehow managed to slip by the deputy on duty downstairs, they'd still have to get past her.

It would take more than luck to accomplish that one.

Reilly's sketch had hit the press today and the manhunt was already underway.

As much as she itched to be a part of the hunt, this time her place was here. Standing between a killer and her brother.

Going down the hallway, she paused outside Reilly's closed door. No sound came from within. Hopefully that meant he'd managed to fall asleep. She had no illusions that the sleep would be peaceful or lasting, but even a small amount would go a long way to removing the hollow look in his eyes.

She headed downstairs, poked around the kitchen until she found a mug, and poured a cup of coffee from the freshly brewed pot on the counter.

One sip of the hot liquid brought a grimace. It had the consistency of mud after a heavy rain. Except the mud might taste better.

Only one person could make this kind of coffee. Alex.

Maybe some cream would help. And sugar. Lots of it.

She opened the fridge. Hazelnut flavored creamer and a bottle of butterscotch ice cream topping waited on the top shelf.

Alex knew her so well.

A dash of creamer, a few squirts of butterscotch, and several spoonfuls of sugar made the coffee palatable.

She pulled a barstool to the bay window overlooking the driveway and sipped her coffee as a light rain misted the glass. Propping her feet on the windowsill, she cradled the mug in her hands and let the warmth seep into her fingers.

She assumed the others were settling in, except for Alex, who was drawing up a schedule for the next few days.

Footsteps tromped down the stairs and crossed the entryway, heading toward the kitchen. She glanced at the doorway as Rodriguez walked in.

"You already unpacked?" Surprise tinged his voice.

"I'll do it later." She nodded at the mug. "Of the last thirty-six hours, I've slept about seven. I needed something to keep me going."

"You make the coffee?"

"Alex."

A grin slid across his face. "Not afraid to take your life into your hands, I see."

So Alex's toxic coffee was well known. She couldn't help smiling in return. "We all have to go sometime, right?"

"Better believe it." He glanced in the cupboard by the fridge before moving on to the next one.

"To the right of the sink."

"Thanks." Retrieving a mug, he poured himself a cup of sludge and chugged it.

"And you called me brave? You're drinking it straight."

Broad shoulders lifted in a lazy shrug. "It's an acquired taste."

"I don't know about that. I worked with Alex for three years and never got used to it."

He refilled his mug before pulling a chair over to join her. "So Reilly must be your stepbrother?"

"No. Just my brother."

"Lana's adopted." Alex's voice came from behind them.

Maybe she should get it tattooed across her forehead. *Adopted.* Save everyone a lot of trouble.

She didn't bother hiding her irritation as she slid her attention to Alex.

A wry grin twisted Alex's lips. "Come on, Lana. Everyone's gonna find out anyway, you know that. Rodriguez happens to be the nosiest one."

"Hey, now."

Alex grinned at Rodriguez's protests. "Not my fault it's true."

Setting his cup on the windowsill, Rodriguez crossed his arms over his chest. "Nothin' wrong with bein' adopted anyway. My girlfriend is."

Time for a change of subject, before Rodriguez asked for more details than she was willing to give.

"You finish the schedule?"

A nod answered her question. "I only worked up a schedule for the next five days. Now that the press has that sketch… well, we'll see how the dust settles. We may not be staying here long."

Lana's phone vibrated in her pocket. Pulling it out, she glanced at the caller ID, but didn't recognize the number. "Excuse me."

She slipped into the living room and accepted the call.

"Sanders here."

Wonders never ceased to amaze. "Detective Sanders. There's news?"

"We made a positive ID on the body. Some old codger who lived in the upstairs apartment. Initial cause of death looks like smoke inhalation."

"What was he doing in Reilly's apartment?"

"Fire ate through the floor. Looks like he fell through."

"Any leads?"

"We're still working the scene. I'll let you know."

She pocketed her phone. Another innocent casualty.

And another death for which Reilly would blame himself.

⁂

The police had a sketch.

Frank Rosetti swallowed past the Sahara lining his throat as he stared at the vividly accurate picture on his television. It was only a matter of time before someone connected that sketch to Doug Garrett.

Then they'd connect Doug to Al.

And Al to him.

He slammed his fist down on his desk.

What an idiot! To use someone who was a known associate of his brother, who currently worked for Rosetti Construction, had been the worst decision Frank had made in years. Possibly his whole life.

It wasn't all his fault. That imbecile Doug deserved equal blame. If not more.

"Frank?" Ginger's soft voice broke into his thoughts.

Turning, he found her standing in the doorway, her large hazel eyes inquisitive. She tucked her copper hair behind her ears, the light twinkling off the diamonds dangling from her earlobes.

"Is everything okay?"

He cleared his throat. "Uh, yeah, babe, everything's fine."

Silence beat a second too long, long enough for her to make sure he knew that she wasn't buying it.

Then she smiled. "If you say so. I'm headed downtown for an appointment. Do you need anything while I'm out?"

"I'm good."

She gave him one of those smiles that still, even after five years of marriage, stole the air from the room.

"Love you, babe."

Her heels padded across the carpet as she approached. Placing one hand on his chest, she stretched up to offer a lingering kiss. "I'll see you later."

It didn't take her nearly long enough to cross to the door. She paused and blew him a kiss before stepping out of sight, her heels click-click-clicking down the tiled hallway.

For several seconds he found it impossible to remove his gaze from the doorway she'd exited.

If he went down for this, he'd lose her.

Would Doug talk if they caught him?

So what if he did? Frank could deny everything and no one could prove he had anything to do with it. It would be Doug's word against his and with Doug's record, no one would believe him.

Ginger would stand by him through any investigation. Her loyalty was one of the things that had drawn him to her.

Of course, her killer looks hadn't hurt, either.

They wouldn't tie him to this mess. He'd make sure of it.

If he had to, he could always bring in a professional. He *wouldn't* go to jail. He'd remain a free man, no matter how much it cost him.

Or who else had to die.

Three

The days had settled into a comfortable - if somewhat frustrating - pattern. Only four days since they'd arrived at this place and she was already going nuts.

Lana sat on the front porch in the deepening shadows, listening for anything that didn't sound right. All she heard were the normal night noises: the faint rustling of the wind in the swamp grass, a muted splash as something either entered or exited the marsh, the throaty singing of countless frogs.

Sitting there in perfect stillness, she blended with the night around her, wishing, praying, that a break would come soon.

At least one good thing had come from all of this. She now knew that Alex had a capable team backing her up.

It lifted a huge burden from her spirit to know that her friend was in good hands.

She could do without Peters and his attitude, but the rest of the team had tucked her in as though she'd been working with them for years.

"Tanner."

Her breath caught in her throat as a male voice sounded behind her. Man, she had not been expecting that.

It was almost like Peters knew she'd been thinking about him.

Thank God it was dark enough that he likely hadn't seen the way she started at the sound of his voice. "Yes?"

"Alex got an update." The words came out clipped.

Typical.

He didn't speak to her often, but when he did it was usually the minimum required to get his point across and always in a tone that said he'd rather be talking to anyone but her.

She pushed up and headed toward the door, which Peters had already vacated. Stepping through the doorway, she locked the door behind her and turned to find everyone gathered in the living room.

"Good news. The cops arrested a guy tonight. We'll be transporting Reilly downtown tomorrow morning to view a lineup."

They had someone in custody? "Who is it?"

"They didn't say. They wanted Reilly to view the lineup before they release any information."

Of course. The smallest slip could give a good defense attorney enough ammunition for an acquittal.

She was almost afraid to hope, but couldn't temper the anticipation of tomorrow morning. Hopefully by tomorrow night, they'd all be sleeping in their own beds.

And Reilly would be free from this threat.

⁂

"Number three."

Lana's gaze flew to the man Reilly had so definitively identified. Light blond hair, square jaw, small nose.

Calm eyes stared straight ahead.

The man didn't shift or fidget, hardly even blinked. It took experience to remain that calm while in police custody.

This wasn't his first time inside.

Detective Sanders called for suspect number three to step closer to the one-way glass. Once he'd done so, Sanders' eyes slid to Reilly. "You're sure?"

"No doubt. That's the guy." Reilly didn't remove his attention from the blond suspect. "How'd you find him?"

"A call came in on the tip line. Name's Doug Garrett. Works for Rosetti Construction. Turns out he's a known associate of Al Rosetti."

Reilly finally turned away from the glass. "I knew it. And Frank Rosetti put him up to this, didn't he?"

"Garrett's not talking. Got a rap sheet with a bunch of small-time stuff on it, but this one could put him away for life. We're hoping he'll cop a plea."

Pushing off from the wall, Alex joined them. "What're the chances that this guy was acting alone?"

"Between you and me?" Sanders glanced at Garrett. "Slim to none. He and Al had some dealings together, but not the kind of stuff you pull a revenge hit for. Plus, we found five grand in cash hidden in the guy's dirty laundry. We're digging into Frank Rosetti to see if he's short five grand. 'Course, it's also possible that Al lined it up from inside the prison."

Both options were equally awful. Lana struggled to keep her face impassive.

All hope that they'd be back in their own beds tonight had died at the mention of Rosetti's name.

Rosetti would try again. No doubt about it.

Only next time, he'd hire a professional.

The grim set to Alex's lips confirmed they'd reached the same conclusion.

Alex shook Sanders' hand before herding Reilly out of the room. Peters and Chow fell into step with them outside the door.

Once they were all safely in the bullet-proof SUV, Alex broke the silence. "Time to relocate. We'll leave as soon as possible."

"My client said the deadline is the end of the month."

A tremor shook Frank Rosetti's hand. He clutched the cell phone tighter. "Until?"

"I don't want to know." A rasping cough followed the woman's words. Garrett's lawyer sounded like she smoked at least a pack a day. She cleared her throat, which did nothing to ease the huskiness of her voice. "Doug said you'd understand."

He did understand. All too well.

Month end. That gave him only twenty days to find a way to get Garrett out of this mess.

But how?

Al would've known what to do, but Al was in prison. Waltzing in there and discussing this under the guards' noses wouldn't be his smartest option.

"Mr. Rosetti?"

"Yes. Tell your client he has nothing to worry about."

"Very good." A click signaled the end of the call.

Frank dropped his phone on the desk. Twenty days. If he didn't come up with some kind of plan, Garrett would turn on him.

What would it take to keep Garrett out of prison?

Sources told him that they hadn't found the murder weapon. While Garrett owned a gun of the right caliber and drove a car that fit the description, the evidence was circumstantial at best. The gunpowder residue forensics had found on the passenger door was a little trickier, but they could still come up with a reasonable explanation.

The most condemning evidence was Reilly Tanner's positive identification.

If he could fabricate a solid alibi and eliminate the only eyewitness, there wouldn't be enough to make the charges stick.

The alibi would be easy. Getting rid of Tanner, who'd surely gone into protective custody, would be a bit harder.

No more screw-ups. Time to call in a professional.

Lucky for him, Al should have contacts that could put him in touch with the right man for the job.

He strode across the office to a tall bookcase. The dust-covered dictionary waited on the bottom shelf. Grabbing it, he flipped it open to the Qs, where a single sheet of paper nestled between the pages.

A dozen names and phone numbers. Which one should he call?

Maybe Al had put them in order of usefulness. He'd start at the top and work his way down.

The first two numbers had been disconnected. He punched in the third. A smooth, heavily-accented voice answered on the fourth ring. "What."

"Uh, this is Frank Rosetti. My brother, Al–"

"I know who your brother is. Why are you calling?"

How much was safe to reveal over the phone? "Yours is one of the numbers Al left for me should I need… advice."

"Can't help you."

"Can't or won't?" Frank drew in a deep breath. "What's it going to cost?"

"Ain't 'bout the money. Don't call again."

"Wait!" Frank paused long enough to hear the man breathing before plunging ahead, "Al said if I ever need help–"

"You got a Zed on your list?"

Frank glanced down the list. There, about number seven or eight. "Yes."

"Call him. And burn this number." The line went dead.

A measured breath eased through Frank's lips. He forcibly relaxed his grip on the phone.

Zed. The name didn't inspire much confidence. But what choice did he have?

He punched in the number.

A sandpaper voice scratched across the line. "Yeah?"

"Zed?"

"Who's askin'?"

Almost as good as an admission. "Frank Rosetti. Al left me your number."

"Al, huh?"

"He said you might be able to help me clear up some of his business affairs."

A harsh laugh burst across the line, erupting into a cough halfway through. "His affairs, yeah. Maybe we oughta get together to work it all out. Have a drink for ol' Al's sake, huh?"

The place Zed suggested made his stomach lurch. The daily special at that place? Cockroach burgers served on buns that expired last year paired with salmonella salad. Yum.

On the upside, he wouldn't run into anyone he knew at that dump.

"Fine. Two hours."

Lana stepped into the room she and Alex had shared for the last week and closed the door. No matter how much Reilly wouldn't want her to have this conversation, it had to be done.

Folding a shirt precisely in half, Alex set it on top of a stack of similarly folded shirts in her suitcase. She glanced up. "Is Reilly packing?"

"Yes. Do you know where we're going yet?"

"Maxwell sent over some files, but I haven't had time to go through them." Narrowed eyes regarded her for several seconds. "What's up?"

Lana massaged her right temple. "Did you hear that Reilly almost died that day?"

"Kinda the reason we're all here. What of it?"

"For reasons that had nothing to do with bad guys and

bullets?"

Alex stilled, serious eyes locking on her. "I didn't hear about that."

Big surprise. He'd always tried to keep his asthma a secret. "Reilly has severe asthma. The shooting triggered an attack. If EMS hadn't arrived when they did, he wouldn't still be with us."

Pointer finger brushing her lip, Alex nodded.

The look was one Lana had witnessed many times as Alex processed new information.

Easing down on the mattress, Alex locked her gaze on Lana. "And stress makes it worse."

"Much worse."

"Then we'll have to avoid stressful situations, won't we?" Alex leaned forward, elbows resting on her knees. "I'm assuming he has an inhaler."

"And some pills he can take if the inhaler isn't cutting it." According to Reilly, the pills had been in his briefcase at the time of the attack. Across the parking lot, but not close enough to do him any good.

"Okay. We'll make sure he has an ample supply of both. Anything else I should know?"

"That's the most critical." Lana sank onto the bed across from Alex.

"Have you already finished packing?"

"I never unpacked."

Picking up a stack of files, Alex dropped them on the bed beside her. "Well, if you'd like to help, maybe you could sort through these. See which one looks best to you."

"Sure." Lana scooted further onto the bed and sat cross-legged before grabbing the closest file.

It seemed weird that they would even have options. Wouldn't it make more sense for Maxwell to simply assign a location?

Well, no matter.

She'd go through these and make a suggestion, just like Alex had asked. Not that she knew what she should be looking for, but as long as it was a government safe house, it shouldn't matter.

She shot up a quick prayer for guidance, then opened the first folder.

Each file took only a few minutes to study. Containing pictures, specs, and information on the surrounding area, it felt a lot like house shopping.

Except that she wasn't spending any of her own money. Even better.

She reached for the last file. Really, any of these places would suffice…

Lincoln City, Oregon.

Her gaze froze on the location printed on the top of the first page in the folder. Lincoln City.

She and Reilly had visited there years ago. A friend, who'd lived in Portland at the time, had suggested meeting up in Lincoln City.

While it'd been over a decade, she remembered feeling like the town was small and charming. Swarming with tourists, which would help them blend in.

Might be a good fit. She skimmed the specifics on the house.

Seized four years ago in a drug bust. Located on the beach at the end of a dead-end street. Five bedrooms. Three bathrooms. Custom built with a security system and panic room.

Nice.

"Must be a good choice. You're sure taking your time looking it over."

"Yeah. I've been to this town. It's been a long time, but if my memories are correct, it might be a good place to lay low." Lana summarized the house, handing over the file when Alex extended her hand.

Several seconds passed before Alex looked up. "I like it. Nice choice."

Not that she'd necessarily chosen it, but she let it ride.

Alex glanced at her watch. "We need to get in the air. Check on Reilly, will you? I'll touch base with the team."

Frank shut his car door, armed the alarm, and turned to face the building in front of him.

A crooked sign hung above the door. The Shady Palm Restaurant.

They had the nerve to call this dive a restaurant? Someone had a sick sense of humor.

No paint remained on the walls, assuming the walls had ever been painted, of course. Maybe they'd always had that third-world-country vibe.

Next to the building, flies smothered a dumpster overflowing with rotting food.

Ugh. It smelled like something had died. Maybe it was the last patron who actually ate something here.

Dodging the broken glass scattered across the parking lot, he pulled open the solid wood door and stepped into the dim interior.

His stomach pitched and bile burned his throat.

Charred meat mingled with years' worth of cigarette smoke. The stench of old grease hung in the air. And he'd thought the dumpster was putrid?

The door thudded behind him like the lid of a coffin.

He waited until his eyes adjusted to the dim light before moving further into the room.

About a dozen people occupied the various tables, all silent, staring at him with unmasked suspicion. Even the frizzy-haired woman behind the grill watched him, a metal turner in her hands.

This place obviously didn't see normal people very often.

Now which of these losers was Zed?

A green hat sitting on the corner table snagged his attention. He crossed the room, transferring his gaze from the hat to the man sitting in the shadows behind it.

"Rosetti?" The gravelly voice matched the one he'd heard on the phone earlier.

"Zed?"

The man nodded. Knocking a French fry off the bench, Frank slid in on the opposite side.

Stringy blond hair brushed the tops of his shoulders. Dozens of piercings caked his lips, nose, and eyebrows with metal. Surprisingly sharp eyes regarded him.

"I knew it hadta be you 'cause ya look like Al. How's he doin' anyway?"

Was Zed some kind of idiot? Maybe he thought he was being funny. "Al's in prison. How do you think he's doing?"

"Could be better, huh? Can't believe they finally nailed somethin' on Slippery Al." He leaned back, crossing his arms over his bony chest. "So whaddya need? I'm thinkin' this got nothin' to do with stuff Al did, huh?"

"Uh..." Sweat made his palms sticky. He rubbed them on his pants and tried to steady his voice. "I need to hire someone who can clean up a mess I've made."

"A mess." Zed stared at him, his metal-spiked face unreadable. "You tryin' to say you need a hit man?"

Letting out a shaky breath, he nodded. "I need the best."

Zed's eyes narrowed as he regarded Frank with fresh suspicion. "Al said his kid brother was gonna do okay and stay outta trouble. Why're you gettin' mixed up in junk like this?"

"Personal reasons." His kept his voice level, faking a calm he didn't feel. "I didn't think something through and now I have a problem I can't handle myself. Can you help me or not?"

After a few seconds of scrutiny, Zed nodded. "Yeah. I can help you."

He grabbed a napkin and pulled a pen out of his pocket.

While Zed wrote, Frank looked around the room, feeling a small measure of relief to find no one that seemed interested in him or Zed. Zed pushed the napkin across the table and Frank unfolded it to reveal a name and phone number scrawled in sloppy block print.

"This got anything to do with Al's trial? Lookin' to snuff out a witness?" The pause said more than Zed's words. "Or the DA?"

So Zed wasn't as stupid as he looked.

Not that Frank had any intention of confirming the truth. "That's not something I'm comfortable discussing."

A smirk tweaked the corner of Zed's mouth. "Well, you want the best, that's him. But he ain't cheap."

"I don't care." Pushing himself to his feet, Frank pulled out several hundred dollar bills and tossed them on the table. "Thanks for the information. Enjoy your meal."

Zed's long, bony fingers clamped onto his arm. "You be sure to tell 'im you've got yourself a pest problem when ya call. Use them exact words or he might hang up."

Frank couldn't tear his attention from the hand dampening his arm.

What, being in this filthy dump wasn't bad enough? He'd have to scrub his arm with searing water and bleach to feel clean again.

But given that this wasn't yet a done deal and he might need Zed's help again, he couldn't risk alienating him.

Clearing his throat, Frank forced a small smile. "Thanks for the tip. Pest problem, right?"

He waited for Zed's nod, left without a backward glance, and headed straight for his car. He popped the trunk and took out the pre-paid cell phone he'd purchased on his way here, then leaned against the side of the car and stared at the device.

Turn it on and dial. The command repeated through his head, but never made it to his frozen fingers.

This was stupid. What had he been thinking?

Criminals hired assassins. Not men like him.

He should bag the whole thing. Go home and have a nice dinner with Ginger.

And if Garrett turned him in, so what? A criminal's word versus a legitimate businessman's was a no-brainer.

Except that the FBI had been looking into him for a while now. Waiting for him to slip up.

He couldn't afford the exposure.

Or take the chance that someone would believe Garrett.

He had to see this through.

His hand trembled as he reached into his pocket, withdrew the napkin, and read it for the first time. The only name listed was Stevens, probably a last name, and a long distance phone number.

The phone took less than a minute to power up. Not nearly enough time for him to plan out what he was going to say.

He'd figure it out on the fly. Before he could talk himself out of it, he punched in the numbers.

One ring. Two. Three. Four.

The knot in his gut slowly eased.

Looked like Stevens wouldn't answer. That wouldn't solve his problems, but at least he'd have more time to prepare–

"Hello?" The soft voice contained an underlying current of steel.

"I'm looking for Stevens. I have a pest problem."

Silence roared for so long that he began to wonder if the man had hung up. What would he do if Stevens refused to help?

"What kind of pest?"

He didn't know whether he was relieved or more nervous than

before, but he couldn't turn back now. "A prosecutor. I hear you're the best."

"I am." No arrogance, just fact. "Who am I dealing with?"

Frank shifted his weight from one foot to the other and rolled his shoulders in a futile attempt to loosen his drenched shirt from his back. The phone slipped in his hand and he tightened his grip.

What if this was an elaborate trap?

The guy on the other end of the phone might not be a hit man at all. He might be a Fed.

He forced himself to breathe. "I'd rather not say. Anonymity is a good thing sometimes."

"Not when you're working with me. Play by my rules or we're done."

What a choice. Either tell Stevens his identity or go back in and talk to Zed again.

Trying to stall, he blurted the first thing that came to mind. "You're not what I expected a hit man to sound like."

"No kidding. I suppose you expected some idiot that dropped out of grade school. Probably figured I must be about as primitive as a caveman, right?" The words dripped with contempt.

"Uh, yeah, I mean, no." Great. Now he'd made the hit man angry.

Time to make a decision.

Trust this voice on the phone, get the hit taken care of, and return to his life, or hang up now and hope that he had some of the luck Al used to have.

The options weren't great either way.

Before he could say anything else, Stevens spoke. "Level with me or I'm gone."

"No." Frank couldn't stop the desperation from edging into his voice. His brother had trusted Zed and he had no other option. "I'm Rosetti."

"Rosetti?" Stevens' voice reflected surprise. "Well, Al's in prison, so you must be the younger brother he mentioned."

Al knew Stevens? Impossible!

Wasn't it? "My brother, uh, hired you for something?"

"Several times." Stevens paused. "But he once told me his brother was clean, so I have a hard time believing you're a Rosetti."

For crying out loud. Had Al told the whole criminal

underworld about him? "Al always took care of things like this so I wouldn't have to. But, uh, I've gotten in a little trouble and… how did you know my brother was in jail?"

Could Stevens be local?

The number was long distance, but that would make sense for a man like Stevens. It'd make him harder to track down.

Stevens chuckled. "When you've been in this business as long as I have, you make contacts who keep you well informed."

Words failed him. "Oh."

"Fill me in," Stevens commanded quietly.

⁂

"I… I don't think I should say too much over the phone."

Obviously Rosetti was in way over his head. Typical for a pampered rich kid.

"Are you on your cell phone?" Stevens told himself to be patient, but couldn't hide the irritation bleeding into his words.

"It's a prepaid phone."

"Then you're fine."

"But…" Rosetti's tone dropped several notches. "Can't the FBI still listen in?"

Great. Another one of these. "You think sending the information via email is safer? Trust me, the electronic trail on email is something their most inept computer geeks could trace."

"I was thinking I could mail–"

"You do that and you delay this thing by a week. At least. Tell me now and I can get started right away."

"Oh."

Silence.

Forget this.

He had better things to do than sit on the phone all afternoon. "You're wasting my time. Good luck taking care of your problem."

"Wait!" Rosetti's shallow breathing came across the line. "I'll tell you. I've just, uh, never done something like this before."

No kidding. "Who's the target?"

"Reilly Tanner."

He confirmed the spelling before writing the name down. "And you said he works for the prosecutor's office?"

"Yeah. After Al's trial, I sent two of my guys to, uh, teach him a lesson. They missed him and shot some intern instead."

Amateurs. "And this Tanner guy witnessed the kill?"

A pause. "Yeah. My guy's in prison now and said he's going to cut a deal if I haven't fixed this by the end of the month."

He glanced at the date on his watch. Month end. That gave him about two and a half weeks to track down this target and complete the hit. Shouldn't be too difficult.

Especially with a fresh trail.

"I imagine Tanner's in protective custody."

"The Marshals have him stashed somewhere." Rosetti cleared his throat. "But I may have someone on the inside who can give up their location. I'll let you know what I find out."

Rosetti had contacts inside the US Marshal's office? Interesting.

Maybe the schmuck wasn't totally worthless after all.

"Fifty thousand. Wired to my account. Half up front, half upon completion."

"Fine."

He recited the number for his account in the Caymans. "I'll get started as soon as I see the first payment."

He clicked off his cell phone and tossed it on the sofa next to him. If Rosetti could get him a location, it'd make his job that much simpler.

While some people in his business thrived on the challenge of the hunt, he wasn't one of them. No, his favorite moment was when he stood behind the barrel of his rifle, knowing that he held in his hands the power of life or death.

Leaning back, he stared at the mindless program flashing across his TV. He would check out Rosetti, make sure this thing was on the level, but his gut told him it was legit.

Still, he could never be too careful.

Fame had its price, especially for the infamous.

Maybe it was time to consider retirement. He wasn't getting any younger and always looking over his shoulder took a toll.

He opened his laptop. As he waited for it to boot, his mind drifted to thoughts of what he'd do if he hung up his rifle.

Maybe he'd take up sky diving. Or learn to fly. Or treasure hunting.

Sunken treasure. Yeah, that'd be fun. He could finally put that scuba certification to good use.

Retirement.

The word sounded more appealing after every job. Maybe this time he'd actually do it.

Right after he finished this hit.

Four

Longest trip ever. Lana rocked her head from side to side, trying to work the kinks out of her neck.

While she'd flown across the country before, the flight from Jacksonville to Portland, Oregon seemed longer than most. Add to that the two and a half hours spent in the car from Portland to Lincoln City and she was wiped.

Too bad it would be hours before she could catch any sleep.

The town slipped by outside her darkly-tinted, bullet-proof window. It looked different than she remembered. Larger.

Of course, it had been over ten years since she'd been here. Naturally, the town would have grown during that time.

They left the main roads behind and navigated the side streets, passing houses of all sizes and conditions. Ahead, off in the distance, the ocean sparkled under the early evening sun.

While she'd normally appreciate the diamonds glittering on the surface of the water, right now she was much too tired.

"We have arrived."

Lana jerked at the sound of Chow's voice.

Through the windshield, the road ended at a small weed-covered lot. A rocky hill rose beyond the lot, jutting down the beach and into the ocean.

They pulled into the last driveway on the right. Well-maintained older homes surrounded them. Not a single person was in sight, but at this time of day, they were probably focused on dinner.

She turned her attention to the house in front of them.

Two-story, beige paint, chocolate trim. Newer than the surrounding houses. A covered porch ran the length of the front of the house, with a dark brown door set dead center.

As the vehicle eased to a stop, Alex reached for the door handle. "Okay, guys. You know the drill. Chow, Peters, you cover Reilly. Everyone else, with me."

Well, almost everyone knew the drill.

Lana bit back the urge to ask for more details. No need to remind everyone that she had never worked witness protection before.

Chow shifted into park but didn't kill the engine.

Okay, so at least she knew that the drill included being ready to make a quick getaway at the first sign of trouble.

Earpieces were distributed, as well as communication devices. With the microphone clipped to her collar and the earpiece tucked inside her ear, Lana followed Alex toward the house.

The silence seemed unnatural. Ominous.

Shouldn't there be noise from people on the beach? Neighbors? Traffic?

Anything?

Alex paused by the door and listened.

The only thing Lana heard was the distant pound of waves hitting the sand.

Alex inserted a key into the lock. The scrape seemed as loud as a gunshot.

Leading the way inside, Alex hit the switch and flooded the interior with light. She paused by the alarm panel long enough to punch in the code and deactivate the alarm, while Rodriguez and Beckman conducted a brief sweep of the room.

A high-ceilinged living room opened in front of them. Hardwood floors, leather furniture. Very big TV.

At least the guys would be happy.

Nestled against the wall to her right, stairs led up to a loft overlooking the living room. Beneath the stairs, a short hallway contained three closed doors. A kitchen was visible through an open doorway across the living room.

"Rodriguez, Beckman, take the main floor." Alex jerked her head toward the stairs. "Lana, you're with me."

As Rodriguez crept toward the kitchen and Beckman angled for the hallway, Lana followed Alex up the stairs.

Two rooms opened off the loft. Lana slipped into the first while Alex moved toward the second. A bedroom. Two twin beds, one dresser, a closet.

An open door on the wall to her left revealed a bathroom.

Not many places for someone to hide.

Leading with her gun, Lana inched toward the closest bed. She lifted the bedspread with her foot.

The mattress sat on a solid wood platform.

She checked the second bed. Same setup.

"Kitchen's clear."

Even though Rodriguez's voice was barely a whisper, Lana started at the sudden sound.

"Roger that." Peters. Sounding more civil than she could remember hearing him.

Rounding the second bed, she approached the closet. Also empty.

She edged into the bathroom, not surprised to find that it connected to the bedroom Alex was searching. The Jacuzzi tub, freestanding shower, and linen closet were all clear.

Jacuzzi tub? No wonder Alex liked working this job.

Most of the furnishings were probably left over from the previous owner. After all, a drug dealer could afford the best, right?

Alex met her inside the doorway of the other bedroom. "We good?"

"Yeah."

Alex pushed the button on her communicator. "Second floor is clear."

"Roger."

As silence descended on the earpiece again, Alex jerked her head toward the room behind her. "Check this out."

Lana stepped onto the plush carpet in the master bedroom. The king-sized bed with massive headboard and matching cherry-wood furniture probably cost more than she made in a month. That mattress looked thick enough to hide a body.

Alex stepped inside the closet, turned on a light, and led the way toward the closet's back wall.

Kneeling at the right rear corner, she lifted up the edge of the carpet to reveal a red button that sat level with the surrounding floor. With one hand, Alex pressed the button and with the other, she pushed on the back wall.

The wall swung silently inward.

Unbelievable. It looked like some kind of hidden passage. The kind she might expect to find in an old British castle, not a modern beach house.

"First floor clear." Beckman's voice filtered through Lana's thoughts.

Alex stood and let the carpet fall back in place, then pushed the button on her communicator. "I think I found the entrance to the panic room. Lana and I are going to check it out, the rest of you hold your position."

A flick of the light switch inside the passage illuminated the space in the white glow of florescent tubes.

At about three feet wide, the passageway allowed no extra space. Unfinished walls lined either side and Lana strongly suspected the walls and ceiling had been soundproofed.

They'd only gone a few feet when Alex stopped. "Looks like we're going down."

As Alex began her descent, Lana saw that the passageway dead-ended at a square hole. Two looped handlebars, similar to a swimming pool ladder, jutted over the edge.

A glance down revealed a ladder attached to the side of the shaft.

Lana gripped the handles and stepped onto the top step. Halfway down, another passage intersected with the shaft. A first floor entrance, unless she missed her guess.

Looked like the drug dealer hadn't been willing to take any chances. Lucky for them.

A few seconds later, her feet landed on solid concrete. She turned to find Alex standing in front of a solid steel door.

The digital keypad chirped to life under Alex's fingers. After keying in a series of numbers, a dull clunk came from the door, which slid open an inch.

Alex grabbed the handle and pulled the door toward them. Stepping inside, she felt around for a few seconds before the room flooded with light.

Plush carpet covered the cement floor. An open door on the opposite side of the room showed a small bathroom. The musty room contained two futons, but no other furniture. A thermostat was mounted on the wall next to the door and two vents, probably hooked up to a separate HVAC than the one that serviced the house, would ensure that anyone locked in here remained at a comfortable temperature.

Alex shook her head slowly. "I'm thinking our guy was a little eccentric."

Eccentric was furnishing every room in your house in polka dotted furniture. This was obsessive.

Once they got settled, she'd be sure to come back and put some of Reilly's asthma medication and a spare inhaler down here.

And maybe a cell phone.

Just in case.

Although it'd be a small miracle if it even got reception down here.

Turning off the light, Alex stepped from the room and shut the vault-like door behind her. "Let's see where that other passage lets out."

They climbed the ladder to the first floor entrance, which put them in a coat closet underneath the stairs. Rodriguez and Beckman met them in the living room.

"Steel-core doors on the exterior." Rodriguez gestured to the large windows surrounding them. "But the glass isn't bullet-proof, if you can believe that."

Weird.

Lana shot a glance at the windows. At least the blinds blocked line of sight.

Alex got on her communicator. "House is clear. Let's bring him in."

ꟷ ꟷ ꟷ ꟷ ꟷ

"Why don't you turn in?"

Reilly rolled his head to look at Lana, but didn't move from his position on the overstuffed beige leather couch. "That'd require energy."

She understood the feeling.

All too well. The last few days had been some of the longest of her life.

Settling into a chair opposite him, she curled her legs up under her. "What do you think of this place? Pretty cushy, huh?"

"I'm thinking this stuff cost a fortune. My tax dollars at work?"

"Actually, the house was acquired after the DEA arrested some big shot. From the looks of this stuff, I'm guessing they left the furniture."

Reilly propped his feet up on the glass-topped, wrought-iron coffee table. "At least it's comfortable. For a prison."

"Oh, come on. It's not that bad."

"Easy for you to say."

As much as she wanted to argue, she could see why he felt the way he did. They'd spent the last hour with Alex and the rest of the team as Alex highlighted emergency plans, escape routes, and strategies. It'd been an intense discussion on what to do if a threat presented.

"You think Branden's still in Portland?" Not that they could see him, of course. Too risky.

Still, being in Lincoln City brought back fond memories of the kid who'd been one of Reilly's good friends in high school.

"I don't know." Reilly yawned. "We kept in touch for about a year after that trip, but then he just dropped off the map. Then I started working for the prosecutor's office and, well, time went by."

Too bad. They'd been good friends at one point.

Maybe after this was all over, she should try to look him up. Sure, they'd be back in Jacksonville by then, but it'd be good to reconnect.

"Maybe I will turn in." Removing his glasses, Reilly rubbed his tired eyes. "Thanks for doing this. It helps having you here."

A lump the size of a mango lodged in her throat and she struggled to remain in control. "There's no place I'd rather be."

But what if she couldn't protect him? She couldn't lose him, especially not to a sniper's bullet.

Lord, help me.

He pushed up from the couch and turned for the stairs.

"One more thing."

Pausing, he met her eyes and waited.

"I want you to lock the main door to the bedroom, but don't lock the connecting door to the bathroom."

"When I'm asleep? Why?"

"If someone manages to get upstairs, they'll still have to get by me."

Narrow eyes and tight-set lips told her what he thought of the idea, but he didn't put those thoughts into words.

"Thanks. I know this isn't easy." A smile tickled the corners of her lips. "But it's about time I get to call the shots. You've been bossing me around for years."

"I have not."

It was good to see him smiling again, even if it wouldn't last. "Oh yes, you have. *You're* older and you never let me forget it."

"Oh yeah? When was the last time I told you what to do?"

"How about last week when you said I should rip out my fence and put in a taller one with a lock on the gate?"

"Your job's dangerous. I was looking out for you."

"Of course you were. It's your self-imposed duty."

"I'm pretty sure it's in the official big-brother handbook."

She arched an eyebrow. "So there's an official handbook now."

"Of course. You just wouldn't know about it." A yawn swallowed his face. "Well, I'm heading up. Night."

"Good night." She watched him trudge up the stairs, hoping he'd be able to sleep most of the night.

It wasn't likely to happen, but maybe exhaustion would trump the trauma.

She headed into the kitchen to find Alex sitting alone at the table, pad of paper and pen in front of her.

"Where's everyone else?"

Alex set the pen aside. "Peters is in the security room, Beckman's patrolling outside, and Chow and Rodriguez are resting up for the late shift."

"I haven't really examined the security room yet. How's the camera placement?"

"Adequate. They seem to cover the entire exterior, but don't have night vision."

As she passed the table, Lana nodded at the paper. "Working on a schedule?"

"Trying. I'm so tired, I'm feeling cross-eyed."

"I hear you. The only way I'm going to last the night is by flooding my system with coffee." Lana hesitated. "Can I make a scheduling request? Outdoor patrol at sunset?"

Alex leaned back in her chair. "Reilly know you're requesting the front lines at shooter prime-time?"

"He doesn't need to. Besides, he's the one who wanted me here."

Retrieving a mug from the cabinet by the sink, Lana poured herself some coffee. Hmmm, didn't look like the tar that construction crews used to refinish roads. Must not have been made by Alex.

"I'll do what I can, but it won't be every day." Alex rose and refilled her mug. A grimace crossed her face as she took a drink. "I knew I should've made it myself. This is weak."

"Just because it doesn't stick to your insides doesn't make it weak." A detour to the fridge and a little doctoring turned Lana's coffee from bland to delicious.

"Lemme try some of that."

Lana jerked her attention up to Alex. "Really? In all the years I've known you, I've never seen you drink your coffee any way but black."

Taking the butterscotch syrup from Lana's hand, Alex squirted in a generous amount. "Trust me. Nothing can make this coffee any worse than it already is."

"Who knows? You might even like it."

"Now you're talking crazy." Alex swirled the coffee in the cup to stir in the syrup and took a sip. "Better."

"You could try a little hazelnut creamer. It's pretty tasty."

"And ruin perfectly good butterscotch?" Crossing the kitchen, Alex reclaimed her seat at the table. "Shoo. I need to draw up the schedule."

Tired as she was, she'd wait to see the schedule before going to bed. Yes, she needed sleep. Even more, she needed to know Reilly was well-protected.

₪ ₪ ₪ ₪ ₪

Lana jerked awake. The blue numbers on the digital clock next to the bed glowed 5:17. A.M. Given that her shift had ended at four, she'd only been asleep for maybe an hour.

So what had woken her?

She listened. No unusual sounds. Steady breathing from the lump in the other bed indicated that whatever she'd heard hadn't disturbed Alex.

Maybe it was nothing. Still, she'd feel much better after checking on Reilly.

She pushed the covers back and swung her legs over the edge of the mattress.

The sound of movement drifted through the open bathroom door. Followed by mumbling.

But no sign of light.

Nausea churned her empty stomach. Reilly wasn't one to stumble around in the dark.

Snagging her Glock off the nightstand, she rushed to the bathroom. A glance found the room empty.

She slid across the tile and bumped his door open.

Arms flailed. The covers thrashed. A pillow landed on the floor with a soft thump.

But Reilly was alone.

A nightmare.

Which, by all appearances, rivaled the ones she'd endured most of her childhood. The ones which still occasionally regurgitated the unsettled questions in her past.

Jagged wheezing propelled her feet into motion.

"Ri." She spoke as softly as she could. "Ri, wake up."

No response.

Weird. Especially given that he'd always been a light sleeper.

"Ri." A little louder this time. "Wake up."

His limbs stilled, but his breathing didn't become any less labored.

Knowing that an arm or a leg could fly her direction at any time, she eased closer. She put a hand on his shoulder and gently shook. "Reilly."

His eyelids flipped open. Jerking upright, his gaze darted around the room. "Look out-"

Movements slowed. He surveyed the room one final time before turning back to her. "A dream?"

She scooped up the inhaler and thrust it toward him. "Breathe."

Several minutes passed, broken by nothing but the puff from the inhaler and the slowing of his breathing.

He disentangled his legs from the covers, clicked on the light, and set the inhaler aside. Hollow eyes stared out from his colorless face.

"Man. That was…" As he ran his fingers through his tousled hair, she couldn't help noticing how his hand shook. "That was intense."

She sat down next to him and wrapped an arm around his

shoulders. "You okay?"

A brief hesitation answered her question. "Getting there."

While definitely vague, it was a more honest response than he would've given most people. She decided to push a little more. "I know it's cliché, but it really does help to talk about it."

"It was the shooting. Over and over again. But there were other people around, too. Des, you, mom and dad."

"It's okay. We're all fine."

A little of the color had returned to his cheeks. "It felt real, you know?"

"I do. Believe me."

He shifted to look at her. "How long's it been?"

"Maybe two months."

"Really?" Snatching his glasses off the nightstand, he put them on and scrutinized her. "You're still having the nightmares?"

"Just the shadow one." After years of comforting her when they were kids, he'd know exactly which dream she meant.

Images flickered through her mind.

A dark room. A shadow standing silently next to her bed. Fabric in her mouth.

She tried to push the feelings down, but they kept coming.

A strong chemical smell, heat, a bitter wind.

None of it made any sense. It only made her miserable.

"You've been having that dream for thirty years. Ever think it's more than a dream?"

She blinked him back into focus. "The thought's crossed my mind, but it doesn't add up. Say I was abducted. Why didn't anyone try to find me? Why wasn't there a missing persons report? And what about the note?"

While her parents had never kept the adoption a secret from her, they'd waited until she was older - and pressing them for answers - to show her the note they'd found with her.

I can't take care of her anymore. You're a man of God, so I'm trusting you to find her a good home.

Like she was a dog or something.

She shook it off. "The note could've been from anyone, but abducted kids get reported. And besides, kids don't typically get abducted and dumped. There's usually a ransom."

Or a darker, more self-serving purpose.

She never allowed herself to dwell on that thought for long, especially since she was pretty certain she hadn't been abused.

"I agree, but reoccurring dreams tend to mean something. All I'm saying is that maybe you shouldn't discount it completely."

"Well, I'm not going to figure it out at five in the morning." Especially running on only one hour of sleep.

Reilly's attention shifted momentarily to the clock. "I didn't realize it was so early. Sorry."

"Don't be. It's about time I returned the favor."

"Go back to bed. I'm fine."

A brief examination found that his color was almost back to normal and the tremors had stopped. Most importantly, he seemed to be breathing fine. She held his gaze with her own. "You sure?"

"Yeah, I'm good. I think I'll try to catch a little more sleep. I should be done with the nightmares for now."

Not likely, but for his sake, she hoped he was right. "If you need me, for anything, don't hesitate to come get me, okay?"

"Got it."

Right. She'd believe it when it happened.

Sliding off the bed, she let her feet sink into the plush carpet. "Sleep well."

If only she could believe it would really happen. For either of them.

But with a killer nipping at their heels, sleep deprivation was the least of their concerns.

Five

A cool wind whipped Lana's ponytail into her face. Fighting off a chill, she zipped her jacket.

Was this place always so cold? She didn't remember it being like this when she visited before, although maybe time had dulled the memory.

If this was summer, she'd hate to feel their winter.

A few people dotted the beach in front of her, but thankfully, most of the tourists were further down the coast.

She had little trouble spotting Peters down by the water.

Shifting her attention, she took in the rest of the terrain.

About a hundred feet to her left, the beach ended at a rocky cliff that stretched into the ocean. It would be difficult for trouble to approach from that side.

Difficult, but not impossible.

Still, out of all the potential directions from which a sniper could advance, that one was the least of her concerns.

Movement in her peripheral drew her attention to the right.

Peters strode toward her. "Been quiet. You should be able to handle things."

How the heck was she supposed to respond to that? The way he'd said it implied that she had the competency of a two-year old.

He never paused or broke stride as he passed her, pushed through the fence, and approached the house. Evidently he'd neither expected nor desired a response.

Ugh. She was having a really hard time seeing whatever it was that Alex saw in him.

Be the better person. Let it go.

She refocused on the beach.

A handful of people dotted the landscape. A couple with two dogs - golden retrievers, by the looks of them - walked on the damp sand down by the waves. A family with three young children packed up the remnants of a picnic dinner. And a lone figure pointed something at the ocean. A camera, if she had to guess, but she was too far away to positively confirm that.

Out of all the people in her field of vision, the only one who seemed like a plausible threat was the photographer. Especially since all of the others were heading away from the safe house.

She broke into a jog, splitting her attention between the house, the photographer, and the surrounding area.

Her attention strayed frequently to the photographer, who appeared to be in no hurry to leave. With the sun sinking beyond the ocean, he was little more than a silhouette near the water's edge.

Definitely male. And tall. Not super skinny, but not ripped either.

What was he doing at this end of the beach? All the hotels were further up the coast. The ocean was the ocean, no matter what stretch of beach he was on. Why come all this way?

Of course, he could live down here.

Or he might be pretending to take pictures while really looking for a place that could be a government safe house.

Maybe she should talk to him. She was good at casually pumping strangers for information.

Her gaze danced across the beach.

The family had disappeared inside a modest one-story house and the dog-walkers were little more than a cluster of dots on the horizon.

Leaving only one unknown person in the vicinity.

A scan of the house revealed no sign of movement. All seemed to be quiet.

Now if this guy would move on, she'd be happy.

Alex had told her to immediately report anything suspicious and this guy was setting off more warnings than she could count.

Turning her head toward the collar of her jacket, she pressed the button on the hidden communicator. "Just a heads-up, there's a guy who seems too interested in taking pictures of the water."

The pause lasted for several seconds before Alex's voice responded. "We've got him. Let us know if anything changes."

Just knowing that the extra camera they'd installed had been repositioned to follow the man's progress made her feel better. She jogged a short distance up the beach before turning around.

Alex's voice came again. "Stay alive, people. He's

approaching."

A glance over found him headed her way.

Okay, definitely not good.

His hand lifted in a half wave.

Would a hired assassin wave?

She strategically positioned herself between him and the house as she slowed to a walk. If this man wanted to kill Reilly, he'd have to go through her to do it.

As he drew closer, she watched for anything resembling a weapon. The camera hanging from a strap around his neck appeared to be fairly new and had a long lens. The camera case slung over his shoulder was definitely large enough to contain a disassembled rifle.

"Great night, huh?" His voice carried across the thirty feet separating them.

A little cold for her liking, but it was easier to agree. "Not bad."

She'd never been more aware of the gun nestled at the small of her back, but she forced her hands to remain relaxed at her sides.

He stopped about two yards away.

Too close, given the circumstances, but at least she could glean enough details to create an accurate sketch should the need arise. About six foot, muscular in a lean sort of way, with chiseled features that enhanced dark chocolate eyes.

As long as he was here, maybe she could learn a bit more about him.

She gestured at the camera. "Are you a pro?"

"Guess you'd say so. I freelance." Half-turning, he nodded at the ocean that glowed like molten lava as the sun appeared to sink right into the waves. "Some of my favorite shots are west-coast sunsets."

"I can see why."

A professional photographer. That might explain why he was at this end of the beach. The area closer to the motels would be much more likely to have charred firewood or litter than this less populated location.

"I don't suppose you're a local." His voice latched her attention.

"Just vacationing." She continued to absorb details. Probably not much older than her, mid to late thirties at most, light brown hair worn short and neatly trimmed, a broad and easy smile. "Why do you ask?"

"Some of the best locations are off the beaten path. Places only the locals know about." He extended his hand. "Nate Miller."

"Lana."

His firm handshake exuded confidence. The smoothness of his skin made her think he was unaccustomed to physical labor, something she'd expect from a nature photographer.

"Nice to meet you." The smile splitting his face appeared genuine. "Do you always jog alone?"

Huge red flag. At least Alex had eyes on her in the camera room. She tried to formulate a reply, but words evaded her.

Red touched his cheeks and he grimaced. "Sorry, that came out wrong. You're probably thinking I'm some sort of creep."

Pretty much.

He didn't wait for a response before continuing, "What I meant was that most women jog with a friend or boyfriend or something."

"I like the solitude." The sun had vanished, leaving darkness in its wake. "I'd better get moving. I still need to get a little more distance in before heading back."

"Sure. Maybe I'll see you around."

Not likely. She offered a smile. "You never know."

She resumed jogging, fighting the desire to look over her shoulder with each step. Part of her expected a bullet to the back at any second.

"He's leaving the area."

Praise God. Alex couldn't have said anything more reassuring than those words.

Except maybe that the threat was past and they were all free to return to their lives.

Lana risked a glance behind her. Amazing how small a six foot man could look when he was a diminishing speck on the beach.

No one else was in sight.

She turned toward the communicator. "We're clear."

"Good." Unusual brusqueness traced Alex's words. "Keep an eye out for another fifteen minutes, then I want you inside for a briefing."

"Will do." Lana jogged a few short laps, keeping the house in full view at all times.

As she moved, she replayed the exchange in her head. Nothing stood out as overly suspicious and her instincts weren't screaming that this guy was trouble.

Night settled around her like a cloak.

A glance at her watch showed almost twenty minutes had passed since Alex's last communication. Twenty minutes with nothing but the crash of the waves and the harsh wind for company.

She turned toward the house, approached the back door, and knocked. While it'd be more convenient to have a key, no one was allowed to take one outside. At least if a sniper got the drop on one of them, they weren't handing him easy access to the house.

A moment passed before Alex opened the door. Lana stepped inside and secured the locks on the door before following Alex to the kitchen table.

"Okay. Tell me everything."

Lana recounted the conversation word for word while Alex scribbled some notes on a pad of paper in front of her.

When she finished, Alex leaned back, tapping her pen against pursed lips. "What does your gut tell you?"

"That he's a lonely guy who spends his life traveling, saw a woman jogging alone, and awkwardly started a conversation."

"Sounds likely." Alex blew out a breath. "Well, he's made our official watch-list. If he shows up again…"

He might be trouble. Alex didn't have to finish the thought for Lana to get the weight of it. "I'm going to see how Reilly's doing."

She crossed the living room, cutting between Rodriguez and whatever police drama he was watching.

Seriously? Didn't he get enough of that in real life?

At the top of the stairs, she spotted Reilly sitting in one of the two chairs situated by the waist-high wall of the loft, an open book in his hands. He looked up as she approached.

"Hey, you."

"No, hey, you." A smile attempted to curl his lips, but didn't quite make it.

"What're you doing up here all alone?"

"Tired of the TV, I guess. This seemed like a good place to relax."

Although the noise from the TV below drifted up, it didn't

seem to bother him. At least, not until the sound of gunfire battered their senses. Reilly's shoulders stiffened, his jaw clenched, and his fingers tightened on the book.

They might have to implement a comedy-only rule until Reilly's mental state improved.

Sinking into the chair across from him, she placed her hand on top of one of his. "How are you holding up?"

His eyes narrowed and his lips flattened. "Would you stop asking me that? I'm fine."

"You aren't sleeping, you're confined to a house being guarded by six US Marshals, and possibly being hunted by a professional assassin. That's anything but fine."

"At least I'm alive. I think your phone rang while you were gone."

She accepted the comment for the subject change it was and retrieved her phone from the table next to her bed.

Not just one missed call. Two.

She rejoined Reilly and sank into the chair next to his before scrolling through her call history. The same number both times, spaced about an hour apart. But not a number she recognized.

Wait a second. She'd seen it before.

She scrolled further back in her call history. There. It had called her two days ago.

Curious. Someone obviously wanted to reach her, but wouldn't leave a message.

"Who was it?"

She glanced up to find Reilly's book closed, his attention locked on her. "No idea, but both calls came from the same source. If it's important, they'll call back."

"They didn't leave a message?" Suspicion laced his words.

"It's no big deal."

He leaned forward, his elbows resting on his knees, his fingers interlocked. "How often do you get calls from unfamiliar numbers?"

Not often, but he was so paranoid right now that he didn't need to hear that. "It happens. Don't worry about it."

"Some freak calls you, twice, won't leave a message, and you expect me to shrug it off? You need to report this."

"Ri, calm down. The GPS chip has been removed from my

phone, so it would take some serious access and time for someone to track me down."

"It's still suspicious."

"No, it's life. It's probably someone from work."

"They'd leave a message."

"Maybe, maybe not." In all honesty, they probably would leave a message, but again, hearing that would do nothing to ease Reilly's concern. Time for a diversion. "You're getting kinda scruffy there. Trying out a new look?"

He rubbed the stubble covering his normally clean shaven chin. "Not intentionally. Whoever packed my stuff forgot to throw in my razor."

"Well, we're not out in the sticks. We could probably pick up a new one for you."

"Too bad you can't pick up a haircut while you're at it. That Rosetti trial kept me so busy I didn't even have time to cut my hair. It's way too long."

"And here I thought maybe Desiree had convinced you to grow it out a little." Reilly's artistic girlfriend might like his hair a little longer.

"Yeah, right. I don't think even Des could talk me into that one."

"Well, you're in luck. Alex knows how to cut hair."

He arched an eyebrow. "I know how to cut hair, too, but I want it to actually look good."

A chuckle slipped from her. "Relax. She took cosmetology classes when she was younger. I think she can handle it. In a few days when things calm down, we'll see what we can do."

"I'll hold you to that." Serious blue eyes zeroed in on her. "And if that number calls again, I want to know about it."

⁂ ⁂ ⁂ ⁂ ⁂

Lincoln City, Oregon. Smart move on the Marshals' part, hiding their witness in a town where tourism was a year-round business.

Little did they know that he was very familiar with this town.

Stevens flipped open the file he'd started on his latest project. Reilly Tanner.

Only two photos had come up in connection with Tanner's

name: one a dramatic shot taken in the courtroom, evidently during a case that was open to members of the media, the other the DMV photo he'd hacked through several firewalls and encryption software to get.

Even though he'd examined the pictures many times already, he mentally traced them again.

He had to be able to recognize Tanner instantly, just in case his window of opportunity was only a second long.

After a minute, he set the photos aside and turned to the other papers in his stack. Tanner's name had cropped up in several different newspaper articles, none of which he'd taken time to read, but all of which he'd printed off to peruse later.

Later had arrived.

He skimmed the first one, some piece on the trial of a repeat sex offender. The jury had found him guilty. Go figure.

The next one covered a drug smuggler's trial. Again, guilty.

But it was the third one that really made him pause. Written as a human interest story, it featured a brief interview with Tanner, one that the reporter stated had been given reluctantly and only after Tanner's boss, the lead prosecutor, had ordered him to do it. The reporter called it humility, but Stevens wasn't buying it.

It contained a surprising amount of information for something only a few paragraphs long. The son of a preacher, Tanner had never been married, was close to his parents and younger sister, and still attended his dad's church.

A co-worker described him as a quick-thinking man of integrity who pursued the truth with ferocity, possessing an uncanny ability to turn the best defense attorney's words against him.

When asked why he'd joined the prosecutor's office when he could've made more money in private practice, Tanner had stated, "God calls His people to seek justice and He put the love of justice in me. This job allows me to pursue that passion while obeying God."

Self-righteous do-gooder.

Well, Reilly Tanner, let's see your love of justice save you from me.

Six

A yawn popped Reilly's jaw. Even from across the room, Lana could see the exhaustion cutting deep lines around his eyes.

"You okay?"

He dipped his head in a half-nod. "Just tired. I didn't sleep very well last night."

And it was only a little after noon. Maybe he'd fall asleep in front of the TV this afternoon. "Before or after the nightmare?"

"Was there a difference?"

The nightmare had hit around 2 a.m. and if his response had been any indication, it had been a doozy. He'd refused to talk about it, but it had left him pale, trembling, and struggling to breathe.

Seeing him like this physically hurt.

If she could take the burden from him, she'd do it. Without hesitation.

The phone on the table in front of her vibrated against the glass. She plucked her cell off the coffee table and glanced at the display.

Her heart tripped at the unknown number.

"Same one as yesterday?" Tension oozed from Reilly's words.

"Yeah." Meeting Reilly's steady gaze, she accepted the call.

"Milana?"

Her full name. Spoken by a man's voice. Not familiar.

The thoughts fired through her brain like an M16 on full auto. She focused on keeping her tone steady. "Yes. Who is this?"

"What, you don't recognize my voice?"

The teasing tone triggered familiarity in her mind, but she couldn't tie the vague memory to any specific person.

A gray hue covered Reilly's face. His fingers pressed into the arms of his chair with enough force to leave permanent impressions.

Time to get this nutcase off the phone so Reilly could relax. "Do I know you?"

"You sure used to. I'll give you a hint–"

"I'm sorry, but I don't have time to play games. Please don't call again."

"No, wait! It's Elliott."

No way. "Elliott? Really?"

"Yeah, really. Man, I knew I should've looked you up sooner."

Offering Reilly a smile, she mouthed *it's okay* before returning her attention to the phone. Reilly had never met her best friend from college, so telling him who was on the phone would offer no reassurance.

"I meant to stay in touch after college, but then I got married and life happened and now it's been what, ten years?"

Close.

How did she know this was really Elliott? Sure, the voice sounded right, but voices could be faked, especially over the phone and especially given the years that had passed. Until she knew for sure, she'd have to be careful to not reveal anything personal.

Which meant keeping the conversation focused on him. "You're married? Congratulations."

He snorted. "Don't bother. It lasted two years. I thought the next one was going better, but she left me after five years."

"I'm sorry."

Unfortunately for him, that sounded like the Elliott she remembered. He'd always had tumultuous relationships with members of the opposite sex, so being twice-divorced in a ten year period didn't strike her as unlikely, not for him.

"Yeah. They both said I was distant and closed-off, if you can believe it."

Now that sounded nothing like the warm, fun-loving Elliott she remembered. Unsure how she was supposed to respond, she opted for a different subject. "What are you up to these days?"

"I'm still a techie. Travel a lot doing systems trouble-shooting for a company with offices all across the country. Another of my exes' complaints."

"I imagine that's hard on relationships."

Actually, it took no imagination at all. She knew very well how hard it was to maintain relationships when you spent a good portion of your life away from the ones you loved. It was one of the main reasons that, no matter how much Alex pushed or persuaded, she would never permanently make the jump to working witness protection.

Sure, she traveled some in her position, but wasn't gone for weeks or months at a time.

"Harder than I thought it would be, that's fursure."

Fursure. Only one person she'd ever met said "for sure" with such an odd pronunciation, running the two words together every single time. Elliott.

Any relief at having his identity confirmed was quickly extinguished by concern.

How had he gotten her number? It wasn't like she'd posted it on the internet.

Now to phrase it so it didn't convey the suspicion she couldn't stem. "I didn't know you had my number."

He chuckled. "I didn't. And let me tell you, it wasn't easy to find. But techno geeks like me have ways of tracking people down."

Tracking people down. A chill shuddered through her core. Could he have picked a worse choice of words?

Relax. It's Elliott.

Yes, but if he could track her down, couldn't an assassin?

"Milana? You still there?" Elliott's voice shattered her thoughts.

She cleared her throat. "Uh, yeah. Sorry. Distractions. You know."

"If it's not a good time, I can call back later."

"No, no, this is fine. So who do you work for?"

"Private sector. I'm the official company trouble-shooter. They call me to fix whatever problems their people have created."

She smiled, hoping the action would carry through in her tone. "Which, when you're dealing with computers, can be a long list."

"Fursure. What about you?"

"I'm in acquisitions. My employer tells me what they want and I track it down." The standard answer to that question slid effortlessly off her tongue. It was general enough that it fit a wide variety of job descriptions while still encompassing much of what she did. "How's your dad?"

"Not bad. A few health things, but nothing major."

They talked for a few more minutes before she said she needed to get going. After terminating the call, she looked up to find Reilly watching her, speculation etched on his face.

"Elliott?"

The inquiry came as no surprise. "An old friend from college. I haven't spoken to him in years."

"I think I may remember hearing the name. Didn't you guys date for a while?"

"We were just friends." No need to tell him that they'd gone on one date, to which she'd agreed mostly to get Elliott to stop asking, and there'd been no sparks. After that, their friendship resumed as if the date had never happened.

"Time changes things."

Sheesh. Ever since Reilly started going out with Desiree, he seemed eager to pair her off with someone, too. "He's not a Christian."

"Oh." A second slid by. "You know, I never realized how good you are at deflecting personal questions."

"Force of habit."

"Doesn't it get old? Never being able to be yourself?"

"It is what it is. Besides, I am being myself. Did you hear me say anything that wasn't true?"

"I didn't hear you say much about yourself at all."

"I knew what I was getting into when I joined the Marshals' office." Not being able to tell Elliott everything didn't really bother her.

What did bother her was the timing of his reestablishing contact. Why now?

Could he possibly be working with Rosetti? He'd been vague about who he worked for and Rosetti did operate a large corporation. In the private sector. Maybe Rosetti had discovered the link in their past and was exploiting that to track down Reilly so his goons could finish what they'd started.

No. That was ridiculous. The odds of Elliott working for Rosetti were astronomically low.

No matter the odds against it, that fraction of a chance couldn't be completely dismissed. A background check on Elliott should turn up the answers necessary to either ease or fortify her suspicions.

⁂

"Why do *you* always have to patrol the beach?"

Lana glanced up from her shoelaces to find Reilly leaning against the doorframe, arms crossed over his chest, eyebrows pressed low over his eyes.

"We have to secure the area. You know that."

"It shouldn't be you. Let Peters or Rodriguez do it."

"You mean let one of the guys handle it, don't you? I've never known you to be sexist before."

Color flooded his cheeks. "It's not sexist. It's common sense. It's bad enough you jog alone at home, but here you don't even know the terrain."

An argument was the last thing she wanted.

Especially since this had little to do with her jogging alone.

She finished tying her shoelace and pushed up from the bed. "I appreciate the concern, but I'm perfectly safe. Earpiece in my ear, communicator clipped to my collar, gun near my fingertips, running shoes in place."

"None of which will stop a bullet."

"Come on, Ri. Look at me. Would anyone who doesn't know me instantly think, 'hey, I bet she's a Fed? Seriously."

The scowl twisting his features was one she suspected he normally reserved for defense lawyers. "Maybe not, but if a hit man is out to get me, couldn't you be a target, too?"

It was possible, and a concern she was certain the rest of the team shared. "Until we know who's been hired, we work under the assumption that you're the only target."

"I don't like it."

She slid past him. "You don't have to like it, but I have a job to do. Remember, you're the one who pushed for me to be here. What did you think this would look like?"

"I'm going to talk to Alex." He fell into step with her as she descended the stairs.

"Go ahead. But if you want to do something really productive, you could pray. This is all in God's hands."

A sigh seeped from his mouth and his shoulders sagged. "Be careful, okay?"

"I always am."

In the kitchen, Rodriguez pushed up from the table and let her out the back door.

Moisture laced the air, chilling through her jacket even as the deadbolt scraped into place behind her. At least the rain that'd plagued them most of the day had tapered off during dinner.

Mist shrouded the beach, shadowing the restless ocean in a gray haze.

She crossed the damp lawn, pushed through the gate, and stepped onto the wet sand.

The beach appeared to be mostly deserted, no surprise given the weather.

Several shapes rose out of the mist like formless monsters. The shudder that rocked her body couldn't be suppressed; the image too closely resembled one of those creepy movies Reilly occasionally got the urge to watch.

Much as she hated those movies, she'd gladly watch a marathon rather than live this horror story of her own.

Focus.

It was only a horror story if something happened to Reilly. And she wasn't about to let that happen.

One of the figures drew closer. Features slowly formed. Chow.

He paused several feet from her location. "All is quiet out here."

"Thanks." Moving past him, she jogged through sand that shifted beneath her feet. As she approached the packed sand, she studied the people in her field of vision.

Two people, most likely a couple judging by the lack of space between them, strolled by the ocean's edge. Though she couldn't see them well enough to discern any details, she could tell they were walking away from her.

Another person - diminutive size indicated a woman - jogged with a dog by her side. Also moving away from the target zone.

The only other person was significantly larger. He had something in his hands.

Damp air stuck in her lungs.

A gun? She was too far away to confirm or disprove that suspicion.

He lifted the object.

She reached for the weapon at her back. The cold metal of her Glock met her fingers.

Wait - he wasn't aiming at the house. Whatever he held, he was directing it toward the ocean.

Confusion melted away.

Because it wasn't a gun. It was a camera.

Which meant that the man was probably that photographer from last night. Miller.

What was he doing down here again?

Once she could've overlooked, but twice? If he were staying at a hotel - likely, since he'd indicated he didn't know the area - he'd traveled a reasonable distance to come to this section of beach. And for what, a few pictures?

And why tonight? By his own admission, he liked shooting sunsets. It would take nothing less than x-ray vision to see the sun go down tonight.

Raise the alarm or let it go?

Ugh. Peters was in the camera room tonight. If she said something, he'd be the one most likely to respond. And if it amounted to nothing, as she suspected it would, he'd probably accuse her of being an alarmist.

The last thing she needed to do was give Peters more ammunition in his quest to have her sent home.

For now, she'd be quiet and watch for suspicious activity.

She casually altered her course. Away from the ocean and toward the more loosely packed sand.

Barely ten steps into her plan, he turned and pointed his camera at the houses lining the beach. Her pulse almost drowned out the sound of the crashing waves.

What was he doing?

He'd said he liked sunsets and nature. Houses were neither of those things.

Time to alert the team.

She paused with her hand on the communicator. Exactly what was she going to tell them? That there was a man who might attack them with his camera?

"Hey!" A hand lifted in a half wave.

Dang. He'd spotted her. Maybe she could pretend she hadn't heard–

"Lana!"

Nope. He was too close for that card to work. Ignoring him at this point would only draw attention and undue suspicion.

She responded with a small wave of her own.

Well, as long as she was now obligated to converse, maybe she could get answers to some of the more troubling questions.

"It's good to see you."

She wished she could say the same.

Instead, she forced a smile she didn't feel. "I'm surprised to see you out tonight. No sunset."

A light shrug danced across his shoulders. "This fog creates kind of an interesting effect, don't you think?"

If by interesting he meant eerie and challenging to secure the area, then yeah. Sure.

He didn't seem to expect a response as he continued, "I especially liked the way the fog wrapped around that one there."

Following his finger, she surveyed the house to which he pointed. The large two-story needed to have the paint stripped and reapplied. Overgrown weeds filled the yard. More importantly, it was only three houses down from the safe house.

"That one? It looks kind of, I don't know, decrepit."

Straight teeth flashed from his full grin. "Exactly. Doesn't the fog give it a mysterious hue?"

She examined the house more closely. It looked like something out of a B-grade thriller movie, not what she'd consider art. But if there was one thing she'd learned from spending time around Reilly's girlfriend, it was that creative types, artists especially, saw the world through different eyes.

Shifting her attention from the house, she found Miller watching her.

Was he waiting for her to say something?

She offered a small shake of her head. "Sorry. I don't see it."

A laugh bubbled from him. "That's okay. Not many people would. But if you saw the print once I develop it, I think you'd understand."

"I'm surprised you come this far down the beach. It's quite a walk from the hotels."

"I like the view down here."

Really? He was going to leave it at that? "Hate to break it to you, but it's the same ocean. The view can't be all that different."

"You'd be surprised. Fewer people to ruin the shots, less litter and debris, plus those great old houses. It's a photographer's paradise."

"I guess you would know."

"Is this your first trip to Lincoln City?"

"Second visit. How about you?" As the words left her mouth, her eyes scanned the area. No one else was on the beach. At least not as far as she could see.

The only visible threat to Reilly's safety at the moment stood directly in front of her.

"I've been here a time or two. I travel up and down the coast any chance I get." His attention didn't stray from her face. "Are you traveling with family?"

Why did he want to know?

Relax.

It was actually a pretty normal question, one she wouldn't give much thought to any other time. "Yeah. We needed an escape from the daily grind, you know?"

"I get it. Are you guys sticking around for a while?"

Wait a second; she'd wanted to get more information from him. How did this conversation become about her? "Another week or so. What drew you to this area? Family?"

Hardness flitted across his face and darkened his brown eyes. "I don't have any family. I grew up in a group home."

Words abandoned her.

A humorless laugh seeped from him. He blinked several times and managed a smile that didn't reach his eyes. "Not an experience I'd recommend."

The light attitude he faked failed miserably, colored by a pain few people would ever understand.

But she was one of the few.

"I never knew my parents either." The words escaped like a convict after a prison break.

Why had she said that? Way too personal.

Besides, while it might seem like they shared common ground, what did she really know about him anyway? They might have completely different backgrounds.

His voice halted the tirade inside her head. "Wish I could say the same. I knew my mom, but it would've been better if I hadn't."

Well, since he'd started this conversation, she might as well keep it going. Maybe she'd learn something useful. "Most days I'm able to say I don't care, but… I don't know, there's always this part of me that wonders what they were like."

"Well, take it from me, sometimes it's better not knowing. My last memory of my mom was when she dropped me off in front of the group home. I was five. She told me to be a man and she'd be back. Yeah, right."

How awful. "What about your dad? Where was he during all this?"

He dug the toe of his shoe in the damp sand. "I don't even think Mom knew who he was. Probably one of her johns. Or her pimp. Never did like that guy."

Johns.

Pimp.

Whoa. Bad enough that his mother had been a prostitute, but he'd known enough to be able to connect the dots as he got older.

What did a childhood like that do to a kid?

"So you actually met, uh…"

Wow. What was she thinking?

There was no tactful way to ask a question like that, nor was it any of her business.

"Oh yeah. She used to lock me in the closet when her clients came over. Seemed that pimp was never far away."

"I-I'm sorry." Lame. Was that the best she could offer?

"You know the saying. What doesn't kill us makes us stronger, right?"

"So they say." The image of a brown-haired little boy cowering in the back of a closet haunted her thoughts.

"Now that you've heard my story, what's yours?"

Not high on the list of things she wanted to discuss, but how could she not answer after what he'd told her? "I was abandoned on a stranger's doorstep when I was little. They adopted me."

"So this brother you're traveling with…"

"Adoptive."

"Lucky you. Are you the oldest?"

"No, he has a few years on me. And he reminds me of it every chance he gets."

"Tanner. Everything okay?" Peters' voice barked in her ear.

She blinked. When had it gotten so dark? No wonder they were checking up on her.

Time to get away from Nate. "I had no idea it was so late. I better get going."

His hand gently caught her elbow. "I'm glad I ran into you."

Measuring out a breath, she tried to relax the muscles that had stiffened automatically at his touch. "Me, too."

The words rolled off her tongue automatically.

"So, I, uh, wasn't only at this end of the beach for the pictures. I mean, I was, but I had kinda hoped I'd run into you again." He dropped his hand, fidgeted, and ran his fingers through his hair. "Would you like to grab dinner? Maybe tomorrow?"

Whoa. He was asking her out.

She should've seen that one coming, but it still caught her off guard. "It sounds like fun, but our situation is, um, well, it's complicated. My time often isn't my own."

"That's cryptic." He quirked an eyebrow, but the lighthearted gesture didn't completely mask his disappointment.

"I know. I'm sorry. I'd like to, but–"

"Lana, you okay?" Alex. Probably wondering why she hadn't checked in yet. Or responded to Peters' inquiry.

She focused on Miller. "I'm sorry, I need to get going."

"Well, how about I walk you back to your hotel?"

"Actually, I'm headed that way." She nodded toward a public beach access point several houses away.

"Oh. Okay, then. Maybe I'll run into you again?"

"Maybe. Well, have a good evening." She stole a surreptitious glance at the safe house. The fog and the dark made it difficult to tell for sure, but she was reasonably certain no one was in the vicinity. As much as she hated to do it, she started jogging in the opposite direction.

Once she was a safe distance away, she got on her communicator. "Things look good out here. I'm headed back."

"Stinking fog. We couldn't see you." Tension laced Alex's words. "Where have you been?"

"Everything's fine. I'll explain when I get there."

Good thing Alex was a friend. If Peters was in charge, she would probably find herself on the next plane back to Florida.

Of course, if Peters was in charge, she never would've made it to Oregon in the first place.

When she reached the public beach access, she looked back. Nate's form was barely visible down by the water, walking away from the safe house in the direction of the hotels. She jogged to the road and followed it back to the safe house.

As she jogged, her thought drifted to Nate. Something about him drew her.

Not many people understood the feeling of being on the outside. In fact, in many ways, she didn't feel like she understood it herself. The Tanners had accepted her and loved her so fully that she hardly ever remembered that she wasn't biologically a part of their family.

But when she did, those old feelings of abandonment, questions of why she hadn't been worth keeping, rose to the surface like a corpse in the water.

Nate understood those feelings. In a way no one else she'd ever met before could.

Reaching the house, she circled to the back and surveyed the beach. All clear. "I'm at the back door."

The door opened as she reached it. Concern etched Alex's face as she let Lana inside.

"What happened? It's not like you to go silent. Or be late."

"Nate Miller."

"The photographer?"

She answered with a curt nod. "One of the only people on the beach."

"What did you learn?"

Ah, Alex knew her so well. She recapped the conversation quickly, leaving out Nate's dinner invitation.

Short fingernail tapping her lip absently, Alex studied her face. "Seems odd to me that he would return to this particular area."

"The same thought occurred to me."

"Did you ask him about it?"

"He claimed he likes the seclusion and the old beachfront houses." A small *humpf* slid from Alex's mouth. "It sounded a little off to me, too."

"And he gave no other reason?" Concern narrowed Alex's eyes. "I wonder if we've been made, although I don't know how."

Dang. No getting around it, was there? "He did say that he'd hoped to run into me."

"Really." Mischief laced the single word and all traces of suspicion fled. "So he was trying to find *you*, is that what I'm hearing?"

"So he claimed. Although, if he is an assassin, that could be a convenient excuse."

In fact, the more she thought about it, the more the idea fit.

She leaned against the counter and looked at Alex. "Do you think we have enough to do a background check? Name, approximate age, and the fact that he was in the system as a kid?"

Alex rubbed her forehead. "I don't know. Nate Miller isn't exactly an uncommon name. We'll try, but I'm not holding out a lot of hope."

Unfortunately, she wasn't either.

Unless she could get more information, like where Miller had grown up or lived now, they'd be more likely to find a winning lotto ticket than learn anything about the mysterious Nate Miller.

"Okay." Alex came down the stairs, pocketing her cell phone as she reached the bottom.

Activity stilled. Everyone was in the living room, except Peters, who had security room detail, and Beckman, who was patrolling the exterior. The call from Alex's superior had come about ten minutes earlier and Lana had no doubt all of them were anxious to hear what progress had been made.

If any. It was only Monday; how much progress could've been made over the weekend?

Alex surveyed the group. "They found the weapon. Buried in the suspect's backyard."

Not exactly the brightest place to hide incriminating evidence.

"Ballistics confirmed that it's the murder weapon. Between that and Reilly's testimony, the prosecutor's office is confident they can secure a conviction."

What she didn't say felt as heavy as what she had said. Because Reilly's testimony was still critical, none of them would be headed home soon. Unless the suspect pled guilty.

Unfortunately, she doubted that would happen.

Only four days in this house and she already felt trapped. What would her sanity look like if this lasted for months?

At least *she* could leave the house. What about Reilly's sanity?

She couldn't worry about that right now. They had more pressing concerns. "Any word yet on who's been hired?"

"Not so far. We've been instructed to carry on as usual."

Watch and wait. Oh, and pray that an assassin's bullet didn't penetrate their carefully constructed hedge of protection.

Man, did he hate down time.

Soft cloth in hand, Stevens rubbed the barrel of his rifle. Not that it needed cleaning. Heck, it hadn't been used all week. But cleaning his weapons felt productive, so that was precisely what he did.

The so-called inside source had yet to make contact, which left Stevens doing a lot of legwork as he tracked his target. Not an easy task. The trail grew colder by the day and the marshals protecting the target were skilled at masking their tracks.

Masking them, but not completely erasing them.

In fact, he'd made good headway today. He'd located a few houses that fit the profile. His next step: set up surveillance and see who was living there.

No matter the steps taken to hide him, Tanner hadn't disappeared. One way or another, he'd track Tanner down and do the thing he did best.

Kill. With no hesitation, no mercy, and no regrets.

Seven

Another day that had lasted way too long.

If she were in prison, she'd be drawing hash marks on the wall. She'd be up to a whopping six by now.

Had it really only been six days since they'd arrived in Lincoln City?

Lana shut her Bible and pushed it aside. While she'd thought scripture would calm her nerves, she still felt ready to snap.

The team had avoided her all day.

Even Alex, who could usually cheer her up, kept her distance.

Reilly was the only one who seemed unconcerned by her melancholy mood. His nonchalant attitude helped, but she was still on edge and had no clue why.

Maybe it was the nightmare that had awoken Reilly the night before. He'd refused to talk about it, but it had upset him enough that he'd given up on sleep. She'd opted to stay up with him and the sleep deprivation wasn't helping.

The weather might also have something to do with it.

She glanced out her bedroom window, looking at the overcast sky. It had rained almost all day, with a bit of thunder and lightning in the afternoon. The sun never once penetrated the curtain of clouds, leaving a bleak, gray mist hanging in the air.

If she were a sniper, she'd choose to act on a night like this one. Between the empty beach and the clouds blocking most of the natural light, conditions were ideal for a hit.

Stop it!

So far there'd been no hint of trouble and with Chow watching the monitors, they'd see an attack coming before it happened.

She needed to do something, anything, to keep her mind busy.

Maybe she'd patrol the yard. It would give her a chance to run off some steam, spend some time alone.

Alex had moved the evening patrols indoors tonight due to the storm, so going out there would actually feel productive. She pulled a black sweatshirt over her head, put on her tennis shoes, and headed downstairs.

The TV blared and Peters slouched in one of the leather chairs with his gaze glued to the screen. Beckman sat on the sofa, feet propped on the coffee table, head back, eyes closed. The banging in the kitchen told her that Reilly and Alex were still cleaning up from dinner.

Her eyes narrowed as she descended into the living room. The blinds covering one window weren't closed tightly. Who would do such a reckless thing?

Walking toward the window, she froze when she caught a shift in the shadows beyond the glass. She plastered herself against the wall, her eyes trained on the large shrub bordering the property.

"Hey you. What's going on?"

Reilly's voice registered in the back of her mind, but she couldn't tear her eyes from the shape outside.

Barely discernible through the veil of shadows, the silhouette of a man crouched by one of the shrubs. In his hands, a long narrow object pointed at the house.

Her gaze whipped to Reilly, standing right in the line of sight.

"Down!"

She slammed into Reilly as the shot rang out. They tumbled to the floor. Pain seared her arm. Glass rained around them.

"You okay?" she asked, her head only inches from his.

"Yeah."

Acid ate at her right arm. She hadn't been fast enough.

But Reilly was fine. Nothing else mattered.

"Lights!" she yelled to Alex. Another gunshot thundered as the room went dark.

First priority. Get Reilly locked in the panic room.

If the shooter had any kind of night vision equipment, he'd likely see them opening the closet door.

That left the entrance in the master bedroom.

She whispered in Reilly's ear. "Upstairs. Stay low."

"Got it."

Pulling her gun, she eased off him. Fire blazed through her arm with each movement but she couldn't focus on that now.

Boom, boom!

The gunshots sounded like cannon fire in the living room. As she reached the stairs, she risked a glance behind her. It looked like someone – probably Alex – was drawing the assassin's fire.

Going around Reilly, she led the way to the top.

She pulled him into the closet, shut the door, and hit the light switch.

The all-too-familiar sound of Reilly's inhaler froze her movements. "Ri, how you doing? Do you need your pills?"

He shook his head. "I'm okay."

"Try to stay calm. Alex is the best there is. She has everything under control."

She knelt in the corner and jerked up the carpet, her mind assessing Reilly's breathing as her muscles moved instinctively. A bit raspy, but not bad. She jabbed the button on the floor. The door swung open.

The florescent lights flickered to life and she led the way to the ladder. Clenching her teeth against the pain stabbing her arm, she descended with all the speed she could muster.

At the bottom, she keyed in the code and jerked the door open. Even though it felt unnecessary, she swept the room.

Empty.

She pulled Reilly inside and pointed to a lever on the wall to the left of the door. "This disables the keypad so the door can only be opened from the inside. Don't open the door until one of us comes for you, got it?"

"Got it." His fingers landed on her arm. "Be care–"

He yanked his hand back as if she'd burned it and stared at the blood staining his fingers. "You were hit?"

"Just a scratch."

His face paled a few shades.

His breathing shallowed. A shaky hand brought up the inhaler and forced a puff into his mouth.

"Ri, look at me. I'm fine. I've cut myself worse slicing vegetables."

"You're sure?"

"Definitely." Grabbing a handful of her sweatshirt, she gently wiped the blood from his fingers. "Hey, would I have been able to handle that ladder or open this door if I was bleeding to death? It's no biggie, really."

A bit of an exaggeration, but it seemed to help.

She needed to get back upstairs, but didn't want to leave Reilly when he could so easily have a massive attack.

Turning her head toward her collar, she got on her communicator. "What've we got?"

"No more shots. I think he's gone." Alex's whispered voice carried through her earpiece. "Chow, can you see anything on the monitors?"

"No, it is too dark."

She met Reilly's eyes. "The shooter's gone. I'm going upstairs to help secure the scene. Stay here. And only open the door for someone on the team, okay?"

"Got it."

"Are you going to be alright?"

"I think so."

Not good enough. She unclipped her communicator and removed her earpiece. "If you need help, push this button and speak. It goes straight into our earpieces and someone will be right down. This," she held up the earpiece, "will let you hear what's going on so you'll know we're all okay."

After waiting for his nod, she shoved the door closed and headed for the ladder.

She gritted her teeth as she scaled the ladder. Okay, so maybe she'd downplayed her injury a lot. This hurt!

Turning off the light, she closed the access panel and felt her way toward the closet door.

Once in the living room, she crawled over to where Alex crouched by the wall. "I gave Reilly my com device in case he has an attack. What's the plan?"

"Lana, Rodriguez, outside. Beckman, guard the front door, Peters, the back. I'll cover Reilly from the living room." Alex spoke through the coms so the whole team could hear.

Lana scurried through the kitchen, snagged an extra earpiece and communicator from the security room, and backtracked to the hallway where Rodriguez waited. They slipped into the closest bedroom.

The window slid open silently and she pushed the screen out.

Her feet hit the sandy soil with a soft thud. Rodriguez landed behind her and she motioned for him to take the front of the house while she checked the rear.

The back yard was deserted, the beach beyond void of life.

That left the far side of the house. Assuming the shooter had remained in the area.

She crept toward the corner, her heart drumming a frantic rhythm.

The assassin could be watching her right now, lining her up in his crosshairs, tightening his finger on the trigger.

She reached the corner, stopped, and listened.

An engine roared. A dog barked. Waves crashed.

Behind all that, growing louder by the second, she heard the most beautiful sound of all. Sirens.

Scanning the brush for any sign of movement, she cautiously approached the fence.

Rodriguez came around the other side of the house and she lowered her gun.

The fact that the two of them were in plain sight and still standing proved that the shooter was gone.

She approached the shrubs the shooter had used for cover.

The flattened area suggested that the shooter was a larger person. A man, judging by the shadow she'd seen. Several shell casings littered the area, but the would-be killer had vanished.

"He's gone, but the local PD is here." Rodriguez's voice competed with the sirens as swirling lights drew closer.

Chow was the first one to speak. "There is a reason I did not see him. There is a narrow section of the yard that is not covered by a camera."

Impossible!

She'd checked the camera positioning herself and knew that the cameras all had overlapping coverage. How could this spot not be on any monitors?

Alex's voice came through the earpiece. "So you can't see Lana or Rodriguez right now?"

"Not at all. There is a whole strip there, I would guess maybe several meters wide, that I cannot see on any monitor."

"Good to know. Rodriguez, you're sure we're clear?"

"Oh yeah. This dude's long gone."

"Okay. I'm gonna let Reilly out. You two stay out there and smooth things over with the locals."

"Got it."

Dealing with the police was the last thing she wanted to do right now. Snooping in the camera room currently topped the list.

Scratch that. Downing a couple of pain killers would be her first priority.

Red and blue lights chased shadows across the yard as a police car whipped into the driveway.

Holstering her gun, she withdrew her badge and started toward them, Rodriguez right behind her. The first car jerked to a stop, with two others close behind.

What'd they do? Dispatch half the police department?

The doors on the closest car flew open.

Blinding light bathed the area and she could barely make out the shape of an officer training his gun on her. "Drop your weapon!"

The voice came from the passenger side of the car and she focused her attention there. "Deputy Tanner, US Marshal's office." She held her badge a little higher.

The officer eased forward, weapon still drawn and ready, and inspected both her badge and Rodriguez's. He slowly lowered his gun. "Got a report of gunfire. Is the situation under control?"

"Yes. The shooter escaped before we could get to him." Lana glanced over as another officer joined them. "Who called this in?"

"A neighbor. Was outside smoking and heard the shots," the first officer said.

Rodriguez put his badge away. "Thanks for getting here so quickly. I don't suppose you saw anyone leaving."

The officers exchanged a brief look. "No. What happened here?"

"Some dude shot at us."

The first officer snorted. "You don't say. Know who it was?"

"No idea." Lana stepped in before Rodriguez could offer another snarky reply. "Is CSU on the way?"

"Yeah, he should be here soon. Have you contained the scene?"

"We'd just finished looking for the shooter when you pulled up. The shots came from over here." She turned, leading the way toward the trampled bush.

The officers inspected the scene and conferred quietly. Frequent glances danced from her to Rodriguez to the house and back to the bush.

One of the officers finally cleared his throat. "We'll need to get statements from each of you."

Thunder grumbled overhead.

Lana glanced upward, but couldn't see anything other than darkness. A single raindrop splashed on her cheek. "How about we do a grid search before the rain washes away any evidence?"

"My thoughts exactly." An older officer with a weathered face and silver beard waved over the rest of the responders. "We're fighting the clock here. Fan out."

Alex's voice came from behind her. "Rodriguez, you got this? I need to talk to Milana for a minute."

The tone of Alex's voice, if not the use of her full first name, instantly put her on edge. She watched the officers follow Rodriguez away, waited until they were out of earshot, and turned to Alex. "Is Reilly okay?"

"He's a little shaken up, but not hurt. I can't say the same for you though, can I?"

"Reilly told you, didn't he?"

"He confirmed it, but I already knew. I saw blood on the floor. If Reilly had been hit, you would've demanded an ambulance. I knew it had to be you."

"It grazed me. No big deal."

Alex didn't look convinced. "Where is it?"

"My right arm."

Sirens approached. Probably the ambulance. Certainly less than a minute away.

Alex held her gaze with fierce eyes. "You're gonna sit this one out. And you're going to let the EMTs do their job."

As much as she wanted to argue, the burning convinced her that she shouldn't. "You're right, but they take care of everyone else first."

Alex's face showed her displeasure. "Sometimes you drive me crazy, you know that?"

"Was anyone else hurt?"

"Some flying glass nailed Beckman, but I think that's about it."

"Don't forget Reilly. His head hit the floor pretty hard when we went down. And I want the EMT's to check his breathing, too."

"Fine, first Reilly, then Beckman, then you. But if you think you're gonna hang around out here, you're crazy."

"Really? You're sidelining me? When you need me to help-"

"What I need is for you to keep that wound clean. You're out." Alex didn't wait for a reply before getting on the communicator. "Peters, Chow, we need your help out here. Beckman, relieve Chow in the camera room."

The sirens stopped as the ambulance parked on the side of the road. Two EMTs jumped out. Alex waved them toward the house.

Wait, if Peters and Chow were coming out here and Alex was with her... "Who's with Reilly?"

"Don't worry. He's locked in his room and I'm headed there now to cover him." Putting a hand on her back, Alex gave her a gentle push. "Go inside. That's an order."

Lana and Alex reached the back door as Peters and Chow stepped outside.

While Alex walked to the living room, Lana headed for the security room. She had to see the camera placement for herself. She watched over Beckman's shoulder as Chow and Peters rounded the corner of the house. Seconds later, they walked off the screen and disappeared from sight.

The blind spot wasn't huge, but it was obviously big enough.

Somehow the shooter had known about it.

The truth attacked her like a rabid dog.

The camera hadn't moved on its own.

It'd been manually repositioned or electronically adjusted. The former would be hard to do without being detected and the latter required access to this room.

No. There had to be some other explanation.

Maybe the adjustment controls had been bumped and whoever did it hadn't noticed the different camera angle.

Or maybe the wind had shifted the camera. Would have been one heck of a wind, maybe hurricane force, but it could happen, right?

Right.

And it just happened to cover the exact area with bushes big enough to conceal a man with a rifle? Right outside the only window where someone *accidentally* forgot to close the blinds?

No way. There were too many variables involved for her to buy the idea that this hadn't been intentional.

A sick feeling settled in her stomach.

One of them was a traitor. How could this happen?

She had to get out of this place before she emptied her stomach onto the floor. Heat coursed through her body and her breathing shallowed.

The kitchen wasn't much cooler than the security room, but at least the air didn't feel as thick. She headed through the living room, nodded at the brown-haired EMT descending the stairs, and stepped outside.

The light mounted next to the door was turned off, basking the covered porch in darkness.

She sat on the top step, a cool breeze washing over her as she stared at the multicolored lights playing off the surrounding houses.

Curtains moved in almost every house within sight. Something told her the neighborhood hadn't seen this much activity since the DEA took down the man who used to own this house.

All her remaining energy evaporated. It'd be so nice to lean her head against the railing next to her and close her eyes.

But she couldn't.

She had to keep watch, make sure no one tried to use the confusion to launch a second attack. Unlikely, but it could happen.

The chatter coming through her earpiece was a sore reminder of her uselessness.

Someone had found the escape route, the shell casings had been collected and tagged, and so far no fibers had turned up.

Great. It didn't sound likely that they were going to find any leads. Worse than the shooter getting away with attempted murder was the reality that he was free to try again.

Eight

"Deputy Tanner?" A smooth voice drifted from behind her.

Lana started, a gasp lodging in her throat.

She swiveled, catching a glimpse of a navy uniform and a nylon bag. The EMT. Of course.

What had she expected? That the shooter would return and politely ask permission to kill her brother?

Now if she could find the strength to stand, she'd be good to go. "Uh, yeah. Give me a second."

"Let me help." He came down the steps and extended a hand.

She glanced up at him. Inky black eyes glittered at her from a face that had the tanned look of a Mediterranean. Spiky coal black hair blended in with the night around them.

Taking his hand, she slowly rose. "Thanks. It's been a long day."

"Getting shot doesn't help matters, huh?" He nodded toward the ambulance. "Best lighting is in there."

She followed a few steps behind him, climbed in the back, and sat on the gurney.

The snap of his latex gloves seemed loud in the enclosed space. He picked up his scissors and turned to her. "Must be the right arm."

"How'd you guess?"

"You gave me your left hand when I helped you up."

Yeah, that would've tipped him off. Man, she was more tired than she thought.

"I'll need to cut the sleeve off. This is gonna hurt."

As opposed to the level of comfort she'd been enjoying. Great. "Go for it."

Cutting all the way around her arm, he gently peeled the fabric back from the wound. Her whole body tensed and a wave of nausea threatened to drown her.

The EMT watched her intently. Probably to make sure she

didn't pass out. Or throw up. No doubt those dark eyes had seen everything, but he remained quiet as he pulled the sleeve over her hand and tossed it in a small bin. He examined her arm closely before leaning back.

"Doesn't look too bad. They probably won't even keep you overnight."

"Whoa. You're taking me to the hospital?"

"Standard procedure for gunshot–"

"You said it wasn't too bad."

His eyes held hers for a few moments. "You need to have a doctor look this over. Might need a few stitches, maybe a tetanus shot."

Going to the hospital would amplify Reilly's feelings of guilt. She'd purposely downplayed the injury to keep that from happening.

More importantly, she couldn't protect him if she was nowhere near him.

Forget it. She stayed with Reilly.

"My tetanus is current. Do what you can right here. I'm not going anywhere."

"Look, I get it. No one likes going to the hospital. But sometimes–"

"If I hadn't been here, someone would be dead right now. I'm staying."

He pulled off his gloves, tossed them into the bin, and crossed his arms over his chest. Not a word passed his compressed lips.

Did he really think he could bully her into submission?

"If you won't patch me up, I'll grab a first aid kit and have someone else help me. It won't be half as good as what you could do, but I'm *not* going to the hospital."

Silence spread between them. A twitch moved his jaw. "Then maybe you should do that."

"Fine." She pushed off the gurney and headed toward the rear doors.

His voice stopped her after only two steps. "Wait."

Turning back to him, she said nothing. He studied her, resignation lingering in his eyes. "You win. But if you experience *any* excessive pain, redness, or swelling, you drop whatever you're doing and head to the ER. Got it?"

"Of course."

A small smile tweaked the corners of his mouth. "You know why I hate working on cops? Stubborn. Every single one of you."

"Comes with the badge, I guess."

Picking up a bottle of clear liquid, he set it on the stretcher and reached for some gauze. "This is gonna sting like heck."

The gauze touched her arm. Tears burned her eyes and blurred her vision. She bit down on her lip to keep from crying out.

If he'd picked up a hacksaw and gone to work on her arm, she doubted it could've hurt any worse.

The ambulance tilted and she closed her eyes against the sudden lightheadedness.

"You okay?"

Opening her eyes, she found that his hands had stilled as he watched her face with concern. "You weren't kidding about that stuff."

"The hospital could've given you something for the pain."

"I'll live."

"I'm about done. Let me know if you need to take a break." He worked efficiently and didn't fill the silence with mindless chatter.

After the day she'd had, she was grateful for the silence.

Another minute of misery passed before he set the antiseptic aside. With a light touch, he pressed some cotton against her skin. While he bandaged the wound, her eyes wandered to the name stitched on his uniform.

Dimitrios.

Something about him put her at ease. In fact, she felt more relaxed with him than she did when seeing her own doctor back home. Weird.

Maybe it had something to do with the fading adrenaline.

A voice pulled her out of her thoughts. "How's it going?"

She whipped her head around to find the brown-haired man she'd passed earlier standing outside the ambulance doors. The EMT uniform identified him as Dimitrios' partner.

"We're done." Dimitrios glanced at her as he started cleaning up. "Change the bandage daily for the next five days. And remember, if it doesn't look or feel right, get to a doctor. You might need antibiotics."

She climbed out of the ambulance and turned to face him as he stepped down behind her. "Thank you."

"No problem. You watch that arm and don't do anything to stress it, okay?" He gave her a tight smile and headed for the driver's side of the ambulance.

Okay, now that her arm had been taken care of, she could see how everyone–

"Milana Tanner? Seriously? I don't believe it!"

Her hand went to her gun and she spun to find an unfamiliar man coming toward her.

Lights from the police cars gave her a clear view: mid thirties, about 5'10" with short, curly blond hair. His smile reached all the way up to his gray-blue eyes. "So is Reilly here, too?"

The gun was aimed at him so quickly that he blinked.

Smile faltering, he held up his hands and took a step back. "Wha–what's going on?"

"Who are you?"

"You don't remember me?" He shook his head. "Course you don't. It's been years and with the surgery and all–"

"Answer the question."

"Branden Flint."

Her gun never wavered as she examined his face closely. "You don't look anything like Branden."

"I was in a bad car accident about a year and a half after our trip here. Lots of plastic surgery after that." Turning his head a little, he showed her some faint scarring along his jaw line. "They did a pretty good job of not leaving scars, except for this one."

She scrutinized his face, watching for some shift or twitch to indicate he was lying, but saw nothing. Still, the story sounded fishy.

Well, he clearly didn't have a rifle. His jacket and jeans weren't bulky enough to hide one.

That didn't mean he hadn't ditched it somewhere before circling back.

"Prove it."

"I've got ID." He reached toward his pocket.

"Don't do it."

He froze. "I'm just going for my wallet."

"ID's can be faked."

He swallowed hard, his eyes flicking from the gun to her face and back again. "Uh, exactly how do you want me to prove it then?"

"Tell me something only Branden would know."

"Okay. I, uh, asked you to homecoming, like most of Reilly's friends. 'Course you turned us all down and went with that senior, then knocked him flat on his face when he tried to kiss you. We were all a little scared of you after that."

That senior had been thinking of more than a kiss. Her martial arts training had come in handy that night.

The story wasn't conclusive proof, but it helped. How would a sniper know about that?

Besides, there was something familiar about his eyes.

"Why are you here?" Her voice contained a hard edge, betraying none of her thoughts.

"I moved here after college. A job opened up and I'd always liked Lincoln City–"

"No." She swept her hand to indicate the surrounding area. "Why are you *here*?"

"I'm a reporter. I monitor the police calls and move on anything that sounds interesting." His eyes had stopped moving and were glued to her gun. "Uh, do you think you could put that thing away? Guns make me nervous."

"You have nothing to be nervous about if you're telling the truth."

Time for a little test. She thought quickly, trying to come up with the right question. "Your dad was a car salesman, right?"

He licked his lips, his eyes never leaving her hands. "I think your memory's going. Dad was a major. He was pretty mad at me when I decided to pursue journalism rather than join the Army."

Too easy. She needed to think of something harder, something that wouldn't be on public record. A memory flashed into her head. "Remember that day when we went to the beach and I found a pet? What was it, what did I name it, and what did you call him?"

Not even her parents would know the answer to the last question. It was the perfect test, something that only Branden or Reilly would know.

He didn't even have to think. "A kitten. You called him Driftwood. Woody for short. I said you should call him Drifter because he was so small he'd probably drift away in the wind."

So. It really was Branden.

She relaxed her stance, but didn't holster her weapon. The sniper could still be nearby.

He let out a shaky breath. "I finally passed the test, huh?"

"Yeah, sorry about all that. I guess I'm a little on edge."

"What're you doing here?"

If he monitored police scanners, he probably already had a pretty good idea. Still, she wouldn't confirm it, especially not to a reporter. "I'm afraid I can't tell you."

His look told her she'd given the expected answer. "Can you at least tell me what happened? The dispatcher said there were shots fired. Were you hit?" He looked pointedly at the bandage on her shoulder.

"I can't tell you that either."

Like he didn't already know the answer. The bandage left little room for speculation.

She glanced around before lowering her voice. "But if you were ever our friend, you'll forget you heard anything about this. You don't know I'm here and you don't know where to find me, understood?"

"I always had a bad memory." He stared at her for a long moment. "I've wondered how you guys were doing, but my phone was lost in the accident and I didn't remember Reilly's number."

"Lana? Everything okay?" Alex's voice came through her earpiece.

She pressed the button and spoke into her collar. "Yeah, it's fine."

Branden studied her closely but she offered no explanation.

"I need to get back. It was good to see you."

"What, that's it?" A hand lightly caught her uninjured arm before she could walk away. "I stumble across you guys again and all I get is 'it's good to see you'?"

"Sorry. This isn't a good time."

"Obviously. Maybe we can get together later. Grab coffee or something."

Sounded like fun, but she didn't see any way of making it work. "I don't think–"

"Come on. It's just coffee. You can even pick where and when."

"I can't promise anything, but why don't you give me your

number? Just in case."

He pulled out a business card and jotted a couple of numbers on it. "That's work, home, and cell. Now you have no excuse."

Sure. No excuse except the giant bulls-eye painted on Reilly's back.

Without looking at the card, she tucked it into her pocket. "I need to get back inside." She'd already spent way too much time talking to him.

"Okay. You'll call, right?"

"Maybe." She turned and headed for the door, pausing at the top of the porch to watch him drive away.

The door opened and Beckman stepped out. "There you are. Alex wants to brief us on our next move."

"Got it."

The team had gathered in the kitchen. Alex studied Lana's face for a second, probably to make sure she was okay, then cleared her throat when Lana offered a small nod. "Okay, everyone. Operation Plain Sight. I want us out of here within the hour."

Without a word, the team dispersed, leaving only Alex with her in the kitchen.

Operation Plain Sight. What the heck was that?

"So… you plan to hide in plain sight?"

Alex's smile looked a little forced. "Operation Plain Sight is one of three major contingency plans. I discussed it with Maxwell and we think it's the right move in this instance."

Something told her she should have requested a handbook on all this when she was drafted for this assignment. "And it entails…?"

"Relocating within the same city."

What? They were staying in Lincoln City?

Alex held up her hand to stop the argument that she clearly saw rising on Lana's face. "Hear me out. Your first instinct is to pack the car and zoom out of town. Logical, right? Well, our shooter is going to think the same thing. He may already be headed to Portland, expecting us to show up at the airport there since it's the largest airport nearby. He won't expect us to stay here."

True. It did have the element of surprise. "And this contingency plan, it's been tested before and proven successful?"

A brief hesitation. "By my team, no. We actually haven't had to put our contingency plans in place because our location usually remains a secret. I honestly don't know what happened this time or how he found us."

Nate Miller's face flashed into her mind. She pushed it aside. It might be him, sure. But she'd done nothing suspicious, nothing to tip him off.

There was also the matter of the blinds and the camera placement to address. No way Miller could have gotten in here and adjusted those things.

Only someone on the inside could have done that.

That was something she'd look into. Sooner rather than later.

"You're sure this is the right move? Because you're right. I want nothing more than to jump in the car and get as far away from here as possible."

Alex locked serious eyes on her. "I understand. I do. I can only imagine how I'd feel if it were my brother locked in that room upstairs. This method has been used a time or two by other teams and it worked. I think it's our best bet right now."

She pulled in a deep breath. The logic made sense and if it were anyone else, she'd probably roll with it. The fact that the life at stake was Reilly's clouded her thinking. "Okay. Looks like everyone else has some kind of assignment. What do I do?"

"How about you keep an eye on Reilly. That'll free me up to get us ready to roll out."

Protect Reilly. There was nothing she'd rather be doing. "Got it."

Lana headed for the stairs. If her energy level had been at zero before, it'd dropped into the negatives now. Putting one foot in front of the other, she trudged to the landing and knocked twice on Reilly's door.

She jiggled the knob. Locked. Good for him. "Ri?"

The door flew open and she found herself crushed in a hug. At least his breathing sounded – and felt – normal.

"You need to stay in your room." Her words muffled into his shirt.

He pulled back and examined her, his gaze resting on the bandage on her arm. "How bad is it?"

She gently pushed him back into the room and locked the door behind her. "Like I told you – it's a scratch. I'll be good as new before you know it."

"You're not saying that to make me feel better?"

"Really. You can even see it in the morning when we change the bandage if you want. I'm fine."

He studied her for a moment before nodding. "Okay. What's the plan?"

"For now, get your stuff together. We leave as soon as possible."

The pictures on the wall shook as Stevens slammed the door behind him.

He'd missed.

He *never* missed.

His eyes roved the room, desperately looking for something he could punch or rip up, anything to release the tidal wave swelling inside.

The evening ran repeatedly through his head.

The waiting, the watching, and finally, taking aim.

It'd been an easy shot. Tanner should be dead.

If he hadn't been spotted by that woman… how had she managed to see him in the dark anyway?

He hoped he'd hit her. Maybe that'd teach her not to get in the way next time.

Unlikely.

Law enforcement training seemed to breed foolish attitudes of self-sacrifice.

He almost wanted to take her down. No one made him miss.

Too bad that wasn't his style. It had always been the target and the target alone; he wouldn't change that now.

Besides, even if he wanted to deviate from the norm, he hadn't actually seen her.

Pacing vented some of his anger, enough to return him to a normal level of sanity. He measured out a long breath.

Nobody was perfect. Not even him.

Tanner may have gotten lucky this time, but next time, the luck would be on his side. And if that woman interfered again, she wouldn't live long enough to regret it.

Nine

"Be careful." Reilly's voice sounded loud in the darkness.

Lana glanced behind her to find him at the window, watching her as she navigated across the steep roof.

What was he thinking? He was a perfect target standing right there.

"Get away from the window!" Her voice came out on a hiss, loud enough for him to hear her but not for anyone else. "I'll be right back."

He disappeared from view, although she had no doubt he stood adjacent to the window, listening for any sign that she was slipping or in trouble.

The sooner she checked the camera, the sooner she could get back inside.

She slowly picked her way across the damp shingles, praying with each step that she didn't take the express route to the ground below. While only a one-story drop, it was still enough to break bones or do serious damage if she fell.

While the rest of the team did whatever they needed to do to implement Operation Plain Sight, she was determined to check the camera, interior camera controls, and the miniblinds for prints.

If there was a traitor in their midst, she needed to flush him out.

She reached the corner of the house and shone her high-powered flashlight at the camera.

Layers of dirt, sea-salt, and grime coated the exterior.

No sign of any smudges, much less fingerprints.

In fact, she'd guess that this camera hadn't been touched in years, except maybe a quick swipe of the lens to clean it.

It certainly hadn't been manually adjusted, not unless someone knew how to do it without disturbing the grime.

She made her way back across the roof and climbed inside.

Reilly glowered at her from a few feet away. "Was that really so important that you had to risk breaking your neck?"

Yes. Although she couldn't fully tell him why. "I needed to examine the camera. See if there was a reason that we couldn't see the shooter."

"And was there?"

"Not that I could see." She needed to get downstairs and look at the control room. "Finish packing. And lock the door behind me."

She headed downstairs. The living room was empty. Now was as good a time as any to dust the blinds for prints.

With a quick prayer that no one would come into the living room before she finished, she dusted the wand.

Nothing.

Not that she was surprised. If someone had adjusted it - and she'd bet money someone had done just that - he would have wiped it clean when he was done.

She used a rag to clean the wand, wiping away all evidence of her suspicion.

Now to check the camera room. She crossed the kitchen and entered the camera room, where Beckman sat in front of the monitors, keeping an eye on the exterior.

Not that their shooter was likely to make another attempt tonight, but they couldn't let their guard down.

Beckman glanced up at her as she entered the room. "You find anything on the roof?"

While she hadn't wanted to announce her plans, she'd had to. There was no way he wouldn't have seen her examining the camera, especially when she pointed her flashlight at it. "Nope. The camera wasn't manually adjusted."

Beckman nodded. "I couldn't see how our shooter would have gotten up there, but it's good we know for sure. Maybe all this wind just slowly moved it."

"Maybe." Not that she believed such a thing. Not for a second. "You want me to cover so you can go pack up?"

Beckman glanced back at the screens in front of him. "Sure. I'll be back in a few minutes, okay?"

"Take your time." She sank into the chair he vacated and waited for his footsteps to fade before pulling out the fingerprinting equipment and dusting the controls that adjusted the exterior cameras.

There should be multiple prints here. Probably from all of

them.

Nothing.

She dusted again.

It wasn't possible! They'd all moved the cameras, particularly the one positioned to watch the beach.

Everyone's prints should be on here!

Instead, she found one partial. Probably Chow's, from when he adjusted the camera after the shooting.

She lifted the print anyway. She'd run it, even though she was pretty sure she knew what she'd find.

Now to clean up the mess. She didn't want anyone to know she'd dusted for prints.

She'd barely finished cleaning up when footsteps approached.

"I'm all packed up, so I can take over here." Beckman's voice came from behind her. "Thanks for covering."

"Of course." She rose and moved out of the way. "We're a team."

Even if she suspected that one member of the team didn't have everyone's best interests in mind.

"My family's vacationing with my best friend and her family. We were planning to travel down the coast, but y'alls town is so cute. We thought we'd stick around if we can get two suites. I'm hopin' y'all have some vacancy for the next week."

Lana paused, listening as the hotel employee at the other end of the line navigated the system. Hopefully the Texas drawl would not only sell the act, but also serve to misdirect, just in case the assassin had put out feelers at any of the hotels.

Seemed unlikely, but she'd take no chances.

The hotel where they'd stayed last night was adequate for one night, but not long term. All seven of them were crammed into one two bedroom suite.

Plus, the suite was ground level. Not as easy to secure.

The man on the other end cleared his throat. "Looks like you're in luck. We have four two-bedroom suites available. Top floor and two of them are even beachfront, so you'll have a great view."

Top floor was good news.

The hotel was one of the larger ones in town and stood five stories tall. It'd be hard for a sniper to get a bead on Reilly with four floors separating them.

"Ain't you the sweetest thing! I don't s'pose they have that door inside that connects 'em, do they?"

"Actually, some of them do. I'll see that you and your friend are put in adjoining rooms. You said a week, right?"

"That's right. You're such a doll!" She gave him Alex's name and credit card number to secure both rooms and made arrangements to check in that afternoon.

Hanging up the phone, she breathed a prayer of thanks for God's provision. Things had fallen into place nicely, giving her a peace she hadn't experienced since before the shooting last night.

"That's a pleased look. I take it you got something worked out?" Alex dropped onto the mattress beside her.

"Adjoining suites, fifth floor, each with two bedrooms. I booked it for a week."

"Sweet." Alex fell silent and studied Lana for several moments. "I've gotta ask. What made you look out the window last night?"

"I saw movement."

"No, I get that, but why then? I mean, think about it. Out of all the times you could've looked out there, it just happened to be at the right time to see a sniper before he fired. You've gotta have about the best luck of anyone I've met."

"It wasn't luck. It was God."

A doubtful expression crossed Alex's face. "So what, God said 'hey Lana, check out that sniper in the bushes'? Come on. That's stretching, don't you think?"

She couldn't help chuckling at the mental image. "That's not quite how it happened, but orchestrating something like that would be simple for Him."

"Sounds more like a coincidence than God."

"Coincidences are acts of God. They may seem random to us, but they aren't to Him. If I'm going to believe He's all powerful – and I do – then I have to believe He's in control of everything that happens."

"Even the bad stuff? I thought God was supposed to be good."

Lana shifted to give Alex her full attention. "He is, but you know better than most people that there's a lot of evil in the world.

He could've made us puppets, but He wanted us to be able to make our own choices. Choices have a way of affecting others."

"Oh yeah? Then what about natural disasters? Nobody chooses for an earthquake or a hurricane to happen."

"No, but He protects countless people during those events. Who knows how many casualties we'd be looking at if He didn't intervene. I know it doesn't really answer all the questions, but part of faith is believing that God knows what He's doing and trusting Him even when we don't understand."

The room fell silent for a few moments. Alex didn't ask any more questions, but neither did she seem to be dismissing it as easily as she had in the past.

Sensing she'd said enough for today, Lana changed the subject. "What I really want to know is how the shooter found us."

"And how the camera's position changed."

"And who opened those blinds."

Alex had asked everyone, even Reilly, and they all denied opening the blinds.

But someone had opened them and that someone made Lana nervous.

Dropping her voice, she leaned closer to Alex. "I've worked the options in my head a dozen times. Rosetti has to have someone working on the inside.

Alex's look could've cut steel. "Not possible."

It had to be hard, knowing her team couldn't be trusted. "Look, I get it–"

"No. You don't. I know these guys. They've all been part of my team for over a year now. None of them would do this."

"Then how do *you* think this happened? How did the camera get repositioned? How did the blinds get left open on the exact night a sniper was waiting outside?"

"Mistakes happen. Coincidence." Alex tossed her hands up in the air. "I don't know!"

"It's the only explanation that makes sense and you know it. Somehow Rosetti got to one of them." She pulled in a deep breath. Alex was the one person on this team that she knew she could trust. "I dusted the wand on the blinds last night. And the camera's control panel."

Alex stilled. "What'd you find?"

"Nothing." Lana let that word settle like shrapnel. "There was one partial on the camera's control panel. I ran it in the system and it belongs to Chow, which makes sense since he positioned the camera after the shooting."

Silence smothered them for a moment.

"There should've been more." Alex's words had a hollow feel. "I've touched that control myself. I think we all have."

"My point exactly." Lana glanced at the open door and lowered her voice to a whisper. "Someone wiped it down. Now why would any of us do that unless we were trying to cover something up?"

Alex lifted a shaky hand to sift her hair. "I can't believe that one of them would do this. That they'd put a witness - all of us - in danger. And for what? Money?"

People had sold out their own family for less. Why not some random witness that they didn't even know?

She said nothing as she let Alex process the news.

A sigh burst from Alex. "I'll tell Maxwell. He can have someone dig into things quietly on the back end."

Good. While he did that, she and Alex could keep an eye out for anything suspicious here.

Since she couldn't quiet her misgivings about the team, Reilly needed his own source of protection. Her backup pistol should do the trick. Not having it on her was a little risky, but she'd never had a problem with her Glock. And right now, it was more important for Reilly to be able to protect himself than for her to have a backup.

As if he knew she was thinking about him, Reilly poked his head into the room, looking from her to Alex and back again. "Did you find us a place to stay?"

"Yeah." She motioned him in, quietly shutting the door behind him.

How much did she want to tell him?

The less he knew, the better.

If she told him, he may start treating the team differently, tipping off the mole. Or stress himself out and trigger another asthma attack.

But he did need to be prepared to defend himself should something serious happen.

Retrieving her spare gun from her suitcase, she pulled it out of the holster and inserted a full magazine. "Don't ask a lot of questions and don't let anyone else know, but I want you to keep this on you."

"No way. I'd probably shoot myself."

"You won't." She gave him a rundown on how to use the weapon. "Trust me, after a few hours you'll hardly know it's there."

"I've never fired a gun before. What makes you think I could use it to protect myself?"

"You could do it. Humor me, okay?" She handed him the empty ankle holster. Too bad she didn't have a different holster. One easier for him to access should something happen. "Put this on."

He lifted his pant leg and strapped the holster to his ankle. Gingerly taking the gun from her, he slipped it inside. "Don't you need this?"

"That's my backup."

"Yeah, but don't you usually carry it?"

"I'll be fine." She couldn't help smiling as he moved carefully, as though afraid he'd accidentally discharge the gun if he moved the wrong way. "Ri, you need to act normal. It won't fire unless you rack the slide, which can't be done by accident."

He nodded. "I'll try, but it feels funny."

"You get used to it."

"I don't know." He took a few more tentative steps. "Really, I think I'm well protected with the six of you watching my every move."

"Probably."

If there really were six of them watching out for him, she'd feel a lot better, but she didn't believe all of them had his best interests in mind.

She needed to figure out who was against them. Fast. Before the sniper took another shot at Reilly.

Wind rustled Stevens' hair as he stared at the turbulent ocean. The restlessness inside him rivaled the merciless way the waves pounded the beach.

If only he'd been able to take care of Tanner last night.

It should've been simple, but it'd all fallen apart.

The knowledge of that failure hung so heavily it hurt.

His anger had long since burned away, leaving only a deep sense of disappointment, all directed at himself. He was supposed to be the best, but he'd really blown it last night.

Now he had to start from scratch.

Laughter drew his attention to the water, where two kids built a sandcastle while their parents watched from a few feet away. One part of the castle collapsed and the dad knelt to help the smaller child rebuild it.

What was it like to build a sandcastle?

He'd never played in the sand as a kid. He'd never done a lot of things. Family activities hadn't been a priority to his parents.

Part of him wanted to kneel in the sand and try it for himself, but he'd look like an idiot.

He turned.

No matter what he wanted, the fact remained that he had a job to do. There would be no time for fun until he'd completed this hit.

At least the morning hadn't been a complete loss.

Time online had allowed him to check out all the airports within a hundred mile radius.

After hacking into each of their systems, he'd learned that very few private flights had left during the night and none of the groups had been large enough to be Tanner and his security detail.

Of course, it was possible that they'd fly out today. He'd keep an eye on the airports for a few days, just to make sure, but odds were good that they would've left last night if that was their intent.

If they weren't traveling by plane, but were driving to their new destination, that would be a lot harder to track.

The only other possibility was that they had remained in town.

A gutsy move on their part, but tactically smart. It'd be the last thing he would expect.

Which brought him to his next option - examining the area's many hotels. Given that a group like that would need either several rooms or a suite, it shouldn't be too difficult to pinpoint, but it would take time. There were a lot of hotels.

At least time was something he had in abundance.

No one who made it on his radar survived. Tanner wouldn't be the first. Soon enough, the prosecutor would be dead.

Ten

"I can get my own suitcase. See those little round things on the bottom? Wheels. Makes it easy."

Reilly ignored her as he collapsed the handle on her suitcase and plunked it up on the bed. "This where you want it?"

"No, but I'll take care of it."

"Tell me where it should go."

"Sheesh, Ri. I'm not an invalid."

Blue eyes narrowed behind his glasses. "Weren't you told to take it easy?"

"Moving a suitcase isn't hard."

"It could still reopen the wound. Now where should I put this?"

She nodded to the floor next to the dresser. "Right there is good. I won't really be unpacking anyway."

"How come?"

"It's easier to leave in a hurry if we need to."

"Oh. Should I leave my stuff packed?"

"No, it's fine."

He turned away from her and regarded Alex. "Make sure she doesn't try to do more than she should, okay?"

The grin Alex tried to hide slid through. She offered a mock salute. "Yes, sir."

"I don't know why I bother." The words, muttered through Reilly's clenched teeth as he exited the room, elicited a chuckle from Alex.

Alex waited a few seconds before commenting, "He's right, you know. You need to take it easy."

"So I'll keep the karate to a minimum. He's being overbearing and you know it."

"Overbearing, but not wrong."

"Thanks for not taking his side when he was standing right there. The last thing he needs is any encouragement."

A weighted pause hung between them as Alex removed a

cosmetics bag from her suitcase and set it on the dresser. When she spoke, all traces of humor had vanished. "He's concerned about you and dealing with a heavy load of guilt. Babying you is his way of processing. It's also a good distraction from everything else that's going on. Let him fuss, okay?"

Alex had a good point. If Reilly focused on her, the murder wouldn't constantly play through his mind.

"Fine, but I wish it wasn't so annoying." Leaving her still-zipped suitcase on the floor, she headed out of the bedroom and into the living room of suite 501.

Across the living room, the door to suite 503, where the rest of the team would sleep, yawned open. While not as cushy as the house they'd just vacated, the two suites would suit their needs nicely.

The only person in the living room was Peters, who had a laptop open in front of him.

Maybe she'd check on Reilly. It beat hanging out with Peters.

She spun and headed back down the hallway, past her bedroom and the bathroom, and poked her head into the room at the end of the hall. "How's it going?"

"Fine." Turning from his open suitcase, he assessed her. "Did you need help?"

"Nope. Only saying hi." She crossed the room and drew the heavy drapes closed.

"Hey. I kinda liked the sunshine."

"There's a shooter on the loose, remember?"

An eyebrow arched. "You really believe he can get us on the fifth floor?"

"I believe in caution. Don't open these at any time for any reason." Time for a distraction. "And be ready to go at five, okay?"

"Go?"

She grinned. "Did you think I'd let your birthday slide by without some kind of celebration? We're going out for dinner."

"Really?" The look of anticipation deflated as his gaze landed on her arm. "Sure it's safe?"

"Absolutely." Somehow she managed to exude more confidence than she felt.

Taking him out was risky. Sure, they had a plan in place, a private room reserved, and multiple escape routes, but so many variables couldn't be adequately anticipated. What if something went wrong?

Leaving Reilly's room, she headed back down the hallway to her own room. She leaned against the doorframe, watching as Alex stowed her suitcase in the closet.

"Everyone else knows about the dinner plans?"

Alex nodded. "Yeah. Peters and Chow will leave about fifteen minutes ahead of us to scout everything out and secure the room. They'll do the same when we're ready to leave so they can make sure things are good here, too."

The biggest risk would be getting to and from the vehicle. Simple, right?

Too bad nothing about this was simple.

"So tell me about this friend who showed up last night."

Lana moved to sit next to Alex on the bed. "Reilly and I knew him back in high school. He and Ri were pretty close until his dad was reassigned. They kept in touch for a while, but eventually lost contact."

"And now he just happens to be a reporter in the town we're hiding out in?"

"Kinda questionable, huh?"

"A little." Alex pushed off the mattress. "But it should be easy enough to verify. I'll send Peters to the local paper and have him talk to security. Maybe they can even tell us what time he left last night."

ꟷ ꟷ ꟷ ꟷ ꟷ

"Invite him to dinner."

Lana stared at Alex, sand filling her throat. Alex couldn't have said what Lana thought she'd heard. "Come again?"

"Peters confirmed Branden's story. Security tapes show him leaving the office at 7:27. That's about five minutes after the attack. There's no way he could be the shooter."

"And we're sure he was there the whole time?"

"As sure as we can be. Even so, the newspaper office is a good ten miles away. Unless he can freeze time, there's no way he could've taken that shot and been leaving the office when the footage says he did."

Okay. Chances were good he wasn't the shooter. But he was still a liability. "We can't let him see Reilly. He'd be able to identify him."

"He could probably identify him anyway. I doubt Reilly's changed that much since high school. And he recognized you, so his memory obviously isn't terrible."

Not the point. "We don't know he can be trusted. He *is* a reporter."

"That doesn't mean he's untrustworthy." Alex leaned forward. "Just invite him. It'll give me a chance to stress the importance of keeping what he knows quiet."

"I told him last night that he couldn't tell anyone about this. He said he wouldn't."

"I think observing him for the evening, and letting him see the seriousness of the situation, is a prudent move. And won't Reilly be surprised to see his old friend? It'll take his mind off that bandage on your arm, at least for a few hours."

Reilly *would* enjoy hanging out with Branden.

Under the circumstances, it'd be one of the best gifts she could give him.

Besides, Alex dealt with security issues every single day and she thought it was safe. Time to trust the expert.

"Okay. I'll give him a call."

"Don't tell him where we're going. You'll pick him up." Alex grinned. "My trust only extends so far."

Going into their room, she closed the door before retrieving the card Branden had given her. A distracted male voice answered on the third ring. "Yeah."

"Branden?"

"Is this Milana?" The voice perked up instantly.

"It is. How's it going?"

"Another day in the life." Papers shuffled in the background. "So what's up?"

"Well, I know it's last minute, but would you be free for dinner tonight?"

"Going out for Reilly's birthday, huh? Sure thing."

Wow, fifteen years later and he still remembered? It lent credibility to his story. "I can't believe you remembered after all these years."

"What can I say? My memory is one thing that time hasn't changed." He chuckled. "Of course, the fact that it's exactly ten days after my dad's birthday doesn't hurt either."

She'd forgotten that detail.

"When and where?"

"Actually, I'll pick you up about six." She smiled, not that he could see it, but she hoped it would come through in her voice. "If that's okay with you."

"Still don't trust me?"

The lightness in his tone sounded forced. Possibly covering up hurt. Or perhaps annoyance.

"Maybe I want a chance to talk to you before we meet up with everyone. Besides, that way if our plans change, I don't have to call you at the last minute with a new location."

A lame excuse. They both knew it, but neither pointed it out.

The three-second pause spoke volumes. "From what little I know about your situation, I doubt your plans change at a moment's notice, but I'll let you have this one. How about you pick me up at work?"

"Sounds good. I'll text you when I get there."

After confirming the time, she ended the call and joined Alex in the living room.

Alex glanced up. "I take it we're good to go?"

"Picking him up at six."

"Good." Alex gave a curt nod. "And you already made arrangements to enter the restaurant through the service entrance?"

"Yeah. I told the manager it's a surprise party and we wanted to sneak a special guest in through the back. He thought I was a little weird but seemed to buy it, especially with the extra money I put down for the inconvenience."

"Well, I think you're a little weird too, but I don't hold it against you."

"How generous." The sarcasm helped relieve some of the tension coiled within her.

"Seriously though, good cover. Shouldn't raise too much suspicion among the staff."

At least not until they left, but she'd cross that bridge when she came to it. She had all night to come up with a believable story.

"After we get Reilly settled and the room secure, you'll take the car to pick up Branden."

Meaning he wouldn't see the Suburban used to transport Reilly. Smart.

"Try to pump him for information and if anything feels off, and I mean anything, abort. Trust your gut."

Lana ran through the plans in her head. Arrive at five-thirty before most of the dinner crowd. Lock the room's restaurant entrance since the wait staff would use the room's rear entrance. Sneak Reilly in and out the back.

They should be perfectly safe. So why couldn't she settle her nerves?

Trying to push the anxiety aside, she cleared her throat. "Okay, so when we go to leave, we do the same thing, but in reverse."

Alex shook her head. "Not quite. I'll have Peters and Chow run Branden back on their way to the hotel. We'll wait about a half hour before leaving."

Silence descended like the fog that sometimes blanketed the beach. She tried to relax but almost felt sick.

In spite of careful planning, so much could go wrong tonight.

Between the risks associated with leaving the hotel to bringing Branden into direct contact with Reilly, she had plenty about which to be concerned. However, the lingering suspicion that someone on their team was playing both sides weighed more heavily than anything else.

She had to flush him out. It wouldn't be easy since everyone else trusted him. But at this point, she could think of few things more dangerous than a traitor.

⌐ ⌐ ⌐ ⌐ ⌐

Lana drummed her fingers on the steering wheel, her eyes straying from the door to the parking lot and back again.

The windows of the newspaper office, the few she could see, were dark. Light illuminated the lobby, but the double glass doors didn't reveal much of the interior.

A shadow crossed into that light seconds before Branden stepped into view.

He pushed through the doors and scanned the parking lot.

Okay. No turning back now. She opened the door, stood, and

waved him over.

A smile flashed across his face as he strode toward her.

He lowered himself into the car. "I gotta admit, I'm disappointed. I expected you to be driving some big van with dark bulletproof windows. You know, something that screams federal agent."

"I think you watch too many movies. Besides, who said anything about the Feds?"

"Come on. You're not really going to try to sell me on that one, are you?"

Holding back her answer, she pulled into traffic. How much Alex planned to reveal was unknown, but it was Alex's call, not hers. For now, she was nothing more than the chauffeur. "How's the newspaper doing in the digital age?"

"Better than some, but you're not getting off that easily."

The glance she shot his direction found him angled toward her. "What do you mean?"

"What agency are you with? FBI? DEA? I know that place you were staying used to be a drug hotspot."

"What makes you think I work for any of them?"

"Seriously? You pulled a gun on me!"

"Hey, a girl can't be too careful these days."

"I've had job interviews less intense than your questioning. It was practically an interrogation. While holding me at gunpoint, in case I failed to mention that. Oh, and let's not forget you were shot."

This was crazy. She should've asked Alex what she planned to tell him.

Instead, she forced a light tone and dodged the question. Again. "You've changed a lot since I last saw you."

"Look, forget I'm a reporter, okay? I'm not going after a story. I'm concerned about you. That's all."

A sigh slid out. "I get that, but I can't really talk about this right now. Maybe we can revisit it later?"

Part of her hoped there wouldn't be a later for this conversation.

She didn't wait for his response before changing the subject. "How are your parents?"

"It's just my dad now. Mom's been gone for eight years. Breast cancer."

"I'm sorry."

The half-hearted shrug he managed was almost convincing. "Dad's good. Still as bossy as ever, but I doubt that'll change." A chuckle slid out. "Since I disappointed him with my career choice, he's made it his mission in life to see that I do everything else right."

"Oh yeah?" Sliding a look his direction, she couldn't help grinning at his chagrin. "And how's that going?"

"Well, he hasn't disowned me yet, so I guess it could be worse."

That sounded like the man she remembered from her childhood. "Does he live near enough to meddle often?"

"Portland. Near enough that I can still see him, but not close enough to give me a lot of grief."

"How long have you lived in Lincoln City?"

He rubbed the back of his neck. "Wow, I guess it's been about five years or so."

"Small-town life doesn't drive you crazy?"

"Nah, I think I've always been a small-town kind of guy. And it's nice being right by the ocean."

A grin twisted her lips. "A cold ocean. I can't believe how windy it is here. Always."

"A bit of a change from Jacksonville, isn't it? I take it you're still there?"

She hesitated. Safe or unsafe?

"Or is that another question you can't answer?"

"Maybe later?"

He shook his head slowly. "I think that's your favorite word."

At least he didn't sound angry. "Sorry. It beats lying."

"True enough. And I've seen firsthand that this thing is serious. How's the arm?"

"Okay." The response slid from her mouth as if automatic.

"Of course. It's not like you were shot or anything."

She eased the car to a stop as the light in front of them changed to red. "Grazed. It burns a bit and the bandage is irritating, but it's not the worst thing that's ever happened to me."

"I don't even want to know about that one."

The green arrow lit up and she turned left before making a sharp right into the restaurant's parking lot.

"The Wet Noodle. Good choice. Great pasta. Which I know

Reilly likes."

"We all do."

"At least some things haven't changed."

She turned off the engine and opened her door. "That one probably never will."

The restaurant's heavy wood door swung toward them as they approached. Branden snagged the edge of the door, holding it wide for the man coming out with a couple of takeout boxes balanced on his hands.

"Thanks."

She knew that voice. "Hi, Nate."

"Lana? Hey." The smile she heard in his voice crinkled his brown eyes, but dimmed slightly as his gaze shifted from her to Branden and back again. "You'll have to try the lasagna. Best in town, trust me."

"I'll take it under advisement, but I have to admit, I'm really looking forward to a good Alfredo sauce."

Nate's attention slid to Branden again, who at some point had released the door and taken a step closer to her side. Were they seriously sizing each other up? The tension sparking the air confirmed it.

Men.

"How rude of me." She shook her head and offered a small laugh as though she'd just remembered her manners. "Nate, this is Branden, a friend from school. Branden, Nate's a freelance photographer."

As she'd suspected, that detail snagged Branden's attention. Although instead of diffusing the tension, it seemed to supercharge it.

"Really? I work for the local paper." Challenge lined Branden's words. "Maybe I've seen your work."

"I doubt it." Nate's thin smile barely bordered polite. "My specialty is nature."

"I read a lot of magazines. Where all have you been published?"

"Some calendars, outdoors magazines, a few home and garden issues." Nate shifted the takeout boxes and looked at her. "I should get going before this cools too much. See you later?"

The weight of Branden's speculation shifted to her. She ignored it, offering Nate a smile instead. "I doubt it. I have some family things going on tonight."

"Okay, well, have fun." He dodged them and started across the lot. "And I was serious about the lasagna."

Opening the door, Branden gestured for her to precede him inside. The door whooshed closed behind them.

"I didn't know you knew anyone else in town."

The suspicion lacing his tone made her want to laugh. "I've gone jogging on the beach a few times. He's usually out there taking pictures."

"And I suppose you held him at gunpoint, too?"

He couldn't let that go, could he? "Don't be silly. I save the special treatment for old friends."

She led the way across the dining room and down a short hallway, stopping outside a closed door. She slid a glance both directions. The restroom doors were both closed and while she could hear things clattering beyond the swinging doors leading into the kitchen, there wasn't anyone in sight.

She knocked twice before pulling her phone from her pocket. It vibrated in her hand a few seconds later.

That you?

She punched in a quick reply to Alex's text and pocketed her phone. The door clicked open and they slipped inside.

As Alex closed the door behind them, she sidestepped next to Lana and lowered her voice. "No problems?"

"We're good." At least she sure hoped so.

Reilly slowly rose. "Branden? Is that you?"

Shoving his hands into his pockets, Branden nodded. "At least *you* recognize me."

"I can't believe it. Lana, where'd you find this guy?"

It'd been a while since she'd witnessed a smile like that on Reilly's face. All the preparation and worrying had been well worth it. "Honestly, he found us."

"Sometimes it pays to monitor the police scanners." At Reilly's lifted eyebrows, he added, "I work for the paper. The only thing that would've made this any better was if I'd been able to write a story about it."

"Speaking of which, we need to go over a few things." Alex gestured toward the table. "Let's have a seat."

Lana claimed the chair next to Reilly, leaving Branden the one at the end of the table.

"Is this where you threaten to make me disappear if I talk?"

Alex forced a stiff smile in response to Branden's humor. "Close."

A server stepped into the room from the kitchen entrance. "Are you folks ready to order?"

While others placed their orders, Lana quickly scanned the menu. So many options.

In spite of Nate's recommendation, she went with the Alfredo.

As the server left the room, Branden faced Alex. "You don't have to worry. My friends are more important than my career. Last night proves that this is serious."

"Very. As far as everyone else is concerned, you haven't seen us, you don't know anything about what happened at that call last night, and you certainly don't know who was involved, got it?"

"Did you see this morning's paper? If I had planned to report on last night, it would've been on the front page."

"Keep it that way. You can't tell anyone. Not your editor, your family, your priest, heck, even your dog is off limits."

If the situation hadn't been so serious, Lana would have laughed at the idea of Branden confiding his deepest secrets to a dog.

"Silent as a corpse." Branden winced. "I could've worded that a little better. But don't worry. I get it. Trust me."

"You wouldn't be sitting here if I didn't."

"Sooo...." A slow grin spread across Branden's face. "Does that mean I get to learn more about what's going on here?"

Alex shook her head. "Not a chance."

"Figured it couldn't hurt to ask." The casual tone said he'd received the expected answer.

Silence lingered a few seconds before Reilly filled it. "So what's with the new look? Running from the mafia?"

"And my secret's out." Branden sobered. "Actually, it was a car accident. Messed me up to the point that plastic surgery wasn't really optional."

The accident.

Branden had mentioned it last night, but she'd had too much going on to get details.

Time to change that. "What happened?"

Murmuring across the table evidenced that Alex and her team had moved on to other conversations, but she tuned them out to focus on Branden.

"Guy in a moving truck fell asleep at the wheel and forced me down an embankment. I don't remember much after that. The police said the doctors hadn't expected me to even survive, much less make any kind of recovery."

"How long did that take?"

"A long time." Branden shifted slightly. "But by the grace of God, I recovered fully."

"The grace of God? Now there's a phrase I never thought I'd hear from you." She did nothing to mask her surprise.

"Yeah, well dark times have a way of changing your perspective a little. And there were a lot of dark times in the three years after the accident."

Reilly nodded, but didn't say anything.

"I, uh..." Branden cleared his throat. "I got hooked on painkillers. I managed to hide it pretty well for about two years, but Dad eventually found out. He convinced me to go to rehab." A hint of a smile pinched his eyes as he added, "In his usual gentle way, of course."

Gentle. Right.

Unless he'd changed considerably in the last fifteen years, Lana imagined that meant Branden's stubbornness had been no match for his father's.

"But you're good now?"

Leave it to Reilly to voice the question she'd been thinking but had hesitated to ask.

Branden nodded. "Seven years clean. I met Christ in rehab. Dad did, too."

The waiter arrived with their salads and the conversation stalled for a few minutes as food became the focus.

Swallowing a bite, Branden turned to Reilly. "What've you been up to?"

"Just life. Work's been crazy–"

Lana placed a hand on his arm. Better to not bring up work than to have to duck a bunch of questions.

"I take it that's on the list of forbidden topics?" Branden's gaze locked intentionally on her hand.

"I know it stinks. Hopefully it won't be long before we can give you the full story."

"I'll hold you to that one." Directing his attention to Reilly, he asked, "I take it you never went to culinary school?"

"What makes you think that?"

"I doubt many chefs end up with a fully armed team protecting them."

Reilly quirked an eyebrow. "Because no chef could ever witness something..."

Clamping his lips together, he drew a few deep breaths through his nose.

Poor guy.

Lana kept her sympathy to herself, knowing it would only make things worse.

"Anyway." The word croaked out and Reilly cleared his throat, forcing a smile that failed to remove the haunted look from his eyes. "Dreams change. I still like to cook, but decided that wasn't the field for me."

"Big jump from chef to prosecutor."

What? Lana's fingers twitched as she halted their movement toward her gun. Could he somehow be involved with Rosetti after all?

"Breathe." Branden focused an intense stare at her, almost as if he could read her thoughts. "I googled him. An article about him witnessing that murder was the first thing to pop up."

Of course, Branden had done his research. Why would she have thought any differently?

Now if she could calm her stampeding heart, everything would be fine. Sort of. "I'm sorry, we can't–"

"–talk about it. I know."

The conversation meandered through a bunch of light topics – covering everything from Branden's church to Reilly's almost fiancée, Desiree.

While the food was great and the conversation interesting, Lana's energy waned. The stress of the last twenty-four hours and the long night with little sleep had finally caught up to her.

She had only to meet Alex's gaze to know she wasn't the only one.

Time to call it a night.

Alex took control of the situation before Lana could. "It's getting late. Branden, remember, not a word of this to anyone or we will lock you up. Got it?"

"Don't worry about me. I'd never do anything to put these guys in danger."

"See that it stays that way. Peters and Chow will drop you at your vehicle."

Branden looked at the two deputies rising from their chairs before turning to Lana. He opened his mouth, but snapped it closed a second later.

A chuckle slid from Reilly. "Don't look so worried. Chow's a good driver."

Peters smirked. "Too bad I'm driving."

"Oh." Reilly couldn't hide a grin. "In that case, I hope your life insurance is paid up."

Standing, Branden glanced between Lana and Reilly. "It was good to see you guys. Maybe we can do this again while you're in town."

"Probably not this trip," Lana interjected before Reilly could agree. "But now that I have your number, we can at least keep in touch."

Once the door closed behind Branden, Peters, and Chow, Alex assessed the group. "Peters is going to give me a call when they've had a chance to sweep the hotel. Once we get the all-clear, we'll head out."

The waiter dropped off the check, exiting as unobtrusively as he'd entered. Lana scooped it up and reached for her purse. "I'll settle up the bill so we're ready when they call."

Alex followed her to the door and closed it behind her. The lock scraped into place.

Something solid slammed into her back, forcing her forward several steps.

Her hand flew to her gun, her fingers resting on the grip. Someone had been waiting for her!

"I'm sorry." A man's voice came from behind her. "I guess that's why I shouldn't text and walk. You okay?"

Whirling, she stared at the tall, dark-haired man behind her.

Dimitrios? What was he doing here? Could he somehow be

connected to the shooter?

Maybe he was the shooter. Here to finish what he'd started last night.

Behind him, a woman exited the ladies room, brushing by them with barely a glance.

She exhaled the breath she hadn't even realized she'd been holding.

He wasn't lurking or trying to finish anything. Most likely, he'd come from the restroom. And now he stared at her like she was some kind of weirdo for not answering his question. Great.

With movements as casual as possible, she relaxed her arms to her sides. "I'm fine, thanks. Just startled."

"Good. If I hurt someone while texting, I'd never live it down."

"By the way, thanks for your help last night. The arm's already on the mend."

"I'm sorry, your arm?"

It'd only been last night. How could he have forgotten in such a short amount of time? "Yeah. We argued about going to the hospital, you threatened not to help… remember?"

A grin stole across his face. "You're thinking of my brother. Dimitrios."

Twins?

Of course. Why hadn't she noticed the subtle differences before? Dimitrios had a more muscular build and eyes haunted by too many calls gone wrong. The man in front of her wore his hair a little longer and didn't look nearly as burdened by life.

"I'm sorry. I bet that happens all the time."

"At least our parents can finally tell us apart. I'm Cyrano."

She took his offered hand. "Lana."

The hand gripping hers stiffened and his smile faltered. A second slithered by before he released her hand.

"Uh, it's good to meet you." Strain punctuated the words and he cleared his throat. "So Mitri, uh, patched you up, huh? What happened?"

"No big deal, just a little accident."

The tension smothering them was so thick she suspected anyone passing by would be able to feel it. What had brought about the sudden change in character?

That mystery would have to wait.

She needed to get moving or Alex would be wondering what was keeping her. "Well, I should get going. It was nice meeting you."

"Likewise." His smile didn't quite conceal the troubled expression underneath.

She headed for the counter, bill in hand, but her mind lingered on Cyrano.

What had *that* been about? She replayed the conversation, weighing her responses to see if she'd said something to warrant his discomfort.

Everything had been normal until she'd given him her name.

The realization slammed through her.

If a professional assassin had been hired, wouldn't he know the names of Reilly's family? Had she put her brother in danger by giving a complete stranger her name?

Ridiculous.

All official records would have her full name. Milana.

Her nickname shouldn't have set off alarms, even on the incredibly slim odds she'd run into the man gunning for Reilly.

Still, maybe they should leave the restaurant now. They could drive around until Peters called.

While the lady behind the register ran her credit card, Lana casually surveyed the room.

Spotting Cyrano was easy. He sat at a small round table in the center of the room. Across from him, a red-haired woman leaned in, nodding every so often to whatever Cyrano was saying.

Seeing him *with* someone provided a little comfort. A hit man would likely be alone.

Seeing him inside, sitting at a table, made her feel even better. At least he hadn't run straight out to his vehicle to grab a rifle.

She signed the charge slip, pocketed her copy, and headed back toward the room.

Maybe he hadn't grabbed a rifle because he'd planted a tracking device on her. No reason to hurry now if he could simply pick up her signal later.

Insane. Certifiably, tinfoil hat, maybe-Elvis-is-alive-and-working-at-a-library-in-Boston crazy.

She wasn't in a spy movie. They weren't dodging a hostile foreign government or hiding from the CIA.

They were avoiding a hit man.

It was unlikely that he'd even *own* fancy tracking equipment, much less plant a device on someone who may or may not know where his target hid.

And the chances that he would have known precisely where they were and been around at the exact moment she exited the room were next to nothing.

So why couldn't she stem the fear clouding her thoughts?

Caution never hurt anyone.

She detoured to the bathroom, locked herself in a stall, and made a thorough sweep of her clothes and hair. No trace of anything foreign, much less some kind of signal emitting device.

Leaving the bathroom behind, she quickly texted Alex, who opened the door seconds later.

"That took forever. Where'd you have to go to pay? Italy?" Alex's tone may have been teasing, but the creases at the corners of her blue eyes told the story.

"Sorry. There was this guy." She eased out a breath. "I'll fill you in later. I think we're good here, but what do you say we take off, just in case?"

"Sure. Peters should be calling any time." Alex tossed the keys to Rodriguez. "Bring the car around back, would you?"

"No sweat. Text you when I'm in position."

The silence left in his wake felt ominous. They couldn't get back to the controlled safety of the hotel soon enough.

Eleven

Dusk settled on the horizon as the SUV halted adjacent to the hotel's side exit. Lana stepped from the vehicle, closing the door firmly behind her.

A soft breeze swirled the salty scent of the Pacific around her.

It'd be a perfect night for a good run, but Lana suspected her beach-running days were through for now. Patrolling the beach was no longer a necessity.

She inserted her key card into the door's lock, which softly clicked open.

An empty hallway stretched before her.

She nodded at the SUV and Beckman climbed out. Brushing past her, he strode down the hall and pushed the button for the elevator. A ding signaled its arrival.

At Beckman's thumbs up, Lana waved for Reilly and Alex to enter. The back door of the SUV popped open and Alex propelled Reilly into the building. Lana let them inside, then brought up the rear.

The SUV's engine roared as Rodriguez pulled away to park the vehicle.

As the elevator approached their floor, Alex guided Reilly into the most sheltered corner and positioned herself and Beckman in front of him. Lana took up position in front of the doors as they slid open.

Another empty hallway.

Well, empty except for Peters, who leaned against the wall outside their suites.

"All clear."

The group hurried into the suite. As Peters slid the deadbolt behind them, Lana rolled her shoulders to try to loosen the muscles.

"Thanks, guys. I needed that." Reilly surveyed the group of deputies before his gaze came to rest on Lana. "I know it took a lot of work on everyone's part and I want you to know I appreciate it."

Lana smiled at him. With any luck, he'd never know how much tension still coursed through her. She really needed that run.

Too bad it wasn't going to happen.

Besides, they still had one more order of birthday business to cover.

Detouring to the bedroom, she retrieved a bag from her closet and rejoined the group in the living room. She removed a wrapped package out of the bag and plopped it down in front of him. "It doesn't feel like a birthday without something to open, right?"

"True story." His grin, not to mention the way he ripped into the package, reminded her of a six-year-old child, not a prosecutor who'd turned thirty-six. He laughed when he saw the Ferrari model car kit inside. "You finally got me a sports car."

The bag she held in her hands rustled as she removed a jar of red paint and tossed it to him. "And it's red, too."

"Some assembly required."

Any doubts she'd harbored about the gift vanished at the amusement on his face.

"Sooo...," Alex's voice snagged her attention. "I take it there's a story behind this?"

"Every year when I ask what he wants for his birthday, he tells me a red sports car. Looks like now he'll have to come up with a new dream."

Reilly glanced up from the box. "Man, it's probably been at least twenty years since I've put one of these together. Although I always used spray paint."

"Can't spray paint indoors." Besides, painting by hand would take him longer, a good thing when his entertainment options were so limited.

Reilly headed back to his bedroom with the kit and paint.

She followed him. Leaning against the door frame, she held up the brush. "You might need this."

"Suppose you're right." He took the brush from her fingers and set it on the dresser next to the paint.

Heaviness lingered in the way he paused. Something was on his mind and, knowing him, he was trying to figure out the best way to say it.

"So."

Incoming! That one word, spoken in a sly tone, combined with the arched eyebrow, made her want to search for cover. Whatever was coming next wouldn't be good.

"A nature photographer, huh?"

Dang. Much as she wished for the contrary, she should've known they weren't done with that topic. "I think you pretty much heard everything there is to tell."

"Not why I had to learn about him from Branden. You should've been the one to tell me."

Branden had a big mouth. "Tell you what? That there's a nature photographer who likes sunsets? Do you want a rundown of everyone I see each day?"

"Only if you're on a first-name basis with them."

Touché.

She lifted her shoulders in a slight shrug and tried for nonchalance. "So he knows my name. Big deal."

"For you, it kinda is. More than that, it sounds like he's got your schedule down." Stuffing his hands into his pockets, he silently assessed her.

"He's a suspect. We're trying to get more information so we can look into him. I can't do that if I don't stop to talk to him."

As she'd expected, the word suspect sobered him.

"Besides, Alex knew." Why was she still defending herself?

"But I didn't."

"You had enough on your mind."

"Well, the secret's out now. Tell me what you do know about him."

"I think you heard everything." They'd covered his photography… but not his background. "Except… he carries this pain around him. You can almost see it."

"What kind of pain?"

"The kind that–" *Only people like me can understand.* She stopped short of saying it out loud. "He was abandoned by his mother."

"Really." Doubt laced the single word. "And how did that topic come up in casual conversation?"

Wow. Talk about a role-reversal.

She was normally the skeptic. "I never thought I'd see the day when you're more suspicious than I am."

"I'm playing the big brother card on this one. It could be a pick-up line designed to gain instant sympathy. I'm just saying."

Could he be right? She mulled the conversation with Nate over in her mind.

While she couldn't remember every tic and expression, she recalled one thing with vivid clarity – the sense he'd been telling the truth.

Pain that deep was incredibly difficult to fake.

"If it is a line, he's the world's best con artist. You'd have to meet him to understand."

They both knew that Reilly wouldn't be meeting any new people for a while.

Her mind drifted to a different stranger. The man from the restaurant. Cyrano. Now that guy really set off her internal alarms. What was it about him?

"Okay, Lana. Spill it."

"What?"

"You've been distracted since we left the restaurant. What's up?"

Sometimes she hated that he could see through her so easily. No one, not even Alex, could read her as well as Reilly could.

"There was this guy at the restaurant."

Reilly arched an eyebrow. "Another one? Sheesh. How many guys are you hiding from me?"

In spite of herself, she smiled. "Not like that. Tonight was the first time I ran into him."

Literally.

Leaning back against the dresser, Reilly crossed his arms and waited.

"You remember the EMT?"

"Which one?"

"Dimitrios. The dark haired one."

A slight nod from Reilly prompted her to continue.

"I ran into his twin at the restaurant tonight. Honestly, I thought it was him, otherwise I probably wouldn't have said anything."

How could she explain that she felt something was off when she couldn't even figure out what that something was?

"Did something happen?"

"No. That's just it. But he gave me this look."

"A look?" Reilly cocked his head to the side. "I'm-an-evil-maniac-who-will-hunt-you-down-and-kill-you-while-you-sleep kind of look?"

"Not even close."

Recalling the expression Cyrano had worn, she tried to find words to convey her concern. Nothing came.

A pithy laugh slid from her, one that contained no humor. "Listen to me. I sound crazy, huh? I don't even know how to describe it. It was weird. I think it had something to do with my name."

"Your name? What would that have to do with anything?"

"Don't ask me. But it wasn't until he heard my name that he started acting strange."

"You wanna know what I think? You probably remind him of someone."

That didn't explain his reaction to her name, but maybe the timing of that was more coincidental than anything else.

Right. Like she'd told Alex, she didn't believe in coincidence. Not one bit.

Reilly didn't wait for her to respond. "Honestly, that EMT kind of reminded me of you. I'm thinking you guys have the same ethnic background. Maybe Italian."

Hmmm. Could he be right?

Maybe it really was that simple.

And it might explain the sense of ease she'd felt around Dimitrios. "But that still doesn't explain the name thing."

"Who cares? Might've been a delayed reaction or something. Heck, you could even remind him of someone named Lana."

"Right. Because it's such a common name."

"It could be in whatever country he's from."

Possibly. "Maybe I'll see if I can track down his last name. Do a little digging, just to make sure." Getting a last name shouldn't be too difficult since she knew where Dimitrios worked.

Reilly shook his head. "I don't know how you do it. Don't you get tired of being suspicious of everyone?"

"You get used to it." A yawn snuck up on her. "I should get some sleep. Have to be up for the midnight shift."

While it was her least favorite shift, the solitude would give her time to think. And pray.

And maybe dig into the background of a certain EMT and his

twin brother.

ꟷ ꟷ ꟷ ꟷ ꟷ

Lana drew in a deep breath of the crisp sea air. Not far from where she stood, the waves slapped the shoreline as the tide pounded in.

Although Alex almost had to push her off the balcony to get her out of the suites, she'd grudgingly agreed to leave.

And Alex was right. She'd needed this release.

While she still didn't trust everyone on the team, Alex had promised to personally keep an eye on Reilly until she returned.

Besides, their assailant had likely moved on. He wouldn't have expected them to stay.

She stretched, then broke into a jog.

It felt like ages since she'd put in a good run. Had it really only been two days since the attack at the safe house?

The bandage on her arm, not to mention the pain she endured when she moved the wrong way, assured her that not much time had really passed.

Cold air slapped her face as she sprinted up the packed sand.

The area had more activity than she was used to seeing. Probably due in large part to the string of hotels lining the beach.

She slowed to a jog, her mind returning to the questions that had weighed on her almost constantly.

"Who told him?" The whispered question was lost in the wind, drowned out by the waves breaking not far from her feet.

Someone on her team had to be playing both sides, but who? And how could she find the mole without alienating the whole team? After all, as far as they were concerned, *she* was the outsider.

No one had said or done anything suspicious. Not before the attack and certainly not since it.

The crime scene itself hadn't turned up any good leads, either.

All they had to work with were the bullet casings and a man's shoeprint, size 13. The shoeprint was a popular style and the manufacturer had confirmed they'd sold millions in this country alone.

As for the bullet casings, they were basically worthless without the weapon.

A shiver bristled up her back and down her arms. It had nothing to do with the weather - she was being watched.

She glanced around. A man with his dog, a group of college kids playing an intense volleyball game, a couple of children looking for seashells while their parents watched from a few feet away.

Nothing suspicious.

Under the pretense of stretching, she glanced behind her.

Ah, that explained it. Heading straight for her, camera slung around his neck, was Nate. Her heart rate slowed a notch.

Maybe now would be a good time to get more information. Something they could use to dig into his background better. She'd have to be subtle, of course. If he was a killer, pumping him for information would raise his suspicions.

While she waited for him to join her, she took a moment to catch her breath. By the time he reached her, she was able to speak without sounding winded. "Hey."

"Hey yourself. Haven't seen you out here for a while."

"Family's been keeping me busy." Time to divert his attention. "Did you get some good shots tonight?"

He lifted his shoulders in a slight shrug. "Nothing special, but I uploaded some from the other night and there are a few that show a lot of promise. I was thinking I'd print them off tomorrow morning."

"You should bring them with you sometime. I'd like to see them." It'd provide some good, solid confirmation that he was who he claimed to be.

"Sure. Maybe over a pizza tomorrow night?"

Whoa. He must've misunderstood. Well, she'd set the record straight right now.

Or maybe she should say yes.

Sitting down for a meal would provide a convenient setting for her to learn more about him. She could find out where he came from, where he lived now, and maybe even his age. All things they could use to run a background check on him and either confirm him as a suspect or rule him out.

"Unless of course your boyfriend has a problem with it."

"Boyfriend?" It took her a minute to make the connection, but when she did, she chuckled. "You mean Branden? He's just a friend, so it doesn't matter what he'd think. But I don't know what my family has planned for tomorrow."

Even though she wasn't technically on duty at the moment, instinct had her scanning the area.

The man and dog had traveled much further down the beach and the family was drawing near to one of the motels. The only people remaining in the area were the volleyball players, whom she suspected would be packing up soon, and Nate.

"Okay, okay, I get it." He held up his hands and grinned. "But you can say no. You don't have to make excuses."

She'd hurt him.

Oh, he tried to hide it behind a smile, but she'd caught the flicker in his eyes. Not to mention that his teasing sounded forced.

"No, it's not that at all. My family has some, um, unusual circumstances. Getting away isn't as easy as it sounds."

"You manage to make it out here almost every night."

"For a brief window of time. Someone else takes over the responsibility of watching out for my brother so I can stay in shape."

"What, like babysitting him? I thought you said he was older…" He smacked his forehead. "He's disabled, isn't he? Man, I'm a jerk."

"You couldn't have known." Besides, she was the jerk for letting him believe the lie. She hated being a party to half-truths, even when it was necessary.

"So you're his primary caregiver? No one can fill in for you to take a night off?"

"Evening is seriously the worst time for me to get away."

"Okay, how about lunch? I promise I'm not an axe murderer or anything."

She laughed. "Because that would've been my first thought."

"You never can tell these days. So is that a yes?"

Why was he being so persistent?

Could he be the shooter? Maybe she'd accidentally said something that had raised his suspicions.

Then again, why would an assassin waste time flirting with a jogger when he should be out targeting his prey? Especially considering his previous failed attempt.

Unless he'd seen her that night. Or heard her voice and

recognized it.

No, if that were the case, he'd simply lay low and try to follow her back to the hotel.

"You still there?"

She blinked him into focus. "Sorry. Just running through tomorrow's schedule to see if I can get away."

Taking an hour off wouldn't be a problem. Everyone else on her team had used some of their free time to explore the town.

But with a mole in their midst and a shooter on the loose, she wasn't comfortable leaving Reilly, not even to check out a potential suspect.

"Look out!"

She whipped around. A volleyball filled her vision. She wrenched left.

The world tilted. She tried to regain her balance, failed, and felt herself falling backward.

Nate's hand closed over the still tender gunshot wound. Clamping the inside of her lip between her teeth, she swallowed the cry that clogged her throat.

The cry almost broke free as he eased her back to her feet.

Pain blazed through her arm. Tears pricked her eyes and she fought to hold them back.

She would not cry.

Nate had only wanted to help and he'd tried to be gentle. There was no way he could've known that even a pillow would hurt right now.

A shaggy-haired guy jogged over, his cheeks rivaling the fiery sun as it lowered into the ocean. "Sorry 'bout that. You okay?"

She pasted on a smile. "Fine. Thanks for the heads-up."

The guy retrieved the ball. "I didn't mean to smash it so hard. Sorry."

He jogged back to where his friends stood laughing. One of the guys shook his head. "Dude, you have *got* to find a better way to meet chicks."

He appeared to ignore the comment. "It's dark. Let's head out."

A dull ache replaced the burning and she gingerly felt her arm. If she had to guess, she'd say the wound was bleeding again.

Great. Now she'd have to ask Alex or Reilly to look at the wound to make sure more damage hadn't been done. Worse, she'd have no choice but to sit through the lecture that would accompany changing the bandage.

"You okay?" Nate's words broke through the pain clouding her mind.

She'd almost forgotten he was there. "Uh, yeah. Yeah, I'm good. Thanks for helping."

"Did I hurt you?" Concern darkened the eyes scanning her face. "I'm sorry. I was just trying to help."

"It wasn't you. Really. I scraped this arm the other day and it's still pretty sore." Dropping her hand, she concentrated on keeping the pain off her face as she moved her arm. "See, better already."

Shafts of pain shot up her arm. She stilled.

"You call that better, huh? I'd hate to see your definition of worse."

"It'll be fine." Eventually.

"If you say so. But now I definitely owe you lunch. What do you say?"

All she wanted was to get back to the hotel and pop a few painkillers. Or break down for a good cry.

Maybe both.

She had to get rid of Nate quickly. "I don't know."

The pain subsided to a pertinacious throbbing that hurt her entire arm. Dang. Hopefully it wasn't as bad as it felt or Alex would send her to the ER.

Wait - had Nate said something?

The expectant gaze locked on her said he had. But what?

Given their previous conversation, she could probably guess what he'd asked. No matter how much she might be able to learn over the course of a meal, Reilly's safety came first. "I don't think so."

A smile split his face. "Great! Then they shouldn't mind if I steal you for an hour or two, right?"

Whoa! What'd happened?

"How 'bout if I meet you at the pizza place by that big motel, do you know which one I'm talking about?"

Darn it. He must've asked if she had other plans for tomorrow. That's what she got for assuming she knew the question instead of asking him to repeat it. "Yes–"

"Good. 1:30 work for you?"

Not good.

Now to get herself out of this mess. "Just a sec. I think we're on two separate pages here."

His smile slipped. "Uh, what do you mean?"

The excitement and hope she'd seen in his face evaporated and his eyes held the sadness of one who'd been let down many times before. Why did she feel like she was kicking a cowering child?

"I can't just…" A sigh slipped out. "I'll have to check."

"Sounds reasonable. If you aren't there by 1:45, I'll know you couldn't get away."

"I'll try. That's all I can promise."

"That's good enough for me."

Years of training screamed at her to give him a firm no, but something inside, she thought it might be the Holy Spirit, kept her from saying it. But why would God care if she had lunch with Nate tomorrow?

Maybe because he was a killer and she'd learn something critical during that meal?

The now-empty beach, not to mention the receding light, confirmed she'd been out too long. Way too long. "I'm sorry–"

"But you need to be getting back. I'll walk you."

"Only if you can keep up. I won't be walking."

"Maybe I'll pass. Running with this thing," he held up his camera, "isn't the most comfortable. Are you sure it's safe for you to be out here alone?"

"I have belts in Karate, Ju-Jitsu, and Tai Kwan Do. I can take care of myself."

He blinked. "Remind me not to get on your bad side. On that note, I'll see you at lunch tomorrow."

"Maybe."

Ignoring her hesitation, he shot her a smile before heading down the beach.

She jogged a short distance, but the jarring only aggravated the pain in her arm. She was done running, for tonight anyway. A glance back found Nate as little more than a speck in the darkness. She cut across the sand and approached the hotel.

To keep her mind off the pain, she focused on Nate.

Life had handed him a lot of disappointment. She hoped she didn't become one of them.

The thought was followed by a more pressing concern. Why did she care?

No answer had surfaced by the time she reached the suite.

Alex let her in, her eyes narrowing in concern. "What's wrong?"

"What makes you think–"

"I've seen corpses with more color."

So much for keeping things quiet.

Reilly glanced up from the book he was reading, but his blank expression indicated he'd heard none of their conversation. She planned to keep it that way.

Dropping her voice, she turned her face away from him so he wouldn't see anything he shouldn't. "I think we need to put on a new bandage."

"Did something happen?"

"Later. Can you look at it now?"

"Sure." Alex led her to the bathroom and flicked on the light.

While Alex gathered first aid supplies, Lana unzipped her jacket.

Ugh. This wasn't going to be pleasant. Too bad there wasn't a way to get the jacket off without moving her arm. She slid her uninjured arm out and maneuvered the sleeve down her other arm.

Okay, not too bad. At least she wore a short sleeved shirt, so she didn't have to remove any other clothing.

Alex peeled off the bandage. "You okay?"

Not trusting her voice, Lana simply nodded.

"Liar." Alex leaned in to examine the wound.

"How does it look?"

"It's bleeding a little, but not too badly." Alex gently dabbed at the wound. "Now will you tell me what happened?"

The story took little time to relate and she finished as Alex opened a fresh gauze pad.

"How'd he find you here?" Suspicion laced Alex's words.

"I wondered the same thing. It seems like he turns up everywhere we go." She watched as Alex placed a clean gauze pad over the wound. "But really, we are less than a mile up the beach from the house."

"I think you should meet him tomorrow. This is the perfect chance to pump him for information. Find out if he really is a threat." Alex ripped off a strip of medical tape and adhered it to the bandage.

Stinging rippled down her arm as Alex pressed the bandage over the wound. Lana pulled in a sharp breath. "He's not the only threat."

Alex dropped her voice. "Look, I get that you have some reservations about the team. Frankly, I'm not sure how I feel. But you trust me, right?"

"Of course."

"Then I'm telling you I'll stay so close he'll think he has a second shadow. He'll be fine." After gently pressing down the final piece of tape, Alex stepped back. "Done. Let's check this in the morning to make sure you don't need medical attention."

No point in telling Alex that she wouldn't seek medical attention, not with Reilly's safety at stake. Besides, she didn't have the energy for the argument it would create.

She rubbed her forehead. It was bad enough that her arm was killing her; now her head had to get in on the act. "I think I need a few painkillers."

What a night. All she wanted was to crawl into bed and shut out the world.

Too bad she still had a job to do. And an assassin to stop.

Twelve

Rain drummed a steady beat on the roof of the car as Lana slid her phone from her pocket. The lighted display showed 1:25. Five minutes until she was due inside the pizza place in front of her to meet Nate for lunch.

Plenty of time to call Barker.

While she knew Alex shared her concern about an inside man, she wondered if Alex wasn't too close to the situation to see it objectively. Barker, being completely separate from this team, might be able to find information that Alex and her boss would miss.

"Barker."

"It's Milana Tanner."

"Tanner? How's it going out there?"

Loaded question. "Did you hear what happened?"

He grunted. "How would I have heard anything?"

Of course he hadn't heard. What did she think? That there was a "What's happening in WITSEC" newsletter that circulated the offices?

She recapped the shooting, leaving out the fact she'd been hit, but highlighting every reason she had for suspecting an inside man.

Silence lingered for several heartbeats after she finished.

"And Deputy Hill shrugged off your concerns?"

Oh boy. The last thing she wanted was to get Alex in any kind of trouble. "No, sir. But she's busy trying to run this op and keep Reilly safe. She's spread too thin to run much of an investigation. I thought maybe you could do a little digging."

"I'll do some digging, all right." The words growled across the line. "Stay alert. I'll see what I can find out and keep you posted."

ᘎ ᘎ ᘎ ᘎ ᘎ

"You made it."

Lana slid across the bench opposite Nate. "I was able to get away. How are you?"

A grin swallowed his face. "Can't complain."

"How'd your pictures come out?"

"Hit and miss. That's the way it goes. How's the arm?"

"Better."

"You guys decided yet?" The waitress, a pretty brunette who couldn't be any older than twenty, snuck a glance at Nate, interest painted in her eyes.

A smile twitched the corners of Lana's mouth, but she fought it back.

It was easy to see what might attract the waitress to him. Funny thing was, Nate seemed oblivious to the attention.

"Wanna split a large?" Nate looked up at her innocently.

"Sure."

They ordered a large deep dish with grilled chicken, olives, and peppers on her half, but only cheese on his.

"Just cheese?" she teased as the waitress walked away.

"Guess I'm a man of simple tastes." Nate retrieved a manila envelope from the bench beside him. "Here're some of my better shots from the last few days."

"Good thinking. I'd hate to leave greasy fingerprints." She opened the envelope and slid out a small stack of 4x6 photos.

Gorgeous sunsets displaying every imaginable shade of orange and purple met her eyes. She recognized some of the well-known coastal landmarks such as Haystack Rock and the Devil's Punchbowl, but many showcased deserted beaches with waves pounding the shore.

Seeing the photos validated his claims. A hired assassin wouldn't waste time sightseeing, walking the beach, and talking to joggers, would he?

"These are beautiful." She glanced at him before returning her attention to the stack in front of her. "Do you purposely avoid photographing people?"

"I do better with nature. I'm not much of a people person."

Really? Somehow, she found that hard to believe. "I suppose if someone were in the picture, you'd have to get their permission to use it. Complications."

"Yeah." He was quiet until she neared the bottom of the stack. "I saved the best for last."

She uncovered the last photo and her breath froze in her lungs. As in all the others, vibrant colors painted the sky, but this picture had the silhouette of a runner at the water's edge.

Her silhouette. She looked up to find him watching her closely.

"I took it a few nights ago, just before you saw me."

"It's great."

Except that the shadows didn't completely hide her face. Her features were dark, but it was still obviously her.

She'd made enemies during her career, some who likely hated her enough to want her dead.

What if one of them saw the picture and went after Nate in an effort to get to her?

She fought to keep her voice casual. "You're not going to actually do anything with this, right?"

"Wasn't planning on it. I snapped it on a whim."

Thank goodness. A smile overtook her face before she could stop it. "Good."

He shot her a strange look and she scrambled for an explanation.

"I don't like drawing attention."

"Huh. Well, I hate to break it to you, but…"

The arrival of the pizza broke the awkward moment. "That smells good."

"This place is the best." Nate reached for the pizza and picked up one of the cheese slices. "So is taking care of your brother a full time job or do you have a career outside of that?"

She'd figured this would come up eventually. Good thing she'd already prepared an answer. "Right now, it's full time, but I'm hoping things will get better soon."

"That's cool. I couldn't handle doing that kind of work."

"It's not exactly glamorous, but I like it." Time to shift the focus away from herself before he asked a more difficult question. "Did you always want to be a photographer?"

"Nah. I've always liked photography, but I never thought I'd actually make money doing it. I've worked all the basic jobs: fast food joints, toll booths, stuff like that. I spent a lot of my spare time taking pictures and finally sold some to a magazine. It's gone up from there."

"I can see why. You seem to know what to shoot." She reached for a slice of pizza. "My dad played around with photography some before going into seminary. He had a terrible eye."

"I think it's something that's acquired." Nate stopped to take a drink of his root beer. "I forgot you told me your dad was a pastor. I guess you must be pretty religious."

Was that a slightly confrontational tone she heard in his voice?

Might be wise to tread carefully. "I don't know about that, but my relationship with God is very important to me."

"If God's as great as people say He is, why doesn't He answer prayers? You know, remove someone from a bad situation?"

"Like when you were in the group home?"

"Yeah. I was a good kid, never picked a fight or made fun of the other guys the way they made fun of me, and I prayed. Every night. I wasn't even asking for much, I just wanted the bullying to stop, but things got worse before they got better."

A pained look flickered across his face. Probably still heard the taunts of the other kids.

"But things did get better eventually?"

"When I finally got a growth spurt, yeah."

She smoothed the napkin she'd placed across her lap. "God doesn't necessarily answer our prayers in the way or time we want Him to, but no prayer goes ignored. You said it yourself, it was rough, but it made you stronger. That might've been His plan all along."

He studied her for a minute. "Well, it stinks."

"Sometimes it does. But it's always helped me to know that God goes through the bad times with me. No situation is too big or hard for Him to handle. I've seen Him do some pretty amazing things."

"So He plays favorites." Nate took a big bite out of his pizza and studied her across the table.

"I've seen Him work in the lives of people who don't follow Him, too. Life's tough, but He's there to carry us through the challenges."

"I guess I'll have to take your word on that one."

"Where was the group home?" She kept her tone soft and compassionate and prayed the topic change wasn't so abrupt that it made him suspicious.

"Las Vegas." His jaw clenched. "I left there the day after I graduated high school and have never gone back."

"I can see why. Where'd you go?"

He shifted. Was the topic making him uncomfortable? Or was it simply the bad memories?

"I joined the army, but it wasn't for me. It didn't take long to figure out I couldn't shoot someone." He lifted his shoulders in a limp shrug and averted his eyes, as if the inability to kill was a sign of weakness.

Was that story true? Or a cleverly concocted lie to make him seem like the least likely person to be an assassin?

Well, it shouldn't be too hard to find out.

She forced a light tone. "I don't think that's a bad thing at all. It *should* be hard to take a life, even in times of war."

A single dip of his head acknowledged her words. "It wasn't all bad. I learned some skills while in the service though, and that helped me find work."

"Is that when you got into photography?" She took a bite of the rapidly-cooling pizza while she waited for him to answer.

"No, that came later." A smile curled his lips. "Actually, it was my buddy Matt who got me started on that path. He asked me to take engagement pictures of him and his fiancée. I'd hardly held a camera a day in my life, but it turned out I had a knack for it. I saved up, bought a good camera, and began snapping pictures any chance I got."

Matt. She hadn't heard that name before, but it could be important. "Did you and Matt keep in touch?"

"Oh yeah. We grew up together. In the group home. He always had my back." A hard look briefly flitted across Nate's face, but he masked it quickly. "More like brothers than friends, really. He lives near me, we take vacations together, get together on holidays, that sort of thing."

"Sounds like a good friend."

"He is. He's actually here now. In Lincoln City, I mean." Nate grinned. "We rented this cool cabin on a bluff. Great panoramic view of the ocean."

Hmmm. If Nate were an assassin, would he really bring his buddy along on the hit?

Probably not. Although Matt could be nothing more than a ruse used to throw off suspicion.

"It's hard to find friends like that. Is he into photography, too?"

"Matt? Nah. He's a freelancer, so he's can work wherever he wants."

Generic. Felt kind of like an answer she'd give when she was trying to keep something secret.

"How'd this become all about me?" Nate grinned broadly. "Tell me about you. How'd you end up as your brother's caregiver?"

Ugh. Not exactly the safe topic she'd hoped to discuss. "I had the training, so when he needed some extra help, I was the logical choice."

"And it's just the two of you?"

That should be safe enough to answer. "Just us. We're pretty close."

"Well, I'm glad you didn't end up in a group home. It was rough."

"How did Matt end up there?" Not that it likely mattered to her, but the more she could learn about Nate, the easier it would be to find out if he presented a threat.

"His dad was an abusive drunk. When he beat Matt unconscious, the state took him away. His dad never even tried to regain custody." Nate took a swig of his root beer before continuing, "He died in a drunk driving accident when we were fourteen."

What a horrible thing. She really had been sheltered growing up. "I'm sorry. That's a rough hand."

He shrugged it off. "We had each other. Matt was always tougher than me. He'd take on the other guys when they were giving me a hard time. Eventually, I got a growth spurt and passed a lot of them up and they learned not to mess with Matt and me."

What did an upbringing like that do to a kid?

She wasn't sure, but the man in front of her seemed fairly stable and well-adjusted. Or maybe adept at hiding his brokenness.

Either way, the way he and Matt had both risen from the ashes of their troubled upbringing was commendable.

She'd learned a lot about him. Enough to get a background check started.

And, surprisingly enough, had enjoyed getting to know him.

Part of her hoped he wasn't a hired killer. He might have the potential to become a good friend.

ꟷ ꟷ ꟷ ꟷ ꟷ

"How'd it go?" Alex asked as she walked through the door.

Lana set her purse down as Reilly walked closer and leaned his elbows on the counter. "It went fine. I learned enough to get that background check going, I think."

She gave Alex the pertinent details.

Alex jotted them down, then pulled her phone out of her pocket. "Let me call this in. The techs should be able to get something from this."

Without another word, Alex walked into the bedroom and closed the door.

Hopefully they'd find something. One way or another.

"What's he like? As a person, not a suspect." Reilly's question drew her attention back to him.

Where did she even begin? Nate had revealed quite a bit about himself. "He likes to travel, although that's not so surprising for a photographer. He pretty much likes all music styles, but favors jazz and reggae."

Reilly's eyebrows shot up. "Kind of an odd combination."

"He's full of them. He likes action movies, but thinks society has grown too violent. He goes to the theatre fairly often, but then tells me he isn't much of a people person. Honestly, I don't know what to make of him."

Just when she thought she had Nate figured out, he threw something new at her and she had to scrap her previous impression.

She was normally so good at reading people; why couldn't she read him?

Reilly's voice broke into her thoughts. "That doesn't mean he's up to no good. He's a little quirky. Like all of us."

How did he do that? Know exactly what was on her mind and what she needed to hear?

Sometimes she thought he knew her way too well.

"Maybe. Or maybe he's full of contradictions because he's hiding a secret life as an assassin."

Trusting him, even a little, was way too risky.

It wouldn't be long before he realized she'd managed to reveal surprisingly little about herself.

And then he'd probably begin asking questions she couldn't answer. At least not with any degree of honesty.

Before that happened, she needed to learn absolutely everything about him, his past, his work, and anyone connected to him in any way. If there were any skeletons lurking in his life, they would be unearthed.

"You're grinning like an idiot."

Nate shook his head at Matt's teasing. Although he couldn't stop smiling, so there was probably some truth to Matt's words.

"I take it she showed. Either that, or the food was awesome."

"Let's just say the food was good, but not *that* good." Nate settled on the couch.

"Man, she must be something special. Show me this photo you said you took."

Nate opened the envelope he'd taken with him and shuffled through until he found her picture.

The picture didn't do her justice. Why hadn't he noticed before how dark it had come out? He'd have to do some digital retouching to see if he couldn't enhance the quality.

Or maybe sneak another shot when she wasn't looking. Not that he needed an image to remember every detail.

Reclaiming his seat, he handed over the picture without a word.

Matt studied it for a few seconds before looking up. "Not what I expected. You usually go for redheads."

"Tell me about it. But there's something about her."

"Oh, yeah? What's that?"

"I don't know." He told Matt some of the things he'd learned, which, now that he thought about it, wasn't much. She excelled at keeping the conversation focused on others. Whether it was intentional or she was simply more interested in other people, he couldn't say. She had a big heart so he suspected the latter.

"Dang. You've really got a thing for her. You don't even know her that well." Matt's tone may have been mild, but concern lined his face.

"I know. Can't explain it, but I feel like she gets me."

"Just watch it, okay? Remember what happened with Ashley."

"Don't worry. Lana's nothing like her." Everything about Lana – from her looks to her temperament – was a far cry from his last girlfriend. Lana was petite, Ashley had been tall. Ashley loved being the center of everyone's attention, Lana seemed to prefer the fringes. Ashley had been shallow and self-absorbed, but Lana focused on others.

"So you think. You just met her. She could be hiding a whole other life from you."

"She's not."

Or was she? What about those times when she'd seemed rather evasive?

Nah, not evasive. Cautious. She'd answered every question he'd asked. Besides, his years in the group home had taught him how to detect a liar.

And she didn't seem to be lying.

Matt regarded him with raised eyebrows.

"Seriously. She's a preacher's kid."

"Oh, and that automatically makes her trustworthy, is that it? You ask me, that makes it worse. She'll probably end up force-feeding Jesus to you."

"She's not like that. I guess you'd have to meet her. Honestly, she's too good for me."

"Hey." The word sliced the air between them. "No one's too good for you. You got that?"

"Yeah, yeah. I hear you." Not that he agreed.

"And next time you see her, ask her if she's got a friend. Maybe someone blonde and leggy…"

Persistent ringing wrenched Lana from a sleep that'd been painfully short.

She tugged her eyes open. The glowing bedside clock read 8:03.

Ugh. Why couldn't they have called on a morning when she wasn't coming off the graveyard shift?

She fumbled for the phone and tried to shake off the remnants of sleep.

The display lit with Barker's name.

Sitting up, she answered the call seconds before it would've gone to voicemail. If he noticed the sleep-induced huskiness of her voice, he made no comment.

"You alone?"

She glanced at Alex's bed, barely able to discern its emptiness in the dim light.

Of course. Alex had been the one to relieve her at six a.m., which meant she was still standing guard in the living room.

"Yes, sir."

"Still working on the people on your team, but that's not why I called. Downplayed the severity of your situation, didn't you?"

Was he referring to her getting shot? How could he possibly know about that?

He must've spoken to Maxwell, Alex's supervisor. "It's just a flesh wound. I didn't think–"

"Wait. What's just a flesh wound?"

He *didn't* know? Maybe her thinking was muddy from lack of sleep, but this wasn't making any sense. "I was shot. Pushing Reilly down. The bullet grazed my arm."

The silence seeped disapproval. "And you didn't think that detail was worth mentioning?"

"I'm healing. Now what were you referring to?"

"The Shadow of Death."

Psalm 23 slid into her mind, but she doubted Barker was quoting scripture. "I'm sorry, sir, I'm really not following–"

"The assassin. Also known as Stevens."

Stevens.

The name squeezed her heart like the cold-blooded viper the hit man was known to be.

It couldn't be him.

No. No, she must've misheard.

But deep down, she knew there was no mistake. Not only had Barker clearly said both the assassin's name and the moniker law enforcement had given him, he would be a logical choice for someone with Rosetti's power and wealth.

"Stevens doesn't miss." The argument sounded flimsy, even to her.

Stevens was good, but nobody was perfect. Logic dictated that sooner or later he would miss. Why not now?

"You got lucky." Barker's blunt statement mirrored her thoughts. "Face it, if you hadn't looked outside when you did, he probably would've succeeded."

She wanted to argue, but the wound on her arm evidenced how close she'd come to losing Reilly.

This could *not* be happening!

"So, you didn't know?" Barker's voice cut through her denial.

"About Stevens? No. How would I?"

"Maxwell knew. I figured he would've told you."

Alex's boss knew they were facing one of the worst threats possible and had chosen to withhold that information?

"How did we get this intel?"

"The guy sharing Garrett's cell. He said Garrett was spouting off on how he wouldn't be in there long because someone had hired Stevens to take care of the problem."

"And he's reliable?"

"We can't take the chance that he isn't."

True enough. Besides, what little evidence they'd recovered from the crime scene supported the Stevens theory. The casings, the time of day, even the fact that he hadn't attempted to take out anyone but Reilly all fit Stevens' MO.

Perfectly.

Her thoughts flitted back to Alex's boss. "Are you sure Maxwell knew?"

"Yeah. Prison records confirm he met with Garrett's cellmate."

So many questions, but Barker had his own workload to manage and she didn't have time to go through each of the questions that dogged her.

Like how Barker had come across this information.

Why Maxwell hadn't told them who had been hired.

What the penalty would be if she took Reilly, ducked security, and went on the run.

Focus. "How well do you know Maxwell?"

"Look, kid, I know where you're going with this and I'm telling you, don't. He's well-respected and has been doing this job a long time."

"That doesn't mean he doesn't have a price."

"And it doesn't mean he's dirty. I'll handle this. You focus on keeping our witness safe."

Her hand shook as she set the phone on the nightstand.

Stevens.

The name echoed in her mind.

Such a simple name. Common even.

Yet belonging to one of the world's best assassins, a monster that traded human life for money.

Suffocated by the air surrounding her, she struggled to draw in oxygen.

Worrying about the integrity of the people around her was bad enough, suspecting Alex's boss might be involved was even worse, but this... it didn't get much uglier than knowing a hit man like Stevens pursued them.

Going to sleep now was out of the question.

She slid out of bed, grabbed some clothes and prayed her way through a shower. Tears mingled with the water running down her cheeks.

It seemed impossible.

Stevens had never been photographed. No one had ever seen him and lived to give a description. Stevens could be a first name, last name, nickname, or pseudonym. For that matter, they didn't even know for sure that Stevens was a man.

How could she possibly hope to protect Reilly from someone with no identity?

Trust God.

Worrying didn't accomplish anything except to demonstrate a distinct lack of faith. God was bigger than this problem.

She managed to get her tears under control, but not the fear that had caused them. Not even reminding herself of all God had done throughout history could banish that. Because shielding them from an assassin was surely more difficult than creating the universe, parting the sea, or raising the dead.

Why did it have to be so hard to leave her problems in God's hands?

After pulling her damp hair into a messy bun, Lana headed toward the living room. Alex sat in one of the chairs, watching some program with the volume turned so low it was a wonder she could actually hear it.

"Have you heard anything from Maxwell?"

Alex glanced up as Lana sank onto the sofa cushions opposite her.

"Not since the shooting." Alex's eyes narrowed as she stared at Lana. "What are you doing up anyway? You got, what, two hours of sleep?"

If that. "Barker called. I couldn't sleep after that."

"Really? What's going on?"

"He knows who's been hired to kill Reilly." Lana fought the pressure building behind her eyes. "It's Stevens."

Several seconds passed. The narrowing of Alex's eyes confirmed she'd heard the words and the tilt to her head said she was processing it. "Good to know."

That was it? "We're talking about Stevens. The Shadow of Death. You know the one, right?"

"Who doesn't?" Alex rolled her head from one shoulder to the next. "Over two dozen confirmed hits, no witnesses, no sightings. Yep, I know the one."

"This is bad. The man is practically a ghost! He never fails."

"Oh and we do? Yeah, Stevens isn't the best news we could've gotten, but we can handle him. I'm not about to be the first deputy to lose a witness and your brother sure as heck isn't going to be the first rule-abiding witness to die under protection."

There was no way Alex could guarantee that. Not definitively.

But she appreciated the pep-talk nonetheless. "Thanks for trying. But–"

"No buts. Besides, this is a good thing. We may not know what he looks like, but we know how he operates. Always strikes at dusk with a high-powered rifle, kills with a single heart shot. Since we know what to watch for, we can better prevent future attacks."

True. Even though Stevens posed a formidable threat, there was power in knowing the enemy.

"Best of all–" Alex's voice cut through her thoughts. "He doesn't go after family. Your parents are safe."

The one bright spot in all of this.

Now there was the question of why she'd heard about it from Barker.

The question had to be asked, but how could she say it without sounding accusatory? "So, uh, I guess Maxwell knew about this. Why wouldn't he tell you?"

Alex hesitated. "Maybe with everything that's happened, he hasn't gotten around to it."

What, because it took so long to pick up the phone and say "Stevens was hired"?

She stamped down the cynical thought. "Okay, we know who we're dealing with. What are we going to do now?"

The question hung in the air for several seconds. "We'll change our strategy. Alter Reilly's appearance. Maybe you could swing by the store and pick up what I'll need to make it happen."

"After that?"

Alex offered a half shrug. "We'll do what we've been doing. With any luck, we can change his appearance enough to confuse even the best assassin."

Given that the best had been hired, she could only hope Alex succeeded.

Of course, all this effort would only help if the people with them could be trusted. If there was a mole, then changing Reilly's appearance wouldn't solve anything since the mole could pass that information along to Rosetti or Stevens.

"How does Reilly feel about contacts?"

"He used to wear them, but stopped a few years back. I think he decided they were too much trouble or something."

"Well, he's about to change his mind on that one. I'll see what Maxwell can do about getting that prescription updated, filled, and overnighted to us. We'll probably go with colored lenses."

Oh, Reilly was going to be thrilled. But at the moment, she was more concerned about his safety than his happiness.

"What about routines and protection strategies? Any revisions to those?"

"A few." Alex rubbed her forehead. "Since Stevens strikes at dusk, everyone will be on duty then. Someone will be posted at that little alcove by the stairs to keep an eye on the elevator and stairs. I'll post you outside to keep an eye on the exterior–"

"Cause, what, you think he might rappel from the roof?"

"Unlikely, I know. But we have to consider every option. He could also break into another room and somehow get from that balcony to ours."

Sounded like a suicide mission to her, but it was better to be overly cautious than regret being lax later. Besides, the man killed people for money. No telling what his twisted mind might think was sane.

"That'll leave the rest of us in here. He'll be well covered," Alex continued.

Well covered or not, until this whole thing was over, no amount of protection would be good enough.

Thirteen

Okay. Razor. Check. Aftershave. Check. On to the hair dye.

She wandered down the aisle, her eyes scanning the rows and rows of boxes. Why'd there have to be so many options?

Temporary.

The word leapt off the box of one of the brands.

She picked up the box and read the back. Lasted about a month. At which point they'd probably have to re-dye his hair due to visible roots anyway.

Now to pick a color.

The color in her hand was medium auburn. Why not?

As she approached the end of the aisle, a highlighting kit caught her attention.

Ooh, an opportunity like this was way too good to pass up. And since Reilly would hate whatever they did, she might as well have some fun with it. She reached for the box.

"Lana?"

She jerked. Her hand smacked the box of highlights, which tumbled off the shelf.

Unfamiliar voice. Her name.

Thoughts slammed through her brain even as she whirled.

The stranger stood a few feet away. Mid-fifties, gray-streaked black hair, olive skin, dark eyes. Not someone she knew or had ever seen before.

Wait.

Dimitrios. Cyrano. This man looked like an older version of them. Likely their father or some other relative.

But how did he know her name? And why would he talk to her?

Best to fake confusion. "I'm sorry?"

She bent to retrieve the box, but her focus never strayed from his face.

Blinking, he cleared his throat. "No, I'm sorry. You remind me of someone and I… but that is your name, isn't it?"

The way his gaze drank in her face flooded her veins with ice. "Do I know you?"

"No. No, we haven't met. But you've met my sons, Dimitrios and Cyrano."

Okay, identity confirmed. But the mystery was far from solved. Why would Dimitrios and Cyrano talk to their father about some random stranger?

She could solve that puzzle later.

For now, she needed to act natural and get rid of this guy fast. "Yes, of course. I can see the family resemblance."

"I'm Theo Lykos." He offered a firm handshake.

"Lana." Felt a little unnecessary since he obviously already knew that, but she said it anyway.

Digging out his wallet, he withdrew a tattered picture. "You remind me of my daughter. This was taken about thirty years ago, just before we lost her."

Whoa. Hold up.

Friendly conversation was one thing, but why would he bring up his dead daughter? He couldn't possibly expect her to serve as some sort of stand in simply because she bore a faint physical resemblance. Or could he?

It'd be best if she simply offered condolences and walked away.

But something, probably the same kind of morbid curiosity that made people look at road kill, rooted her feet in place. Her eyes drifted to the proffered photograph, which was too far away for her to make out any details.

After a moment's hesitation, she slowly reached to take the picture.

Five people smiled back at her. A much-younger Theo Lykos stood beside a fair-skinned woman with light brown hair. In his arms, he held two dark-haired children, one boy and one girl, while the woman held a second dark-haired boy. The children all appeared to be about the same age, maybe two or three years old. Triplets?

Her gaze slid back to the girl in question, the daughter that Lykos had said they'd lost. "What happened to her?"

"A fire. Arson. They told us she was dead."

Why was he telling her all this? Maybe the stand-in theory had some merit after…

Wait. He couldn't possibly think *she* was his daughter, could he?

Of all the psychotic ideas! His daughter was dead! What kind of man would still be looking for a child he'd buried thirty years ago?

The picture shook in her hand as she returned it. Time to get away from this lunatic.

She watched his eyes move across her face, practically drinking in the details. "Is Lana short for anything? Milana, maybe?"

How could he possibly know that? Unless….

No. No way.

There couldn't be any truth to his theory. It wasn't possible. She had a greater chance of getting struck by lightning than accidentally stumbling across her family, especially in the middle of such an important case in such a small town.

Serious dark eyes watched her closely. "It is, isn't it? Milana."

She couldn't do this.

Not now.

Probably not ever.

Even if she was related to this man, what did she care? She liked her life the way it was and she didn't need these people screwing it up, complicating things with their probing curiosity or need for closure.

Besides, his daughter was dead. D. E. A. D. Dead!

And she was most certainly alive. She'd never been dead, nor brought back from the dead, so she couldn't possibly be his daughter. Even if their coloring was similar and he did know her name.

Calm down.

So he knew her name. So there were certain physical similarities.

It didn't mean anything.

The hope that had flickered in his eyes now blazed. "And your family? I mean, were you, uh, were you–?"

"Adopted?" Her tone was sharper than she'd expected. "It's really none of your business."

"I'm sorry, but I, well, I think she'd look just like you."

Her heart pounded a furious beat and she fought to breathe. "I have to go."

"Please."

She turned and started to walk away but the pain in his voice stopped her.

"I miss my girl. So much. If there's any chance at all." A breath shook from his mouth. "I look at you and I see my sons. And my wife. You have her nose."

How could she walk away?

The agony of losing a child probably wasn't something anyone ever got over completely.

But what about the agony of abandonment? What about all the pain she'd felt over the years? Was she supposed to forget about that?

Her eyes slid shut as she debated what to do. Walk away and forget the whole thing or at least consider the possibility?

What possibility?

So she and his daughter had the same name. There were other Milanas in the world.

But other Milanas with her coloring that had no contact with their birth families?

Opening her eyes, she turned back to him. "You're wrong. I mean, it–it's not possible. I'm not from around here."

"I see." A muscle in his jaw twitched and moisture lined his eyes. "But maybe we could compare stories. Rule it out for sure?"

She didn't want to compare stories. She wanted to walk away from this man. And never look back. "I–I need to go."

"Can I call you? I could give you a few days to think things through and then we could talk."

No way would she give her number to this man. What if he was some kind of nut?

"I'll call you." Reaching into her purse, she pulled out a small notepad and a pen.

"Thank you." He took them from her and jotted down his name and number.

Without even glancing at it, she slid the paper back into her purse.

"I need to go." Now she was repeating herself. And in a high, crackly voice she'd expect from a thirteen-year-old boy, no less.

His arm jerked slightly like he wanted to reach out for her, but it remained at his side. "You'll call, right?"

She wanted to say no. No, she wouldn't call. Not today or tomorrow or ever.

The words even sat on her tongue, ready to lash out at this man who had suddenly tipped her world upside-down.

Somehow she couldn't force them out.

She couldn't keep from looking at the picture he held lightly in his left hand, his thumb unconsciously stroking the little girl's face.

To lose a child so young; she couldn't even imagine that kind of pain.

This was the last thing she needed right now.

"Please. Just to compare stories."

How could she refuse?

This man hadn't asked to lose his daughter any more than she'd asked to be abandoned. And, as unbelievable as it seemed, what if it were true?

She cleared her throat, but her voice still came out raspy. "Give me a day or two. It's… I need to think."

Without waiting for a reply, she slipped past him and hurried toward the checkout counters. She had to get out of here. Tremors shook her legs and threatened to spill her to the floor, but she forced them to move faster.

Oh, Lord. What are You doing to me?

Peters wordlessly let her back into the suite, barely waiting for her to enter before bolting the door behind her.

Brushing past Mr. Personality, she carried her bag to the kitchen table.

Alex sidled up next to her as she unpacked the contents of the bag. "That took a while. No problems?"

Depended on your definition of problem.

If you defined a problem as running into some guy who wanted you to be his dead daughter and whose story had enough credibility to make you think it might be true, then yeah. She'd run into a problem. A very big one.

But she'd already determined to keep this whole little drama a secret. For now.

"Picking things out took a little longer than expected."

Reilly saved her from further questioning by joining them. "Okay, what crazy color did you get me?"

Reilly. How could she tell him she'd met a man who might be a blood relative?

"You okay?"

Snap out of it. She blinked and forced a smile. "It was a difficult choice between purple and green, but green goes better with your eyes."

"Okay, spill it. What's wrong?"

"It's a long story."

One better saved for later, after she'd had time to check out this Theo Lykos guy and see if there was anything to his story. Maybe the guy was some head case who got his thrills by upsetting strangers.

She probably couldn't get that lucky.

"Okay, okay." Reilly's voice pulled her back. "I know better than to push. But when you're ready to talk, you know where to find me. Not like I'm going anywhere."

The dry tone made her smile, but didn't shrink the boulder that had settled in her gut.

She couldn't deal with this.

Not now.

Not when all of her attention, every ounce of focus, needed to be spent guarding Reilly from the world's best hit man.

Reilly picked up the box of hair color and skimmed the front before noticing the highlights. "You can't be serious."

"Highlights are trendy. Besides, it'll help hide the fact that your goatee is lighter than the rest of your hair."

"Goatee? Really."

"You might like it. You haven't worn one in years."

"Yeah. Because it wasn't my thing."

"Precisely the point."

"Gee, I can hardly wait. When does the torture begin?"

"We'll get started on your hair after lunch." Alex shifted her attention to Lana. "And Maxwell called while you were out. He's overnighting the contacts to the hotel so we should have them tomo – no, tomorrow's Sunday. We should get them Monday."

She tried to offer a reassuring smile as she turned to Reilly. "By the time Alex finishes, not even Mom and Dad will recognize you."

The lines around his eyes softened as the tension slowly slid from his face.

Huh. Her words must've at least sounded convincing. Too bad she couldn't sell herself on it as easily.

All their plans, the disguise and secrecy, would only fool those on the outside. If they had an internal problem - as she suspected - then no amount of planning could truly protect Reilly.

Unbelievable.

Lana stared at the stranger in front of her. She knew it was Reilly. Heck, she'd helped Alex with the transformation. And yet, he looked so unlike the brother she'd always known that her mind refused to connect the two.

Silence settled as Reilly absorbed his reflection in the bathroom mirror.

It wasn't often that he was totally speechless. Not that she could blame him.

The color had turned out more auburn than brown, a far cry from the blond hair he'd always had. The highlights kept the color from looking too dark for his skin tone and the messy style Alex had created subtracted about five years from his age. The full goatee even helped disguise his face shape.

But his blue eyes anchored her. Good thing there were brown colored lenses on the way or all Alex's hard work might've been for nothing.

Reilly grunted. "At least I'm not going into a courtroom looking like this. No one would take me seriously."

Where he got such an idea, she wasn't sure, but she didn't argue. "It looks good."

"I look like some surfer dude."

"Nothing wrong with that."

He studied the mirror a few more seconds before running his fingers through his hair. "I guess it's not too awful."

"Not too awful? Alex did a great job. In fact, once we get those contacts, I'll have to take a picture for Des. She'll flip when she sees this." Not that she'd be likely to see it anytime soon, but when this was all over, Lana knew Desiree would enjoy seeing this new side of Reilly.

"Well, you better take a picture because as soon as this is over, it's all going away." He turned from the mirror. Humor glinted in his eyes. "Maybe you oughta call that photographer friend of yours. Have him take the picture."

"Dream on."

"Predictable."

They stepped out of the bathroom and into the hallway. Reilly turned toward the living room, but she stopped him with a light touch to his arm. "I was hoping to run something by you."

"It's about time." He studied her face. "Kitchen?"

Too public. "Your room."

Not waiting for a response, she led the way down the hall. She still didn't have as many facts as she'd like, but the small amount of digging she'd done earlier had convinced her that Lykos was neither crazy nor someone who habitually accosted young women.

Sitting at the end of the bed, she tucked her legs under her. Reilly eased the door closed and joined her.

How did she even begin a conversation like this?

Silence lingered.

Reilly cleared his throat quietly. "What's up?"

"When I was in town earlier, I met this guy." The words wedged in her mouth, fermenting on her tongue like rotting fruit.

"Another guy? I'm gonna have to keep a closer eye on you."

She worked up a smile in response to his teasing, even though it did nothing to lighten her mood. "He thinks I'm his daughter."

Okay. Not quite how she'd imagined saying that, but at least it was out there.

Reilly stared at her, mouth slightly open, eyes wide behind his glasses. "I did not see that one coming."

There was so much more she could say, things she should say, but the words wouldn't come. Thoughts froze inside her mind as she watched Reilly process the information. How would he handle this?

Probably better than she had.

"So we know what he thinks. What do you think?" The calm in Reilly's tone soothed her nerves.

"I–I don't know. There's so much that doesn't add up."

"What's his story?"

"He thought his daughter died in a fire when she was little. Probably about two or three, judging by the picture he showed me."

"Wait, he showed you a picture? Did it look like you?"

"All kids look alike at that age."

The corner of his mouth tweaked up. "I'll take that as a yes."

"It proves nothing."

"Says you. But if he thought his daughter was dead, why is he looking for her? And how did he track you down?"

"I don't think he *was* looking." A chill shot through her and she rubbed her arms to fight it off. "And it appears he stumbled across me. But he'd heard about me, which must've gotten him thinking–"

Reilly held up a hand. "How exactly did he hear about you?" Concern weighted the words.

"He's Dimitrios' and Cyrano's father." How had she forgotten to mention that oh-so-important detail?

"Really. Now I wish I'd paid more attention when Dimitrios was checking me over." Reilly searched her face, his eyes moving over her features as if seeing them for the first time. "You know, that might explain a lot. Like the weird feeling you got at the restaurant."

And the level of comfort she'd experienced around Dimitrios, not that she'd told Reilly about that.

"Did you check him out?"

She nodded. "Yeah. Married, three kids. Triplets. Two boys and a girl. The girl was declared dead after a fire started in her room when she was two. I guess it destroyed half the house."

"If she's dead, why would he think you might be her?"

That was the question of the day. "I have no idea. But he claims I look like his sons and his wife."

"I don't know. He sounds a little mental to me."

"There's no apparent history of mental illness."

She paced to the window, inching the drape back to peek out at the sun-drenched day. The air conditioner kicked on and she rubbed her arms against the sudden chill.

Too bad the chill was more than skin deep.

She turned and met Reilly's calm stare. "Her name was Milana."

The TV down the hall provided the only noise for what seemed like an eternity.

"Did he–" Reilly cleared his throat. "Did he say that before or after he learned your name?"

"Before."

"What does he want?"

"To compare stories. See if there's any chance." Memories of the anguish in his voice assaulted her. She offered a limp shrug and shook her head. "You should've heard him. I don't think he's crazy. And I don't think he's done something like this before."

"Do it."

The firmness in his tone surprised her. "What?"

"Meet with them. Compare stories."

"Are you nuts?"

"What's it going to hurt?"

"Maybe them." Not to mention what it might do to her, but she left that part out. "They get their hopes up that their daughter's back from the dead only to find out she's not."

"What if it's true? Face it, you have the same name–"

"There are other Milanas in the world." None that she'd met, but still, there had to be other people with that name.

"–about the same age, same physical characteristics and coloring. You might be her."

"Oh yeah? And how'd I get from Oregon to Florida at age two? Sleepwalk?"

"We lived in Denver until you turned four, remember?"

She'd forgotten that little detail. But it changed nothing. "That's still a lot of miles in between."

"He might be able to explain that. You won't know until you talk to him."

She tried to erase the memories from her mind. The familiarity around Dimitrios. The look in Cyrano's eyes. Lykos' tears.

They told us she was dead.

Lykos' words rang in her ears. Hadn't he seen the body for himself?

None of it made sense.

"If it was my child, I wouldn't give up until I knew for sure that she was gone. Until I had the body in front of me."

"I hear you, but everyone deals with loss differently. If you really want answers, it's not me you should be talking to."

Unfortunately, she had no desire to talk to the man who did hold the answers. "Well, then maybe I don't care. I haven't needed to know before and I don't need to now."

"You should hear him out. There could be something to this."

"Or it could be nothing. Bodies don't disintegrate in a fire. And get this. He was a firefighter. He'd know that!"

He scrutinized her. "You know what I think? I think you're afraid to learn the truth."

Dang it. Why'd he have to be so good at reading her?

She turned away from his probing gaze. No point in denying it. "Sometimes it's easier to believe a lie."

"Sometimes the truth is better than you expect it to be."

"And if it's not?"

"At least you'll know. Besides, we don't even know for sure that there's any relation between you and this family. All this anxiety might be for nothing."

"I'll think about it."

"Do more than just think about it. Pray about it."

Pray. What a novel idea.

Worrying had distracted her from the one thing that would have helped her the most.

God, please give me wisdom to know how to handle this. And strength for whatever comes next.

Peace bled into her anxiety.

This encounter, no matter how much it had surprised her, was not a surprise to God. She could rest in that.

Even if everything else in her life felt like a washing machine stuck on spin.

Fourteen

"I don't like you going out there alone. Especially with someone like Stevens around."

Lana zipped up her jacket before meeting Reilly's scowling eyes. "Relax. Stevens doesn't even know I exist."

"The man's been hired to kill me. You don't think he's done his homework on my family?"

"Actually, I don't. Stevens has never gone after family."

"What if he starts now?" He crossed his arms and leaned back in his chair.

"Even *if* he knew about me and found a picture so he'd know what I looked like, he'd expect me to be back home, not here. People see what they want to see."

"I still don't like it."

"You don't have to like it. It's part of the job." Coming up behind him, she gave his shoulders a small squeeze. "It's okay. I have my gun, a knife, an earpiece and communicator, plus my cell phone. Not to mention my mad martial arts moves."

At least that one earned her a small smile.

The smile didn't mean he agreed, however. She didn't wait for a rebuttal before crossing the room and exiting the suite.

Wind blasted her as she stepped outside, the sharp chill biting through her jacket. Fighting the wind with every step, she headed a short distance down the beach.

The tricky part would be to keep the hotel in view while maintaining her cover. Running into Nate tonight might make that task easier, as she'd be able to position herself to see both him and the hotel, but it would also distract her.

Of course, he might not even show up tonight. The cold wind would be enough to keep any sane person inside.

She jogged for a few minutes, her gaze fixed almost constantly on the balconies along the top of the building. Once she could no longer unobtrusively watch the top floor, she turned around.

Her attention locked on two figures strolling toward her.

Not many people were in sight, but the two figures appeared to be headed straight for her.

Her pulse tripped. Her eyes darted from one side to the next, weighing escape options and looking for cover.

Relax. She pulled in a deep breath. No one would be coming after her.

There would be no reason for anyone to be after her. Not here, not now.

As the gap between her and the figures closed, details clarified.

Both men.

In fact, one of them reminded her of Nate. The gait, the build… it even looked like he had a camera around his neck.

But Nate always came out here alone.

The man lifted his hand in a wave.

It was Nate.

With him, a man with close-cropped sandy brown hair walked with his hands in his pockets. The man stood an inch or two shorter than Nate, but had a stockier and more muscular build.

"Hey, Nate." She slowed, carefully positioning herself so Nate and the other man stood between her and the hotel. The balconies, visible between them, would be in her peripheral so she could watch them without being obvious.

"Hi Lana. For a minute there, I thought we'd have to run to catch up to you."

"I move pretty fast for a short thing, huh?"

He chuckled. "Not quite what I was thinking, but yeah. I mean, yeah, you're fast, not that you're short–"

She laughed as his face matched the sinking sun. "It's okay. I came to grips with being vertically challenged a long time ago."

The color lingered on his cheeks. He jerked his head toward the man beside him. "This is my buddy Matt."

An easy grin glided across his face as Matt offered his free hand. "Ah, the infamous Lana. I've heard stories."

She chuckled. "Sounds dangerous. But at least we're even."

"Yeah. Although I wouldn't necessarily believe everything you hear." Matt shot a sideways glance at Nate. "This guy's been known to tell a story or two."

"I can imagine." She let her eyes travel between them, scanning the balcony as she did.

All clear.

Big surprise. It seemed unlikely Stevens would choose such a visible method of attack.

Of course, within a few minutes, it would be too dark to tell if someone was up there. He could probably parachute in wearing blue spandex and a cape and she wouldn't be able to see him.

Matt elbowed Nate. "Guess I'll have to stop teasing him about his imaginary friend Lana."

"I don't know, he could've paid me to pretend to be this Lana."

Matt laughed, a hearty sound that came from deep inside. "True enough."

A brisk wind whipped her ponytail into her face and sent a shiver through her limbs. "I think the temperature dropped ten degrees in the last five minutes. I'm going to call it a night."

"Hey, you free for lunch tomorrow?" Nate's question came before she could get away.

Darn. She'd hoped he wouldn't ask again.

Because honestly, a part of her wished she could say yes.

"I'm sorry. My family has some stuff going on tomorrow."

Matt shifted awkwardly. "I'll see you back at the car. Nice meeting you, Lana."

"Likewise." She turned back to Nate as Matt walked away. "He seems nice."

Nate nodded. "I don't think I'd have survived without him."

"I'm glad you have someone like that in your life."

Hesitation rolled off Nate like the waves on the sand behind them. "So I just have this feeling that some night I'll come out here and you'll be gone."

He was right, obviously, but how should she respond to that?

"What did you think would happen? We're both on vacation. At some point, we'll both be headed back home." Now might be a good time to try to find out where he lived. "I don't even know where home is for you."

"California." He shook his head slowly. "But it doesn't have to be. With my job, well, I could relocate. For the right reason."

Whoa. Talk about a heavy topic.

They hardly knew each other and clearly his mind had already moved to thoughts of permanence. Maybe it was a casualty of his upbringing.

She swallowed hard.

Regardless of whether or not Nate was an assassin - which she seriously doubted - there wasn't a future for them. There couldn't be. Not as long as he stood on the opposite side of the faith line.

"Look, don't get me wrong." The words rushed from Nate in a flood. "I'm not proposing or anything. I know we just met, but I... well, I feel this connection. I'd like to get to know you better and see if there's something there. You can feel it, right?"

"Yes." Even if she knew that it could never be anything more than friendship, she couldn't deny a pull toward him. "I don't know where to go from here."

"Maybe I could have your number? That way if I miss you out here, we could still keep in touch?"

The US Marshal in her said no. Absolutely not.

But something in her spirit countered that.

Lord?

Peace stole over her.

She'd give him the number. Why, she wasn't sure. But she sensed the Lord leading her to do it.

Besides, as she'd told Reilly, he couldn't track her phone.

"That would be great." She pulled out her phone and punched in his number, then shot off a text. "There. Now you have my number, too. If you don't see me out here, feel free to reach out."

The sun had descended into the ocean, but Nate's smile flashed white in the fading light. "Cool. Thanks."

"I need to get going, but we'll talk soon, okay?" How she'd explain this to Alex, or Reilly, she wasn't sure. Maybe she didn't need to.

He nodded, then headed toward Matt as she jogged away from the hotel.

It pained her to have the hotel - and the balconies - at her back, but she couldn't give away the location. Just in case.

She jogged a short distance before looking back.

Only two figures in sight. It had to be Nate and Matt. They moved away from her, approaching the public beach access.

She turned back, her eyes going to the balconies, but it was too dark to see anything.

With her attention divided between the balconies and Nate and Matt, she slowly jogged toward the hotel.

Once Nate and Matt disappeared from sight, she picked up the pace and approached the building.

She let herself inside, then rode the elevator to the fifth floor.

A soft ding indicated her arrival. As she exited the elevator, she glanced toward the sitting area by the stairs where Peters had been posted.

The chairs were empty. As was the couch.

What the heck? Alex had told Peters to watch the area until ten p.m., when Chow was scheduled to relieve him. So where was he?

She stopped in the middle of the hallway.

The only sound was the ding and whirr of the elevator descending.

The doors to both suites were closed. She hadn't heard any chatter to indicate any kind of trouble. In fact, communication had been at a minimum tonight.

Which could mean things were quiet.

Or it could mean that a highly-skilled assassin had taken the team out one-by-one.

An arctic blast pumped through her veins and a block of ice lodged in her throat. The silence surrounded her with a presence that was both oppressive and ominous.

She reached for the button on her communicator, but stopped short of pressing it.

If Stevens had breached their defenses, he might be listening.

She couldn't let him know she was out here.

With a glance down the empty hallway, she slipped her gun from the holster and eased toward their suites.

The soft swish of her shoes on the carpet seemed deafening.

She paused by the stairs leading to the lower floors and looked over the edge of the four foot wall. Though she couldn't see every part of the flights below her, no trace of movement caught her attention.

A clunk echoed in the enclosed stairwell directly beyond the stairs.

Those stairs only led to the roof, nowhere else. There shouldn't be anyone in there, especially not at this time of night.

A faint cough sounded from behind the door.

Her fingers tightened around the gun's grip. She inched forward.

Careful. It could be Peters.

Or it could be someone else. Why would Peters be hanging out inside the rooftop access stairwell?

The door opened when she was only five feet away. She whipped up her gun and sighted on the solid man stepping through the opening.

Peters.

Recognition dawned as irritation-laced words flew from his lips.

"You better point that thing somewhere else."

That was all he had to say for himself? She bit back irritation of her own. "I wouldn't have even had to pull it if you'd been at your post. What were you doing?"

"Thought I heard something."

"Did you let anyone know?"

His scowl confirmed her suspicions. How could he be so negligent?

As if reading her thoughts, he crossed his arms over his chest. "I don't answer to you."

Praise God for that. "No, but your actions impact all of us. What is your problem, anyway?"

"You. You shouldn't even be here."

Of all the narcissistic... "If it weren't for me," she drew in a deep breath and lowered her voice, "the witness would be dead right now."

"The witness is your brother. This thing has conflict of interest written all over it."

"No one else seems to have a problem with it."

"Or maybe they aren't saying so."

Ugh! Like arguing with a tree. "Well, you might as well get used to it, because I'm not going anywhere."

She brushed past him and approached the suite.

Putting up with his attitude had been bad enough, but this time he'd put everyone at risk. Including himself. Stevens could've been waiting in there, slit his throat, and stolen his earpiece before any of them even knew anything was wrong.

She'd tell Alex about this and if Alex wouldn't do something, she'd take it higher. File an official complaint.

Too bad reassignment wasn't likely to happen.

Alex granted her access to the suite, nodding at Peters before securing the door. "Things good outside?"

"Fine." The problem was inside. More specifically, sitting in a chair by the stairs.

"Doesn't sound like it. What's up?"

"It's..." She glanced at the couch, where Rodriguez sat watching TV, and nodded toward the kitchen. Stopping beside the sliding glass door, she dropped her voice. "It's Peters. He left his post. And I've had it with his hostility."

An understatement of phenomenal proportions.

"I've noticed the weirdness. What's going on?"

She recapped the incident in the hallway. "It's like he goes out of his way to pick a fight with me. How do you put up with him?"

Alex's light eyebrows scrunched. "I don't get it. He's not normally like that."

"Great. So I'm special."

"I coulda told you that a long time ago." The teasing tone sounded forced. Alex sighed. "Let me talk to him."

"No. I don't want it to seem like I ran crying to you." The last thing she needed was Peters thinking she couldn't fight her own battles. Besides, bullying 101 dictated that involving a third party normally made matters worse.

"I'll tell him that I've noticed some things and approach it from that angle."

"Please don't. We're all adults here–" Not that Peters was acting like one – "and can be professional, even if we don't get along."

Sober blue eyes studied her. "If you're sure."

"I am."

"Okay, then. And for the record, while he should've let us know about the stairwell, it's not a big problem." Alex paused for half a beat. "Did you run into Miller tonight?"

"Yes. I learned he lives in California, although he didn't specify where. And I got his phone number." Both of those things should assist in the background check. She pulled out her phone and jotted down the number.

Alex glanced at it and nodded. "Good. Anything else?"

"He had a friend with him, so we didn't talk much."

"A friend?" Alex's gaze sharpened. "Well, that makes him look less suspicious. I can't see an assassin of Stevens' caliber bringing a friend to work."

"Me, either."

"What's the friend's name?" Alex poised her pen to jot the information down.

"Matt..." Huh. Nate hadn't said Matt's last name. "He just introduced him as Matt."

Alex wrote it down, not that a name like Matt was going to do them much good. "That's okay. It's probably not important anyway."

Probably not. "Have we heard anything on him yet?"

While she was pretty sure Nate wasn't Stevens, it'd be nice to have confirmation that she hadn't given her phone number to a killer.

Alex shook her head. "Not yet, but it's a little too soon. The California connection should help."

A little. There were probably thousands of Nate or Nathan Millers in California.

If anything, the phone number would probably prove the most helpful.

With any luck, they'd have some answers by end of day tomorrow.

₪ ₪ ₪ ₪ ₪

A hand flashed in front of his face and Stevens jerked to the side to avoid smacking into it. Raucous laughter erupted from somewhere to his left and loud voices swirled around him in an off-key symphony.

Who knew the pub would be so busy tonight?

He wove between the tables, heading for an unoccupied stool at the very end of the bar. The bartender took his order for a beer on tap and Stevens leaned his back against the wall behind him.

A few other loners nursed drinks in silence further down the bar, but the bulk of the people in the room sat in groups.

Judging by the loud voices and unsteady movements, a number of these people wouldn't remember much in the morning.

Crazy the way some people relinquished all control.

One of the loners pushed up from the stool and staggered past

Stevens, muttering under his breath about the noise.

Yeah, it was loud, but after the solitude of tracking his target, the volume didn't bother him. A man could only spend so much time alone before going crazy.

Across the room, a girl with curly blonde hair stared at him.

He let his gaze pass right over her, doing his best to ignore her unspoken invitation.

If she weren't a hooker, he might've been interested. But the low cut pink v-neck and leather skirt that looked like it had been painted over her bony hips, not to mention the attire of the women on either side of her, confirmed her occupation.

"Hey, honey. You drinkin' alone?"

He glanced over to find her approaching, swinging her hips as she strode toward him.

Scratch that. Even if she weren't a hooker, he wouldn't be interested. She was probably only sixteen.

If that.

Her skeletal frame and the red marks on her arm told the rest of the story. Most likely a runaway who got hooked on drugs and started turning tricks to support her habit.

When he didn't answer, she sidled closer, purposefully bumping his knee with her hip. "Bet you'd find that I'm real good company."

He scanned her face. "You're what, fifteen?"

A coy smile curled her painted lips. "Honey, I can be whatever you want me to be."

She leaned in and ran her finger down his chest. Surprise flickered across her face as he knocked her hand away.

"Get lost. I don't go for kids."

"Why you…" Heat flashed across her face, in stark contrast with the ice in her words. "I am *not* a child."

Without waiting for a reply, she whirled, shoes clacking an angry beat as she stormed away.

Good riddance.

While he might spend a good deal of time alone, he'd never be lonely enough to sink that low. Not after–

He tried to stop the onslaught of memories, but it was too late. Her face already filled his mind. And with it, memories of the betrayal. The depth of the love he'd had for her. The millions of pieces his heart had been in after the truth had come to light.

Had he known she was selling her body on the side, he never would've asked her out, much less dated her for close to a year.

Or purchased the diamond ring that currently collected dust in his bottom desk drawer.

He still didn't know how she'd managed to keep it a secret as long as she had. Sure, he'd spent a fair amount of time out of town, but they'd talked on the phone when he wasn't around. There should've been some warning.

"You want another?"

He blinked the bartender into focus before glancing down at his empty glass. Huh. Hadn't even realized he'd finished it. He nodded.

While the bartender refilled his mug, he pushed all thoughts of the past from his mind.

The present needed to be his focus. And the present revolved around his mark. Tanner.

He'd hacked the registration systems for several of the area's motels, but unfortunately a lot of people had checked in on the day following the shooting. And of course, none of the rooms were registered to the US Marshal's service.

Assuming they were even at a motel. One of the town's many rental properties would provide a greater level of privacy. There might even be other government safe houses in town.

His phone vibrated against his side. An unfamiliar number lit the display.

No one was close to him and with the noise, they'd have to be right next to him to hear his end of the conversation.

He accepted the call.

"It's Rosetti."

Ah. Of course he didn't recognize the number. The little wimp was probably using a burner phone. Or a pay phone. "Yes?"

"Is it…" Rosetti cleared his throat. "Is it done?"

He glanced around before answering in a soft tone. "Still looking. I'll let you know."

"I'm running out of time! The FBI's always on me. And the deadline's only a little over a week away."

"Searching takes time. I'm narrowing the field."

"I'm trying to get you a location, but I'm having trouble

reaching my guy on the inside."

Right. The inside guy. Stevens still had some qualms about that one. "How do you know your guy's not a plant?"

"Let's say I've got the right leverage. No way he'll cross me."

"So you say. Are you sure he even knows the location?" Could explain why Rosetti was having trouble reaching him.

Rosetti chuckled. "Oh yeah, he knows. He's *with* Tanner."

Interesting. And very suspicious. But that would explain why the blinds hadn't been drawn when he'd attempted to take Tanner down the other night. "Well, if you hear anything, let me know."

Stevens didn't wait for a reply before terminating the call.

If Rosetti wanted to hang his hopes on an inside man, fine. Stevens didn't need one. He'd tracked tougher targets than this and had never relied upon someone else to do the work for him. This time would be no different.

With or without help, he'd find Tanner and extinguish every last bit of life from his body.

Fifteen

"It's beginning to look like a car." Lana leaned against the wall as Reilly positioned one of the model car's side panels.

The day had dawned overcast and rainy. Even now, she heard the tapping of rain on the balcony railing outside the sliding glass doors beside her. The drawn blinds kept her from seeing the storm, but the forecast predicted rain all day.

While she'd been going stir crazy, Reilly had been meticulously assembling the model car.

Reilly looked up at her. "Slowly. Now if only I could figure out a way to drive it."

"Good luck with that one." She nodded at the car. "You know, I could see you driving something like that. Maybe you should consider getting a real one."

"Right. I'll just pencil Ferrari into my budget."

"Maybe not a Ferrari. But you could afford a Challenger or Mustang."

"I'll stick with something more practical. Besides, sometimes dreaming about it is enough."

"True."

"You know what we *should* do, though?" His grin told her she wouldn't like what was coming. "Go out for dinner tonight."

"Uh, hit man on the loose, remember?"

"New look, remember?"

"That doesn't mean we take unnecessary chances." And going out definitely qualified as an unnecessary chance.

"It worked out fine the last time. And I looked like me then."

True. But then they hadn't known they were dealing with Stevens. That little detail changed everything.

She shook her head. "Above my pay grade. You'll have to take it up with Alex."

And she was reasonably certain Alex would say no.

₪ ₪ ₪ ₪ ₪

Rain drilled steadily against the roof above her head. A cool breeze swept the hair back from Lana's face and she pulled the blanket tighter across her shoulders. Thunder growled in the distance, but she had yet to see any lightning.

Too bad. She could go for a good light show right now.

Ongoing storms all day had cancelled the outdoor patrol. Lana chose to keep watch from the shelter of the balcony.

Not that she thought any hit man would be crazy enough to go out in this weather.

Then again, sanity might not be something Stevens possessed in great quantities.

Still, the natural light had disappeared about an hour ago. They'd made it past Stevens' primary working hours. Going inside would be okay.

She didn't move.

The solitude, the fresh scent, and the drumbeat of rain held her in place despite the cold.

For the first time all day, she allowed her thoughts to stray to an area she really didn't want them to go.

Theo. Dimitrios. Cyrano. What if everything she'd believed about her past was a lie?

Amazing how quickly life could change.

It'd only been five days since the incident at the safe house. Five days since she'd been shot and had met Dimitrios. Little had she known that incident would trigger a domino effect in her personal life.

She tried to let the falling rain soothe her.

Yeah, right. With the storm in her life making the one in front of her look like a drizzle?

Oh, God. How much do You think I can take?

Throbbing in her eyes precipitated the tear that snuck rebelliously down her cheek. She swiped it away and forced deep breaths.

Now was not the time to fall apart.

If anything, the stress provided all the greater reason for her to hold it together.

She could do this.

Not alone, but thankfully, she didn't have to do it on her own. Reilly was on her side. As was Alex.

And, most importantly, God was with her for every step.

Claiming the promise of James 1:5, she breathed a prayer for wisdom.

Okay. Say those people were her relatives. So what? She didn't have to rearrange her life or change anything.

In fact, it might be kind of nice to know more about her roots. There were certainly strong medical reasons for knowing her family history. To see if cancer, heart disease, or schizophrenia ran in the family, for example.

She should call them. Maybe tomorrow.

The future was too uncertain to wait long. Especially given that her team could leave town at a moment's notice. Much as she dreaded what she'd learn, she also didn't want to live with the regret of chances not taken.

Only a coward would run away. And she was not a coward.

Decision made. She'd call them.

Once she knew the truth, then she could decide whether or not to walk away and never look back.

Finally. He thought they'd never leave.

Frank Rosetti let the curtain slip from his fingers as he watched the last car bearing federal agents drive away. The quiver in his hand irritated him almost as much as the FBI's presence had only moments ago.

They'd shown up with a warrant. How had they gotten the evidence they needed to get a warrant?

The deadline was still eight days away, so he didn't think Doug had talked. But how else would they have gotten a judge to sign off on a search warrant?

Maybe he should've paid to have Doug eliminated.

At least the FBI left empty handed. The hidden file room Al had installed off the wine cellar no longer seemed like actions born out of paranoia.

"Frank?"

He whipped around to find Ginger standing inside the

doorway. *Play it cool.* He flashed a grin. “Hey, babe.”

Ugh. Hopefully his smile was more reassuring than his tone.

Her heels tapped across the room as she came to stand in front of him. She cocked her head to one side, her curls brushing her bare shoulder. Light eyebrows drew together in concern. “Are you okay?”

Toying with a lock of her hair, he tried to keep a lighthearted tone. “Yeah. I’m good.”

“Why was the FBI here?”

He wanted to tell her. The truth of what he’d done wouldn’t bother her, of that much he was sure. Before they’d gotten married, she’d been a major player in one of Al’s enterprises.

But anything he told her would make her an accessory after the fact.

While he might go down for this, he refused to take her with him. “They’re on a vendetta, trying to nail me like they did Al.”

“But they won’t, right? There’s nothing for them to find?”

He pulled her into his arms and kissed her head. “Don’t you worry.”

Her arms slid around his back and she angled her lips to meet his. “I love you.”

“Love you back.”

As their lips met, he vowed to outsmart the Feds. He couldn’t go to prison. Separation from Ginger would kill him.

Stevens had better keep up his end of the bargain. Tanner couldn’t live to see month’s end.

* * *

Two solid days of rain.

Lana let the slat of the vertical blind covering the sliding glass door swing back into place. According to the news report they’d watched last night, the whole Oregon coast was experiencing an unusually wet season.

Figured. Why couldn’t the wet season have started *after* they left town?

Another day of this and she’d go running in spite of the rain. A little water never hurt anyone, right?

How was she supposed to keep her sanity while stuck indoors

for two whole days?

Never mind that Reilly had been trapped for even longer. And that the progress on the case was proceeding about as quickly as a slug performing brain surgery.

Maybe God was trying to instill more patience.

If so, she still had a long way to go.

Or maybe God planned to hold her captive until she finally called Theo Lykos. She'd certainly welcomed any distraction that kept her from doing what she knew she needed to do as far as that whole matter was concerned.

A sigh shuddered from her. She'd procrastinated all day yesterday until the day was gone; now today was half over, too.

Well, no more putting it off. It was time.

She wandered into the living room, where Alex sat alone, half-watching a comedy Lana remembered seeing a few years ago. Banging in the kitchen told her Reilly was in there, probably making the lunch he hadn't wanted to eat earlier.

Dropping onto the other end of the sofa, Lana curled her legs up underneath her. "Where is everyone?"

"Peters and Chow are down at the hotel's gym. Rodriguez should be in the other suite and Beckman's probably asleep."

At least they were unlikely to be interrupted. "I need to talk to you about something."

Alex fixed sharp eyes on her. "Is it Peters again? I'll set him straight if you need me to."

"It's not him." Not that he'd been any more pleasant to be around, but he was the least of her concerns right now. "Something happened on Saturday when I picked up those things for Reilly."

"And you waited three days to tell me about it?" Disapproval tinged every word.

"It's personal. Has nothing to do with Reilly." Or did it? What if this was some elaborate ruse to lure Reilly out so Stevens could kill him?

Not possible. This thing had too much truth and too many variables involved to be a hoax.

"Lana?"

She blinked Alex into focus. "Sorry. This is tough."

Pulling in a breath, she recounted what had happened and what her research had turned up.

Silence lingered as Alex processed the information. Finally, she shook her head. "So what's next?"

"I'm going to call him." It almost hurt to say that. "I know he'll want to meet up. Compare stories."

"Do it. It's hard to believe there could be any connection, but you never know."

Propping her elbow on the back of the sofa, she leaned her head against her fist. "You have no idea how much I wish I could take Reilly with me to this meeting."

Sympathy touched the smile on Alex's face. "Too risky."

"I know. It'd just make it easier to have him there to act as a buffer."

"I have an idea. Set it up for that Mexican restaurant and we'll all go. We can't sit together, but at least you'll know Reilly's close and that he's safe. He's been driving me crazy asking to get out of this place, so you'll be doing him a favor, too."

That wasn't a bad plan.

Not the same as having Reilly sitting next to her, but under the circumstances, it was the best they could do.

The Mexican restaurant was one of the places they'd considered for Reilly's birthday. A number of the tables sat in private cubicles, so they'd be able to sequester Reilly easily enough.

There was only one problem. "You're willing to take him outside? What about Stevens?"

"We'll get inside before sun down and won't leave until well after. I'll put a vest on him and we'll surround him on every side. It should be fine."

"Assuming Stevens sticks to his MO."

"Well assumptions are all we've got." Alex offered a reassuring smile. "Realistically, Stevens is more likely to track us here than if we go out."

True. But at least they could control the environment here. A restaurant was a completely different story.

She tried to smother her worry.

Alex was in charge here. Alex was the one with all the experience. And Alex thought taking Reilly out was okay. That needed to be good enough for her.

"Sounds like it's settled." She forced a peace she didn't feel. "I'll give them a call now."

"You do that."

Pushing off the sofa, Lana headed for the bedroom. A soft click signaled the door latching as she leaned against it.

Her eyes went to her phone.

Or, more specifically, the crumpled piece of paper sitting next to it. Although she couldn't read it from this distance, she knew what it said.

Her hand shook as she reached for the paper. Tightening in her throat made breathing difficult and swallowing nearly impossible. She curled her fingers into a fist and smacked it down on the table next to the paper.

Grow up.

It was a name and phone number, for crying out loud. She was only making an inquiry, not auctioning off her firstborn.

God, I need Your help here.

If only she could feel God's hand on her shoulder, hear His voice telling her everything would be okay. But no warm presence enveloped her; no booming voice reached her ears.

He was waiting for her to obey.

She snatched the phone off the dresser and punched in the number before she could further consider her actions.

The line rang in her ear. Once.

She wandered to the window and opened the curtains as the phone rang a second time. Three times.

Maybe no one would answer. Then she could at least say she'd tried.

A woman answered. Older, judging by her voice. Possibly Theo's wife.

"Is, uh, Theo... Theo Lykos available?" Real smooth. She sounded like an idiot.

But that may not be a horrible thing. Maybe they'd assume it was a telemarketer and hang up.

Silence cloaked the line. "I–is this Milana?"

Dang. "Yes."

Okay, so this woman answered Theo's phone and knew about her. Had to be Theo's wife.

She refused to carry the thought any further.

"I'm so glad you called. I almost went with Theo to the store that day, I wish I had, and I was afraid you wouldn't call." The words mirrored the downpour spattering the window in front of her, but stopped abruptly enough to make the silence shocking.

She should say something. Anything.

No words came to mind.

"I'm glad you called." The woman repeated, her voice softer, heavier, laced with an emotion Lana didn't want to define.

"I almost didn't." Wow. That sounded nothing like her usual voice.

Silence burdened the line. After several seconds, the woman cleared her throat. "Uh, well, let me get Theo."

This was a mistake. The biggest one she'd ever made.

"Milana." Theo's deep voice intruded on her thoughts. "Thank you for calling."

"No problem." Great. And now, to top it all off, she was lying.

"Did you have a chance to think things through? I mean, do you think–"

"I don't know what to think. Thirty years is a long time." The hardness lining her words surprised even her.

She should apologize.

No. None of this was her fault.

If blame should be assigned to anyone, it was them. How could these people do this to her?

"I know." Grief weighted the words. "I've spent every day of those years second guessing my actions that night."

That night.

It could only refer to the night of the fire. The fire that had claimed his daughter's life.

Or so he'd thought.

The hand crushing her cell phone twitched. She fought the urge to hang up.

Stick with the plan.

She'd come this far. She couldn't back down now.

No matter how much she wanted to.

She inhaled a sharp breath. Even the air tasted bitter. "I think we need to meet. Hash all this out in person."

"Thank you. I'm sure this isn't easy for you either."

Dang. It was easier to blame him when he wasn't considering her perspective. And she really wanted someone to blame right now.

She was a jerk.

There was no denying the raw emotion she heard in his voice. His wife's, too. This had to be even harder on them than it was on her.

If she wasn't who they thought she was, she could go back to her life like nothing had ever happened. They, on the other hand, would lose their daughter all over again.

The risk they were taking was so much greater than her own.

"How about over dinner? Tomorrow night?" The words tumbled from her mouth.

"That sounds good. Would you like to come over here?"

"Actually, I was thinking of a Mexican restaurant I saw. I think it was called La Hacienda."

"Good choice. What time works for you?"

"6:30?"

He agreed. Of course. She probably could've suggested meeting on the moon at midnight and he would've found a way to reserve a space shuttle to get there.

After a terse good-bye, she closed the curtains and turned away from the window, but didn't move.

What if they really were her biological relatives? What happened then?

Enough. She couldn't spend the next twenty-four hours - a glance at the clock confirmed it was actually closer to twenty-seven - obsessing about this.

Crossing the room, she jerked open the door and almost smacked into Reilly.

He lowered the hand that had been poised to knock. "Hey you."

"No, hey you."

While seeing him brought some comfort, it didn't completely stop the contortionist at work on her stomach.

A smile spread across his face. "I was coming to find you."

If he'd picked up on her mood, he didn't indicate it. "I was on the phone. What's up?"

A smirk twisted his lips as he looked at the phone in her hand. "Elliott again? That's what, four times he's called in the last ten days? Has he proposed yet?"

Okay, so maybe he had figured out she was in a bad mood.

The teasing lightened her burden a little, but not much. "We've only spoken twice and it's not like that. He's going through some stuff and I think he needs a sympathetic ear who doesn't know his ex. Besides, that wasn't him."

He quirked his head and waited.

She leaned against the doorframe and pulled in a long breath. "I called them."

Confusion flickered, followed quickly by recognition. "The guy from the store?"

"Theo. We're having dinner tomorrow night."

"Good. Even if there's nothing to it, at least you'll all know the truth."

All. The word parroted inside her brain.

In her head, she'd pictured meeting with Theo, but that wasn't likely to be the case, was it? Why hadn't it occurred to her that he'd probably bring the entire family? What if not everyone was as eager to meet with her as Theo? What if they all hated her?

The air around her coagulated.

She couldn't do this. She couldn't. Just like she couldn't seem to get enough oxygen right now.

"Lana. It'll be fine."

She relaxed the hands she didn't even realize she'd fisted and met his eyes. "I wish you could come with me. I'm scared."

Great. Now she sounded like a whiny ten-year-old.

Reilly didn't point out the obvious.

Wrapping her in a hug, he held her tightly. She clenched her jaw and tried to still the trembling in her chin.

No. She wouldn't cry. Not about this. She'd wasted enough tears over this already.

"No matter what, you've still got us."

She pulled away. "I know. Thanks."

"What are you so worried about anyway?"

"That they really are my birth parents."

"I'd call that a good thing. You'll finally have the answers to your questions."

She slid her eyes away, focusing on the textured cream walls. "I never asked for that. Besides, how do you go about getting to know your own family?"

"The same way you would anyone else. One topic at a time."

He made it sound so easy.

"I'll try." Like she had any other choice.

"That's all you can do." He took a step back. "Anyway, I was going to grab a bowl of ice cream. You want some?"

What she wanted was to rewind time and go to a different store to buy those supplies. Too bad that was impossible. "Maybe a little."

As she trailed him to the kitchen, her thoughts turned to the Lykos family once more.

Give her a fugitive on the loose, hand-to-hand combat with a serial killer, a psycho with a gun, and she'd know how to handle the situation.

But tomorrow night's meeting? She didn't have a clue.

It was a good night to have the graveyard shift. She would've been too wound up to sleep anyway.

Lana adjusted her position, ensuring her gun remained only inches from her fingers, and tried to focus on the words in front of her. Normally she loved studying the Bible. She'd been working through the prophets and was halfway into Habakkuk, but tonight she couldn't quiet her thoughts enough to understand much of anything.

All she could think about was tomorrow night.

She blinked at the clock. 4:59. A.M.

Not tomorrow night; the dinner was tonight.

She only hoped she'd actually be able to fall asleep when Peters relieved her in an hour. No way could she handle the stress coming her way if she was running on empty.

How many people would show up to dinner? What did Dimitrios and Cyrano think of all this?

Returning her attention to the Bible, she tried to force her mind to concentrate but the words blurred as her thoughts ran wild.

She closed the book and slid it away, choosing instead to focus on the images on the laptop in front of her.

The wireless cameras they'd hidden in the hallway all showed empty corridors. Balconies were clear. The living room in the adjoining suite was dark and motionless.

All was as it should be.

Rather than worrying, she should try doing something productive. Like praying.

Embracing the silence, she poured her energy and emotion into prayer.

Time slipped by. Peace filtered through the anxiety, not completely replacing it, but easing it enough that she began to feel tired.

A door closed in the adjacent suite. Most likely Peters getting ready to take over.

Still, she curled her fingers around the grip of her gun, ready to act in case someone other than a member of their team stepped through the door.

Several minutes passed before Peters stepped into the living room. She glanced at the clock. 6 a.m. exactly.

Pushing up from the sofa, she stretched and nodded at the laptop. "Everything's been quiet."

A curt nod answered her.

Why had she even wasted her breath? She holstered her weapon, slid her phone into her jeans' pocket, and picked up her Bible.

Peters regarded her for a second. "How's the arm?"

What, he cared all of a sudden? "Healing."

"Good."

Hands stuffed in the pockets of his cargo shorts, he didn't move to let her pass, nor did he advance any closer. Whatever. She was tired and didn't have the patience for this.

She'd begun to skirt around the table when he spoke again, "Look. I've been thinking."

Well, good for him. Did he expect some kind of award?

She paused and studied him. Something was up. The hostility that usually radiated from him was absent. As was his scowl. And the words had been spoken almost lightly, not with the usual blanket of scorn.

Even so, she wasn't ready to call him a friend yet.

When she didn't say anything, he shifted, then pulled his hands out of his pockets and rubbed the back of his neck. "I think maybe I could've been a little nicer."

A terse laugh slid from her lips before she could stop it. "You think?"

"Okay, fine. I know." He studied her for a second in silence. "About a year ago, we were working this detail. A kid gave up the key players in a major gang after his banger buddies killed his dad. Long story. Anyway, the whole family went into WITSEC. The kid, his mom, and three siblings. One of 'em was his older sister. Twenty-five and hot as..."

Red flashed across his cheeks and he cleared his throat.

"Anyhow, I got emotionally involved. Then this one day our guy in the video room sounds the alarm. The camera by the front door went black. We hear footsteps pounding up the steps. We're all thinkin' 'this is it,' but me, instead of standin' my ground and backing the team or covering the witness, I book it down the hall and cover the sister. One of my team was injured. It could've been much worse."

What, did he think that story was going to make her feel sorry for him? The situation was totally different.

His gaze locked on her. "You see where I'm goin' with this? I gotta be able to trust everyone on this team completely. Your objectivity is compromised."

Compromised? How dare he accuse her of not being trustworthy!

"Make no mistake, I will go further than *anyone*," she flung her arm in a wide arc to punctuate the word, "to protect our witness."

Calm. She looked away.

"Exactly. But this detail is not only about our witness. If I'm facing down a hit man with a gun, I need to know you've got my back, too."

Of course she had his back. What a stupid thing to even suggest.

But wouldn't she have been concerned about the same thing? If their positions were reversed?

She didn't even have to think that through.

The same thoughts would have troubled her. Although she liked to think she would've handled it more tactfully than he had.

No matter how much she didn't want to let him off the hook, she had to.

"We're a team. I'll protect anyone in our group, whether it's Reilly or one of you."

"Good enough for me." He turned away and dropped onto the sofa. "Try to get some sleep. Big day today."

No fooling. Of course, he was simply referring to the work involved with dinner out. No one on the team had been told about the trip's ulterior motives.

She headed down the hallway to the room she and Alex shared and slipped inside.

Autopilot kicked in as she moved around the nearly black room. She set her gun and phone on the bedside table, changed into cotton shorts, and slid beneath the covers only to stare into the darkness.

The conversation replayed in her mind.

What could've happened to make Peters apologize? Had someone said something?

Or maybe he'd finally accepted the fact that she wasn't leaving and decided to make the best of it.

Hopefully the attitude would last.

⁂

Success!

Stevens closed the door of his car, satisfaction mingling with the adrenaline coursing through his body. It'd taken a lot of time – the Marshals guarding Tanner were good, he'd give them that – but he was ninety percent certain that he'd isolated their location.

And he'd done it without the help of an informant.

He pulled off the blond wig and tossed it on the seat next to him. Peeling the matching goatee from his chin, he rubbed the skin to make sure no adhesive remained. One of several disguises he'd brought with him, it had turned out to be the perfect choice to use on the naïve college-age girl working the front desk.

Man, had she been easy to manipulate.

A little flirting, combined with some story about being in town for his friend's wedding, but not knowing their room numbers, and he'd had her. She'd probably lose her job if her boss knew how much information she'd given out.

He craned his neck to see the top floor of the hotel in front of him.

Why, he wasn't sure. The target wasn't likely to stick his head out one of the windows and wave.

But the oh-so-helpful woman with whom he'd spent the last ten minutes conversing had given him enough details to make this location a strong possibility. The group in question had checked in a week ago, rented adjoining suites on the fifth floor, and had refused maid service every day since.

Once he headed back to his hotel and changed his disguise, he'd be back to do a little reconnaissance of his own.

And if that checked out, he'd be back at sunset to take his target down.

Sixteen

The world's biggest idiot.

Yep, that title could be officially bestowed upon her. What had she been thinking?

Lana trailed the rest of her team by a fair distance so it wouldn't look like they had arrived together.

At her request, Alex had kept everyone in the dark about the reason for this outing. While there had been curiosity about why she wasn't eating with the rest of them, the team had been in favor of getting out of the hotel for the night.

Of course, that hadn't stopped Rodriguez from casually pumping her for an explanation or Peters from asking flat-out.

She'd refrained from providing any reason.

Each step caused her stomach to churn more violently. As much as she loved Mexican food, she doubted she could handle it tonight.

It wasn't too late to ditch the plan. She could wait in the car. Bypass the awkward meeting with the Lykos family.

It was a tempting option.

She forced her feet to keep moving.

Scents of spicy pepper and melted cheese attacked her senses the second she stepped through the door. The team was being led back as she approached a smiling hostess.

"Just one?"

Last chance to back out... "Actually, I'm meeting some people here."

"The name?"

"Last name is Lykos, maybe under Theo." She hoped. She didn't know Theo's wife's name.

A grin swept across the hostess' face. "I should've known. You look just like Cy and Mitri."

The hostess didn't allow time for a reply before turning and leading the way toward the dining area. "Follow me. So you've gotta be related, huh? I went to school with Cy and Mitri, but they were a few grades ahead of me so I didn't really know them. Not like there were that many twins at school though, so pretty much everyone knew who they were. Mitri's kinda quiet, but Cy was always really friendly. I think he got voted most outgoing or something by his senior class, but it's been a while so I might be wrong."

The words poured out so quickly that Lana couldn't have said anything even if she'd wanted to.

Oddly enough, the rambling chatter soothed her frayed nerves.

They bypassed the tables in the center of the room, heading for the cubicles lining the outside walls. Reilly and the rest of her team were somewhere seated in one of those cubicles. Too bad she wasn't with them.

The hostess stopped next to a cubicle toward the end of the row. "Well, here we are."

"Thank you" slid out automatically as she stepped past the hostess and into the area. Not that she felt the least bit thankful.

Four heads swiveled toward her.

Everything in her wanted to follow the hostess' example and escape.

Her gaze took in the faces she'd seen before: Dimitrios, Cyrano, and Theo. A petite brown haired woman sat to Theo's left and Lana recognized her as an older version of the woman from Theo's photo.

Theo had been right. She and this woman did share similarities in their facial structure.

The silence stole the air from her lungs.

The woman rose from the table and approached, a smile shaking on her face. "Milana. Thank you so much for coming. I'm Michelle."

She shook Michelle's hand on autopilot. "Thanks for meeting me here."

Come on. Get it together!

She blinked and tried to shift into work mode. Detached. Calm. Professional.

It was the only way she'd make it through this dinner.

Two empty chairs waited opposite Theo and Michelle. Dimitrios sat at one end of the table and Cyrano at the other.

As Michelle reclaimed her seat, Lana moved with a grace and

confidence she didn't feel and pulled out the chair closest to Dimitrios. Out of all of them, she'd spent the most time around Dimitrios, making him feel like the safest choice.

Although that didn't say a lot.

Where was Reilly when she needed him?

God, help me!

"How's the arm?" Dimitrios' question broke the silence, but did nothing to ease her tension.

"Fine. Not a big deal." Hopefully no one would question it further.

"What happened?" Concern lined Michelle's words.

She tried to catch Dimitrios' attention to keep him from answering, but he'd turned to look at his mom. "GSW. She refused to go to the hospital."

"Gunshot wound?" Theo's dark eyebrows hiked. "How'd that happen?"

Dimitrios turned to face her.

While she didn't know him well, she was pretty sure regret lingered around his eyes.

Well, it was too late now. Words couldn't be retracted. Hopefully though, he'd think a bit more carefully before saying anything else that might blow her tenuous cover.

Maybe she could pass it off as an accident. After all, Stevens hadn't intended to shoot her.

Before the story left her mouth, Dimitrios spoke up. "Happened right after she rescued puppies from a burning building, defused a bomb, and prevented a ten car pileup. She'd tell you more, but then she'd have to kill you."

His tone was so serious that she almost believed him. His face, however, betrayed him. The corner of his mouth twitched and laughter lurked in his eyes.

Cyrano chuckled. "Wow. So you were shot trying to save the world, huh?"

Best to play along. Even if it only delayed the inevitable explanation. "What can I say? That hero complex will probably be the death of me."

Michelle's smile still contained traces of worry as she examined Lana's face. "Now that Mitri's had his fun, can I ask what really happened?"

You can ask, but I can't answer. Too bad she couldn't really say that.

"His story was more entertaining. I took a bad fall and cut my arm. Dimitrios patched it up."

Okay, didn't quite cover all that happened that night, but nothing she'd said was a lie. She'd simply held back some of the more sensitive facts.

A waiter approached with their beverages, saving her from further questioning. Could he feel the tension that seemed to occupy the empty seat beside her?

The topic of their dead daughter hung as dark as a thunderhead.

No one had brought it up yet, but it was the reason she was here, the reason she'd agreed to a meeting. To find answers. Even if she wasn't yet sure she really wanted them.

Putting it off would benefit no one.

As the server walked away, she pulled in a shaky breath.

"I–" The word scratched out and she cleared her throat before trying again. "I don't know the best way to ask this–"

"You want to know what happened to our Milana." Resignation encumbered Theo's words. Speaking his daughter's name seemed to instantly age him.

Part of her wished she'd waited for them to bring the topic up. Maybe they could've eased into it better.

Too late now. She swallowed the bitter taste skulking in the back of her throat. "Yeah."

"We lost her in a fire. Arson."

Online research had told her that much. "So, if she's, um, gone, why would you think it's connected to me?"

"They never found a body." He released a shaky breath. "But the fire was so hot. I knew she couldn't have survived."

So they had a hot fire, no body, and obvious foul play. And a grieving family who had chosen to give up all hope?

It didn't add up.

"You mentioned arson. Did they catch the guy?"

"Yeah. There was really no question as to who set it. McCrink. He'd lost his daughter in a house fire a few weeks before."

"What did that have to do with you?" She should've tried tracking down the police report or something to get more information prior to tonight. It would've helped her assess how much of his story was true.

"I was the firefighter who found her." The words echoed hollowly as he looked down at his hands. "Hadn't been in the job that long. My first fatality. A girl about the same age as my own kids. There are some things you never get over."

"You found her after she'd died, so he blamed you?"

"Easier than blaming himself, I guess. The guy was a junkie." Theo folded his hands on the table in front of him and leaned in. "The fire at his place was caused by a cigarette. He said he remembered lighting up, but nothing after that. They found heroin in his system and his wife said he shot up all the time. She was at work when it happened."

The oppressive pause carried the weight of years of guilt. She didn't break it, but waited for him to continue.

"I found the McCrink girl in her bed, but she was already gone. Smoke inhalation."

"Then he set the fire at your house and targeted your daughter."

Theo flinched. Michelle rested her hand on top of his and gave a gentle squeeze.

After tucking her hand between both of his, he looked up at Lana. "That night… the explosion woke us. Michelle got the boys out. I went for her. The door wouldn't open and I tried to break it down. By the time I did, the smoke was so thick."

He released Michelle's hands and pulled up one of his sleeves.

Scarring ran down his forearm. "Fire was everywhere. I remember looking for her and a couple guys from work telling me to get out. But I wouldn't leave. The next thing I knew, I was waking up in the hospital and Michelle told me…" A sigh shuddered out. "They didn't find her."

Lana stared at Theo's face. No indication of deception, but maybe he was a really good liar. "So they declared her dead. Even without a body?"

He nodded.

Forensics wasn't her forte, but she knew enough. There should've been at least some trace of a body.

This story had to be little more than a convenient lie to cover up… something.

She wasn't sure what. Or why.

But there had to be more to it than what she'd heard so far.

"Wouldn't there have been something? Bones or teeth, at least?" Amazing how she could keep her tone so mild when her suspicion ran so deep.

Anguish lit Theo's eyes with a feverish hue. "The explosion. It–it happened on the bed. They couldn't even identify all the pieces afterwards. And she was so small. It seemed like the only possibility."

"And you gotta remember that forensics and investigative techniques weren't what they are today." Dimitrios' rough voice startled her.

Theo's damp eyes locked on her intensely, pleading with her to understand.

But she wasn't ready to give her approval or acceptance, not yet.

Maybe not ever.

"So." Anger laced the single word as she dropped all pretense. "You didn't file a missing persons report because you *assumed* she was dead."

"McCrink confessed. There was evidence against him, including an eyewitness who saw him fleeing the neighborhood. We were at the police station when they questioned him. I saw him when they led him away and he looked me straight in the eye and said 'Now you know how it feels.' If you'd seen him, you would've believed him, too."

Much as she wanted to find some inconsistency, some hint of dishonesty, his sincerity and grief convinced her that he'd spoken the truth.

Unless he was a much better actor than anyone in Hollywood.

But a lot of unanswered questions remained. "If he hadn't killed anyone, why would he confess?"

"Another reason we thought he was guilty."

"Is he still in prison? I'd like to talk to him."

Michelle sniffled and dabbed at her eyes. "He died in prison. About a month or two after going in."

"What happened to him?"

"Some kind of terminal illness. I don't remember exactly."

A terminal illness. He'd likely known he was dying and didn't have long. Could he have confessed to a murder he didn't commit because he knew he'd never live out his sentence?

Possible. Hatred and revenge were pretty strong motivators.

This was too much to take in all at once. She needed time to think, do more research, maybe track down McCrink's ex-wife or a previous cellmate and see if he'd said anything to them about the fire and the Lykos girl.

But she didn't *have* time.

Instead, she had this family staring at her, hoping against reason that she might be the adult version of their presumed-dead daughter.

"May…?" Michelle's voice squeaked and she cleared her throat before trying again, "May I ask about your childhood?"

Well, they'd bared their wounds to her; only fair that she return the favor. "I was adopted when I was, well, we think about two. A pastor and his family. They found me on their doorstep in the middle of the night."

"And before that?"

"I don't know. I have no memories before then."

Moisture laced Michelle's eyelashes, clumping them together. Her chin quivered so severely it was amazing she could even speak. "So you don't even know if Milana is your given name."

"We're pretty sure. It was engraved on the back of a necklace."

"A necklace?" The words came out in a rush of air. "W-w-was it a daisy? With an amethyst?"

Lana's mouth parched and her mind blanked.

How could Michelle so perfectly describe the necklace in her jewelry box?

There was only one way.

Nice as these strangers seemed, she didn't want this. In fact, all she wanted was to get back to her quiet life in Jacksonville.

Unfortunately, it was too late for denial. She had no choice but to deal with it.

The pain in her throat felt like a professional wrestler had clamped on with both hands. "We never could figure out why I would wear a necklace to bed."

"You refused to take it off. You loved that necklace." Theo's voice sounded thicker.

He looked like there was more he wanted to say, but nothing

came out.

Instead, he stared at her. They all did. Like she was some rare animal in a zoo.

The waiter arrived with their food. Not that any of them were likely to have much of an appetite. The smells of grilled meat and sauce overwhelmed her.

She was going to be sick.

No one spoke until the waiter left.

"I-I can't believe." Michelle's voice wobbled. "All this time. Have you been close?"

"No. My family lived in Denver."

Fog swirled in her mind. Too much. She couldn't handle this. Especially not now.

Her birth parents weren't the monsters she'd always believed them to be. In fact, they'd mourned her death. For years. They'd likely still mourn over the time that had been lost.

So much made sense now.

The recurring shadow dream. Her subconscious had been trying to remember.

"Denver. What kind of whack job would drive so far for revenge?" Dimitrios' voice penetrated her thoughts.

Pull it together.

She could fall apart later. When she was alone.

"Actually, it's really not that far," Cyrano's voice broke through her thoughts. Thank God he'd saved her from having to reply. "You could drive it in about a day or so."

"Oh. There's so much I want to know." Michelle's smile stretched across her face, a stark contrast to the message sent by the mascara smeared around her bloodshot eyes. "What you do, your hobbies, where you grew up, likes and dislikes, your fa-amily." Her smile dimmed as she stumbled over the word family.

"That's a… a long list." Lana shifted her attention to Theo. "One thing still bothers me. Kidnapping a child and driving several states away to dump her is a lot of trouble. Why didn't he just kill her, uh, me?"

"My guess?" Theo's gaze kept circling her face. "You probably reminded him of his daughter. That was what I noticed when I pulled her out of the fire. She reminded me of you."

"So you were adopted by a pastor?" Michelle ventured in the

silence that followed.

"Yeah. I have a great family." How must it be for them to hear her refer to her parents and her brother and know she wasn't talking about any of them?

She pushed the thought aside.

It didn't matter how they took it. Family, true family, went deeper than genetics or blood.

"Just you? Or do they have other children?"

The intensity of Cyrano's tone, not to mention the look on his face, surprised her. Although, really, she shouldn't be surprised. In a matter of days, he'd gone from believing his sister was dead to learning she was alive and well.

Maybe he even thought she was playing them or had some kind of angle.

"Only one. Justin's a few years older than me." The false name slid off her tongue like she'd been saying it for years.

Everyone had started eating and she mechanically did the same.

"What do you do for a living, Milana?"

The use of her full name sounded strange, especially spoken in Theo's unfamiliar voice. "I work for the government. Basically a paper-pusher, but I get to help people. I like that."

Okay, that was about as vague as vague could get.

Time to shift attention away from herself. Although she held no illusions it would last long.

She let her gaze travel between them. "So it's just the four of you?"

"Yes." Michelle stared at her and Lana briefly wondered if the woman ever blinked. "Well, five counting Donna, Cy's wife."

"She really wanted to come," Cy interjected. "But she caught a nasty bug from her class and can hardly get out of bed right now."

"Cy and Donna are both teachers," Dimitrios' soft voice came from her right.

A cell phone's ring drifted through the room. Lana tensed.

Not good. She and Alex had agreed upon a time to leave and Alex wouldn't call unless something had happened.

Wait, that wasn't her ring.

The thought registered as she saw Cyrano pulling a phone out of his pocket. His eyebrows lowered as he looked at the display and accepted the call. "Hello?"

As he listened to the person on the other end, his jaw tensed and his eyes narrowed.

Hmmm, anger? Concern? Frustration? She didn't know him well enough to interpret the look, but the caller obviously wasn't calling with great news.

"Give me a minute." He pushed back from the table and offered a grim smile. "Sorry, I have to take this."

Silence ensued as he strode from the table, muttering in tones too low to decipher.

She should ask a question, anything to deflect attention from herself and avoid the many, many questions she couldn't answer. Nothing came to mind. In fact, it felt like her brain was slowly shutting down. A headache brewed behind her eyes; this whole situation would be so much easier if she wasn't working.

But she was on the job and had to guard every word.

"So if you live in Denver, you must be on vacation? What made you choose Lincoln City?"

She didn't correct Theo on his assumption that she still lived in Denver. "I'm traveling with some friends. They chose the place and I'm just along for the ride."

A double beep reached her ears as she felt her phone jolt against her thigh.

Her muscles stiffened, which made digging the phone from her pocket challenging.

As she unlocked the screen, Alex's message popped into view.

GET OUT NOW!

Something had happened. To Reilly? Had to be. He was the one wearing a target.

Oh, dear God. Please, no.

She never should have set this up. It was all her fault.

Shoving back her chair, she collected her purse and dropped a twenty on the table. "I'm sorry. I have to go."

Her words came on short breaths that didn't provide the amount of oxygen she needed.

What if Stevens had gotten to Reilly? And all because of her selfishness.

"What?" The heartache in Michelle's word slowed her step. "Will you be back?"

"Not likely."

Dimitrios had risen from his seat, intense stare locked on her. "Everything okay?"

Concern gave his words a rough edge. No doubt he was remembering the last time.

She couldn't even manage a smile. "I'm sure it's fine. Nothing I can't handle."

Really, she was sure of no such thing.

A slow nod responded and he eased back into his seat.

"How will we get in touch with you?" Theo asked before she could slip away.

She didn't have time to deal with this right now. Reilly could be dying, for crying out loud. "I'll call you."

Not waiting for any further reply, she hurried out of the cubicle as quickly as she could without drawing undue attention to herself. She cut across the restaurant and out the main door into the parking lot.

The SUV was gone.

Seventeen

That was good, right? They'd have no reason to leave if Reilly had been killed.

Snatching out her phone, she brought up Alex's number. Alex answered on the first ring.

Lana didn't bother with pleasantries. "Reilly. Is he–?"

"He's fine." A muffled curse drifted across the line as a horn blared. "We're taking him someplace safe."

"What's going on?"

A siren wailed, so close that her ears rang. She looked up to see an ambulance on the main road, turning toward the restaurant. Two police cars tailed close behind.

"Join Chow in the alley. I'll call you."

The call ended as abruptly as it had begun.

She pocketed her phone and looked around. Only one alley nearby, to the right of the restaurant. The few details she had swirled in her head.

Emergency. Moving Reilly. Chow in alley. EMS. Police.

It all painted a very confusing - not to mention troubling - picture. One she wasn't convinced she wanted to see.

She entered the alley.

Behind her, the emergency vehicles screamed into the parking lot, but she couldn't tear her attention from the scene in front of her.

A body on the ground, face down in a puddle of blood.

Blood spatter on the wall to her left.

Chow's gun aimed at Beckman, who sat on the ground next to a dented dumpster.

She looked at the body. Even from the back, she recognized the man. Peters. Had Beckman been the shooter?

She approached the body, but stopped at Chow's voice. "He is dead."

The air squeezed from her lungs. Dead. Peters. She hadn't really liked the guy, but he didn't deserve this. No one did.

Light flooded the alley.

Doors slammed. Footsteps pounded.

"Drop the weapon!"

With any luck it'd be the same officers who responded last time. Might help expedite things.

Chow didn't look away from Beckman. Nor did he lower his weapon. "US Marshals. Here is the man you want."

Turning, Lana squinted against the light. Two shapes moved toward her. "I'm going to grab my badge."

"No need." The voice came from the shape on the right. "I recognize you from the other night."

The officer moved toward Peters. No doubt to check for a pulse.

"You are going to need the coroner."

The officer paused at Chow's words, but proceeded to kneel anyway. After determining Chow was correct, he rose.

"What happened here? Isn't he," the officer nodded at Beckman, "one of yours?"

Lana nodded at the body on the ground. "So was he."

It hurt to say the words out loud. Beckman had shot a member of his own team. Why?

Maybe Peters had been the mole. And maybe Beckman had caught him passing along critical information to Stevens. But if that were the case, why would Chow be holding Beckman at gunpoint?

Unless Peters wasn't the mole.

Beckman.

Either way, it wasn't a story that the Lincoln City PD was likely to hear any time soon.

"I do not know all the details. Beckman had left the table to take a phone call. Peters said he was visiting the restroom. Then he called and said there was a situation and he needed backup. By the time I got out here, he was dead."

After which Alex and Rodriguez had spirited Reilly away.

Not that Chow would say as much to the locals.

She hoped Reilly had his medication and inhaler. And that Alex was keeping a close eye on him.

"So he shot your guy?" The officer sounded as skeptical as she felt.

"I do not know. Perhaps he will tell you once you place him under arrest."

Judging by the glower on Beckman's face, she seriously doubted it.

₪ ₪ ₪ ₪ ₪

Stevens removed the battery from his phone and set both aside. Something told him Rosetti's inside guy had been found out.

Stunk to be him.

Unfortunately, Rosetti had given that guy Stevens' phone number. And while the phone records and billing information would lead them nowhere, the phone number would enable the Feds to triangulate his position. He'd have to get a new number.

Or not.

If he was retiring after this hit, why did he need a new number?

The timing was perfect, actually. He'd really only need to make one more call from this number - to Rosetti, to let him know the hit was complete and give him payment instructions. All he had to do was go to a crowded place, make a quick call, and disappear forever.

Simple.

Rosetti's contact had been able to give him one interesting piece of information before being caught - they'd changed Tanner's appearance.

Good to know.

Anything else the contact might've shared was irrelevant since Stevens had already found their location. In fact, it was about time to head that way now. Although he didn't honestly expect them to still be there when he arrived. They were probably pushing Tanner out the door right now.

But their hotel wasn't far from his location. With any luck, he'd arrive as they were leaving and could plug his mark before the Marshals could hide him again.

He checked his disguise in the mirror and, satisfied that the bearded stranger in the pin-striped suit looked nothing like him, picked up his briefcase and headed for the door.

Maybe he'd have this job wrapped up before the night was out.

₪ ₪ ₪ ₪ ₪

"He says he'll only talk to Maxwell." Lana turned away from the one-way glass of the interrogation room where Beckman sat silently.

Alex's curse carried through the phone pressed against Lana's ear. In all the time she'd known Alex, she could count on one hand the number of times she'd actually seen Alex rattled. It scared her almost as much as knowing that their team was down by two people because one of them had killed the other.

"At least he's already en route. He told us to sit tight until he gets here, then he'll help us relocate." Alex released a slow breath. "You guys might as well get out of there." She gave brief directions to their new headquarters for the night. "The other car's still at the hotel. Maybe you can pick up our stuff while you're at it."

"No problem. And Reilly's okay, right?" Never mind that Alex had already told her as much. She'd be worried until she saw him with her own eyes.

"Fine. Used the inhaler, but didn't need his pills. He's more concerned about the fact that you're not here."

That sounded like Reilly. "We'll get there as soon as we can."

Chow signaled her from the hallway.

"Gotta go. See you soon." She ended the call and walked toward Chow.

"One of the officers will deposit us at the hotel. He is waiting for us now." Chow indicated a uniformed man with the posture of a bulldog.

As she followed the officer, her gaze strayed to a wall clock. Almost eleven. No wonder she was tired. Especially since she hadn't gotten much sleep after climbing into bed that morning.

Had it really only been that morning? The memory felt like something buried underneath layers of time.

The officer dropped them in front of the hotel.

She and Chow rode the elevator in silence, swept both rooms, including the balconies, and got to work.

While Chow disconnected their cameras, she brought up the video feed for the hallway. Since the system was only programmed to record when there was movement, there shouldn't be too much footage to weed through.

People came and went, most of whom she recognized as occupants of the surrounding rooms. She slowed the tape as a well-dressed man in a suit stepped out of the elevator and looked around.

Not someone she recognized.

And that briefcase he carried was large enough to hold a disassembled rifle.

She checked the time stamp. 7:49.

Alex's text - and Peters' murder - had been around 7:30. If Beckman had sold them out to Stevens, and if Stevens had dropped everything to come after them, the time fit.

A retro bowler hat covered his head, a full beard masked his mouth and jawline, and he kept his head angled down as if to avoid hotel security cameras.

Too bad for him that their cameras had been placed much lower.

Unfortunately, she was reasonably certain that the getup he wore was a disguise. Someone like Stevens didn't escape detection for so long by not planning ahead. The suit had a boxy quality about it that camouflaged the man's build and the beard hid his face shape.

The man approached 501 and set the briefcase down. He rapped on the door with his right hand while reaching around his back with the left.

Several seconds passed.

His left hand didn't reappear, even as he knocked again.

After what felt like an eternity, he looked up and down the hallway again before kneeling next to his briefcase.

He edged it open. Not enough for her to see inside, but enough for him to withdraw a small device. He rose and used his body to shield his actions, but she knew what he was doing. Overriding the lock. A few seconds passed before he cracked open the door and slipped into the room.

Her gut clenched.

Stevens had not only been here, he'd been inside.

If she and Chow hadn't already searched the rooms, she'd be clearing out right now.

She tapped a few buttons and brought up the views from the internal cameras. The suited man appeared, a gun in his hand. The extraordinarily long barrel on the weapon drew her attention.

A suppressor. Naturally.

After setting the briefcase down, he moved stealthily through the room. Checking behind furniture, inside closets. It felt like an eternity of searching, although the time stamp revealed less than a minute had passed since he'd entered.

He grabbed his briefcase and headed for the balcony.

A few more key taps brought up the balcony cam. The man dissolved into the shadows in the far corner.

She glanced toward the still-closed balcony door. They'd checked out there. Turned on the light. The balcony had been empty.

While he remained fairly still, he moved enough that the camera continued to record.

She didn't have time for this. She brought up the living room feed again.

The next recorded segment started over two hours after the previous one had ended. The sliding glass door opened and the man stepped inside.

He crept through the living room and let himself out into the hallway at 10:33 p.m. Switching back to the hallway recording, she forwarded to the 10:33 time stamp, where she saw him step into the elevator and descend to the first floor.

Evidently he'd determined that they would've returned by ten-thirty if they were going to return at all.

She leaned back. 10:33. They'd missed him by about a half hour. She didn't know whether she was frustrated or relieved.

The door to the suite beeped once and swung open.

She scooped up her gun and pushed off the sofa. Chow appeared, the cameras in his hands.

Just Chow. She let her gun arm drop.

"Did you see anything on the video?"

"He was here. In this room."

"You are joking."

"Wish I were." What if Stevens had planted a tracking device in their luggage or on their clothes? When he'd checked the bedrooms, he'd been out of the camera's view for several seconds. More than enough time to plant a tracker. "We need to sweep our luggage, our clothes, everything before taking it with us."

Chow shook his head. "That will take a great deal of time."

More time than they had tonight. "You're right. We'll grab a change of clothes for each of us, sweep that, and come back tomorrow to do the rest."

ꟷ ꟷ ꟷ ꟷ ꟷ

Chow parked the car at the far end of the privately owned motel's parking lot.

Alex had driven to Newport, a city about a half hour south of Lincoln City. The motel had a two-story building with exterior corridors, plus a number of individual cabins. From the brief view she'd gotten when their headlights swept the cabins, they appeared to be fairly basic, but they offered the space and privacy their group needed.

Most of the cabins, nestled among sand dunes and tall beach grass, were dark, but light shone around the windows of a cabin that sat back from the lot. She'd guess that was where she'd find Alex, Rodriguez, and Reilly.

She and Chow stepped from the car.

Their shoes crunched on the gravel as they followed the winding path over a small rise.

Two steps led up to a weathered wooden door. At the base of the steps, a rustic sign announced that they'd reached number eleven.

She texted Alex before knocking once.

The door opened and Alex let them in. Lana's gaze immediately found Reilly, who sat on a brown and orange paisley couch that looked like something from the seventies. A small smile tightened his lips when he saw her, but he remained seated.

She turned to Alex. "Where's Rodriguez?"

"Sleeping. I'm supposed to wake him up at six a.m. to take over."

Hopefully Alex could last until six a.m.

"What happened?"

"Wish I knew." Red tinged Alex's eyes.

Man, she looked horrible. At least ten years older than she had that afternoon. Deep creases etched into her forehead, which had a stone-gray pallor. Puffiness gave her a squinty-eyed appearance.

At least Reilly seemed to be handling everything okay.

Her attention flicked to him. A little pale, but his breathing didn't seem hindered.

"Peters told me earlier that he thought something was up with Beckman." The softness of Alex's tone made her voice difficult to hear. "I should've looked into it then, but we were getting ready to leave and I didn't figure waiting a few hours would hurt."

"This isn't your fault."

"Tell that to Peters." Alex massaged her temples. "I mean, I asked him if it could wait until after dinner. He hesitated. I should've known then, but he said it could wait."

Obviously that had been the wrong answer. "So, at the restaurant…"

"Beckman kept looking at his watch. Then said he'd be right back. Really abrupt-like. I remember Peters looking at me, but he didn't say anything. About a minute later, he said he was going to use the restroom. Next thing I know, he's calling my cell, says he needs backup outside, in the alley, right now. I sent Chow and Rodriguez out, locked Reilly in the bathroom, and guarded the door."

Chow offered a tight nod. "I heard the gunshot as I stepped outside. When I went to the alley, Peters was dead and Beckman's gun was smoking. He tried to tell me that Peters was telling someone our location, but I did not believe him."

Beckman must not have heard Peters call Alex or he would've known that excuse wouldn't fly.

"Chow and Rodriguez subdued Beckman, Chow called me, and I texted you."

"Relocating was the right call. I checked the surveillance video. An armed man was in our room tonight. He waited about two hours before leaving."

Alex straightened. "You mean we got video of Stevens?"

"Possibly, but it won't do us any good. He was pretty well disguised."

"Naturally." A small snort accompanied Alex's words. "Heaven forbid this be that easy."

"You said Maxwell was coming?"

Good thing or cause for concern? Lana honestly wasn't sure. Maxwell had been less than forthcoming about Stevens and while it appeared Beckman had been their leak, she had yet to hear a good reason for Maxwell's secrecy.

"He called an hour ago. His flight lands around noon, so he should be here early afternoon. He told us to sit tight until he gets here."

"Did he say why he never told us about Stevens?"

"He said he hadn't wanted to mention it until he'd confirmed the story."

Confirmed or not, he should've told them. They needed to know what they were up against.

Of course, it might be a convenient cover story. Not a very good one, at that.

If Alex noticed her skepticism, she gave no indication. "Once Maxwell gets done with Beckman, he's going to help us clear out."

"We shouldn't wait. We need to get as many miles between us and this place as we can. Right now." Intensity tightened Lana's throat and made her voice tense.

"We will. But right now, we're all exhausted and we're down two people. Moving would be an even bigger risk."

Lana pressed her lips together.

Stevens was out there. Hunting for them. What if he found them here?

A yawn popped Reilly's jaw, the sound seeming loud in the silence.

Alex offered a smile that contained none of its usual warmth. "You guys should all go to bed. Got a long day ahead of us."

"I think you are right. I will hit the straw."

Hit the straw. Not quite how most people would say it, but exactly what she would expect from Chow.

"You and Rodriguez are in the bedroom on the right." As he left the room, Alex turned to Lana. "I figure you guys can share the other room. There's a king bed and a rollaway cot in there."

"And a window, I presume." Not really a question. And definitely a concern, especially since this cabin was ground level. Easy access should Stevens track them down.

"Already took care of that. Rodriguez and I moved the dresser in front of it and put a nightstand on top. If anyone tries to come through that window, they'll have to push the furniture out of the way first."

That was something anyway. It would buy her time to wake up and get her gun pointed at the window.

"You look like you need the sleep more than I do. You go. I'll take over the rest of this shift."

Alex hesitated. "You need to sleep, too."

"I had the overnight shift yesterday, remember? It's been a lot longer since you slept than it has for me." She watched the indecision play across Alex's face. One more push ought to do it. "Go on. I'll grab a few hours after Rodriguez takes over."

Alex couldn't smother the yawn that overtook her. "Okay. Even that cot sounds pretty comfortable right now." She shifted her attention to Reilly. "The perk of being the witness. You get the bed."

"You go on. I'll be there in a few minutes." Once Alex disappeared down the hall, Reilly turned back to Lana. "How'd everything go?"

"Okay, I guess. It was weird."

"What did you find out?"

"It's them." She didn't know how else to say it. Calling those strangers family didn't feel right. "It's late and you're exhausted. Go to bed. We can talk about this later."

He nodded and trudged toward the bedroom, leaving her alone with her thoughts.

Good thing Alex had taken her up on the offer to cover her shift. Lana didn't think she'd be able to sleep anyway. Not with the day cycling through her head.

She hoped Alex would be able to sleep.

Losing someone she'd worked with so closely had to hurt. More so since she'd been the one in charge. And, knowing Alex, she no doubt blamed herself for what had happened.

Poor Peters.

Who would take care of his mother now?

Would she even understand that her son was dead? Depending on how advanced her dementia was, she may not. Which might – in some ways – be a blessing in disguise.

Confined tears blurred her vision, but did nothing to dim the image seared into her memory.

Peters. Motionless in a growing pool of his own blood.

For the first time ever, she knew someone who had been murdered on the job. Not just knew him, had worked with him.

It could've been her. Thank God it wasn't.

How could she even think like that? Peters was dead and all

she could think about was herself? Especially since she knew her soul was prepared for what came next. She didn't know if Peters had been.

And she'd certainly never taken the time to talk to him about it.

Not that he would've been likely to listen to her anyway.

She tried to stamp the thoughts down. Obsessing wouldn't change the facts. It was too late to do anything about it now.

Learn from the past, focus on the present, and live for the future.

She turned her attention to the day ahead and all that had to be done before they left the state.

Like sweeping their things for listening devices and trackers. Packing. Talking to Beckman and hopefully getting some answers. Making arrangements for Peters' body.

On a personal level, she'd have to figure out something in regards to her… family.

She pushed the thought aside. She'd deal with that later, once her brother - her real brother - was out of an assassin's crosshairs.

Eighteen

Time had moved more slowly than frozen molasses all day.

Lana felt somewhat renewed, in spite of running on only a few hours of sleep.

Alex looked better, too. Her eyes still looked like a kindergartener had gone crazy with purple crayons, but she had more color in her cheeks and the whites of her eyes were actually white.

Not to mention she was able to smile.

At least, she had been smiling a few minutes ago. Before her cell phone rang and displayed Maxwell's number.

Maxwell had gotten into Lincoln City a few hours ago and they'd waited anxiously all afternoon for any word. Hopefully, the news Alex was hearing was good.

Alex reemerged from the bedroom, sliding her cell into her jeans pocket.

"Maxwell's getting details squared away for transporting Peters' body. And Beckman's cooperating." Alex's attention shifted between her and Reilly.

There were still so many questions. Lana focused on the one troubling her the most. "Did he say why he did it?"

"Evidently Beckman's wife has some pretty big gambling debts. Someone offered to pay off the bookies she owed."

"Who?"

"He never gave a name."

Lana massaged her temples. "So Beckman did all this for money?"

"Partly. I guess those debts had come due and there were some serious threats of physical harm."

There was still a lot that didn't add up. "Walk me through this. Rosetti–"

"Someone."

"Okay, someone contacts him…"

"At first, he told Beckman to leave the blinds open and realign the cameras. When that plan failed, then he gave Beckman Stevens' number and told him to work with Stevens directly."

"So he gets Stevens' number and then, what? Waits a full week?"

Alex smothered a yawn, giving evidence to how little sleep they'd all gotten the night before. "I guess initially he dodged the call for a few days, then whoever it was got the wife involved. After that, he talked to this person, who gave him Stevens' number, and so on."

Weird. "So Beckman's wife…"

"Is under protection. That's why he wanted to talk to Maxwell. To cut some kind of deal for her."

"And Peters must've heard Beckman talking to Stevens, which is why Beckman shot him." Stupid. Beckman should've known that it would be traced back to him.

"Yeah. He said he panicked when Peters confronted him."

And now Peters was dead.

Lana pushed the thought aside. "Well, at least we have Stevens' number now. That's good news, right?"

"You'd think. Turns out it's a pay as you go phone. There's an address attached to the account, but we're not expecting it to pay off."

Figured. A guy like Stevens likely had contingency plans for his contingency plans. "Okay, so what's our next move?"

"Maxwell told us to pack up here and head for the police station. Chow and Rodriguez will meet us there."

"Did they find anything?" Chow and Rodriguez had been at the other hotel for hours, scanning for bugs and trackers as they packed up the team's belongings.

"No. And they're almost done, so it appears last night's visitor didn't leave anything behind."

And evidently hadn't returned. Which was both good and bad.

Alex pushed up from the sofa. "Let's get moving. We're losing daylight."

And Stevens' preferred time of attack was dusk.

It took under thirty minutes to get the few belongings they'd brought with them packed and the master bedroom furniture put back where it belonged.

Alex picked up the single bag containing the group's possessions and paused by the door. "I'll put this in the car, make sure we're clear, then signal you. Lock the door."

Like she'd really do anything else. Lana simply nodded.

The seconds slogged by.

What she wouldn't give to have a third person here. Someone who could stay with the vehicle while she and Alex escorted Reilly out. Especially since they had to cover some open terrain to reach the SUV.

She watched Alex trek up the winding gravel path, crest the small hill, and slowly disappear from sight. The lowering sun cast long shadows over the sandy terrain.

Dusk crept toward them.

They were moving Reilly during Stevens' favorite hunting time. And that small rise would give him a good vantage point from which he could pick them off as they approached.

It'd be easy for the hit man to take them down.

Too easy.

On the upside, with Alex watching from the top of the hill, she should have a pretty clear view of all directions. Hopefully she'd spot trouble coming before it reached them.

If trouble was coming.

They'd moved to a whole different city. It should take Stevens time to track them here.

She had to assume he'd been able to track them already. Reilly's life depended on it.

Lana ejected her Glock's magazine, confirmed it was full, and slid it back into place.

At least she was ready. Just in case.

Seconds later, Alex appeared at the top of the hill, slowly rotated, then signaled them forward.

Go time.

Her eyes slid to Reilly as she twisted the deadbolt. "Head for Alex. Quickly."

A nod confirmed he'd heard the instruction. The gray pallor of his skin concerned her, but he seemed to be breathing okay and she couldn't take the time to question him now.

She racked the slide and held her gun in front of her, angled slightly downward.

With a hand to Reilly's back, she shoved him out the door. Her gaze swept left, right, forward. She tossed a glance behind her.

No sign of movement anywhere.

They neared the top. Alex scurried toward the SUV.

Almost there. Once Reilly was safely inside the bulletproof vehicle–

A shadow. Behind Alex.

The shadow materialized into a man. Tall. Dressed in black and wearing a ski mask.

A rifle swung up.

Stevens!

The butt of the rifle slammed into Alex's skull. She collapsed without a sound.

No!

A chunky black boot connected with Alex's discarded weapon and kicked it into a shrub.

Lana pushed past Reilly and whipped her gun up. "Drop it. Now!"

The rifle swung Reilly's direction. She tightened her finger on the trigger.

Click.

No boom. No recoil. No bullet.

Impossible!

She tapped the magazine, racked the slide, tried again.

Same result.

"Down!" She shoved Reilly to the side and rushed Stevens.

The rifle's barrel jolted toward her. Wavered, but didn't fire.

She kept moving, left hand closing around the barrel, right hand swinging her useless gun at the masked head.

He captured her hand before it connected with his skull.

Long fingers snaked around her right wrist, yanking her to the side as he easily twisted his rifle out of her grasp.

She fisted her now-empty left hand and swept it up, aiming for his temple.

Dropping the rifle, he blocked the blow and seized her arm.

Both hands restrained. Not good. Not at all.

Maybe she could kick him–

He thrust his arms out, propelling her backward.

The world tipped. Her feet flew out from beneath her as she

went down. Gravel bit into her hands and elbows.

"Lana?" Reilly's voice, behind her.

Stevens reached for his rifle.

"Get in the car!" She shoved to her feet.

As much as she wanted to make sure Reilly was obeying her directions, she couldn't take her eyes off Stevens. He picked up the rifle and swung toward Reilly.

A car door slammed. She glanced toward the SUV long enough to confirm that Reilly wasn't in sight.

She rushed toward Stevens.

After a brief hesitation, he turned and ran for the road.

What?

Veering toward the bushes, she plunged her arms into the scraggly branches. Her fingers connected with metal. Alex's gun.

She ran, racking the slide without missing a step. He might be taller, but she was faster. The gap narrowed.

I've got him.

The thought registered half a second before she saw a white car at the side of the road.

Stevens dove in the driver's door and gunned the engine. The car surged forward, spitting gravel into the air.

She aimed at the tires.

Rubber met asphalt and the car fishtailed.

Moving targets were hard. But not impossible. She pulled the trigger. Again and again and again.

Not one shot connected as the car moved out of range.

Dang it! If he hadn't had a car waiting, she would've caught him.

But as it was, she hadn't even caught the license plate number. The car was a newer model Ford Taurus, but unless she missed her guess, there would be a lot of those in town.

It was probably a rental anyway. Or stolen.

The car vanished around a corner. Stevens was gone.

Reilly. Alex. She whirled and raced back to the SUV.

The back door opened as she approached and Reilly stepped out. "What were you think–?"

"Get back in the car."

Her tone was harder than she'd intended, but it worked. Sliding back inside, Reilly shut the door, but not before she glimpsed Alex in the seat beside him.

She retraced her steps and retrieved her gun.

After brushing the gravel off her seat, legs, and palms, she climbed into the driver's seat and twisted to look at Reilly. "Are you okay?"

He nodded. Her gaze swung to Alex.

While her face was unusually pale, red patches glowed from her cheeks, a sharp contrast to the narrowed icy eyes above them. Several fine scratches ran down the right side of her face from where she'd landed on the gravel.

"Alex? You all right?"

"Fine." She bit out the word. "No. I'm not fine. I'm mad as... how'd he get the drop on us?"

Obviously, she didn't expect anyone to know the answer to that question.

"Okay, I'm going to drop you at the ER, then take Reilly to the–"

"Let's get to the police station and get out of town. That was too close."

While she absolutely agreed, she also didn't want to take a chance with a head injury. "Alex, you took a blow to the head. With a rifle. You need to be checked for a concussion."

"And possibly some stitches," Reilly inserted. "She's got a pretty good gash back there."

"I'll be fine." Irritation bled through her words, making them as sharp as shattered glass. "This is still my op and I'm still in charge. We're going to the police station. All of us."

Lana bit back the arguments that waited on her tongue. If Alex wanted to pull that card, there wasn't much she could do to stop her. Except inform Maxwell of Alex's injuries when they arrived at the police station.

She started the car and backed out of the parking spot.

The silence inside the car didn't last long.

"What happened back there?"

Reilly's question mirrored the one bouncing around inside her own head. "I don't know."

So many mysteries.

Like why her gun hadn't fired. It seemed as though Stevens had anticipated such a thing. But how could he? Maybe Beckman had tampered with it. As soon as she got a chance, she'd have to disassemble her weapon and see what was wrong.

Mystery number two: why Stevens hadn't taken the shot.

Sure, she'd distracted him, but they should all be dead. And yet, there hadn't been a single casualty. Why would a hit man, someone who killed without conscience, show them mercy?

"What did happen?" Alex's voice, softer now, contained more curiosity than anger.

As Reilly filled Alex in, Lana ran the scene through her mind.

Stevens had hesitated. When she rushed him.

Even though she hadn't been able to see his face, he'd clearly hesitated. The wavering of his gun. The way he'd shifted his attention between Reilly and her. Not because either one of them posed a particular threat to the assassin, but because of something else. What, she wasn't sure.

A fixation with Reilly would be natural. After all, Reilly was his target.

But the way Stevens had acted made her think this had something to do with her. The hesitation hadn't appeared until she'd rushed him, until he'd really been forced to look at her.

It didn't make any sense. What would make a hit man hesitate?

Fear of capture, maybe. Or doubts about whether or not he could hit the mark.

Neither of which were applicable in this instance.

Or maybe a personal connection.

The idea settled like a box of bullets in her stomach. Could there be some personal connection? Between her and Stevens?

Nineteen

Slam!

Nate jerked. The bland abstract pictures on the wall of his room shook.

Man. Matt was in a mood.

He set the laptop on the floor, pushed up from his chair, and headed for the main living area of their rented cabin. Stepping into the sparsely furnished living room, he leaned against the wall right outside the bedroom door.

It took one glance to see that Matt wasn't just in a mood. Narrowed eyes glared from a cherry-red face and his lips pressed into a tight line.

Today's assignment hadn't gone well. Clearly.

Matt's glare zeroed in on him.

"What have you done?" The roar echoed in the room.

What was Matt talking about? He'd been here all afternoon.

Matt's chest heaved and his nose made a faint whistling sound as he exhaled, but other than that the room was silent.

So clearly Matt thought something was his fault. But what? "I didn't–"

"I froze! Because of you. All I could think about was the way you talked about her and what it would do to you."

Her?

No doubt Matt referred to Lana – it couldn't be anyone else – but what did that have to do with Matt's job? Nate pushed off the wall and took a step closer. "I'm not tracking."

"She's a cop!"

"Lana?"

"Who else?"

It couldn't be true. "You're wrong. There's gotta be some mistake."

"I had a gun. Pointed at her head. There's no mistake."

Gun pointed at her head. Nate's eyes dropped to the rifle still clutched in Matt's hand. Images of what the bullets could do to Lana's face seared his mind.

"You didn't." The words died on his tongue.

Matt snorted. "The great Stevens couldn't pull the trigger. I froze like some kinda amateur."

Was it horrible for him to be glad?

He'd purposely never spent much time thinking about the people Matt was hired to eliminate.

Heck, he'd pretty much decided that they all deserved what they got.

But if Lana was protecting someone and was even willing to die for that person, then his theory had to be flawed. She wouldn't put her life on the line for someone who was on the wrong side of the law, would she?

Wait.

Details she'd revealed stampeded through his mind. She was helping her brother. It was a recent development. She couldn't leave him alone. Especially at night. Maybe because she knew that an assassin who only attacked at night was after him?

"Your target. What do you know about him?" Nate's voice rasped through his tumbleweed throat.

Sharp eyes slid his direction.

He understood the look. Never before had he asked about the marks Matt had been hired to take down.

Nevertheless, Matt answered. "Reilly Tanner. Prosecutor. Preacher's kid. Both parents still alive. One younger sister."

A younger sister. And she just happened to be the same woman who occupied so many of Nate's thoughts.

But Reilly wasn't the name she'd used. She'd called him Justin.

Then again, if her brother was in witness protection, of course she'd call him by another name.

The facts fit. It had to be him.

"Her brother." Nate cleared his throat. Too bad he couldn't clear his thoughts as easily. "You were hired to kill her brother."

"I don't care whose brother he is." Matt's jaw clenched. "I never leave a job undone."

If Matt killed Lana's brother, it would destroy her. Assuming she survived the attack. It'd be just like her to try to stop the bullet with her body.

Matt turned for the door.

"No!" Springing forward, Nate grabbed Matt's arm. "Let this one go. Please."

The arm under Nate's hand tensed. Matt jerked it away. "Let it go? You got any idea what that'd do to my reputation?"

"So what? You said you were gonna retire after this one anyway."

"All the more reason to get this one right." Matt poked him in the chest. "Face facts, dude. She played you!"

"Why would she do that, huh? She had no way of knowing I had any connection to you."

"So you think. Maybe she suspected you all along." Matt pressed his lips together and pushed a sigh through his nostrils. "Look, I'll try not to hit her, okay?"

Skirting around him, Nate blocked the door. "Don't do this."

The clenched teeth, the ruddy face, the white-fingered grip on the rifle - anyone else and Nate would be concerned. But this was Matt, the guy who'd shielded him from countless bullies. The one person he could trust with his life.

"Get outta my way." The words ground from between Matt's lips, which barely moved.

"No."

"You think you can stop me?"

"I gotta try. You do this, it'll destroy her–"

A fist smashed into his jaw, whipping his head sideways. Nate staggered back a step.

The silence in the cabin was broken only by Matt's ragged breathing and the bells pealing inside Nate's head.

A metallic taste filled his mouth.

Although it'd been years since he'd taken a hit like that, he recognized the taste from his youth. Blood.

He touched the corner of his mouth. The fingers came back streaked with crimson.

The glare narrowing Matt's eyes loosened. He rubbed the back of his neck and stared at the ceiling.

"Think how you'd feel if someone killed me." Nate wiped his fingers on his jeans. "All these years and I've never asked you for anything. But I'm asking now."

The sigh that burst out of Matt seemed to deflate him and he dragged himself to the nearest chair. Collapsing heavily, he let the rifle slip from his fingers and rested his elbows on his knees. "All the chicks in the world and you gotta pick a cop?"

"I didn't know."

But he should've guessed. The signs had been there.

She was skilled at dodging questions while asking plenty of her own. Her eyes always seemed to be moving. It screamed law enforcement. Not to mention all the martial arts training she claimed to have. How could he have missed it before?

He crossed to the couch on legs that wobbled beneath his weight. Whether from the shock about Lana, the betrayal of Matt's punch, or the force of the blow itself, he wasn't sure.

He swallowed, the bloody taste almost gagging him.

When he looked up, he found Matt's attention locked on him.

The firm set to Matt's jaw and his lowered eyebrows screamed the truth. Nate knew his friend well enough to decipher the look. Everything in Matt wanted to pick up his rifle, walk out the door, and end this.

Somehow he had to keep that from happening. He pulled in a long breath and released the words that simmered inside him. "Please. I love her."

"Great." Matt shook his head. "And what're you gonna tell her? 'Hey, Lana. You remember my buddy Matt? Well, guess what. He almost killed you. Yeah, he sometimes goes by Stevens. Small world, huh.' That's gonna go over well."

"I won't tell her anything. And if you're retired, who'll ever know?"

Silence descended.

If he were a praying man, he'd pray that Matt would agree. But even if God was there, He'd never listen to someone like him.

After what felt like an eternity, Matt sagged against the back of the chair. "Fine. But you know that someone else will be hired, right? Someone who might enjoy killing cops."

Dang. He hadn't thought about that. "So don't tell anyone."

"Right. At some point the guy who hired me will get tired of waiting and just hire someone else."

"Maybe they won't find her. I mean, she's good, right? She'll be okay."

"Maybe."

"Will you hear about it? If someone else is hired?"

A pause. Matt rubbed his eyes. "Probably. And if not, I can find out."

"Can you keep me posted?" He wasn't sure why he wanted to know. Maybe some kind of control thing, not that he had any control over the situation.

A short nod. "How's your head?"

About as close to an apology as Matt was likely to offer. Nate forced a small smile. "You kidding? You hit like a girl."

The throbbing in his jaw screamed otherwise.

Matt picked up his rifle and disassembled it, his movements stiff and jerky.

As soon as he finished, he gathered the pieces and left the room without a single word or glance at Nate.

Nate rested his head in his hands. How had it come to this?

A cop. He'd fallen for a cop.

And because of her, he'd ticked off the only family he had.

Had he won that round or did it just feel like it? Even though Matt had agreed to back off, he might change his mind.

Lana was still in danger.

No matter how skilled she was at protecting people, no amount of training could stop a bullet.

"I'm sorry. I don't remember your name."

The man who would've dwarfed a linebacker laughed, his deep voice vibrating through Lana's ribs. "Not a problem. You guys all looked like the walking dead last night, so I'm not surprised. Name's Johnson, but everyone calls me Pint."

"I bet there's a good story behind that."

"You know it. My first gig, the witness was this kid." He sized her up briefly. "Not much bigger 'an you, actually. Anyhow, she had some spunk to her and called me pint-sized the whole time. Pint stuck."

"Nice to meet you. So where are we, anyway?"

"Nebraska."

She would've guessed Kansas, but Nebraska was close. The private airstrip at which they'd landed last night had been surrounded by corn stalks and they'd driven about an hour down a highway that was so straight the vehicle probably could've driven itself.

After waking up thirty minutes earlier, she'd peeked out the window of the room she and Alex shared to find sun-drenched golden fields as far as the eye could see.

"And so you don't have to ask," Pint continued, his voice rumbling from above her. "The guy with the red mop on his head is Gibson, the little guy is Ochoa, and the guy who could stand to lose thirty pounds is Newhart."

Pictures of the other three deputies she'd met last night popped into her head. Pint had described them perfectly. "Noted. Thanks."

Pint leaned his elbows on the counter behind him and surveyed her. "So, I gotta tell you, you're something of a legend. Face to face with Stevens and still breathing. Pretty crazy stuff."

A legend? Already? It'd only been a day! "How the heck did you hear about it?"

He grinned, revealing slightly crooked, but startlingly white teeth. "Word travels fast. Why didn't you take him down?"

"My gun had been tampered with."

"How'd that happen?"

"There was a guy on the inside. Removed the firing pin. He must've messed with it while I was in the shower because I've got it on me the rest of the time."

Pretty gutsy move, too.

Alex or Reilly could've walked in on him doing it. Too bad they hadn't.

"Man, you've got some luck, though. I still don't get why Stevens didn't cut you all down."

"Join the club." The nagging questions continued to dog her.

Why hadn't he killed her? Could Stevens be someone she knew?

A friend?

Or relative? There was a lot she didn't know about her biological family.

She tried to shake off the questions. Her job was to protect Reilly, not solve the mystery of Stevens' identity.

Besides, if Stevens was someone she knew, someone close enough that he'd spare her life, did she really *want* to know who he was? Maybe it was better if she never learned the truth.

ᒥᒧ ᒥᒧ ᒥᒧ ᒥᒧ ᒥᒧ

"News from the home front."

Lana shifted from her place on the sofa next to Reilly so she could see Alex better. The meeting had been called as soon as Alex got off the phone with Maxwell. Hopefully it was to give them good news. Two days in this safe house in the middle of Farmville was more than enough.

Everyone - except Chow, who was monitoring the exterior from the camera room - had gathered in the living room. The air felt thick as Lana waited for Alex to begin.

"First, the good news. Word on the street is that Stevens has retired."

What the...?

That couldn't possibly be true. Could it? The best hit man in the world, retiring abruptly in the middle of his prime?

"For good?" Pint asked the question that burned in her mind.

"According to our informant, yeah. Confirmed by some buzz online in various weapons communities."

"Maybe Stevens is tryin' to fool us. Ya know, lull us into security or somethin'." Rodriguez crossed his arms over his chest and leaned back in his chair.

"Wouldn't make any sense for him to do that. It's not like we'd come out of hiding just because he's not around."

Lana felt the eyes on her. The weight of speculation.

Let them speculate; it wasn't like they were wondering anything she hadn't already asked herself. "Do we know who Rosetti has hired to replace him?"

"No. Maxwell has people looking for that information, but so far we've got nothing." Alex's gaze rested on Lana for a beat before swinging to Reilly. "There's one more thing. Garrett's offering a full confession, including giving up the person behind the shooting, but he says he'll only do it if Tanner's there."

That made about as much sense as Stevens retiring so abruptly.

Even though Reilly worked for the prosecutor's office, it wasn't like he could do anything to help Garrett. Even if he wanted to, which he didn't.

"Why?" Lana's question hung in the air.

"He won't say. Just says that either Reilly's there or there's no deal. Normally such a thing would be out of the question, but given that our witness works for the prosecutor's office," Alex's eyes, which had been moving across everyone in the room, came to rest on Reilly, "The prosecutor thought it would be worth discussing."

"Let's do it."

Reilly's response came as no surprise, but that didn't mean she had to like it. "Hold up. Let's think about this. It could be a trap."

Turning, Reilly looked at her. "Yeah, it could be. But that's why I've got all of you."

"Lana's right." Severity lined Alex's words. "It's incredibly risky. Not only will everyone know where you'll be, they'll know the exact time as well."

"So we come up with a plan to arrive in a manner or at a time that no one would expect. It beats sitting here for a year or more while we wait for this thing to go to trial."

While Reilly had a point, Lana hesitated to agree to something so dangerous. "Ri, we all want to go home. But this isn't the safest option."

Reilly zeroed in on Alex. "What do you think? Can you keep me safe?"

A hint of challenge underscored the words. When she heard it, Lana knew she'd lost.

Alex nodded. "If we take extra precautions, maybe throw in some misdirection, I think we can pull it off."

"Good." Reilly's mouth settled in a grim line. "Let's get it set up."

₪ ₪ ₪ ₪ ₪

"He's hired Freddie Young."

Any interest Nate had in the television program was gone as Matt's words sunk in. "Is he good?"

"Good enough."

Good enough. What did that mean? "So do I need to be worried?"

Hesitation. Never a positive sign.

After a few seconds, Matt sighed. "Young likes to target cops.

And family. Your chick falls under both categories."

Which would make killing her an added bonus.

Matt walked from the room, but Nate barely noticed.

Did Lana even know about Young? Would she take the necessary precautions? Or would she throw herself between her brother and the end of Young's rifle?

He didn't even have to think about that one. Lana would do whatever it took to protect her brother. Not only because it was her job, but because she fiercely protected those she loved.

He was going to lose her.

A vise squeezed the air from his lungs. Swallowing around the sand dune blocking his throat proved impossible.

It wasn't fair.

The future had never held promise for him before. Dreams of a wife and a family were for other guys, but not for him. Or so he'd thought. And then he met her. Only to lose her again.

Maybe Matt would…

He discarded the idea. No way would Matt help protect her. Nate hadn't even been able to convince Matt to dodge Rosetti's call. Or keep his retirement a secret. Heck, it'd been hard enough to get Matt to back off in the first place.

As far as Nate knew, no one else was aware who had been hired. Which meant *he* was the only one who could help her.

The roast beef sandwich he'd had for lunch felt like a slab of meat hanging in his stomach. If Lana had to count on him to protect her, she might as well pick out her epitaph now.

Okay, so protecting her was out of the question. But maybe he could warn her.

The idea ricocheted inside his mind.

The warning would have to be done anonymously, of course. Meaning he'd have to use a pay phone or something so she couldn't trace the number back to him.

Or he could use Stevens' phone. Yeah, that would work. He could even claim to be Stevens.

It'd lend credibility to his warning. Hopefully enough to make her take him seriously.

Twenty

"It's hard to believe we'll be home tomorrow." Lana zipped her suitcase and set it on the floor.

Alex looked up from her own open suitcase. "I hope we'll be able to stay there."

That didn't sound good. "You have doubts?"

"The whole thing's a little off. I can't shake the feeling that there's more going on here."

"Then why did you agree to it? You practically told Reilly to do it!"

A bit of an exaggeration, but she didn't correct herself. Alex had put on this confident front for Reilly, but harbored doubts of her own?

The skin around Alex's eyes creased. "It's our best shot at closing this thing quickly and keeping Reilly safe in the long run. It's a calculated risk."

Calculated risk? That's what she called putting Reilly's life on the line?

Before Lana could voice her frustration, her phone rang. She crossed to the dresser and picked it up. The number looked vaguely familiar, but wasn't one in her phone's stored memory.

She accepted the call. "Hello?"

Silence. Yet she could hear something. Background noises; traffic, voices, and wind. Someone had to be there.

"Hello?" Two more seconds and she'd chalk it up to a wrong number and end the call. Or maybe have it traced.

"Don't hang up."

The words rushed into her ears, spoken by a hoarse male voice.

"This is gonna sound weird, but hang with me, okay?"

Whoever this was, whatever it was about, it wasn't good. In fact, she'd bet money that it was very wrong.

She eased in a breath and worked up a light tone. "Sure. Who is this?"

The tone caught Alex's attention. Abandoning her packing, she approached, eyebrows drawn together and an unspoken question on her face.

The pause on the other end of the line lengthened.

"It's Stevens."

No way. It couldn't be him. Could it? "Stevens? Okay, I'm listening."

She met Alex's eyes and nodded when Alex mouthed "trace it?"

Maybe they'd get a lock on his location. All she had to do was stay calm and keep him talking long enough for them to get the trace.

Whirling, Alex snatched up her phone and scurried into the hallway.

Lana tuned back into the matter at hand as the raspy voice reached her ears again.

"I'm, uh, calling to um, warn you."

What the…?

The nerve of this man! Who did he think he was? Was he seriously so arrogant as to think himself untouchable?

"Warn me? You've been hunting my brother, my team, me, for weeks and now you're calling to *warn* me?"

"I know how it sounds–"

"Do you? Because I'm thinking you don't have a clue." Okay, so much for staying calm. She better watch it or she'd drive him away and they'd never get a trace.

"Look, I'm not a threat anymore. I've retired."

"Like I'm really going to believe a word you say."

"It's true."

"Really. And why would you do that?"

"My motives aren't what's important here."

Was that impatience she heard in his tone?

Before she could needle him further, he continued, "You need to be careful."

"Your concern is touching."

"He's hired Freddie Young."

Young. Why was that name familiar? She pushed the question aside to deal with later. For now, maybe she could get him to give up Rosetti. "Who's hired Young?"

"Not important. What matters is that Young targets his victims' families. And law enforcement. You're both, which will sweeten the deal."

"Gee, I appreciate the concern. But given that you already shot me once, you'll have to forgive me if I'm not ready to be friends."

The words hung in the silence that followed.

Was he still there? Or had her snarky reply cost them the opportunity to catch him?

"I'm sorry. I never wanted to hurt you."

"No. You wanted to hurt my brother!"

"Just watch your back."

Before she could reply, the line went dead. She tossed the phone onto her bed and turned to Alex, who stood in the doorway. "Tell me we got something."

"Tech is working on it. I guess we'll know soon enough."

Something told her they'd come up dry. Stevens hadn't escaped capture this long by making stupid mistakes.

"What was that all about?" Alex rested her shoulder against the doorframe.

"He was calling to warn me. Can you believe it? He actually sounded concerned about my safety!" Exhaustion swept her and she dropped onto the edge of the mattress. Could this get any more confusing?

"Actually, I can believe it." Alex cleared her throat and came to sit next to Lana. "Have you considered the possibility that Stevens is someone you know?"

"Are you kidding? I've hardly thought about anything else."

"Did you recognize the voice?"

"No. But he was trying to disguise it." Proof that he'd been concerned about her identifying him.

Ugh. Was it possible? Could she really know Stevens by some other name?

"Any thoughts?" Alex's voice shattered her musings.

"I don't know. It's hard to imagine that I could know someone who kills people for a living." Thoughts jumbled inside her mind and she struggled to sort through them all. "He'd have to be someone who doesn't know what I do, yet obviously someone who cares about me enough to be concerned for my safety."

"And someone who has your number."

"Or has access to someone with it." Who did that leave?

Possibly countless people from church, although she doubted Stevens frequented a place of worship. Unless he took the whole Sunday Christian thing to a whole new level.

It could also be Elliott. Awfully coincidental that he'd reestablished contact with her at the exact time a hit man was tracking her brother. Perhaps he'd noticed the last name Tanner and it had brought back memories of her. It wasn't a completely uncommon last name and since he'd never met Reilly he may not have even connected the two.

Or what about Nate? Growing up in a group home made him much more likely to get involved in criminal activities. But a hit man? Really? And why drag Matt along with him if he was planning to kill someone? It made no sense.

Maybe it was someone from her biological family. Cyrano had taken that call around the same time that Beckman called Stevens. Coincidence?

It could even be Branden, although she seriously doubted it. Stevens had seemed surprised to see her, but Branden knew who she was and what she did. Even if she hadn't told him in so many words.

Alex's phone rang. The conversation was short and terse and Alex ended the call with a quiet snort. "Big surprise. The trace came up blank. No GPS so either the phone's really old or he removed the GPS chip. They triangulated the call to Lincoln City, but couldn't pinpoint the location. It's the same number they pulled from Beckman's phone, so at least we know it was really him."

Not that she'd suspected anything else.

She sighed. "I better write down the conversation while it's still fresh in my mind."

This information would have to be passed along to Maxwell, since he was in charge of the case, and Barker, since he was her immediate supervisor. There would be questions, an investigation, people prying into every corner of her life to try to track down the one person who could be an international hit man.

She pulled out a notepad and pen and jotted down what she remembered. Some of the exact verbiage escaped her, but she was able to recall most of it.

When she finished, Alex took the notepad from her hand and

skimmed it. "Wait a second. You didn't tell me about Young."

Lana hiked an eyebrow. "What of it?"

"Don't you know who he is?"

"He sounds familiar, but–"

"Lana, his street name is The Butcher."

The Butcher. Of course. That's why he'd sounded familiar. He'd taken out entire families. With ruthless abandon.

Alex pulled out her phone. "We need to get someone on your parents. And what's Reilly's girlfriend's name? We'll have to make sure she's covered, too."

Stevens' words came back to her. Family and law enforcement. Young would go after her with almost as must enthusiasm as he would Reilly.

Although Alex hadn't said as much, her position with the team had changed from protector to protected.

ꟷ ꟷ ꟷ ꟷ ꟷ

Nate's hand shook as he pulled the battery off Stevens' cell phone. Tossing the phone and battery onto the passenger seat, he cranked the engine and shifted into drive.

Had she taken him seriously? It was hard to say.

Her sharp sarcasm sliced through his mind. Trailed by her words about being shot. By Matt.

Had Matt known? And purposely chosen not to tell him about it?

The question still burned in his mind ten minutes later as he strode through the front door of their cabin.

Matt looked up as he walked in. "Where you been, man?"

"You shot her!" The words flew from him before he'd thought them through.

Surprise flickered across Matt's face. "You talked to her? How'd you explain knowing about Young?"

"I pretended to be you." He tossed Matt's phone and the battery onto the coffee table in front of Matt. "Did you know?"

"I thought I hit someone, but I didn't know who. She pushed the target out of the way."

And obviously hadn't gotten out of the way fast enough herself. Nate slowly exhaled.

"Dude, you need to tread carefully. One wrong move and she'll figure it all out."

Nate looked at Matt, noting the concern in his face. "Don't worry. The last thing I want is for her to connect the dots."

"If she does, we've both gotta disappear. She could describe us well enough to give the Feds a sketch." He paused. "You think she believed you?"

Sinking into the closest chair, Nate rested his head in his hands. "I don't know. I hope so."

Thoughts of what could happen made him want to hurl. If Young caught up to Lana and her team, those thoughts would become reality.

⧉ ⧉ ⧉ ⧉ ⧉

"I'm telling you, you have nothing to worry about." Frank Rosetti channeled every ounce of confidence he possessed, glad no one could see the tremor that shook the hand he clenched beneath the table. "He'll never make it inside."

On the other side of the Plexiglas barrier, Garrett leaned forward. "That's good, man. 'Cause if he does, I'll be seein' you in here."

He had no doubt Garrett would tell the cops everything. But Freddie Young had guaranteed him that Tanner wouldn't make it to the prison.

"Stick with the plan. When he doesn't show, you tell them that you had nothing to confess. You wanted the chance to look your accuser in the eye. Remember, without his testimony, they've got nothing on you."

"'Cept the gun." Garrett cursed.

"Evidence can disappear. Get compromised. Keep your mouth shut and I'll take care of everything."

"You better, man. Or else."

Frank clenched his teeth, ignoring the pain that spiked through his jaw. If he could, he'd have Young take out Garrett, too.

And Stevens.

Not a bad plan. Once Tanner was out of the way, maybe he'd hire Young to track Stevens down. Teach him a thing or two about keeping his commitments.

Then once Garrett was free, maybe Young could eliminate the loose end.

For now, though, he needed to keep Garrett on his side. And playing by the rules. "I got this. Hold up your end and you'll be out in no time."

Garrett stared at him, his icy eyes never blinking. Finally, a slow nod indicated acceptance.

Frank hung up the phone and walked away.

Coming to the prison had been a calculated risk. It would look suspicious to the Feds and would no doubt be questioned by the prosecutor's office, but nothing he couldn't handle. He'd simply argue that since the FBI was fingering him for involvement, he'd wanted to speak with Garrett himself to learn whatever he could about the circumstances involving his arrest and incarceration.

Sure, the Feds would have their suspicions, but would lack the evidence to do anything about it. This whole mess would disappear and Frank could get back to life as usual.

Just as soon as Young eliminated Reilly Tanner.

Five miles to go. Then they'd be safely inside the walls of the prison.

Lana hoped Garrett really planned to confess. No one would be very happy if he backed out.

If this didn't end today, little doubt existed in her mind that the team would begin to treat her less like a colleague and more like a witness.

To be honest, she was surprised they'd let her ride along today.

The fact that she sat in the back, behind tinted, bullet-proof glass, was not lost on her.

Traffic snarled ahead of them and Chow brought the vehicle to a halt. Nothing but bumpers and brake lights, a whole herd of them. Great.

At least they'd left much earlier than necessary. The plan was to arrive at the prison two hours before the meeting in an effort to throw off Young. Or anyone else who might be looking to take a shot at Reilly.

Time dragged. The vehicle barely moved.

Lana twisted in her seat to find traffic packed into the lanes around and behind them, too.

They were trapped.

Could Young have orchestrated this? Caused an accident to slow their progress so he could take them out?

Ridiculous. Young wouldn't have any way of knowing what route they'd take.

Then again, was it any more unlikely than Stevens being connected to her in some still unknown way?

A quick scan of the faces inside the vehicle found the rest of the team alert, but not alarmed.

At least someone could be calm.

Because it certainly wasn't her.

She slowly removed her gun from the holster, her gaze brushing across the surrounding landscape.

No one approached them on foot. None of the other drivers seemed interested in anything but getting moving again. There was no sign of a sniper - at least not that she could see - on any of the surrounding buildings, either.

Then again, a good sniper would be well camouflaged.

Her attention swished between the dashboard clock and the windows. The clock, then the windows.

The vehicle inched forward. Stopped. A little further. Then stopped.

What was taking so long?

Almost a half hour passed before they started moving more than a few feet at a time.

As they neared the head of the line, she saw a landscaping truck on its side, the long bed blocking several lanes. Bark, rocks, and gravel littered the edges of their lane, which was clear. The piles off to the side told her that hadn't always been the case.

Well, they'd *had* the element of surprise on their side. But a forty-five minute delay in traffic had reduced that element significantly.

Okay, so they wouldn't be quite as early. So what?

Maybe Young would get caught in the same traffic. Or something worse.

The silence in the car remained unbroken as they closed the gap to the prison. The razor-wire fence rose from the marsh like a mirage, followed by a cold, gray building.

Warehouses lined the opposite side of the street. Cars, ranging from battered to beautiful, parked around them.

They pulled up to the gate and glided to a stop beside the guard's booth.

Chow offered his credentials as he lowered the window. "US Marshals. I believe we are expected."

Taking the badge, the guard peered into the vehicle. "Lemme call this in."

Crack!

The sharp sound resonated between the buildings. Steam rose from the hood. What was–

Crack!

The truth slammed into her as lines webbed across the window on the other side of the car. They were under fire!

Twenty-One

"Everyone down!" Alex's words echoed those darting through Lana's head.

Outside, the guards scrambled into the booth. One of them already had a walkie-talkie in hand, lips flailing as he scanned the surrounding terrain.

Young. He'd found them.

Please don't let him have armor piercing rounds. If he did, their bulletproof vehicle wouldn't shield them for long.

She held out little hope that he'd be using standard ammo.

Alex wrestled a shield from the cargo space and positioned it in front of Reilly. "Chow! Get us outta here!"

"We are blocked in."

Lana strained to see out the back window.

The grill on a large refrigerated truck filled the view.

"Tell 'em to open the gate!"

In response to Alex's command, Chow signaled the guards, but they didn't see him. Or maybe just had no inclination to cooperate.

More gunshots sliced through the morning. Alex got on her phone and yelled for backup.

Backup would take too long.

They had to stop him.

Now.

Before he hit someone.

Thoughts clicked through Lana's mind. The guards inside were likely mobilizing, but they'd be penned in. Young probably had a rooftop vantage point.

Local law enforcement would get here. But would it be soon enough?

She couldn't take the chance.

She pulled out her Glock and backed up to the door.

Lord, shield me.

Young was located somewhere on the other side of the vehicle.

If she could get around the refrigerator truck, she might be able to take him by surprise.

It'd only work if someone distracted him.

"Chow." Her fingers closed around the door handle. "Count to five. Then draw his fire."

Alex whipped her head around. "What're you–"

The door gave way behind her and Lana half-rolled, half-fell from the car. She landed in a crouch, eased the door closed.

"Tanner." Alex's crisp tone snapped through the closed door. "In the car. Now."

Not going to happen. If she pulled this off, Alex would forgive her.

If she didn't, well, dead people didn't need forgiveness.

She slid down the side of the car and paused by the rear tire.

Okay, Chow. Any time.

Nothing.

She knew Alex wasn't pleased with her actions. Had Alex told Chow to ignore her request?

That wouldn't stop her. She'd stick to her plan. With or without support from her team.

Come on, back me up.

A few seconds passed before two gunshots sounded. From the vehicle, this time.

She'd have to remember to thank Alex later.

Without stopping to think about it any further, she ran in a half-crouch toward the truck.

More shots. Nothing seemed to hit nearby. Maybe Young hadn't seen her.

She slipped down the side of the truck to peek around the back.

Movement atop a warehouse caught her eye.

A long barrel. A shape. The barrel jerked about the same time she heard the next shot.

Something smacked into the metal next to her face.

So much for not being seen.

She flitted back and positioned herself by the tire. The last thing she needed was to have her legs shot out from under her.

What to do?

Crawl under the vehicle? She could use the tires for cover, maybe get off a shot before he saw her new position.

Risky. What if the truck's driver suddenly floored it?

Too bad she couldn't communicate with the team. Get them to draw his fire.

She glanced back at the SUV. Rodriguez gave a half wave from where he knelt by the rear tires.

Okay, now she really owed Alex a thank you. Maybe even lunch.

All she had to do was get Rodriguez to understand. She pointed at him, his gun, and the sniper.

A nod. Man, she hoped he got the message.

Turning, he edged down the vehicle and paused by the front tires. He nodded at her. When she returned the gesture, he held up three fingers. Dropped to two. Then one.

He rose.

As she hurried to the rear of the truck, she heard several shots. Some from the building, some from Rodriguez.

She brought up her gun. Peered around the edge and sighted on the figure.

The recoil jolted up her arm as she pulled the trigger.

The rifle fell back and the figure disappeared from sight. She got him. With any luck, she did enough damage that he'd have to back down.

Sirens wailed in the distance.

No sign of movement from the roof. Five seconds turned to ten. She faced Rodriguez. "I'm going in."

He jogged to join her. "Let's do it."

They tore across the street. Man, was she going to get a lecture from Alex after this. Not to mention what Reilly would say.

A clattering sound. From somewhere close. Young making his escape?

"Alley." Rodriguez's low voice sounded behind her left shoulder.

She plastered her back against the building and peered around the corner.

Empty. A fire escape clung to the side of the building.

That explained the noise they'd heard.

They darted down the alley. At the corner, she stole a look onto the neighboring road.

About a block down, a man opened the driver's door on a small white sedan. She caught a glimpse of something long and black as he pulled it from inside the plaid beige, brown, and pea green raincoat he wore.

"Freeze! US Marshals!"

Without giving any indication he heard her, he dropped into the driver's seat. The engine roared to life.

Stop him! She brought up her gun and aimed for the tires.

Rubber protested. The car fishtailed away from the curb.

She squeezed off a shot.

The car flailed across the nearly empty road, oblivious to the white lines painted on the pavement. Smart. The erratic driving prevented her from getting a clear shot at the tires.

She lowered her gun as the car screeched around a corner.

From beside her, Rodriguez swore softly. "Couldn't make out the plate from here. You see it?"

"No." She bit out the word. "We better get back."

"Yeah. S'pose so."

As they turned, she noticed something dark on the ground. She knelt.

Blood. A trail of it.

"Looks like I hit him."

"Good. Serves 'im right."

Maybe his DNA would be in CODIS. They could track him using it.

Unlikely, but the glimmer of hope made her feel a little better.

The blood continued down the alley, stopping in a small pool underneath the fire escape. Looking up, she found the ladder rungs smeared with blood, too. Maybe she'd gotten in a solid hit.

They continued up the alley to where it opened into the street opposite the prison.

Police vehicles packed the area.

The truck hadn't moved, but the SUV was nowhere in sight. Knowing Alex, she'd moved Reilly to the security of the prison's interior as soon as she could.

She and Rodriguez offered their badges to a dozen tense cops.

After showing the responding officers the sniper's perch and the route he'd taken, as well as giving their statements, they were escorted into the prison. Chow let them into a visitation room before resuming his post outside the door.

Narrowed blue eyes locked on her the second she stepped through the door. Yeah, she knew Alex wouldn't be happy.

"Deputy Tanner. A word." Alex's voice contained enough ice to chill a penguin.

Oh, boy. She was in for it.

Alex led the way outside the room and motioned for Chow to go inside. The door clicked shut behind him.

"What the heck were you thinking?"

The fury behind Alex's words made Lana blink. Had she ever seen Alex this angry?

Alex didn't give her a chance to reply. "What part of you being a target do you not understand? Young would just *love* to take you down, remember? And then you go and do something so incredibly stupid as to get out of the car and go after him yourself!"

"We were pinned down. It would've only been a matter of time before he hit someone."

"I oughta report you to Barker. Insubordination."

"Calm down, will you? It worked out okay."

"But what if it hadn't? You could've been killed! I can't let that happen, especially not on my watch."

The angry façade cracked, giving Lana a glimpse of the fear Alex had hidden beneath it. "I'm sorry. I didn't mean to scare you. I just wanted to get you guys to safety."

Heavy footfalls, accompanied by rattling chains, echoed down the concrete hallway. Lana looked up to see a broad man in an orange jumpsuit, flanked by several guards, shuffling toward them. Though too far away to make out any details, the white blond hair confirmed his identity.

Alex's slowly released breath whistled through her nose. "Let's finish this."

₪ ₪ ₪ ₪ ₪

"Rosetti arrested in murder-for-hire scheme."

It seemed everywhere Lana turned, she saw the local paper screaming the good news.

Hard to believe it'd been a week since Garrett had confessed to everything, including the fact that the murder had been ordered by none other than Frank Rosetti. He'd also told them that Rosetti had hired Stevens, followed by Young, the latter of whom had guaranteed that Reilly wouldn't make it to the jail.

Good thing the guarantees of criminals weren't worth the oxygen expelled making them.

"Good to see you again, Lana."

She offered a smile to Tomas, the server she and Reilly always requested when frequenting their favorite restaurant. "Believe me, it's good to be here."

"You guys are big news right now."

"One of us is, anyway." Thank God it was only Reilly's name in the papers.

"Ah, but I bet you weren't far away."

"Guilty as charged."

"Were you there when they made the arrest?"

"Unfortunately, no." But she wished she had been. She would've loved to have seen the look on Rosetti's face when they slapped the cuffs on him.

Tomas nodded at the two empty chairs across from her. "Still waiting on that brother of yours?"

"And his fiancée. Some things never change."

A rich laugh bubbled from him. "The usual? Peach iced tea and a raspberry lemonade?"

That he knew her and Reilly's favorite drinks so well was one of the reasons she requested him. "Absolutely. Better add a diet soda for Des."

"You got it."

He moved away, greeting Reilly as he approached the table.

Pulling out the chair across from her, Reilly loosened his tie. "Des should be right behind me. She said yes, by the way."

Of course she had. "Was there ever a doubt?"

"I never know about you women. You can be kind of unpredictable." Teasing lightened the words.

"Just like to keep you on your toes." Speaking of unpredictable.... "What happened to changing your hair? I mean, that is what you said you were going to do, right?"

While the contacts were long gone and the goatee was history, Reilly's hair still sported the highlighted style Alex had given it.

A hint of pink flashed across his cheeks as he offered a sheepish grin. "Des. Somehow she convinced me to leave it. For a while, anyway."

Tomas dropped off their drinks before hurrying on to the next table.

As he walked away, Reilly leaned in. "You all packed?"

"Just about."

In a few days they'd all be flying back to Lincoln City, for a real vacation this time. Her parents, Reilly, and even Des had cleared their schedules for the trip. The top thing on their agenda was to get to know the Lykos family better.

The top thing on *her* agenda was to finally level with them about who she was and what she did. No more half-truths or dodging questions.

Except maybe the one she really wanted to ask – if any of them could possibly be, or know, an international assassin who went by Stevens. Looked like that was one mystery that would remain unsolved.

For now.

"What's in your head?"

Tracing her finger through the condensation on the outside of her glass, she eased out a breath. "Wondering who Stevens is. If he's somehow connected to them. To be honest, I don't know if I want to learn the truth."

"Maybe God's telling you to let this one go."

Okay, that was the last thing she would've expected from him. "And what about justice? He's killed a lot of people."

"Sometimes God uses us to exact justice, but sometimes He takes care of it Himself. This might be one of those times. Don't waste time obsessing about something you can't control."

He was right. God was a God of justice *and* mercy. Whichever He decided to show Stevens was up to Him.

卍 卍 卍 卍 卍

"I thought you were supposed to be good."

Young flinched. Partly from the tone, but mostly because the words, spat from Ginger Rosetti's perfectly painted lips, contained more truth that he wanted to hear.

She was right. He *was* supposed to be good. Yet here he sat, a colossal failure.

"I am. I just didn't have the time I needed to get the job done." He hated the defensiveness in his tone almost as much as he hated making excuses.

"You assured Frank it wouldn't be a problem."

"I was wrong, okay? That what you want to hear?"

"I want to hear my husband's voice!" Tears glittered in her eyes like broken glass. "I want all this to be behind us. I want Tanner to suffer as Frank has."

Huh.

He'd have pegged her as a gold digger who only married Frank for the status and money, but she really appeared to love her husband. "Oh, I could make Tanner suffer, all right."

She blinked. A tear strayed down her cheek, but she didn't wipe it away.

Instead, she studied him for several seconds. "Does he have a brother?"

Genius.

Why hadn't he thought of that before? "A sister. They're very close."

"Really." Ginger's lips bunched in a scowl. "And do you think you could actually complete this one?"

"Better believe it." It was perfect really. He'd get revenge on the woman who not only made him fail, but shot him in the process. "And I'll take care of her for free."

Twenty-Two

Nate closed the internet browser.

So. Rosetti had been arrested. Reilly Tanner was safe and, more importantly, so was Lana.

Maybe now he could finally call her.

Of course, he could've called her before, but he hadn't wanted to do anything to arouse suspicion. Especially after calling and pretending to be Stevens.

A double knock sounded on his apartment door.

Matt.

Swinging open the door, he let his friend inside. "Did you see the news? We did it."

He turned to find Matt surveying him soberly.

Uh-oh. He'd seen that look before.

"You might hold off on the party," Matt's tone was even. Expressionless, really.

"What do you mean?"

"I mean that your chick shot Young."

So? Young had been trying to kill her brother. And her. Not only was shooting him part of her job, it was self-defense. "Good for her."

"No. Bad for her."

What was he talking about?

Matt planted his hands on the back of Nate's brown leather sofa and leaned forward. "She should've killed him, but she didn't. Now Young's angry. He's goin' after her."

The moisture vaporized from Nate's mouth. "H-how do you know?"

"Got a contact who makes it his business to know. He remembered me askin' about Young before and thought I might wanna know the latest."

"Any chance this guy's wrong?"

"Not likely." Matt straightened and crossed his arms over his chest. "It's what I'd do in his place."

Now what? Lana thought this was over. Would she even be on the defensive?

Probably not.

He could call her.

Memories of their last phone conversation flashed through his head. The more he spoke to her as Stevens, the more likely she'd be to recognize his voice.

Not to mention that he was no longer in Lincoln City, but home in Santa Barbara. Calling her could lead the Feds straight to his home town.

Out of the question. But what else could he do?

Go to her. He didn't know what he'd do when he got there, maybe call in an anonymous tip to the cops or something.

"I don't suppose your source told you where Young is right now?"

"You serious? Dude's not his travel agent."

Of course not.

Well, he had her number. And he'd been thinking about calling her anyway. It shouldn't be too hard to get her talking about her present location. "I'll find out."

"You gonna call and warn her again?"

"No. I'm going to find her and stop Young."

"And how do you plan to do that?"

"I don't know." Nate met Matt's gaze and held it with his own. "I could use your help."

Eyes narrowing, Matt's lips slid into a slit. "Forget it. This obsession has gotta stop, man."

"It's not an obsession."

"Come on, there's no future here. Let it go. You can do better than some self-righteous Fed."

"You don't know her."

"I know she hunts guys like us."

"Guys like you."

Dang. The words had popped out, almost on their own. Why had he said that?

"Says the thief." Matt stomped around the sofa and jabbed his finger at Nate. "Or did you forget about all those heists you pulled?"

"That was a long time ago."

"Doubt you've passed the statute of limitations." Matt rocked back on his heels and shook his head. "I knew I shouldn't have told you about this."

"I'm glad you did." Nate raked his fingers through his hair and released a shaky breath. "I'm going. And I'm going to stop Young. No matter what."

"He'll rip you to shreds and still kill her. Maybe make you watch."

"I'm not gonna let him get close enough to touch her. I'll kill him if I have to."

Matt's mouth curled into a sneer. "Right. You're the one who washed outta the military 'cause you couldn't shoot people remember?"

"Yeah, well maybe I can shoot this guy. I'll figure something out."

"This is suicide, man."

"Well, at least I'll go out trying to help someone." For once.

"Fine." Matt gestured wildly into the air. "Go! Maybe you can save the world while you're at it."

Whirling, Matt stormed toward the door.

"I'll see you, Matt."

Matt jerked open the door and shot a glare his direction. "Not likely."

A gust of wind lifted the fresh sea spray across Lana's face.

She wrapped her arms around her stomach, but didn't turn her face from the wind. Cold as it was, she relished the fresh scent the wind wrapped around her.

Four days in Oregon and each one had been filled with family. Not just one family, but two of them. Sharing a room with Des left her with very little time to herself. She'd come out here to jog, but for now was content to enjoy the ocean and the solitude.

Although if she wanted to get any exercise in, she'd have to do it soon.

The sun neared the surface of the ocean. It wouldn't be long before it set and darkness descended. Half hour, tops.

She'd kind of expected to find Nate out here. In all honesty, had hoped she would. Especially since he'd told her on the phone the other day that he was still in town.

"I don't want to get shot today, so I'm announcing my presence," a man's voice spoke up from behind her.

Branden. Not exactly the guy she'd expected to run into, but that was okay.

She turned. "Don't worry. Friends are on my no-shoot list."

Several steps put him directly beside her. "I guess I didn't need to worry anyway. Now that you're off duty."

"You think that matters?" She quirked her eyebrow. "My favorite accessory is a Glock. Never leave home without it."

Surprised eyes traveled to her waist. "You mean…"

"Better believe it."

"Noted. Reilly told me I could find you out here, but also said I might have trouble catching up to you."

"I was going to jog, but haven't made it that far yet."

"Well, let's go. If you think those short little legs of yours can keep up."

Oh, he thought he could take her on? She grinned. "I'll make you eat that challenge."

She took off down the packed sand, keeping Branden in her peripheral. When she sensed him lagging behind, she slowed slightly. Not enough to lose her lead, but enough to not lose him.

Ten minutes passed before she felt his hand land on her shoulder.

"Think… we could… walk?" The words traveled on puffs of air.

"What's the matter? Having trouble keeping up with these short legs?"

"I've got… a desk… job. What… do you… want… from me?"

She slowed to a walk. Really, felt more like a crawl. But she allowed Branden to set the pace. "You need to get out more often."

"I've been skipping the gym lately." Breathing seemed to be coming a little easier now. "Have to get back into it, I guess."

Silence descended as they walked for a few minutes.

Branden broke it with the question she'd been expecting since he first joined her. "So, now that everything's over, care to give me the inside scoop? Not for the paper or anything, just between us," he added quickly.

Where to begin? She summarized quickly, giving him enough details to bring him up to speed but not compromise what was still an active investigation.

"So what brought you back to Lincoln City?"

"I thought I should get to know my family."

"Your family?"

Hadn't she told him about that? "Yeah. Didn't I tell you that I ran into my biological family here?"

"You failed to mention that one." He studied her briefly before shaking his head. "I can't believe I never saw it before. Cyrano and Dimitrios."

Wait. He knew them?

Perfect. She could pump him for information. Satisfy her suspicions as to whether or not one of them could be a hit man.

"You guys are friends?"

"Nah. More acquaintances, really."

A reporter, an EMT, and… what had Dimitrios said Cyrano did? Teacher, maybe? "How do you know them?"

"Met them through work. I've run into Dimitrios at crime scenes and accidents quite a bit. Then a few years back, I covered a story on Cyrano when he was up for a state teaching award."

A teaching award, hmm? It was hard to believe Stevens could create a cover that believable.

But maybe he was good. Really, really good.

She forced a light tone. "So what're they like?"

"They seem like good enough guys. Like I said, don't really know them well, but the family seems pretty tied into the community."

Not as helpful as she'd hoped.

Ghostly fingers tickled across the back of her neck. A chill sunk into her bones.

Something wasn't right.

It had nothing to do with Branden. Or the things he'd said about Dimitrios or Cyrano. The problem was here. On this beach.

She turned a critical eye to every person within sight.

An older couple walking hand in hand. Three women jogging. A couple with four young children playing in the sand.

Nothing to inspire trepidation.

But the feeling settled like ice in her limbs.

She bent down, pretending to tie her shoelaces, while surreptitiously scrutinizing the area behind her.

"What're you doing?"

Branden's amusement-tinged words were little more than an echo in the background. A lone figure strode down the beach behind them.

Too far away to make a positive ID. But there was something familiar about him.

The jacket.

Her eyes locked on the beige plaid jacket. There couldn't be many coats that ugly. But she did know someone who owned one.

Young.

That didn't make sense. Why would he be here?

Rosetti had been arrested, Garrett had confessed. Reilly should be safe.

Wait a second.

Reilly wasn't here. And Young wouldn't be after Branden. This had to be about her. But why?

The why didn't matter.

What mattered was that he *was* here. That Branden was in the line of fire.

And that she had no backup.

She skimmed the area.

The closest refuge was a maintenance shed. Near a hotel about fifty yards up the beach.

Drawing Young toward an area so populated was risky, but what choice did she have? If it was Young, and if he was out to get her, the beach offered zero options for cover.

She straightened. "That shed. As fast as you can. Don't run a straight line and don't look back."

"What?"

A glance back found the man reaching a hand into his coat.

She grabbed Branden's arm and started running, dragging him a few feet until he fell into step beside her.

"What's going on?" Alarm coated his words.

She risked a look behind her. The man was running now, his attention locked on them.

Something dark hung from his hand. Abnormally long for a

handgun; likely equipped with a suppressor.

If he started shooting, she didn't want Branden caught in the middle. She veered to her left to put distance between them.

Almost there.

She looked back in time to see the man take aim.

Throwing herself at Branden, she caught him around the middle and took him to the ground. Sand flew in her face.

No gunshot.

Didn't matter. It was coming.

"Hurry!" She shoved to her feet and dashed the few remaining feet around the corner of the shed.

A pop, like the world's loudest nail gun, echoed off the building. Wood splintered near her head.

Definitely a suppressed gunshot.

Breathing hard, Branden plopped down beside her. "Who is that?"

"An assassin." She pulled out her gun, racked the slide, and fixed her gaze on Branden. "Go to the hotel. Call the police. Tell them there's an officer under fire. Have the hotel locked down and stay inside."

Branden hesitated.

"Go!"

He pushed up and sprinted across the scrub grass.

Okay. Now to keep Young busy.

Branden raced toward the hotel, fighting the urge to look back with every step.

What kind of friend was he? Leaving her to face a killer alone?

But she'd told him to go. Besides, bringing help was the best thing he could do for her. If he stayed, he'd only get in her way.

Why had he left his cell phone in his car?

He tore around the corner of the hotel, shoes skidding on the asphalt. A line of cars blurred to his left as he approached the main entrance.

He burst through the doors and the lady working the front desk looked up.

"I need to use your phone."

The polite smile she offered told him she couldn't care less. "Of course, sir. What's your room number?"

"I'm not a guest."

"I'm sorry, sir. Our phones are for hotel guests only."

"No, you don't–"

Glass shattered from somewhere in the parking lot.

The woman's eyebrows drew together. "Excuse me. I need to check–"

"No!" His hand shot out to stop her. "He's got a gun!"

"Who has a gun?" Skepticism laced the words.

For crying out loud. They didn't have time for this. "I don't know. But she's out there and he's going to kill her."

More breaking glass.

White washed her face. A shaky hand pushed the phone toward him without a word.

If anything happened to Lana while he hid inside like some kind of coward, he'd never forgive himself.

No matter what she'd said, he was going back out there.

He leaned toward the lady and held her gaze. "Call 911. Tell them there's an active shooter and a cop under fire. Then lock the doors and stay away from the windows."

No color remained in her cheeks. She nodded and picked up the phone with a trembling hand.

Okay, backup was on the way. Now to see if he couldn't do something to help.

A windshield shattered inches from Lana's head. She ducked out of sight and wove around the vehicles.

Ugh! He knew where she was, but she had yet to catch sight of him.

The receding light didn't help.

Pausing by a white van, she knelt on the blacktop, searching for his feet amid the sea of tires.

Nothing but shadows.

Somehow, she had to get away from the hotel before someone was hit by stray gunfire. She hoped Branden had gotten the place locked down.

Straightening slightly, she risked a glance through the van's windows.

The window exploded by her head as the sound of the shot reached her. She dropped back down, praying for divine intervention.

Rolling under the van, she crawled to the other side.

No sign of feet. She scurried to the next vehicle.

What she wouldn't give for a cough. Or sneeze. Cell phone ring. Something.

That darn suppressor made tracking the source of each shot impossible.

Footsteps. Several rows over.

"Yo, Tanner. Come on out."

Right. Like she was really going to walk right up to him.

She slid around a convertible, edging toward the voice.

Wait. Why would he advertise his position?

A smart man wouldn't. Not unless he had a compelling reason.

She peeked under the cars, spotting his feet in the blue glow of a streetlamp.

Not just his feet. Two pairs.

A hostage.

"Better get over here or your boyfriend's history."

Boyfriend?

Branden.

She'd told him to stay inside. How could Young have gotten him?

Branden had probably thought he should help her. Wasn't it just like a guy to think she needed protecting?

How many shots did Young have left? Enough to take them both out?

"You got five seconds!"

No time to think this through.

She stood up. "Okay. Stay calm."

Young swiveled, pulling Branden in front of him as a human shield.

One arm wrapped around Branden's throat. The other pressed the suppressed gun to Branden's temple.

"Git over here. And keep that gun where I can see it."

She put her hands up, the Glock held loosely in her right. Once she eased around a white BMW, less than thirty feet separated them.

All she needed was a small opening and she could take him down.

A slamming door. An engine. Anything to draw his attention away from her.

Where were the police? Even if Branden hadn't called them like she'd told him, someone should've heard the shots. They should've been here by now.

Eerie silence cloaked the night.

"Drop your gun."

Could she get a shot off before he killed Branden?

Unlikely.

"I'll shoot him, I swear–"

"Okay, okay!"

Without her gun, she didn't have a chance. But what choice did she have?

No doubt Young intended to kill them both, but she would be first. Maybe Branden could get away.

Still no sign of help. She was out of time and out of options.

Twenty-Three

Easing to the ground, she set her Glock on the pavement.

"Kick it away."

The kick sent the gun grating across the asphalt, stopped by the tire of a shiny black truck.

His gun angled away from Branden's head. "This one's for my shoulder."

Branden drove his elbow back. A grunt slid from Young and the arm at Branden's throat slackened.

Now or never. She rushed toward the men.

Growling, Young whipped the gun up and slammed the butt against Branden's head.

Branden went limp. Young pushed the unconscious body to the side.

The weapon shifted toward her. She dove to the left.

Behind her, a muffled shot.

Numbness tinged her shoulder as it hit the ground. She rolled into a crouch, then launched herself at the assassin as he swung toward her.

Her hand wrapped around his wrist, her momentum driving the gun up as it went off.

Hot breath tickled her forehead.

Which arm had she shot? The right. She smashed her fist against his right bicep.

A roar ricocheted between the buildings.

With her other hand, she slapped at the gun. It tumbled from his fingers and hit the ground with a thunk.

Red darkened his cheeks. He slammed his forehead against hers.

Pain exploded in her head. Fuzziness edged her vision.

She blinked it away.

Hands crashed against her shoulders. She backpedaled, but couldn't find her footing.

As she fell, she saw him turn toward where he'd dropped his gun. The asphalt knocked the breath from her lungs.

Her gun was her only chance. Rolling to her knees, she pushed up and scrambled toward the black truck.

A bullet would tear into her any second. She wasn't going to make it!

Her fingers encircled her Glock.

She palmed her gun and twisted.

The weapon sighted on Nate.

Nate?

It *was* Nate! Gripped in his shaking fingers was a rock the size of a baseball. Young lay motionless at his feet.

She rose slowly, her gaze roving from Young to Nate to Branden and back to Nate. "What're you doing here?"

Careful.

He'd likely saved her life and deserved to be treated like a hero, not a suspect under interrogation.

Nate pointed to a row of cabins at a motel across the street. "That's where I'm staying. I heard the noise, looked outside, and, well, thought I could help."

How many nature photographers would have the guts to take on a guy with a gun? Then again, Nate wasn't just any nature photographer. He was one who'd grown up with bullying and violence. Maybe a guy with a gun didn't faze him as much as it would most people.

Of course, an assassin of Stevens' caliber wouldn't think twice about such an altercation.

But Stevens would've killed the man, not hit him with a rock.

She crossed to check on Branden. Strong vitals. He'd wake up with a mammoth headache, but he'd live.

"So, uh, you a cop or something?"

She blinked at Nate's question as she turned to face him. Did he already know the answer? "US Marshal. This man tried to kill my brother."

"And now you've got him in custody. Must sweeten the deal."

Sweeten the deal?

The air in her lungs turned to smog. She told herself to breathe, but her body refused. Not a completely uncommon saying, but unusual enough.

Nate swallowed. The color slid from his face. "You okay?"

"It's you." The words slipped out on a breath. "Stevens."

"I… I'm not tracking."

Could she be wrong?

She studied him. Resignation lingered in his eyes.

The secret was out and he knew it.

"You're Stevens." The words came out stronger this time, an announcement that would change both of them forever.

He pulled in a thick breath. "No. Lana, listen to me. It's not–"

"Stevens?"

Young!

Whirling, she found Young on his feet, gun already pointed their direction.

Stupid! Never take your eyes off the target. How could she have made such a rookie mistake?

A rookie mistake that would cost her, possibly all of them, their lives.

"Shoulda known it was about her." Young gave his head a small shake. "Now I get to take down Stevens. That'll do a lot for my rep."

The gun locked on Nate and steadied.

No!

She threw herself at Nate, her shoulder connecting with his ribcage.

A muffled pop severed the night.

Something slammed into her with the force of a freight train.

Pain blasted through her body, then faded as quickly as it came. Her head bounced off the ground but surprisingly, it didn't hurt.

Shadows invaded her vision. She couldn't move, couldn't think, couldn't breathe.

"Lana!" Panic tinged Nate's words.

A cackle. From Young. "Too bad I don't have time for you to watch her die."

Watch her die? Was she dying?

No. He was going to kill her. Or at least try to.

Do something!

Blink.

The parking lot came into focus.

She turned her head. The hand holding her Glock poked into her ribs and she wrenched it from under her body.

Young stood several feet away. Angled away from her, he focused on Nate.

Planting her hands, she pushed herself up.

Her palms slipped. Crimson coated the ground beneath her.

Blood. Hers?

Couldn't be. She felt nothing.

Stop Young.

The words shouted through her head, focusing her scattered thoughts. She rose.

Ringing echoed in her ears and she swayed, but stayed on her feet. A tremor shook her hand as she brought her gun up.

Pull it together.

Young racked the slide on his weapon and leveled it at Nate's head.

She planted her feet, cupped her other hand around the gun, and pulled the trigger.

The bullet caught Young in the temple. He collapsed without a sound.

Get his gun. Even though he had to be dead, she wasn't willing to make the same mistake twice.

Her legs shook like twigs as she half-walked, half-staggered to where Young was splayed across the asphalt. Kneeling, she felt for a pulse. Nothing. Her hand dropped from his neck, but she couldn't find the energy to move.

Why was she so tired?

"Lana." Nate's voice contained a surprising urgency.

"He's dead."

It felt like her brain was shutting down. There'd been something important, something about Nate? Or was it Young?

And didn't Stevens figure in somewhere?

Fog enveloped her mind. A shiver rocked down her body. When did it get so cold out here?

With movements that felt about as graceful as an elephant at the ballet, she pushed herself to her feet. Dizziness clouded her vision and the buzzing in her ears increased to a near scream.

She wobbled.

A hand landed on her back. She looked up into Nate's

concerned face. Red and blue lights pulsed in his eyes. Were the police finally here?

"I'm okay–"

"You've been shot." His sharp tone sliced through her murky mind.

What was he talking about?

Wait. She *had* seen blood, hadn't she? Her gaze traveled down to her hands, where she saw the scarlet coating them.

"It doesn't hurt." The voice sounded like it came from someone else, but she felt the words vibrate from her throat.

"You're in shock."

She stared at him and tried to decipher the unfamiliar expression.

Fear? For her? She looked down again.

Blood snaked down her arm in several fat trails and her shirt clung to her like a second layer of skin. Red skin. Lots of it.

Tremors worked up her body, increasing until they rivaled the violence of an earthquake.

Her knees buckled.

An arm supported her back. Nate eased her to the ground as if she was made of glass.

The world before her blurred, but she couldn't remember how to focus.

"The ambulance will be here any second. Everything's gonna be okay."

She didn't hear any sirens. And Nate sounded miles away.

"No! Lana, stay with me. Come on, look at me."

Gentle patting on her cheeks brought her eyes open, but she saw nothing more than dim shapes.

Sirens. She could hear them now. But they were so far away.

"Over here! Hurry!"

Nate's voice sounded barely louder than a whisper. Had he left her?

Maybe now she could rest. Her eyes slid closed, and this time no one tried to get her to open them again.

Twenty-Four

GSW. Female victim.

The limited information taunted Dimitrios like a recording and filled his mind with way too many images. All bad. And all involving his sister.

He cursed the five-car pile-up that had called all the on-duty police officers and ambulances to the other side of town. Everyone involved in the accident had been okay, but it'd taken time. And had put all emergency services far away from what might be a life or death situation for Milana.

No. Not Milana. He refused to believe it was her.

Just because she was in town, and just because she'd already been shot once, didn't mean that she was the only woman who would suffer a gunshot wound on his shift.

She was off-duty now. No work, no danger. Besides, Lana wasn't even staying at that hotel.

A hotel could mean an affair gone bad. Or something to do with drugs or prostitution.

The arguments did nothing to calm his nerves. Good thing Mike was driving tonight.

Mike jerked the ambulance to a halt in the parking lot.

Three police cars had beat them to the scene. One officer walked around, but the rest congregated in one spot, focused on the ground.

The victim, no doubt.

A body sprawled a few feet away from the group, but no one seemed interested in that one. Likely the guy was beyond help.

Another officer knelt next to a guy sitting on the ground, leaning against a car.

The distance prevented him from seeing any details, but if the guy was sitting up, he likely wasn't critical.

Dimitrios grabbed a kit while Mike pulled out the gurney. One of the officers separated from the cluster and waved them over.

The information from dispatch repeated through his head. Female GSW.

It couldn't be her.

Behind him, another ambulance screeched into the parking lot, but he didn't turn to look.

He jogged toward the group. The officers parted as he approached, but one guy didn't move. No uniform. Blood coated his hands and stained his clothes.

Every ounce of his attention seemed focused on the slight, still body in front of him.

Dimitrios' pulse spiked as he approached.

Don't be her. Don't be her.

The closer he got, the more he could see. Black hair blended with the parking lot. She was about the right size and build.

The now-familiar face came into view.

No!

Blood blackened her chest in sharp contrast to her gray face. Her eyes, identical to Cy's and his own, were closed.

He couldn't move.

He knew he had to. Knew that every second he stood like an idiot was one he could be using to save her, but his legs felt like extensions of the ground beneath his feet.

Mike pushed past him, bumping Dimitrios' shoulder as he squeezed by.

Treat her like anyone else. Do what you have to do.

Wooden legs carried him to her side. One of the officers gently pulled the man away.

Breaths rasped from her slightly parted lips, each one hitting like a dagger in his side. At least they didn't sound moist. Hopefully that meant there was no blood in her lungs.

Mike snapped his gloves on and efficiently sliced open her shirt to reveal a dark, coagulated hole just below her collarbone.

Oh, man.

There was so much a bullet could destroy there. Blood vessels, arteries. How much damage had been done? From the amount of blood she'd lost, he'd guess quite a bit.

For her sake, he had to keep his objectivity.

"Milana. Can you hear me?"

No response, movement, anything.

Mike's hands faltered momentarily as Dimitrios said her name, but then continued to dress the wound for transport.

"She'll live, right?" A man's voice sounded behind Dimitrios' left shoulder.

While he knew he should respond, try to offer some reassurance, he didn't have it in him.

"Let's check her back." Mike glanced up at Dimitrios, his eyes clearly asking if he could do this.

Dimitrios reached for her injured side.

"Her back's clean," the man spoke up again.

Shooting his attention to the man for the first time, Dimitrios assessed him. Grief lined his face. Mingled with hints of panic. But he seemed pretty certain. "You're sure?"

A nod answered him.

So the bullet was still inside her. From a blood-loss standpoint, that was a good thing.

From an injury perspective, it meant more internal damage.

He and Mike loaded her onto the gurney and rushed toward the ambulance. As he climbed in the back and closed the doors, he found the man standing exactly where they'd left him, watching. A police officer stood next to him, saying something that he doubted the man even heard.

He looked back at her. How could this happen?

Mike climbed into the driver's seat and tore out of the lot, siren blaring. The five mile drive seemed longer than ever.

The emergency room staff waited as they pulled up to the doors of the ER.

Even though she was in the capable hands of the trauma team, Dimitrios ignored protocol and ran alongside, his gaze focused on his sister's too-pale face. He stopped only when the gurney was whisked through the double doors of the trauma unit.

Life bustled around him, but he couldn't remember when he'd last felt so alone.

A hand landed on his shoulder. He turned to find Mike standing there, somber expression in place.

"That the sister you mentioned?"

No words would form. He nodded.

How did a US Marshal get shot while on vacation?

"I'll pray." Mike placed a hand on his shoulder and started

praying.

For the first time he could remember, Dimitrios found himself hoping there was something to this God thing that both Mike and his parents had bought into. That maybe God was there. That maybe He was listening.

And that maybe, just maybe, He'd care enough to save Milana's life.

"How're you holding up?"

Nate jerked his head up to find the dark-haired EMT from earlier standing a few feet away. Dried blood crusted on the front of his uniform, a harsh reminder of why Nate sat in the chairs opposite the emergency room.

"Uh. Okay. I guess." Except for the tears backed up in his eyes and the pressure crushing his throat.

"I know what you mean." The EMT leaned against the wall across from Nate's chair. "The first time I saw a gunshot wound, it, wow. It changes you. It's worse when it's someone you know."

Worse still when it was your fault.

He studied the EMT. Something about him seemed familiar, but he couldn't nail down what it was. And honestly, right now he was too exhausted to try.

Pushing off the wall, the EMT extended his hand. "I'm Dimitrios."

"Nate." As he withdrew his hand, he couldn't tear his eyes away from the blood staining his skin. No amount of scrubbing had taken it off completely.

Dimitrios seemed to notice his gaze. "It'll fade."

Too bad the memories wouldn't.

"So how do you know my sister?"

Sister? Nate locked onto the EMT. Yeah, he could see the resemblance now. If he hadn't been so worked up, he probably would've seen it before. This guy had to be part of the biological family she'd discovered down here. "Man, I'm sorry."

Dimitrios stuffed his hands into his pockets and dipped his head. "Is what it is. So you're a friend of hers?"

"Yeah." At least he hoped they were still friends.

He looked toward the ER doors.

Shouldn't they have heard something by now?

A petite woman with gray-streaked hair walked by, her white sneakers squeaking on the tile. Pale purple scrubs identified her as a nurse.

Dimitrios gently snagged her arm. "Margie, any way you can get the scoop on the gunshot victim I brought in earlier?"

Compassion laced her smile. "Sure, hon. Let me see what I can do."

Five minutes later she returned, no hint of a smile on her round face. "Hon, she is one lucky woman. That bullet angled in under her collarbone and fragmented. They're diggin' pieces out of bone and muscle now, but looks like it missed all major organs. It nicked an artery and she's lost a lot of blood, but it's lookin' good."

"Thanks, Margie."

"No problem, hon." Margie walked away, the squeaking of her shoes fading with each step.

Silence descended between them. At least Dimitrios didn't seem to be one who felt the need to fill silence with meaningless chatter.

Minutes ticked by. Why hadn't he thought to ask Margie how much longer this would take?

In spite of the positive prognosis, he wouldn't believe Lana was okay until he could see it with his own eyes.

The elevator dinged. A couple who looked to be in their sixties stepped off, along with a younger couple. Dimitrios excused himself and approached, speaking to the group in tones too low for Nate to hear.

But the grief on their faces told him all he needed to know. He was looking at Lana's family.

A muffled cry burst from Lana's mother and her father slid an arm around her shoulders.

He pushed up from the chair and strode the opposite direction.

This was his fault. That bullet had been meant for him, but she'd stepped into it.

If her family hadn't heard the whole story yet, they soon would. And when they did, they'd hate him. Maybe almost as much as he hated himself.

ꟷ ꟷ ꟷ ꟷ ꟷ

"Nate?"

Nate started, his eyes flipping open.

In front of him stood the man who'd stepped off the elevator earlier. From Lana's family. No visible family resemblance, so likely her adopted family.

"I'm Lana's brother. Reilly Tanner." Reilly shook his hand before settling in the chair across from him. "Dimitrios thought you might've come down here."

"Looking for a quiet place, you know?"

"I hear you. Thought you'd want to know that she's out of surgery. She'll be out of the action for a while, but I doubt it'll be long before she's getting into trouble again." Reilly rubbed the back of his neck. "I tell you, she's going to put me in an early grave. You have any siblings?"

Nate shook his head.

"Lucky you."

Dry humor laced the words. As much as Lana's dangerous job might stress Reilly out, Nate could tell he wouldn't trade her for anything.

"So, no permanent damage?" Nate's throat burned.

"They anticipate she'll make a full recovery."

Fire pricked his eyes. When had he become so weak?

"You all right?"

The concern behind Reilly's words almost undid him. Not trusting himself to speak, he simply nodded.

Reilly leaned forward, elbows on his knees. "My family's in the room down the hall. Why don't you wait with us? The hospital's been good about updates."

So he could look at all of them and feel his guilt compound? No thanks. "I'm good here. Thanks anyway."

"Well, maybe I'll wait with you then." Leaning back, Reilly settled in. "I've actually looked forward to meeting you. Lana's told me a lot about you."

"Probably shouldn't believe everything you hear." Man. Hopefully that wasn't as lame as it sounded to him. "I've heard a lot about you, too. But I honestly expected an invalid."

Reilly chuckled. "Let me guess. She gave you some vague

details and let you draw your own conclusion, right?"

"Something like that."

"It's my fault. She was protecting me." Reilly rubbed his bloodshot eyes. "Some people were trying to kill me. But I'm surprised she didn't set the record straight."

"Maybe she would've but we didn't have time before she was..." The word *shot* froze on his tongue. "We, uh, didn't have time."

An awkward silence descended that Nate desperately wanted to fill.

Or flee, he hadn't quite decided which.

If Reilly noticed, he gave no indication. The smile he'd worn earlier had slipped a little, but still reflected in his eyes.

"You don't have to hang here with me. I know your family's waiting for you down the hall."

"Maybe I like the quiet, too. Besides, you look like you could use a friend."

True as that was, his two friends weren't going to be keeping him company tonight. Matt was back in Santa Barbara and probably still angry; Lana was recovering from surgery because of him.

Maybe it was time to put all the cards on the table. "Look, you don't have to pretend to like me."

Reilly arched an eyebrow. "Why wouldn't I like you?"

"After what I did? Are you kidding?"

A pointed look landed on the blood caked on Nate's clothes. "What you did was try to save my sister's life."

"It's my fault she's here. That guy was aiming for me."

"From what Branden said, that guy was after her long before you showed up."

"But she was shot pushing me out of the way."

"She got shot saving me, too. It's who she is."

"I get why she'd save you, but why me? I'm not some good guy who deserves it. She knows that. Why would she save someone–" He clamped his lips shut before he could say something he'd regret.

A grin slid across Reilly's face. "You know what, my friend? You just witnessed the love of God."

"What're you talking about?"

"I'm talking about a cross on a hill two thousand years ago. When Jesus took what we deserved by dying in our place. What you saw in Lana today is a dim shadow of what God did for you, for her, for all of us."

Huh. He'd never heard it explained like that before.

More than that, he'd never had such a clear visual before now. Could there be something to this whole Jesus thing?

But if there was, shouldn't God have done something to keep this from happening in the first place?

A ding echoed in the room.

Reilly pulled a cell phone from his pocket. "Looks like there's another update. Sure you don't want to join us?"

Much as he'd love to hear the latest, he shook his head. "Thanks anyway."

"Okay. Well, if you change your mind, we're right down the hall."

Reilly was almost out of the room when Nate spoke the words that burned in his throat. "Thanks. For everything."

Vague as it was, Reilly seemed to understand. He nodded. "Stick around. I know Lana will want to see you."

If only that was true. He nodded.

Exhaustion drowned him. A glance at his watch showed it was almost midnight.

He looked down at the blood on his clothes. Maybe he could use it to his advantage. Get the nurses to update him on Lana's condition. Then he could go back to his motel, change out of these clothes, and collapse into bed.

Changing out of the clothes might erase the visual reminder, but he had a feeling that the images burned in his memory, not to mention the guilt, would be much harder to banish.

***

Lana tried to find the strength to reach for her Bible, but her muscles felt like water.

Had it really been a day and a half since the shooting? That's what the nurses had told her. And her family. They all claimed she'd slept a whole day away.

Pain killers made her brain fuzzy and her eyes heavy, but she was tired of sleeping. Actually, she was tired of being tired. When would she regain some of her energy?

It'd taken some doing, but she'd finally convinced her family – all of them – to leave and grab some dinner. No doubt they'd return soon, and in force, but for now she had time to think. Time to decide what to do about Nate.

Stevens. Not Nate. How could she have been so stupid?

She'd have to turn him in. What other choice did she have? He was a killer without conscience and she had sworn to uphold justice.

But the weird thing was that she'd witnessed evidence of a conscience in him.

Sleep threatened a hostile takeover. Her eyes slid closed.

Squeak.

She recognized the sound of sneakers on tile. Probably a nurse. With more medication, no doubt. Would they leave her alone if she pretended to be asleep?

Doubtful.

It took almost all her reserves of strength to turn her head.

Standing inside the doorway, looking like he couldn't decide whether to enter or run, stood Nate.

In spite of her exhaustion, she managed a smile.

"Nate." Her voice scratched from an impossibly dry throat. The water glass on the table beside her bed called her, but she lacked the ambition to reach for it.

He crossed the room, holding a vase with a large tropical arrangement in front of him. "How are you?"

"Thirsty." The word escaped before she'd thought it through or could stop it.

He blinked, his gaze shifting to the water glass. "Oh. Let me set this down."

The large display overshadowed the other flowers on the shelf opposite her bed.

Picking up the glass, he maneuvered it to her waiting hand. After taking a few sips through the white bendy straw, she offered the glass back to him.

Could he really be Stevens? Looking at him now, it seemed so impossible.

Maybe none of that had really happened.

But she knew better, didn't she?

Before she'd been shot, he'd been trying to tell her something.

He deserved to be heard out.

She leaned her head back. "Back in the parking lot, before Young… what were you trying to say?"

"I'm not Stevens." He dropped heavily into the chair beside her bed. "You have to believe me. I'm not."

As much as she wanted to believe him, too many things didn't add up. "You called me."

"I had to warn you and I didn't know how else to get through to you. So I pretended to be him."

This didn't make sense. "How did you even know? About Stevens, any of it?"

He hesitated a moment too long. "I, uh, I just do."

The pieces clicked into place. "Matt."

"He's not a bad guy. Just had some rough breaks."

"He's a killer. And you're an accomplice."

"No. I swear I had nothing to do with killing."

"But you knew what he was doing. In the law's eyes, that makes you an accomplice."

He slumped back in the chair. "I told myself that his targets were bad people. Drug dealers, gang bangers, murderers, rapists. People who deserved to die. I convinced myself he was doing what the cops couldn't. Like a vigilante."

"It doesn't matter."

"You don't understand." Suspicious dampness glistened in his eyes. "Growing up, Matt did everything for me. He protected me when no one else would. I owe him."

She didn't know what to say.

After all, he was right. She didn't know what it had been like for him growing up. The constant abuse and bullying. How much of that Matt had absorbed for him.

But that didn't excuse the things Stevens had done.

Or relieve her of her responsibility to turn them both in.

To what end? They'd never confess. And Stevens had always covered his tracks well enough that there wouldn't be any evidence to solidly tie either of them to any crimes.

It would be her word against theirs.

Her energy lagged.

Arresting him would have to wait. She couldn't even move, much less call the police or put him in cuffs. Not that she *wanted* to do either.

"Why'd you save me? You thought I was a killer and you still pushed me out of the way."

"You're not ready to die."

"And you are? You've got more reasons to live than I do."

Man, was she tired. But this was important. She had to stay focused long enough to share the truth. "If I die, I wake up in heaven. Can you say the same?"

After studying her silently for several heartbeats, he pushed himself to his feet. "You're beat. I should leave."

No matter how much she wanted to deny it, she didn't have the energy to continue. "I'm sorry. I can't seem to stay awake."

"Don't sweat it. Just get better."

Fading fast. But she couldn't let him leave on that note. "Maybe we can continue this later."

"Maybe." He paused at the doorway and turned back to her. "Thanks. I'll never forget what you did for me."

Something about his words felt very final, but she didn't have the energy to figure it out. Her brain screamed at her to stop him from leaving, even as her eyes drifted closed.

Twenty-Five

Ginger Rosetti poured herself another glass of wine. So what if she'd already had three glasses. She might as well enjoy it while she could.

That imbecile Freddie Young had taken her name and phone number with him when he'd gone after Tanner's sister. The FBI had already questioned her once; it was only a matter of time before they returned to arrest her.

She was pretty sure they were outside now. Probably waiting for her to do something ridiculous like flee the country or open fire in a crowded place.

Well, they could watch all they wanted. There wasn't a thing they could do to stop her.

A scream slashed her throat as she flung her glass with all her strength. The glass shattered against the wall, the wine streaking the white paint like blood. Crystal rained on the thick carpet, sparkling in the dark red wine as the liquid soaked in, no doubt creating a stain that would never come out.

Who cared? After today, it'd be someone else's problem.

She snatched another of the exquisitely cut glasses from the wet bar and filled it almost to the brim.

"Ginger?"

Wine sloshed over her hand and onto the highly polished cherry wood bar as she started. Slamming the bottle next to the puddle, she cursed and tried to shake the excess liquid from her hand.

"Everything okay?" Joe Freeze, a man whose intense blue eyes lived up to his name, stood in the doorway.

She'd forgotten he was here.

Regardless of the fact that he'd lost Al's case, he was still one of the best defense attorneys in town. Not to mention an old friend. She'd called him as soon as the FBI left.

"Ginger?" he repeated, his tone gentler.

"Why wouldn't everything be okay? My husband's been arrested, the FBI's parked outside my house, and I'm being fingered for the attempted murder of a US Marshal. Things have never been better."

"I heard… never mind." The thick carpet muffled his footsteps as he crossed to stand in front of her. He took the wine glass from her fingers and set it further down the bar. "Don't you think you've had enough?"

"No! I've not had enough. If I'm going to prison, I might as well enjoy myself before I go."

"No one's going to prison. So Young had your name and number. Big deal. You said yourself that he decided to go after her on his own. No money exchanged hands. We'll beat this thing, no problem."

"Didn't you say same thing about Al?"

His lips tightened into a thin line. "Al's case was different. Lots of evidence, plus a long history of allegations."

Silence descended. Suddenly she didn't feel so hot. She pulled out one of the padded bar stools and sat heavily, leaning her back against the bar.

"Is there anything else I can do for you?" Joe's voice broke the stillness.

"Not unless you can get Frank out of prison."

"Give me time. By the time this thing goes to trial, I'll have more than enough to create reasonable doubt."

Right. She'd believe that when it happened.

"Can I call someone for you? A friend, family?"

Ginger shook her head. "I want to be alone."

Warm fingers captured her chin as he took a step closer. "That include me? I'll stay."

The tender smile he flashed at her left no room for speculation. She licked her suddenly dry lips. "And what would you tell your wife?"

"I always think of something."

His sky colored eyes, which usually looked as hard as gemstones, now invited her in. Made her want to say yes. Forget the past and ignore tomorrow.

But he'd led her down this road before.

"You should go."

Instead of leaving, he came closer. Placing large hands on the bar on either side of her, he leaned down to look into her eyes. "I'm worried about you. I've never seen you drink more than one glass and here I come in to find you drunk."

"I'm hardly drunk." Yet. If he only knew her plans, he'd have good reason to be concerned. She looked away.

He traced a finger down her shoulder. "Don't know why I ever let you go."

"You didn't let me go." Knocking his hand away, she jerked to her feet and pushed him aside. She took two steps then whirled to face him. "You made your choice, remember?"

Sure, he'd had fun fooling around with her, but at the end of the day, she wasn't the one to whom he'd wanted to come home. It'd all worked out okay, though. She'd met Al through him, and Al had introduced her to Frank.

He slowly straightened. "Okay, I'll go. Promise me you'll put the alcohol away. And that you won't do anything stupid, okay?"

"Of course. Go on home to your *wife* and don't worry about me."

"Okay." Skepticism in his eyes told her she wasn't fooling him. "I'll see you tomorrow. And don't worry. I'll get you out of this."

She forced a smile that felt as artificial as her innocence. "Tomorrow."

"I'll stop by in the morning on my way to meet with Frank." Ah, the courtroom voice. The one that inspired confidence and made people want to agree. If she didn't know him so well, it might've worked. "In the meantime, if you need anything, I want you to give me a call. You have my cell, right?"

"On speed dial."

He crossed the room, pausing on the threshold. "Anything else I can do before I go?"

Actually, now that he mentioned it…

She plucked an embossed cream envelope off an end table. "Maybe give this to Frank when you see him tomorrow?"

A pause. For effect, no doubt.

He stared at the envelope, then lifted his gaze to hers. "This a goodbye letter?"

It was, but she'd never tell him that. "If you're going to get him off, why would I need to say goodbye?"

No response. Not an agreement, a question, not even an argument.

The fear in his eyes almost shattered her resolve.

Her throat felt seared from the tears she worked so hard to contain. "It's an explanation. If I'm arrested in a day or two, I might not be able to communicate with him for a while. I want him to understand why."

After several more seconds, he slowly nodded. "I'll see that he gets it. Now you aren't planning anything rash, are you?"

"I'm not suicidal. Besides, I've always trusted you."

That last part was true, anyway.

With a nod, he started down the hallway. As he approached the front door, she halted him. "Joe, thanks. You've always been a good friend. To me and Frank."

"I'll see you tomorrow." He said the words with determination, as if he could make it happen by sheer force of will.

But he knew. She could hear it in his voice.

Tears swirled his suit into a navy blue blur as he stepped into the sunshine and softly closed the door behind him.

Time might be short. He might get to his car and decide he had to stop her. Maybe even call 911 before she had a chance to do what she needed to do. She rushed to the front door, locked the knob and the deadbolt, and slid the chain in place.

Retrieving the wine glass and the bottle, she hurried upstairs to her bedroom and sank onto the edge of her bed.

A slight tremor afflicted her hand as she opened the drawer and removed a bottle of pills. Just days old, the prescription had been written by her doctor to help her sleep.

So the FBI thought they could keep her here by camping across the street, did they? She'd show them. No one could make her do what she didn't want to do. Soon they'd learn that she alone decided her destiny.

* * * * *

"You sure you don't need help unpacking? Or making dinner? I can hang out for a while."

Patience.

Lana tried her hardest, but after dealing with airports and

spending hours on a plane back to Florida, patience was in short supply. If Reilly didn't back off soon, she might have to pull her gun. "Will you stop already? I'm not an invalid."

"I never said you were. But the doctor said to take it easy and I know you."

"You already put my suitcase in my room, so all I have to do is unzip it and take things out. For dinner, I'll order a pizza or something. Seriously. How much trouble can I get into?"

He arched an eyebrow. "You really want me to answer that?"

Probably safer if he didn't.

Just like it was better if she didn't tell him that she wasn't hungry. That would certainly earn her a lecture. "I'll call you if I need anything, okay?"

"You better. I don't care what time it is, I'll be here."

His new apartment was closer to her house than his old one had been. It was nice knowing he was close by, even if she had no intention of calling him.

He headed for the door and stepped out into the early evening sun. After giving a small wave, she locked the door behind him.

Unpacking took very little time, but depleted her energy reserves.

Not that she'd had much left after a day of travel. Man. How long would it take for her to feel normal again?

At least she was in her own home. Everyone in her family had pressured her to stay with someone, but she'd finally convinced them she could handle things on her own. She didn't need as much help as they all obviously thought she did.

She'd barely stowed the suitcase in the closet when her doorbell rang.

What the...? She wasn't expecting anyone. Had Reilly returned?

It'd be just like him to circle back to make sure she was doing okay. If he thought he was going to check on her every hour, he had a tough reality check coming. Older or not, he needed to give her some space.

Normally, stretching up to look through the peephole wasn't a big deal. Today was another story. She stood to the side of the door. "Who is it?"

"Alex."

Really? Alex should be in D.C. What was she doing here?

Knowing her, she probably came all this way to give her a lecture about getting shot.

She let her friend in and secured the door before leading the way into the living room. "Shouldn't you be in Washington?"

"Funny story." Alex settled on the edge of the sofa cushion. "I quit."

"You what?"

"Actually, transferred is more accurate. You know Barker's had an opening for about a month now, right?"

Of course she knew, but she never would've seen this one coming. "Really? You're moving back to Jacksonville?"

"After what happened with Peters and Beckman, I couldn't do it anymore. Besides, it was good working together again. And we both know you weren't planning to switch positions." Alex slid back on the sofa and scrutinized her face. "You look a little pale."

"Getting shot will do that to you. But the doctor says I'm recovering well."

"You better be. What the heck were you thinking, getting shot like that?"

"It's not like I planned it. Young showed up and tried to shoot Nate. I had to do something."

"And that was the best you could come up with? I thought you were more creative than that." Alex's scowl slid. "Nate, huh? How'd he get tied up in this mess with Young?"

"Long story." She summarized as best she could, but was even more exhausted by the time she finished.

"Wait. So you're telling me Nate is best friends with Stevens?"

"Crazy, huh? It's the reason Stevens didn't kill me and Reilly that day."

"I don't know." Alex's eyes betrayed her skepticism. "Sounds pretty unlikely that Stevens would back off a hit for a friend."

"I know, but they've got this special bond. Some kind of brotherhood thing. I think you have to go through the abuse they suffered as kids to really understand."

"You didn't *let* him get away, did you?"

"No way. I was going to have him arrested. I even contacted the police and told them where he said he was staying, but no one was registered under his name." Lana leaned back into the cushions. "He came to see me in the hospital, but I was too tired to stop him from leaving. That was the last I saw of him."

Probably the last she'd ever see of him.

He had to know that she'd take him in if he ever showed his face again.

"I didn't really think you'd let him off that easy, but I had to ask." A trace of apology laced Alex's words.

"It wouldn't have been easy. He'd become a good friend."

A sly grin stole across Alex's face. "Just think what would happen if you let your guard down more often. Maybe you could reform dozens of cold-blooded killers."

She shook her head slowly, well aware that Alex didn't mean it.

On the other hand, if she'd played by her own rules, both she and Reilly would be dead right now. Who would've thought such a simple investment of time could have such an impact?

She prayed that her investment had also planted seeds of faith, seeds that God would water through others who might invest in Nate. Because only God could give Nate the love and acceptance he'd always been denied.

Too bad she'd never know.

Nate was long gone. Gone, but not forgotten. Never forgotten.

Dedication & Acknowledgements

Dedicated to Jesus Christ,
Savior of the world and the only one worthy of praise

Thank you doesn't begin to cover the appreciation that is due to the many people who have supported this dream over the years. A very special thanks to my family, especially my Mom, who has read every word I've written (at least once), and to my special friends Janet and Del, who have helped mold this book into what you see here. I am so blessed to be surrounded by such a wonderful group of people.

The greatest thanks, however, must go to the ultimate Author and Lord of all. Thank you, God, for sparking within each of us a desire to create something of value. Anything we create shows the touch of the Creator. If you haven't read His book lately, I'd encourage you to do so. It's my favorite book and worth reading every single day!

A Note from the Author

Thank you so much for joining me on Lana's journey! I hope you enjoyed getting to know her and her friends as much as I enjoyed creating them. Her story isn't over, though; join her on her next adventure in *Deadly Devotion,* book two in the Deadly Alliances series. A sneak peek of that novel begins on the next page.

If you enjoyed this story, would you do me a huge favor and write a quick review? Reviews are a blessing to me and can help other readers decide if they want to read this book.

Would you like to receive notification about new releases? Sign up for my newsletter "Keep me in suspense!" In it, you'll receive a monthly update on my current work in progress, an inspirational thought for the month, as well as suggestions on other Christian books you may enjoy. Visit candlesutton.com to sign up.

Have you ever asked yourself why God uses people to change the world? It's not like He actually needs us. He's God - He can do anything and, quite frankly, can do a better job than we can even dream of doing. Yet He chooses to use us, in spite of how messy and messed up we are. It's truly amazing.

As I wrote this book, I was struck by the impact one person can have on another. Yes, Lana is a fictional character and realistically, the chances of any of us changing a hardened criminal are pretty unlikely. But who knows? What may seem like a small thing to us - smiling at the barista at the coffee shop, saying "hi" to the single parent at church, conversing with the person ringing up your groceries - can impact people in ways we might never know.

So as you go about life as usual, I'd challenge you to join me in reaching out. It doesn't have to be major or earth-shattering. Just look beyond yourself and see someone else.

Who knows? Maybe God will use you to be Christ to them.

Thanks for reading. If you enjoyed this story, I hope you'll tell the other readers in your life about it.

May God bless you. Seek Him and let Him guide your paths.

Excerpt from Deadly Devotion

Book two in the Deadly Alliances trilogy, available exclusively through Amazon

Prologue

Night crept in with a predator's stealth. He welcomed the cold embrace of darkness, which felt far warmer than that of the woman who held his heart.

Light leaked from the windows of the house across the street.

He tried not to think about what was going on inside, but found himself consumed with little else.

How long had they been in there? Minutes? Hours? It felt like it had been days since she'd started a movie and closed the drapes.

The front door opened and a man stepped out, the circle of the porch light illuminating him. Tall, broad shoulders, dark hair. Beyond the man, he caught a glimpse of her. A smile engulfed her beautiful face and she stepped into the man's arms.

He longed to look away. Yet he couldn't even blink.

She was practically making out with that jerk.

And on her doorstep no less! It was bad enough that she rubbed his nose in her unfaithfulness, but now she was flaunting it for the whole world to see.

How could she do this to him?

His fingers curled around the smooth ivory handle of the antique hunting knife resting on the seat beside him.

He'd teach her a lesson, one she'd never forget.

After one final kiss, she flitted her fingers in a small wave - meant as yet another cruel taunt solely for his benefit, no doubt - and closed the door.

The dark haired man walked down the porch steps, an idiotic grin on his face and a bounce in his stride.

What a chump. He better enjoy it while it lasted because with her, it wouldn't last long.

It never did.

Part of him wanted to jump out of the car and plunge the blade into the man's chest, but none of this mess was that guy's fault. He likely didn't even know she was using him as her pawn. Just another victim of her heartless games.

The loser climbed in his car and backed out of her driveway.

As soon as the taillights disappeared around the corner, the man threw open his door and stepped into the balmy evening air.

He glanced up the street. The night was still as death.

Weed-filled cracks littered the path leading to her front door, further evidence that she wasn't the woman he'd thought she was. The lack of care for her property reflected the carelessness in her heart.

Tremors vibrated down his fingers as he pushed the doorbell. Chimes echoed inside.

He stepped into the shadows to the left of the door.

A chain rattled. The lock clicked. The door opened.

"Back so soo–"

He slapped a hand over her mouth and thrust her inside, kicking the door closed behind him.

A scream slid past his fingers as she stumbled. He caught her arm and jerked her to her feet, pressing the flat part of the knife against her neck.

The scream died in her throat.

Her eyes flicked down, futilely trying to see the blade she could feel against her skin, before resting on his face. Tears glittered in her dark eyes.

Shaking in his grasp, she looked so small, so weak and helpless.

How could he feel sorry for her after all she'd done? He'd given her his heart and she'd thrown it to the dogs.

"Please don't hurt me." The breathy words spilled from her perfect lips.

Was that repentance he heard?

Maybe. But it'd take a heck of a lot more than a simple "I'm sorry" to smooth this over. She needed to know, to truly appreciate, exactly how much she'd hurt him.

Let her be scared for now. She deserved it.

"Please. Don't hurt–"

"Shut up!"

She clamped her lips together.

"Down. On your stomach." Growling the command, he lowered the knife and pushed her back a few steps.

"Wh-what do you want?"

"I said shut up. On the ground. Now!"

She dropped to the floor. Her body quaked. A sob hiccupped, the sound echoing off the polished hardwood beneath her.

"Hands behind your back."

The sob morphed into a soft wail.

"Shut up!"

Kneeling beside her, he set the knife aside, pulled a roll of fishing line from his pocket, and lashed her hands together. He grabbed her arms and yanked her to her feet.

"Here's how this is gonna play out. You're coming with me. You make one sound and I'll slit your throat, got it?"

Light danced up the edge of the blade as he held it up. Her wide eyes rested on the weapon before focusing back on him.

She nodded.

Pressing the knife against her back, he shoved her out the door.

The street appeared deserted, but that didn't mean someone wouldn't turn the corner at any second. Not to mention the threat of being seen by one of the neighbors.

They needed to hurry.

Opening the driver's door, he pushed her toward his car. "All the way across."

She crawled in, falling over the center console, and landed sideways on the passenger seat. Not waiting for her to right herself, he slid into the driver's seat and cranked the engine.

Ragged, shallow breaths shuddered from her, the noise drowning out the hum of the tires on the asphalt.

Five minutes passed before she broke the silence. "Whe-where are you t-taking m-me?"

Frankly, as much as she liked to talk, he was surprised she'd waited so long to say something. "Someplace where we can talk without being disturbed."

"Ta-talk about what?"

Was she serious?

He whipped around to look at her. "You and me. Him. The future."

Fresh tears scrolled down her cheeks. "Why me? What did I ever do to you?"

"What did you…?" He fought to keep his attention on the road, but couldn't stop his eyes from straying to her. "How can you ask me that? After that scene back at your house?"

"Scene?"

She couldn't be serious. "Oh, come on! You know what I'm talking about. Your infidelity. You didn't even try to hide it!"

"Infidelity?"

"Yes, infidelity." Was she acting dumb just to irritate him? If so, it was working. "I saw him leaving your house. Did you seriously think I wouldn't find out?"

"I don't even know you!"

Don't. Even. Know. You.

The words ricocheted inside his mind as he stared at her. "Why would you say that?"

"I've never seen you before."

Aiming for the curb, he jerked the wheel to the right and slammed on the brakes. She flew forward, her body slamming into the glove compartment before crumpling to the floor. A yelp escaped.

Good. Served her right.

The pain she felt was a fraction of what she'd inflicted upon his heart.

She struggled to get back on the seat, but lacked the leverage to do so. With her back against the door, she drew her knees to her chest and stared at him.

"I don't know what kind of game you're playing, but it's over. A connection like ours–"

"There is no connection!"

The words knocked the air from his lungs. No connection? It was like he didn't even know her.

Maybe he didn't.

Maybe she'd been putting on a show this whole time. Maybe the woman he loved didn't really exist behind the false front she'd shown him.

The dome light blinked on and she tumbled out of the car.

No! Somehow the little tramp had managed to get the door open.

He grabbed the knife as she stumbled to her feet.

"Help! Help me!"

The screams bounced off the empty buildings lining either side of the street. Too bad for her the businesses had long since closed and no one ventured into this area after dark. The only witnesses to what was about to happen included a delivery van, tractor trailer, and graffiti-covered dumpster.

It was a good place to die.

One

The scream severed the silence.

Paul Van Horn jerked his head up. Another scream followed the first, slamming him like a fist to the gut.

The raw fear in the woman's voice evidenced greater terror than most people experienced in a lifetime. Certainly more than he'd ever known. And he'd been through a lot.

The noise choked off as abruptly as it had started.

He paused. The echo faded, but it sounded like it might be one or two blocks to his left.

He ran.

Not away, although that might've been the smartest thing to do, but toward the source of the sound.

He'd never claimed to be a genius anyway.

A boarded-up business flew by on one side. A graffiti tagged warehouse on another. A pawn shop with bars on the windows, a paper manufacturing plant, a mom-and-pop deli. All closed.

In fact, there was no sign of any living person. Except the unknown source of the scream.

The woman needed help. Unfortunately for her, it looked like she was stuck with him.

He rounded a corner.

Two blocks up, headlights illuminated a figure kneeling over something on the sidewalk.

As he neared, he saw that it wasn't something. It was someone. His gut told him it was the woman who screamed.

That same gut told him that the figure leaning over her wasn't trying to help.

The creep touched her.

"Get away from her!" The words rumbled through his chest before he'd thought them through.

The man jerked his head up.

Time stalled as he felt the man's appraisal, then the man jumped to his feet and bolted to the car.

This guy wouldn't get away. Not if he could help it. Paul charged down the block.

The car door slammed.

Even as Paul's brain told him that the guy was going to escape, his feet kept carrying him closer.

He had to at least try to stop him.

The engine roared. The headlights swept him as the car whipped a U-turn and sped down the block.

Paul faltered, watching the taillights recede until they were pinpricks in the darkness.

If only he hadn't yelled. Maybe he could've gotten the drop on the guy. The guy had been so focused on the victim… the victim!

Paul snapped his attention to the still form on the ground. Was she alive?

She was perfectly still. Too still.

And there was so much blood. Pooled beneath her. Coating the exposed skin on her arms and neck. Staining her pink shirt.

Even the bare feet poking from under her long skirt were etched with red scratches.

It was hard to believe all this blood had come from such a small woman.

In spite of the Florida humidity, a shiver rocked his body.

Images flashed through his mind, a slideshow of one of the worst days of his life, the only other time he'd seen so much blood firsthand. The day he'd almost watched a friend die.

Focus. She might still be alive.

Forcing the memories back into the recesses of his mind, he jogged toward the woman, careful to avoid the blood and spatter surrounding her. Midnight hair tangled around her head. Eyes stared sightlessly at the black sky, her mouth frozen in a silent scream.

He didn't need to feel for a pulse to know she was dead.

Still, he knelt beside her and pressed two fingers against her neck. His stomach pitched as the fingers slipped in the blood smeared on her skin. Fighting the instinct to rip his hand away, he moved his fingers to the right spot and felt for any flicker of a heartbeat.

Nothing. The woman was long gone.

ꓷ ꓷ ꓷ ꓷ ꓷ

Blood ringed Paul's fingernails. He rubbed at it, as he had so many times in the past hour, but the color seemed tattooed on his skin.

The hard curb hurt his tailbone, but he couldn't find the energy or motivation to move.

At least *he* could still feel pain. That woman–

"Paul?"

The voice poured over him, warming him like fire, even if it didn't completely chase the chill from his bones.

She'd come.

Of course she'd come. She'd told him she would. And in the year since he'd met Milana Tanner at her father's church, he couldn't think of a single time she had failed to keep a commitment.

Just one more trait on the already long list of things he loved about her.

Police lights bathed her in a blue and red glow as she approached, the colors dancing on her olive skin and shiny black hair.

He pushed to his feet and enveloped her in his arms. "Sorry I disrupted your night."

"Don't be. This isn't your fault."

True. But choosing to call her, knowing she'd give up whatever she had going on to help him, was his fault.

He hadn't considered calling anyone but her. Even if she hadn't been his first choice, she was probably the only person he knew who wouldn't be completely horrified by what he'd witnessed tonight. Years of working for the US Marshals' service guaranteed that she'd seen things like this before.

Probably much worse.

"You okay?" Her words muffled into his shirt.

"Yeah." As much as he didn't want to, he released her and stepped back. "Better than her."

Both of them turned to look at the body, not that they could see much. Between the police, medical examiner, and distance, the body was little more than a speed bump. But he didn't need to see her. The woman's pained face burned his mind.

He looked down at his blood-stained fingers.

"It'll wash off." Lana's soft words carried a wealth of compassion that brought tears to his eyes. He forced them back.

She was right. The blood would wash off his hands. But would he be able to wipe it from his memories as easily?

"There was so much blood."

"Usually happens with a stabbing."

That explained a lot. The amount of blood, the tortured scream. Not to mention the lack of a gunshot.

He looked up, meeting eyes so dark they appeared black. "She was stabbed? How did you…?"

"I listened to the police scanner on my way over. What were you doing down here anyway?"

"I was walking back from the police station."

"What happened?" Her eyes narrowed slightly, intensity shining in their depths. "And why were you *walking*? Where's your car?"

"Some punks slashed the tires." The night swirled in his head.

If he'd known what kind of day today would turn out to be, he would've stayed in bed. Not that avoidance would've prevented any of this from happening.

"So you went to the police station to report the vandalism?" Confusion laced her voice.

"I wish. Austin was arrested." The words cut like a knife to the heart.

"Gangs?"

"It always is with him. He was part of a drive-by tonight. Thank God no one was killed." He rubbed the back of his neck and sighed. "I failed him."

"Hey, you did everything you could. It's hard to help someone who doesn't want to be helped."

The truth didn't make him feel any better. "I don't know what I'm gonna tell the other kids."

The faces of the kids in his group home filled his head. At sixteen, Austin was one of the oldest and, when not around his gang buddies, a pretty good mentor to the younger kids.

"How about the truth? That there's right and there's wrong, that choices have consequences, and that those consequences can last a lifetime. It's never too early to learn that lesson."

Didn't he know it.

Here he was in love with someone way out of reach because of mistakes he'd made in the past.

"I guess you're right. But it's not going to make the conversation any easier."

"It never does." She turned to look at the cluster of police surrounding the body. "Have they taken your statement or said when you'd be free to go?"

"They took my statement, but didn't say much after that."

"Let me see if I can take you home."

Home sounded nice. Especially considering the headache building behind his eyes.

She pulled her badge from her pocket and strode across the asphalt. Several heads turned as she made her way toward the detective, but none of the uniforms moved to stop her.

At only a little over five feet tall, it amazed him that she could command the authority she did. Heck, half the kids in his home were bigger than her and yet, here she was, moving through a sea of cops as though she called the shots.

Then again, a high level of confidence was probably a necessity in order to be taken seriously in what was still largely a man's world. Especially since she looked a whole lot younger than thirty-seven.

As she stopped beside the detective, Paul sank back to the curb and rested his head in his hands.

Man. What a day.

After today, he'd probably be on a first name basis with the cops at the local precinct.

He drove the events of the day into the background and focused on more pleasant things instead. Like Lana. Her quick smile and slightly upturned nose. The way she smelled like mangos. How she always dropped everything to support the people she cared about.

"Okay. Let's get out of here."

He jerked, his eyes flipping open to find Lana a few feet in front of him, looking every bit as good as she had in his mind.

"Hey. You okay?"

"Uh, yeah." Pushing up from the curb, he tried to smile. "I think the long day's getting to me, though. So we're good here?"

"He wants you to come to the station tomorrow for a formal

statement, but he said you can go for tonight."

Yay. Another trip to the station.

He fell into step beside her as she led the way around the police tape to where her white Toyota Corolla waited. As she started the car, his eyes fell on the clock.

"Aw, man." 11:03 p.m. "I should've called Dale to let him know what was going on."

At least it was summer. Dale and Annie Webber, his live-in staff, wouldn't need to be up early to get ready for school. Sometimes it paid to be a teacher.

"You can fill them in when we get there."

"Yeah, but Dale gave me a lift to the police station. He was expecting me to call him when I finished up so he could come get me, but I was so keyed up I decided to walk."

Funny how such a seemingly small decision could so dramatically impact his life.

He leaned his head back against the headrest. "I bet Jason and Stef will still be there, too."

"They were there when the police told you about Austin?"

"Yeah."

"I take it they haven't figured out who they want to adopt yet?"

"Not yet." The Pools had been getting to know his kids for a few weeks now and were always over helping out.

Which was fine by him. Not only was it nice to have an extra set of hands, the more adults who invested in those kids, the better.

"You should've called me. I would've gone with you."

"Like I'd make you drive halfway across town to help me deal with one of my kids. It's bad enough I called you for this."

"You can always call me. You know that."

"I know. But you've got your own problems to deal with." The last thing she needed was to absorb all his issues, too.

She pulled to a stop in front of the group home and quieted the engine. Silence fell for a few seconds before she broke it, her voice soft and serious. "The police think this is the work of that serial killer."

Serial killer?

The truth tore through him like a flash flood. What were they calling him? "That Jacksonville Ripper guy?"

"That's the one. And you're the only witness."

Also Available by Candle Sutton

Deadly Alliances Series
- Deadly Alliances
- Deadly Devotion
- Deadly Redemption
- Deadly Deliverance

The Fallen Series
- Silent is the Grave
- Broken is the Grave
- Empty is the Grave

Sinister Secrets Series
- Nameless
- Faceless
- Relentless

Shadow of the Storm
(Prequel to the *Shadows* Series)

Shadows Series
- Midnight Shadow (Coming Summer 2022)
- Avenger's Shadow (Coming Winter 2022)

Made in the USA
Columbia, SC
15 August 2022